Keeping Christmas

VOLUME ONE

CHAUTONA HAVIG   CATHE SWANSON

OLIVIA TALBOTT   KATHLEEN J. ROBISON

DENISE L. BARELA   MARGUERITE MARTIN GRAY

NAOMI CRAIG

CELEBRATE
Lit

ISBN: 978-1-951839-73-4

Celebrate Lit Publishing

304 S. Jones Blvd #754

Las Vegas, NV, 89107

http://www.celebratelitpublishing.com/

In castles far and near, long ago and yesterday, find happily-ever-afters wrapped in love and tied with Christmas joy.

***The Lights of Castlebourne* (by Cathe Swanson and Chautona Havig):** He bowled her over at first sight--his dog, that is. Sydney just wanted a chance to do the landscape design at Castlebourne. She never dreamed the owner's electrician would light up her heart at Christmas.

***The Girl From Dalarna* (by Olivia Talbott):** She's the most beautiful woman in Sweden, but she doesn't want to be. A simple life among milk cows is all she desires. Will a scandal upend her plans and ruin her chances for love?

***The Cross at Morioka Castle* (by Kathleen J. Robison):** In the ancient land of shoji screens and tatami mats, Ariko finds the stone ruins of Morioka Castle, and the mysterious cross that holds the secret of a Christian faith extending far deeper than Ariko ever imagined.

***The Ghost of Christmas...* (by Denise L. Barela):** Abbigayl needs to get away for Christmas this year. No family, no questions about why she's still single, no suggestion about being set up with someone's friend. What will happen when Neuschwanstein Castle's past converges with Abbigayl's future?

***Crystal Clear* (by Marguerite Martin Gray):** Rosalind's muddied past and foggy future crystalize in Château Chenonceau, a refuge from gossip and more. Watch as the château and Christmas work their magic and break the bonds of propriety, and rejoice as Rosalind experiences the crystal-clear hints of peace, joy, and hope all around her.

***The Weary World Rejoices* (by Naomi Craig):** Behind the elaborate furnishings of Herod the Great's palace, conspiracy and distrust run rampant. Mysterious visitors from the east challenge everything

Amal thinks he knows as palace scribe. Will his quest to uncover the Truth free him from the ornate shackles of palace life, or will he be the next victim of King Herod's maniacal jealousy?

The Lights of Castlebourne

CHAUTONA HAVIG AND CATHE SWASON

One

～⤳～

T he lack of a moat and drawbridge should have been a sad disappointment, but Sydney's obsession with princesses and pretty dresses hadn't survived first grade, when she grew her first bean plant in a red plastic cup. The overgrown shrubbery and barely-discernible flowerbeds fascinated her now. Someone had cared for this not all that long ago. Bindweed and creeping charlie swarmed over rock walls and slate paths, but they hadn't yet destroyed them. At least kudzu hadn't invaded, although despite what people claimed, St. Louis most definitely *did* have patches of it. There was that carriage house up the river a ways...

Sydney tightened her grasp on the folder, resisting the urge to bend over and start tugging out the weeds. She hoped Mr. Bradford wouldn't call the police and charge her with trespassing. Sydney didn't mind making the trek up the hill, but it would be depressing, and humiliating, if she had to walk back down to her truck after an ignominious dismissal. If he really wanted to keep people out, he should lock the little building next to the iron gates at the end of the castle's driveway.

Glad she'd decided on the "hardworking landscaper" look instead of the "female entrepreneur" style her mother kept pushing, Sydney stepped over a pothole. She'd had to walk at least half a mile from where she'd left the truck. Even if the driveway were in better condition, she couldn't have done it in heels. She'd have looked ridiculous trying. Of course, the female entrepreneur could march up those steps and bang the knocker with confidence. The gardener had to use the servants' entrance.

Sydney considered the castle. Did they even use the front door? Those steps might be elegant, but the dead leaves and dirt looked undisturbed. Mr. Bradford probably drove into the garage and used whatever door was most convenient. According to her mother and her mother's friends, Mark Bradford was rude, proving inexplicably elusive. A single man in possession of a castle (even if only one overlooking the Mississippi River) ought to make an effort to meet people, especially attractive women. But he'd refused all their invitations. Maybe he could give Sydney some pointers on how to accomplish that.

She turned in a circle, pondering her options. She'd passed two roads branching off the main driveway on her way up here. One or both must go around the castle to a garage or parking area in the back. This part of the driveway was just a single lane that made a loop in front of the double doors, suitable for carriages delivering ladies to a ball. Sydney would put a fountain in the lawn there. She tipped her head and squinted at the oval space. A simple fountain, flanked by two stone benches and symmetrical boxwood hedges. Grass, but no flowers or other trees. This would have been so much easier if she'd been able to check out the grounds ahead of time and present Mr. Bradford with some detailed drawings at their first meeting. Or if she'd been able to find a phone number or email for him and make an appointment.

Still... nothing ventured, nothing gained. If he said no, she'd only wasted a little time. But she really wanted this job. This *opportunity*. Having Bradford's Castle in her portfolio would impress potential clients more than a bunch of suburban lawns and an expensive academic degree. *I really need this, Lord. Don't You think?*

Onward. Sydney walked across what had once been a rose garden and around the side of the castle. She glanced up at the windows, hoping no one would spot her until she found a door to knock on. She hadn't realized how awkward it would be to arrive and have to hunt for the owner.

She stopped, peering into a scraggly cover of raspberry brambles. A traditional herb garden? It looked like horseradish had taken over one whole bed, and mint had spilled out into the path. The ubiquitous clump of chives had mushroomed into a bush.

Sydney walked closer and squatted, examining the plants. Bare patches and broken stems indicated that the local wildlife saw the herb garden as a tasty salad bar. Something that might be a variety of sage remained untouched in one corner. She set the folder on the path and gingerly reached through the raspberry canes, squeaking when the thorns scraped her hand.

Sydney knelt, glad again to be wearing her jeans. She steadied herself with one hand and leaned forward, pulling away chickweed as she tried to see what was growing in the back. Thyme? Maybe.

She stretched further, just as a male voice shouted, "Stop! Murphy!" Sydney scooted back, but something struck her from behind, propelling her through the plants into the dirt. A dog. A big dog, judging by the weight on her back, pressing her into the thorny branches. Even in the angst of the moment, there was no mistaking the dog's joyful barks for anything menacing. He wanted to play.

"Murphy! Stop! Get back here!" The man sounded panicked now. Or was that anger? So much for making a good impression. Sydney rolled to her back, pushing at the dog, and trying to sit up.

He licked her face. She shoved. "I am so sorry. Are you all right? Down, Murphy!" The man seized the dog's collar and dragged him away. "I hope he didn't hurt you."

"No." Sydney got to her feet.

"You are hurt!" He let go of the collar and grabbed for it again before Murphy could leap at her. "You're bleeding!"

Sydney touched her face. It stung. "Just scratched." She wiped her fingers on her jeans. He probably wouldn't want to shake hands. "I was looking at the herb garden."

"Herb garden? Down, Murphy!" He looked at the garden. "That's an herb garden?"

Mark Bradford didn't know gardens. Was that a good thing or bad? Sydney picked up the folder. "Yes. It's a traditional herb garden in the

English style. I'm Sydney Elliott, of Elliott Landscapes. I would have called, but I couldn't find your number."

No, that sounded flaky—or maybe even accusatory. She rushed on, trying to recall her practiced spiel. "I'm a licensed landscape architect, and I'm building a portfolio for my business."

"A landscape architect? You need a license for that?" He let go of the dog's collar, and Murphy bounded off toward a cluster of oaks. "Yes," Sydney said firmly. "I'm well-qualified to create and implement a landscape plan for Castlebourne."

"Is that why you're here?" A frown creased his brow. "Are you sure you're okay?" He pointed at the side of his face. "You did get scratched up."

And slobbered on, by his stupid dog. She was dirty, scratched up, bleeding, and slimy, and she probably had dog drool in her hair. Sydney shuddered and then straightened. If she didn't get herself under control, she'd be crying too. Just as well she hadn't gone the female entrepreneur route... she'd rather look like an idiot in jeans than in a suit.

"Yes. I've put together a proposal for work here. Because I'm still establishing my local business, I'm willing to design the plan for the grounds at no cost and implement the initial phase of it for the cost of materials."

"Wow, that's generous of you." He sounded sincere, not sarcastic.

Encouraged, Sydney continued. "In exchange, I'd like to use photographs and video from the project in my portfolio and marketing."

"Smart!" he nodded several times.

"This place would be perfect for that." Relief washed over her. How had this guy got a reputation for being curmudgeonly? He seemed perfectly friendly to her. Charming, even. Sydney beamed. "I think it would be mutually beneficial. I've written a proposal with all the details. Do you have time to go over it now?"

"Oh, I'm sorry. I think—" He broke off as Murphy erupted in agitated yaps and howls, twisted in midair and pelted toward them, barking.

"That is the dumbest dog I've ever met."

Sydney opened her mouth to reply and choked. No. Just no. Not fair. She tried to get out of the way. It was Bradford's dog. He should be the one knocked down and covered in second-hand skunk. She gasped at the impact and tumbled to the ground, squeezing her eyes shut against the squirming mass of wet black fur. Not fair.

"Murphy, what on earth..." He gagged and pulled Murphy off her again. "Go away. Get out of here!"

Sydney knew he was talking to the dog, but the urgent need to escape banished any remaining sensible thought. She scrambled to her feet and thrust the folder at him. "Tomato juice. I hear it works."

Despite two V-8 juice baths and a concoction of hydrogen peroxide, baking soda, and dishwashing liquid, the stench of skunk still lingered after Philip finally finished his last shower of the day. Murphy whined outside, but the troublesome oaf could just stay out there and think about what he'd done—or whatever Philip's sister always said to her kids.

The fridge offered him the tantalizing choice between cold pizza and frozen burritos. As any wise man would, Philip opted for both. Grains, protein, dairy, fruits—if you counted tomatoes as fruits—vegetables, and legumes all in one perfect meal.

Murphy whined again, and he stared at the unappetizing plate. "I agree, buddy. A burger sounds better, but since I like the way my truck smells, we're staying put."

The old carriage house had been remodeled into a garage and upper apartment sometime in the eighties. Formica butcher block stretched across a short expanse of one wall, and as Philip slid a paper plate across it, he almost pushed off the crumpled, soiled, and still somewhat odoriferous proposal Sydney Elliott—it was Elliott, wasn't it? He glanced at the letterhead. ELLIOTT LANDSCAPES

Yep. She'd gone before he could tell her that landscape decisions weren't his purview—practically ran from the place, and who could blame her. Still... those eyes had struck him as hopeful... eager. Warm, brown eyes that made a lasting impression. And Mark really did need someone to do something about the place. It was an overgrown jungle of dead plants and weeds. Even worse, it was as much of a fire hazard as the jumbled mess of old knob and tube wiring, damaged wiring, and downright idiotically installed "updates" in the old castle-like mansion.

When Philip had moved in, the old furniture that had inhabited the apartment for decades—wood-framed stuff with rustic scenes of old barns and water wheels—had been relegated to a donation center. While he'd decided to live with the ancient appliances and even the clunky waterbed platform for his mattress, Philip hadn't been able to stomach staring at something that reminded him of his childhood babysitter's house every single night. Man, that woman had been scary. Instead, he stretched out on his sleek but comfy sofa, his plate balanced on his belly, and pulled out his phone.

Mark answered just as Philip decided it would go to voicemail. "Hey, how's it going?"

"Steady but slowly."

"Glad I'm paying you by the job instead of the hour."

After a bite of flaccid pizza, he decided to break the ice with the story of Murphy's accident. "So, your dog got in a fight with a skunk, attacked a woman with the stench, and earned himself a few nights outside, where I hope—rather than believe—he'll have learned not to tangle with skunks again."

"Skunk? Great. Just—wait. What woman?"

Out tumbled the story—from Sydney getting mowed into the bushes, the bloody scrapes, the skunk attack, and most important, her offer of free work on the grounds. When he caught himself holding his breath for a reply, Philip decided to examine the why of it later. Right now, his job was to make sure Mark agreed. He'd figure out that why later too.

"That sounds like a great offer, but I don't want the grounds changed. It's perfect for paintball weekends. Can't you see it? We'd have all kinds of great hideaways."

Pointing out the fire risk almost failed. Mark just didn't care... at first. "Look, it's a *stone* castle. It's not going to burn down if someone sparks something somewhere. We'll put it out with a hose or something, not that I think it would actually happen."

Big guns. He needed them. But what? The oak paneled walls did little to inspire ideas.

"Philip?"

To give him time, he mumbled that he had a mouthful of food around said mouthful. After swallowing, taking a drink, pretending to choke on that drink, and clearing his throat a few times, he nailed it. "You may think it's no big deal to you—just risking your own property and all—"

"Exactly!"

"But fires spread. Fast. I'd be surprised if you didn't have the city out here demanding a cleanup eventually. Better to beat them at the pass. You could always tell her you'd want it to have viable spaces for paintball. She'd be able to use that in her portfolio too."

That sent Mark on a tangential tirade about overreach of local governments and something about property taxes meaning no one really owned anything. Philip knew his friend, though. Let the guy just keep talking. Get it out of his system. Then go in for the kill when he was all wound down again.

Mark surprised him, though. Instead of Philip having to bring up Sydney the landscape architect—that title still threw him one—Mark asked what the cost was again. "I really don't want to throw a ton of money into landscaping that I don't care about."

"She said design and personal labor would be free in exchange for being able to use videos and photos for her portfolio. You'd be responsible for materials—plants, equipment..." Philip didn't exactly know what those materials would be. He ended with a lame, "Stuff like that."

A bite of his burrito made his stomach sink. If he talked Mark into it, he'd tie up Murphy and go to Culver's for a burger.

"That could still be pricey, but I suppose I could just find out her estimated budget and whittle it down..." A deep, heavy, "I can't believe this is happening to me" sigh followed. "Are you *sure* we have to change anything? I like the rugged wilderness look of it."

"At the back of the property, that's great. At the front, great too. We'll tell her to keep it as natural as possible, but around the house, it just looks tacky."

Aaannnd, it had finally happened. He'd become acclimated to living at a castle. He'd just said, "the house" like a forty-some-odd-room castle was a suburban split-level near a Walmart.

Somewhere in the world, someone was watching *Jeopardy* reruns. He could hear the theme song growing louder with each passing second. The next sigh gave him hope. Since when did Mark sigh, anyway?

"You know what? Fine. Get me that estimate, but the only way I'm doing this thing is if you run interference. I'm not dealing with it, so if you don't want the hassle, tell her we're not interested."

The conversation drifted to Mark's mission work in Honduras, area clean up and rebuilding houses in the wake of a tropical storm, and Philip thought the guy said something about the irony of paying someone to update the electrical in his house while he wired houses in another country. Then again, he couldn't be sure. As he gave Murphy his leftovers, he held his breath and discovered it was hard to concentrate while fighting off the gag reflex.

But he didn't care. He'd done it... he'd earned that burger, and tomorrow he could call a certain blonde-haired, brown-eyed woman with lips that turned up in a natural smile and request a real estimate.

Two

"I'm sure the girls would understand if you needed to skip book club this afternoon. We know how busy you are, setting up this new business of yours." Virginia Elliott entered the bedroom, straightened a pillow on the bed and strolled back to the doorway. Had her mother just sniffed her?

Sydney closed the closet door and regarded her. If she'd known that's what it took to get out of her mother's book club meetings... well, no. Getting skunked was too high a price even for that.

Lengthy hot showers and half a dozen internet remedies—none of which included tomato juice—failed to eradicate the ephemeral whiffs that haunted Sydney's nostrils. She'd bundled up her shoes and every stitch of clothing and tossed them into the dumpster behind Taco Pronto, but the truck...

"If you're sure you don't mind," Sydney began, "I do have work to do."

"Absolutely, dear. You will be... um, available for next week's Friends of the Library meeting, though, won't you?"

"I don't know, Mom. I'm hoping to have a job lined up by then."

Sydney pushed her hair behind her ears. There was no way Mr.

Bradford would accept her offer after Monday's fiasco. He'd probably pitched the proposal straight into the trash.

"Don't let it take up all your time." Her mother wagged a finger. "We have civic responsibilities, Sydney. The Elliott and Dawson women have been pillars of this community for generations."

And that's what her mother expected of her. Four years of college and an internship had fooled Sydney into thinking she was an independent businesswoman with a career she loved, but her mother would always see her as a Dawson-Elliott woman. As a cute kid, she'd been a great fashion accessory for her esteemed mother. It hadn't occurred to her that she'd still be serving in that capacity as an adult. A pillar-in-training.

"I'm hoping to build Elliott Landscapes into a successful business, Mom, and you know how much work that is, being self-employed and running a small business."

Her mother didn't know that, at least not in real life. She supported local businesses by shopping. "Yes, but your work will be done in the office, and you can adjust your hours according to your own schedule." She wagged the finger more playfully this time. "You're the boss."

Sydney blinked. Had she really given her mother that impression? "I don't even have an office yet, Mom, except the spare bedroom, and before I get an office, I'm going to need a place to store equipment."

"Won't it fit in the garage?" No, her mother didn't get it. Did she think landscape architects sat in offices and drew pictures of gardens all day? It would be unkind to disillusion her all at once, but she'd have to adapt to the idea that her daughter would be digging holes, mowing yards, and trimming shrubs too, as well as meeting with clients. She might even get knocked down by dogs and sprayed by skunks.

"Actually, Mom…" She hadn't intended to say anything, since it would be embarrassing if it—when it—fell through. "I went out to Bradford Castle the other day—to talk to the owner about doing some work there."

Her mother straightened. "Really! Mark Bradford? You met him?"

Sydney nodded. "That's where I encountered the skunk. His dog got sprayed, and then the dog jumped on me and shared it."

"What was he like?" It took Sydney a few seconds to realize her mother was talking about the man, not the dog. "He seemed pleasant. Younger than I expected."

"Miranda Forrester-Smith said he was rude. She sent him invitations to dinner and then that dancing event they had last month, but he refused both of them. She had to mail the invitations, because he's never in town, and she didn't have a phone number for him."

Her mother gave a genteel snort. "He mailed his responses too, even though she put her number on the invitations. Then she would have had his number, and I assure you, she would not have shared it with the rest of us."

He hadn't been rude to her, but the circumstances had been... absurd. "I thought he was nice. The skunk put an end to our conversation, but I left him some information, and I'm hoping he'll call me back."

"Then you'll have his number!"

"It wouldn't be very professional to give out his phone number," Sydney began.

Her mother lifted a hand. "Say no more. I completely understand. I need to get ready for this afternoon, and you must want to get... er, cleaned up."

Sydney gazed mournfully at her beautiful truck. It was meant to be a work truck, of course, but having that "new car" smell replaced by skunk musk, after only two months of ownership, was just wrong. The car wash attendant claimed it was gone, but she could smell it. She'd probably smell it forever.

She hoped her mother didn't find out. The words "squandering your inheritance" and "better ways to invest that money" had been repeated all too often lately. Mom was right about one thing... her aunt Lucille would turn over in her grave if she knew Sydney was using that money to fund a landscaping business instead of as husband-bait.

Her phone rang as she climbed inside, and she answered it with one hand while turning the key in the ignition. "Elliott Landscapes!" She loved the way that name sounded. Like music.

"Hi. Is this Sydney Elliott? Stop, you stupid dog!"

Sydney sat up. "Yes, it is."

"Sorry about that. Murphy was just fine a minute ago. I think he recognized your voice."

Great. Still, if she got this job, she could handle a badly-behaved black lab.

"This is Philip Ward. I don't think I got a chance to introduce myself the other day."

Sydney leaned back against the seat, closing her eyes. "I thought you were Mr. Bradford."

"Yeah, I thought you might have, and I was going to say so, but then Murphy came back after the skunk, and… well, I forgot."

"Oh, I see." Even with her eyes closed. "What can I do for you?"

"After you left—after I got Murphy and myself cleaned up—I talked to Mark on the phone. He's down in Honduras on a work mission, cleaning up after that big hurricane they had a few months ago. He said I should call you and ask for a real estimate." He raised his voice to be heard over the dog.

Yes! Sydney thumped a fist against the steering wheel and tried to compose herself. It was hard to sound professional when she was grinning broadly and wanted to squeal with delight. "I'd be glad to do that. Can I come out today? I need to take pictures and make notes."

"Sure! I'll be here. I wanted to call you yesterday, but the dog got sick. The vet said he's allergic to the shampoo I bought to get the skunk smell out. If Mark had told me the dog would be more work than the castle, I might have thought twice about moving in here."

He lived there? Sydney waved at the attendant, who was impatiently motioning her to move the truck so the next customer could enter. "I'll be there in about an hour. Is the gate open so I can drive up?"

"I'll go do that right away. Thanks!"

Why had she said an hour? The castle was half an hour from the edge of town, and she'd have to go home to pick up her cameras and notebooks first. A few minutes with a comb, a toothbrush, and lipstick would be necessary too. And who was Philip Ward? They'd only talked for a few minutes, and most of that time was taken up with Murphy and the skunk.

Tall, lean—but not skinny—with a friendly smile and brown hair that sprang back from his forehead. A five o'clock shadow. Attractive. Maybe she'd noticed him a little more than she'd realized. If Mark Bradford was as cranky as reported, it might be easier to work with this man. Sydney bounced in her seat and accelerated. Things were working out just fine.

With his clipboard pressed against the wall, Philip wrote FRIDGE in block letters on one breaker sticker and WEST WALL OUTLETS on the next. "Do you know what I think, Murph?" That question usually earned him an eager, "Arf," but not today.

When he glanced over his shoulder, he remembered. Outside. The dog had stayed outside with Sydney. She'd arrived early wearing a billowing lightweight white shirt, jeans ripped at the knee from hard work rather than in a factory, and a wide-brimmed hat stuffed down over what he suspected was a French braid. He'd learned that trick from his sister. Girls wore French braids under hats because they didn't bunch up so much that the hat didn't fit.

Not that his knowing that factoid would impress someone like Sydney. Clipboard in hand, he strode up the basement steps to take a look outside. Just to be sure Murphy wasn't being a pest, of course. From the kitchen window, he watched her fiddling with a box, but she never looked at the box.

Hoping she needed a knife or something, he strode out the back door—a ridiculously ordinary thing to say about a forty-ish-room castle —and across the drive and what passed for a lawn these days, to Sydney's side. *Now* Murphy "arfed."

"Anything wrong?"

Sydney turned to smile at him. Those brown eyes... Van Morrison's voice and the tinny sound of an electric guitar filled his mind, but Philip shoved it back. No cheesy seventies rock at a time like this. He'd drive her off for sure.

"Just recording the layout of the grounds so I can come up with a reasonable estimate."

That's when what she held made sense. A controller... for a drone, no less. Impressive. "That's cool."

"It really helps give me a good overview. We're spoiled with all of today's technology. I almost feel guilty about it." Sydney grinned at him, and for half a second, Philip thought she'd wink. "Almost."

Her attention reverted back to the sky where she brought the drone in for a landing... on the roof of her truck cab. Philip couldn't resist a chuckle. "Smart move there. Murph would probably have it buried before you could get to him."

"I'll make a note to add in ten percent to the estimate." She ruffled the dog's ears before heading toward the truck. Calling back over her shoulder, she added, "To either cover the cost of a metal detector to find all the tools he buries... or to replace them."

Something about that woman got under his skin and in all the best ways. He wanted to follow, to ask about her ideas—anything to keep her talking. A job awaited, though. He had a Sub-Zero refrigerator to install as soon as he finished up in the basement. Although why Mark needed top-of-the-line appliances when the guy barely baked a frozen pizza, Philip couldn't imagine.

On the kitchen counter, he saw the clipboard and grabbed it. Down the basement steps and over to the circuit box, he pulled off the first sticker and heard a squeal from somewhere above. After slapping on those stickers, he raced back up, only to see Sydney wrestling with Murphy in the overgrown grass. He'd have to mow that if she didn't get to it first.

Certain that all was well, back he went to finish attaching wires to circuits so he could finally install that fridge. One thing at a time. If he got that fridge in and cooling, he could justify going outside to "rescue her from Murphy," or whatever better excuse he could come up with by then. Philip wasn't particular about the reason aside from it sounding plausible enough not to make him look like an idiot.

That fridge slid into place seconds after he plugged it in. Only opening the door to show a light proved it was on. The thing was quiet! The harvest gold monstrosity in his apartment—not so quiet. Then again, it worked as white noise while he slept, so there was that.

By the time he got outside again, Sydney's hair had come loose from the tie. Half had already unraveled, and if her mock scolding meant anything, a tussle with Murphy was to blame. Sure, it was too soon. Wasn't that how things always worked with him—too soon or too late? But when the thought, *I'd have done that for you if you wanted,* crept in and settled into long-empty chambers of his heart, Philip made a decision.

He'd find out—find out everything. What made her laugh, what made her angry (if for no other reason than to avoid that), what made her feel special, and most of all, if she loved the Lord as much as he hoped she did—if all that made up someone he could invest in. She was the first woman in years that had interested him beyond five minutes. It was time to find out if he had a chance with someone like her, and this time he wouldn't give up *too* soon.

That decision cemented itself in his soul the moment she turned her eyes on him. He'd probably be forced to confess to his mother that he's first noticed and fallen for those eyes. Mom knew how to extract that kind of information. She also knew how to ensure that she extracted it at the most awkward and embarrassing moments. Moms had skills like that.

"Hey... I brought lunch with me—brought extra. Are you hungry?"

"Oh, yeah. I have—" He swallowed hard and thought fast. Did you offer to contribute to an unplanned picnic? Was that rude? He'd have to chance it. "I have sodas in the fridge—fruit too. Also have a few bags of chips I could contribute."

Sydney didn't respond. She cocked her head as if thinking, just like Murphy did, in fact. Call him crazy, but he could almost feel the zing of connection. No, he definitely felt it, although whether she did was still up for consideration.

Delicate eyebrows drew together. Her nose twitched. "Um..."

If he still smelled like skunk, he'd send Murphy to a kennel for a week.

"Do you smell smoke?"

She'd barely gotten the "smmm" from smoke out when the sound of crackles registered in his mind. He knew those crackles. Feet pounding across the grass, Philip flung open the back door and nearly threw himself down the basement stairs. A coughing fit began as smoke filled his lungs. Flames engulfed the wall—or so it seemed. They couldn't, of course. The basement walls were all stone and cinder block. However, the electrical "map" of the castle and the enormous sketch pad he'd used to make it on burned even as he pulled the pin from the fire extinguisher and coated the whole area just to be certain.

That's when he heard the coughing behind him. "What happened?" Another coughing fit.

"Not sure... Unless I hooked the kitchen wires up to the wrong circuits—not likely, but possible—I can't say."

"Did I hear sparks?"

"Yeah." With a carpenter's pencil, he poked at the panel for some idea of what had gone wrong.

"Didn't know electrical panels could spark like that, much less cause a fire. Isn't that the point of a breaker box?

"Well, those weren't the sparks I was hoping for..." The words trailed off as Philip realized he'd spoken aloud. Sydney gave him a lopsided smile but said nothing.

Three

The fragrant dirt, deliciously warm in the late afternoon, crumbled in her fingers. Sydney peeked over her shoulder before sitting cross-legged on the ground and scooping up dirt in both hands. She still had plans to draft and plants to order, but sometimes, she just needed this... this time, not exactly in prayer or even focused strictly on God, but alone in His world, close to the ground, in the dirt. Some people had mountaintop experiences, but Sydney found God in the soil. God liked gardens. He did a lot of important stuff in them.

She picked up a rock and rubbed the dirt off it. So many of her classmates had preferred the design process over the actual work. They'd wanted careers like architects, not gardeners, but Sydney would hate to be stuck in an office every day.

"There you are!"

Sydney scrambled to her feet, embarrassed to be caught playing in the dirt like a child. "Hi, Philip."

"Hi."

He smiled at her, and Sydney shifted from one foot to the other, flashing back to junior high and the awkwardness of an adolescent crush. Even from six feet away, on the other side of a chest-high hedge, something about the way he looked into her eyes when he smiled felt almost intimate.

"I feel like we should get interrupted by Murphy right about now," Philip said. "You could get him to dig that hole for you. Don't you have a shovel?"

She glanced at the small hole and pile of rocks and felt herself blushing. "I just wanted to see what the soil was like."

"Ah. I suppose that's important. Is it good soil?"

Was this guy really interested in dirt, or was he just making conversation? Their paths hadn't crossed much since the day he set the castle on fire, but she'd got the impression he was... interested. Not in soil and plants or her work at the castle, but actually interested in Sydney.

A frisson of excitement rose in Sydney, followed by a flutter of anxiety. Despite her mother's determined efforts, she wasn't good at this man-woman social stuff. She wasn't even good at light conversation. After their one and only night out together, her exasperated college roommate declared that Sydney had flunked flirting 101 and ignored her for the rest of the semester.

Philip's comment about sparks had been flirtatious. Even Sydney could recognize that, but if she tried to flirt back, she'd say the wrong things, and then she'd have to avoid him because she'd be embarrassed. And she didn't want to avoid Philip.

Sydney took a deep breath. Over-thinking this would only make it worse. She'd talk to him like any other person, as if he weren't making her feel queasy. No... giddy. Nervous. Not queasy, and that was a perfect example of her skills. She'd probably tell him he made her sick.

No, she'd just talk to him like a person. They were both adults, not teenagers. Their hormones were done raging and had settled into a nice simmer.

"What are you smiling at?" Philip asked.

Another perfect example. Sydney tried to think of something clever. She couldn't tell him about the simmering hormones, of course, even if she found it amusing.

"The dirt. It's good dirt." Sydney winced. No, no social skills at all. "I mean, I didn't realize I was smiling, and the soil is just fine." Any second now, she'd be telling him it appeared to be a good aggregate but probably needed some lime and that the presence of burdock might be an indicator that the soil was low in calcium.

"Mark will be glad to—"

Philip broke off, and Sydney turned to follow his gaze. Her cousin Arielle approached, picking her way carefully over the flagstone path, impossibly perfect in a yellow suit that should have clashed with her red hair. Sydney couldn't see her shoes, but it was a safe bet they had three-inch heels. Maybe four.

"Hello!" Arielle waved. "Are you busy working? I don't want to interrupt your work." Without waiting for a response, she turned to Philip. "Are you Mr. Bradford?" She extended a hand. "I'm Arielle Dawson—"

The guy interrupted her. "No, I'm just the handyman. Philip Ward." He shook her hand. "Mark will be back next week."

"Hi, Arielle. Welcome back!" Sydney moved forward to give her a hug. "I've missed you!" She turned to Philip. "This is my cousin, Arielle. I thought you were an electrician."

"I—am, but Mark's putting me up for free until I start my new job in Columbia, and he likes to get his money's worth. Besides, it keeps me busy."

He was moving to Columbia—Missouri or South America? Sydney opened her mouth to demand... er, request more information, and then closed it again. Shouldn't that have come up in conversation already?

"You're moving to Columbia?" Arielle pumped a fist in the air. "Go Tigers! I just moved back from there. I went to the university and then stayed to work with a large events company before coming back here to set up my own."

"Events? Like a wedding planner?"

Sydney clamped her lips even tighter, but the snicker burst through. She'd heard this conversation a dozen times.

"An *event* coordinator," Arielle corrected. "I can do weddings, but I also do corporate events, conferences, charitable fundraisers, conventions... think Boston Marathon or Olympic opening ceremonies."

"You forgot Times Square on New Year's Eve and Renaissance Fairs," Sydney said.

Philip's phone rang, and he pulled it from his pocket, grinning.

"Sorry. I'd never really thought about those things." He glanced at the phone. "I need to take this. It was nice to meet you, Arielle."

They watched him hurry away before Arielle said, "Right now, I'd be thrilled to get a wedding job. I'd rather be on my own than go back to working for someone else, but I might have to. Not only is mine a brand-new business, but I also don't have all the local connections."

"I'm sorry." Sydney gestured toward the ruins of the gazebo. "Let's go sit down. I wasn't being very productive anyhow."

Arielle surveyed the grounds. "It looks like a big project."

"It is, but like you, I need to build up a portfolio." Sydney sat on an iron bench and scooted over to make room for her cousin. "Bradford's Castle will be a good centerpiece."

"Actually," Arielle said, "I did get an offer for a wedding. Your mother said it won't be till next spring, though." She raised one eyebrow. "My feelings are hurt. Why didn't you tell me?"

"Tell you what?" Sydney jerked upright. "My mother said I'm getting married?" Unbelievable. No, it was all too believable. "I am *not* getting married. She's set me up with three different guys in the past few months."

"You went out on dates with them? Why?"

Easy for Arielle to say… Aunt Millicent wrote mushy romance novels and believed that true love showed up unexpectedly. "You know my mom. She's good at making people do what she wants."

"No," Arielle said, "she's good at making you do what she wants. You need to move out."

Sydney sighed. "I just need to figure out how to make Mom see I'm an independent adult."

"But you're not independent," Arielle pointed out, "if you're still living at home. You just inherited a bundle! You can afford a place of your own."

"I wish I could, but you wouldn't believe what it costs to start a landscaping business. The equipment costs a fortune, and I'll have employees soon."

Arielle ignored that. "Still, you don't have to go out with men your mom picks out for you."

"It's not that easy. Right now, she's stuck on Evan Montgomery."

And Evan was stuck on Sydney. "I agreed to a second date with him, and then we sat next to each other at a wedding reception, and now he thinks we're a couple."

"That was the name," Arielle said. "Do you like him?"

Sydney stretched her legs out and crossed them at the ankles. The comparison between her cousin's pumps and her own work boots made her tuck them back under the bench. "He's persistent. He's involved with a lot of the same stuff as Mom, so he talks to her about me. She's thrilled."

"But do you like him?"

"No! He's totally self-centered, and he's... well, he's smarmy." Sydney pushed a strand of hair behind her ear. "The worst part is that he and Mom seem to be working together. I'm pretty sure that's how we ended up together at the wedding."

"Tell her you don't like him!" Arielle insisted. "Tell him you don't want to go out with him."

"I did! Mom doesn't believe me, and he's not taking no for an answer. It's like he doesn't even hear me. He kept calling, so I blocked his number, but he calls the house or talks to me through Mom."

"He sounds like a stalker!"

Sydney shook her head. "Not exactly. I'm not afraid of him or anything like that. He's just annoying. And Mom... well, she's Mom. She means well. She thinks he's perfect for me. Don't worry... I won't be going out with him again, and as soon as I can move out, I will."

"Try not to be trapped into marriage with him." Arielle rose. "But if you do, let me know, and I'll put on a great wedding for you."

"... I'll put on a great wedding for you."

Philip threw down his needle-nose pliers, wiped his forehead with the back of his arm, and draped his arms over his knees. *"... I'll put on a great wedding for you."*

She wasn't dating someone. She couldn't be. Sydney Elliott wasn't the kind of woman to flirt—well, no. She hadn't flirted, exactly. But she'd *allowed* him to without saying a thing about there being a guy in her life. She was the kind of woman who would say, "My boyfriend would like that one" to the joke about sparks or when it was getting late say, "I really should finish up. I'm meeting my boyfriend for dinner." Just an off-hand comment so he'd know she was taken.

But Sydney hadn't done that. She'd smiled, even blushed a little. She'd sought him out without trying to be too obvious. Philip wasn't exactly a ladies' man, as his dad would've put it, but he knew when a girl was interested. So what was the deal?

He rose, dusted off his jeans, and started for the stairs. A moment later, he went back, picked up the pliers, and put them in the toolbox. Throwing tools. What kind of juvenile stunt was that?

If he were to avoid juvenile stunts, he'd start with moping about something he overheard. That was the kind of stupid stuff people should leave back in middle school—and didn't. Well, *he* had.

Outside, the day had grown beyond "hot and sticky" to "natural sauna" in just a couple of hours. Sydney had her hands in the dirt again, this time with tubes and things. Probably testing ph. or whatever soil had. He'd never really paid attention to that stuff in school, but his grandfather had talked about soil ph. Hadn't he?

Sydney turned toward him as he approached, and Philip waved. "Hey... your friend gone?"

"Cousin, yeah."

Here went nothing. "Came back a bit early a while ago. Heard something about a wedding and figured it was private, so I turned around." There... honest, mostly. All the things he said were true, although... "Frankly, I didn't want to hear about you being engaged so I took off. Gave myself a lecture on being an adult, and here I am." Philip planted his feet apart, shoved his hands in his pockets, and did his best to look her in the eye as he asked, "You engaged?"

Emotions shifted so swiftly in Sydney's expression that he had trouble following them, but her soft chuckle-like giggle told him he hadn't offended her too much. At least not yet. "That—that was crazy refreshing. Just come out and ask. And no, no I am *not* engaged. I am not even dating anyone, but my mother and her latest choice for me can't seem to accept that."

After setting her tray of tubes down and pulling off gardening gloves, Sydney reached for an insulated water bottle, chugged a good bit, and moved into the shade of the nearest tree. "I could use a break."

"So... Mom wants you to marry her best friend's socially awkward son and has convinced him that you're just shy and not to give up on you?"

Without answering, Sydney examined the ground at the base of the tree, dusted the dirt with her foot, and then plopped down, apparently satisfied that... She gestured for him to join her. "No ants. I checked."

Ants. Of course. Who wanted to lean against a tree crawling with ants?

"You've got it all wrong. I have a socially conscious mother who should have been born back when marriages were brokered to increase wealth and social standing, and girls were supposed to be grateful to have a husband at all."

What did that mean?

As if he'd asked the question aloud, and Philip was quite certain he had not, Sydney kept talking. "She keeps setting me up with "suitable" men. By that she means rich guys who are full of themselves—guys who won't want their wives to have anything to do with something as plebeian as dirt. Her latest favorite thinks we're a couple." The girl nearly snarled out, "We are *not*."

"Well, I'm glad to hear that, anyway."

He hadn't seen it coming. Hadn't heard a thing. One second, he'd been about to tell her how he'd been trying to get a reservation at one of the popular restaurants so he could ask her out with a definite date in mind, and the next, Murphy came flying through the air and toppled her over.

The slobbery kisses commenced—Murphy's, not his. Too bad about that. Well, not the slobbery part, Philip conceded. But as he watched her wrestle with the exuberant dog, laughing at Murphy's antics, he had to admit that if he were honest with himself, kissing her— human kissing, that is—didn't sound half bad.

Another thought followed quickly. Ridiculous. It sounded great.

"This dog of yours..."

"Mark's."

Sydney sat up and wrapped her arms around Murphy's neck—likely more to control the animal than out of actual affection. "Well, he knows how to ruin a moment."

Her cheeks flamed and she started stammering that her words came out all wrong.

Philip stopped her. "Actually, he did. You got that right. I'll just put it out there. I'm interested. I've even been trying to get a reservation at Evvers for a few days now and so far, it's all three weeks out."

"Why would you want—?" She stopped herself. "Um..."

"I mean, I could ask you if you'd have McDonald's with me, but..." Great, now they both had gotten into the unfinished sentence thing.

"Sounds better than Evvers. Pretentious place with snacks masquerading as dinners so you have to go home and make a frozen pizza, or you starve."

Okay, he'd been attracted to her. What guy wouldn't be? Every bit of her oozed authenticity and, well. She wasn't exactly a troll. Everything he'd ever appreciated in a woman, she had. Right down to the "not high maintenance" bit. It sounded like her mother was, though. Still, now she wanted real food? For a real date? Maybe?

"So... instead of Evvers, maybe we could just go over to Dewey's?"

"I thought you were going to say Katie's, and force me to say no."

"Don't like pears, figs, or prawns on your pizza?"

Her smile... she really shouldn't do that. It made him notice those lips, and things were nowhere near that level of "get-to-know-you-ness." Is that where some old book would say, "More's the pity?" Probably. And the old book would be right too.

He reached around the tree, ending up on his knees to do it, and snapped off a sunny dandelion flower. Handing it to her, Philip said. "Sounds like Dewey's it is. Meet you there or pick you up?" Before she could answer, he added, "Any night you name."

Even before she spoke, he saw her answer. And this was exactly why people needed to just talk about things. He could still be in there, sulking over a non-existent fiancé. Instead... pizza and a few hours without Murphy ruining moments. A perfect date if he'd ever heard of one.

Four

If she wore that baseball cap she'd picked up at the church bazaar, she could put her hair in a ponytail and pull it through the hole in the back. Her hair always made that cute flip at the end of a ponytail. Still, a pink and white zebra-striped cap with rhinestones spelling out the word "shine" wasn't exactly professional. And it would look ridiculous with her work clothes. She had to dig today – really dig, with a shovel.

Sydney lifted her hair with both hands, stared at herself in the mirror for a few more seconds and then let out a whoop of laughter. She'd already spent twenty minutes picking out the perfect outfit to wear this evening – clothes that were casual enough for a pizza joint but special enough for a date with Philip – and trying to decide how she should style her hair to work in the garden was over the top. She didn't need to wow him twice in one day. He already liked her.

Still chuckling, she braided her hair and twisted a band on the end. Good enough.

"Are you on the phone?" Her mother appeared in the doorway with a length of green fabric draped over both arms. "I thought I heard you talking to someone."

"Just myself." Sydney pulled a pair of jeans from her dresser. "Getting ready for work." If she repeated that word often enough, maybe Mom would realize she took her new business seriously, like any regular job.

"Oh, good. I was afraid you were busy." She entered the room and shook out the fabric, transforming it into a full-length gown. "What do you think?"

"Pretty. It's a good color for you."

Her mother ignored the disingenuous comment, beaming down at the dress. "I saw it at that little boutique on Olive Street and knew it would be perfect for the concert tonight. It matches your new handbag perfectly."

The handbag her mother had given her yesterday – wait. "What concert?" Sydney tossed the jeans onto her bed. "I don't know anything about a concert. I have plans tonight."

"It's been on the calendar for months, and I know Evan reminded you yesterday. He said he left a message on your phone."

"Hmm..." Sydney had hit the delete button with a cheerful flourish at the opening syllables of his message. "Well, I have other plans for this evening."

"What plans? There's nothing on my calendar."

Sydney opened her mouth to reply and closed it again. This wasn't the time to talk about her adulthood and remind her mother that Sydney did have a life of her own. Because, well... aside from work, she really didn't. Until now.

"I'm going out to dinner." Stop. Full stop. She didn't want to tell Mom about Philip. Sydney reached into the closet and slipped a polo shirt from a hanger. Not now, when Sydney needed to leave for work and hadn't had time to come up with an explanation.

Her mother stood erect, holding the green gown, calmly waiting with one raised brow. Sydney bit her tongue. Her mother's "silent expectation" technique was always more effective than her interrogations, guaranteed to induce babbling in under thirty seconds.

Why put off the inevitable? She caved. "I'm having dinner with Philip Ward. He's the guy I met at the castle. He's house-sitting—castle-sitting—for Mark Bradford." Sydney threw the shirt on top of the jeans and looked at her mother's reflection in the mirror. "He's a really nice guy, and he doesn't know many people in town." Sydney could picture Arielle rolling her eyes and tried for a little assertiveness. "I'm working till four, and then I'll be back to shower and dress before I leave again. I'm meeting him at six."

"But you have the concert tonight. Evan is picking you up at five-thirty so you can eat first."

Why did her mother say that as if it was a straightforward situation rather than an argument? As if Sydney just needed a reminder and should plan to be ready then? "Sorry, Mom. I have other plans."

"Evan is expecting you to go with him." Perfectly calm and a little patronizing, as if Sydney were a little girl who needed to eat her spinach before she could have cake. An apt comparison, really. Philip was definitely cake.

"I don't know why he would." Sydney picked up her clothing. "I know nothing about a concert, and I already have plans for the evening." She walked into the bathroom and closed the door gently behind her. The snick of the latch was quieter than the thumping of her heart.

Sydney stabbed the trowel into the dirt and got to her feet. She'd found a dozen of the sprinkler heads so far, all rusted and useless, but the placement of the lines didn't make sense. There should be a main pipe coming from the pump house, but as far as she could tell... nothing. The sprinkler system didn't appear to be connected there at all. She turned, hands on her hips, regarding the pink flags she'd used to mark the heads. They looked like a child had stuck them in the ground at random.

She hated to add the cost of an automatic irrigation system to the estimate, but it would be easier and less expensive to put it in now instead of trying to retrofit it later. Even if Mr. Bradford didn't want to replace the sprinkler system, the fountain out front needed new water pipes. That would be a focal piece of the landscaping. Despite her efforts to keep it affordable, the list was growing fast. Philip said Mark Bradford didn't have any specific requests except to leave as much wilderness as possible for games. Paintball? Did they play Hide and Seek and Capture the Flag too?

Sydney walked toward the southeast corner. How did the pond get water? She used her fingers to probe for moisture. If there was a creek nearby, it wouldn't take much to divert enough water to fill the pond. Or maybe... She hiked up the pebble-strewn path toward the castle before realizing what it was. Stepping off the path, she squatted and scraped away the rocks, hoping to find a pipe underneath. She'd need another manicure.

No, not a pipe. Sydney squatted on her heels and pondered. The rocky path itself could be a shallow creek, filling the pond and eventually cascading down the pile of rocks into a flowerbed at the edge of the lawn. It would be perfect for something like hydrangeas if she could get the water flowing. She continued her trek, watching for signs of a spring.

"Hi, there!" Philip loped toward her, smiling and waving. "I saw all your little flags. What are you marking?"

"Sprinkler heads," Sydney said, "and hello! How do you think Mr. Bradford would feel about replacing the underground irrigation system?"

He looked around the grounds and visibly swallowed. "Does it need one?"

"It would help. I'd need water to the fountain out front, for sure, and this creek... I'm trying to find its source."

"That's a creek?" He bent to scoop up a handful of pebbles and poured them back. "It's bone dry."

"Yes, but..." Sydney pointed. "It comes around the side of the castle there, and then I think it goes under that overgrown honeysuckle and lilac cluster and comes out over there." She used her finger to trace the path for him. "It fills that little pond and then continues until it runs over that pile of rocks like a waterfall." Only the sheltered parts of the path had pebbles, and some areas were completely grown over. Was she wrong?

"You can see all that? I'm impressed. It just looks like a mess to me. Mark said his aunt did a lot of gardening, but she died years ago, and his uncle didn't keep it up."

That might explain things. "Most formal castle gardens are symmetrical," Sydney said, "so I'd expect to see a matching water feature over there." She gestured toward the opposite side of the yard. "But these grounds are more... natural."

"Ah." He folded his arms across his chest and grinned at her. "You're thinking of those stuffy European castles, not the rebellious colonials."

Roguish. A roguish grin, straight out of Aunt Millicent's romance novels. Sydney had never seen one in real life before, but here it was, instantly recognizable. She swallowed and then had to clear her throat. What had they been talking about?"

"Sorry. I... um..." She cleared her throat again, hoping the heat in her face didn't mean she was turning bright pink. "Water. I'd like to see if that really is a creek. Is there a hose around here?"

"I'm sure there is." Philip tipped his head toward the castle. "Let's go look."

Sydney fell into step beside him. "I'd like to let water flow into it slowly for several hours – not too fast, or it will just make a mess. Do you think we could leave it on for the evening... if you could remember to shut it off when you get home tonight?"

"Home from our dinner date?"

Sydney didn't look up at him. He was probably smiling at her, and she'd start blushing again. "Yes, if you don't mind. I need to leave soon, to get ready... Oh! Would you mind if we meet at five-thirty instead of six?"

The gates at Castlebourne loomed ahead and created a picture so gloomy that it gave the whole place the appearance of a Gothic novel. Surely, some weird woman in a cloak billowing out behind her should appear in his headlights and vanish when he jumped out to see who had invaded the sanctuary of the small—comparatively, anyway—castle. But not one wisp of that gloom could dampen the satisfaction of a perfect date.

It wasn't that Philip Ward had never experienced good dates. But how often did everything line up into a perfect evening of laughter, smiles, and yes... quite a lot of flirting? How often did all that happen with someone you really *want* things to work out with? And on a first date? If he were a proponent of "confirmation theology," he'd have decided right there that Sydney was God's hand-picked woman for him.

He wasn't (a proponent of said theology) and he didn't (decide she was it). That said, he wouldn't complain if it turned out that way. Not a bit. That thought turned those other thoughts into a quick prayer. *Lord... is it presumptive to start asking for more after one date? Because we both know that's what I want.*

So, pulling through the gates with their creaks and shadows, Philip made a mental note to ask Sydney about lighting and maybe trees to arch over and soften the entrance. Make it more romantic. No, that wasn't the word. Ridiculous. Just... welcoming. Yes, welcoming.

With his truck in park beside his little apartment, Philip pulled out his phone and sent a text. He couldn't resist. HAD A GREAT TIME TONIGHT. THANKS FOR COMING. SEE YOU TOMORROW.

He'd made it halfway up to his door when her reply came. ME TOO. THE ICE CREAM WAS EXACTLY WHAT I NEEDED AFTER ALL OF MOM'S TEXTS. SO, THANKS FOR A GREAT TIME, AND THANKS FOR DILUTING HER BARRAGE TOO. Another one pinged before he could come up with a good response. DON'T FORGET TO TURN OFF THE WATER.

Ugh. He wanted to go into his apartment, lie on the couch, and figure out what he could come up with for a second date. Preferably on... say... Sunday. Instead, he turned back to go turn off that water. A bark out by the kennel unleashed a groan. And let out Murphy.

Sydney must have been right about that creek, because as he neared the spigot, he heard water splashing somewhere close. It continued even after he turned it off. With his phone for a flashlight, he peered around the spigot, the foundation, and even into the window to see if something had leaked through. All looked well below—right up to the point where his Mountain Dew can from the other day floated past.

"Oh, no..."

An hour later, after turning off all electrical, getting a sump pump going on the generator, and freeing a now frantic Murphy from his cell —erm, kennel—Philip did what had to be done.

He begged the Lord for grace and pulled out his phone to call Mark. At almost ten o'clock at night. To inform his friend that he'd flooded the castle. Great.

A sunny yellow, classic VW Beetle sped toward him, weaving a bit. Great. A glance at his watch showed just past three o'clock. Someone had been hitting the bottle a bit early. Just as long as he—long red hair became visible as the car neared. Make that *she* stayed on her side of the road. When she got close enough to see, Philip recognized her. Sydney's cousin. Arielle.

He flashed his lights and slowed, rolling down his window. At first, he didn't think she planned to slow at all, but her car came to an abrupt stop beside his. After staring at him, her mascara smudged and her eyes red, Arielle lowered her window as well.

"You all right?"

"No." If it hadn't been for the quivering lower lip, he'd have sworn she was ticked off rather than hurt.

"What happened? Do I need to call someone? Sydney?"

The woman's eyes flashed, and she seemed to pull herself together. "Yeah. You need to tell her that she's fired, and she should be glad. Mark Bradford is a first-class jerk."

Maybe it wasn't very masculine of him, but his insides quivered like a little girl with a snake shoved in her face. It also probably was insensitive of him to even think of it, but he pictured Sydney as a little girl and decided *she'd* be the one shoving the snake in *his* face. He could hear it now, *"See! Isn't it cute?"*

"I don't know how you can stand him."

Uh, oh. Damage control. He needed to do it and fast. "He called? How'd you get the call?" Philip shoved his hand in his pocket, and sure enough. There was his phone.

"No... he drove up and saw me waiting by my car. Sydney's supposed to be here any minute, but she's not answering her phone— probably avoiding Evan, actually. Anyway, he just walked up and started yelling at me, telling me what a lousy landscaper I was and that I was fired."

Gut clenching, Philip shook his head. "Wait. Mark is *here*?"

"Yep. And he's ticked off about the flooded basement—blames Sydney for it. Like it's her fault his plumbing is messed up."

No, no, no... he had to fix this. And fast. First, Sydney could not be fired. Second, Mark could not start blaming her for something like that. Besides, he was working on it. The basement was half pumped out already, and he'd found the busted pipe that leaked in through a crack in the foundation. Combination—detrimental and deleterious to unsuspecting basements. That's what the guy at the plumbing supply he'd gone to said. Sounded redundant to him, but Philip had to admit he wasn't confident of the definition of deleterious.

"Philip?"

Arielle's sharp tone snapped him out of his attempt to evade the problem. "Sorry. Thinking. I'll take care of it."

"Save Sydney's job, and I'll help her sabotage Aunt Clara's mission to marry her off to Evan. I'll even try to convince her that you're an electrical engineer instead of a lowly electrician."

It took more effort than it should have to stifle the smile that tried to form. Sydney must have told Arielle about their date. That was good, right? If Arielle was on his side?

"Deal. Better get to the castle and straighten Mark out about responsibility." Then her words hit. A "lowly electrician?" What was that about? And he *was* an electrical engineer, thank-you-very-much. Before he could ask, Arielle spoke again.

"Do that. Oh, and good luck with Syd. She's the best, really."

Since saying, "No, duh" was both unnecessary and juvenile, Philip just nodded. "I agree. See you later." He'd have raised his window but stopped just in time. "And sorry about Mark. After my electrical fire, getting the call about a flood wasn't what he needed. I just didn't make it clear whose fault it was, apparently. I'll fix that."

"Good." And with a wave of perfectly manicured fingers, Arielle cranked up her window and zipped down the road.

A glance in the rearview mirror showed her staying on *her* side of the road. At least he'd accomplished something. Now to deal with Mark.

Instead of rehearsing his argument, Philip spent the drive up to the castle pondering that manicure. Sydney was probably the least high-maintenance woman he'd ever known, but she too had perfectly manicured nails. Cousinly bonding? Her "one weakness?" Her mother's influence or demands?

And one more thing? Why did he care?

Seeing Mark glowering at the corner of the castle drove all thoughts of polish out of his mind. Philip brought his truck to an abrupt halt and practically vaulted from the cab. "Mark!"

Mark did not respond beyond a glare his way.

Reaching the still-sodden corner of the castle, Philip sidestepped Murphy's greeting and promptly blasted his friend. And boss, but who kept track of relationships at a time like this? "What do you think you're doing going off on Sydney's cousin like that?"

"Sydney? The redhead?"

"No, that would be *Arielle*. Sydney's *cousin*. She nearly caused a car accident driving while upset because *you* blasted her for something that wasn't hers *or* Sydney's fault."

"She flooded my basement for her landscaping. She's fired."

He really didn't want to have to find a cheap Airbnb until the Columbia job, but Sydney needed this opportunity, and he needed an opportunity to keep their relationship...viable. So, tossing caution into the Mississippi, Philip folded his arms over his chest and leveled his most intimidating glare (if he did say so himself) on Mark.

"You want to fire someone? Fire me. I started the water for her, I left it running, I did it all—including getting the water *out* of your basement when *I* blew it. Don't blame Sydney for my mistakes."

"There weren't mistakes before she came. She shows up and we have a basement fire, a flooded basement..." Mark glared back at him. "What've you got against my basement, anyway?"

"Nothing... yet. But I'll be tempted to rig an explosion if you don't call Sydney and tell her she's not fired... Oh and apologize to Arielle. She didn't deserve that."

Having set the record straight and presented his closing argument, Philip waited for the verdict.

Five

Something had to change. Sydney tossed the green leather handbag onto her bed and headed toward the bathroom. How many times could her mother hear the words "I have work to do" without understanding—or rather, without accepting—that Sydney meant them? If she didn't ignore the phrase entirely, she pursed her lips and regarded her daughter as if Sydney had said something rude. And twice, she'd reminded Sydney that it was the weekend.

She couldn't have it both ways – independent but still living with her parents. Arielle had pointed that out last week. Every month Sydney stayed here instead of moving into her own apartment saved another thousand dollars for her business, though, and she'd just placed the order for that new trailer. She had to stick it out a little longer.

A nudge in her spirit prompted a wince as she shut the bathroom door behind her. *Okay... maybe I should've been praying about this for a long time. Here's me asking how to pray about it because I don't even know where to begin.*

Sydney turned on the shower and grabbed two towels from the shelf. The water would be ice cold for at least two minutes. They needed a big boiler, like the one at the castle. Of course... she chuckled, remembering Philip's phone call. He'd made a funny story of the flooded basement, but it must have been a mess. He'd still be bailing water if he hadn't found a sump pump.

Maybe he'd spent the weekend mopping up. She returned to her bedroom and dug the phone from her purse. No call. He'd been busy, of course, and it wasn't like they had the "call every day" kind of relationship. They didn't have a relationship at all, yet. One date—no matter how perfect—did not constitute a relationship.

But that date... if she'd ever been flirtation-challenged, she'd certainly blossomed over pizza. She'd laughed more on Friday night than she had since... well, maybe ever. Despite the incessant pings from her mother's texts, she hadn't felt awkward—not once, even when they said goodbye at the restaurant door, and the thought had crossed her mind that if she'd let him pick her up instead of meeting him there, he might have kissed her goodnight after driving her home.

Her mother would have been watching and possibly waiting when Sydney got inside. Or had she gone to the concert? Sydney didn't know and didn't ask about it the next morning. Didn't care. She needed to start asserting herself. She couldn't blame her mother for not taking her seriously when she never asserted herself. Next time her mother brushed off Sydney's statement of needing to work, Sydney would politely but firmly tell her...

She jumped at the ringing of the phone and snatched it up. Unknown number. Sydney had her finger on the screen to decline the call but stopped just before the swipe, remembering she ran a business and had to answer phone calls even when she didn't recognize the number, even at seven o'clock on a Sunday evening. Even when it wasn't Philip so who cared?

"Elliott Landscapes." She infused the name with enthusiasm. It wasn't the caller's fault she'd been mooning over a good-looking electrician.

"Yeah. Is this Sydney Elliott or an answering service?"

Ah. Just another client who wanted their lawn mowed and hedges trimmed. He sounded cranky rather than elderly, but no one under sixty would even think of an answering service.

"This is Sydney. How can I help you?" She re-entered the bathroom and shut off the water.

"This is Mark Bradford. You might as well go ahead and finish your estimate."

Sydney paused with a hand on the faucet. "I'm sorry. What did you say?" She'd heard him the first time; it just didn't make sense. Was he saying to finish up the estimate quickly and submit it to him? His tone wasn't encouraging.

"You can come back. You're un-fired. Finish doing whatever it is you've been doing out here when you're not flooding the castle."

She straightened. Definitely not encouraging. "I didn't..." but she was at least partially responsible. She'd been distracted, and she'd known Philip wasn't familiar with the hundred-year-old plumbing. "I apologize for that."

"Yeah, whatever. You're un-fired. Let's get it over with."

Un-fired? She'd been fired? Sydney pulled the phone away from her ear to see if there was a voicemail she'd missed and realized he'd disconnected. What was that all about? Should she call Philip? At least she had a valid excuse now.

The phone vibrated, and Arielle's ringtone sounded even as Sydney scrolled to Philip's contact information. That obnoxious Disney song... Sydney clapped a hand over her mouth, overcome with an insane desire to laugh. Flooding the basement...

"Hi, Arielle. What's up?" Sydney knelt and lifted the dust ruffle, looking for her slippers. Hopefully, her cousin hadn't just called for a chat. She wanted to call Philip and find out what was going on.

"Did Philip call you?" Arielle's question sounded more demanding than inquisitive.

"No." Sydney grabbed the slippers and rose. "But our date went well. It was great."

"Yeah, whatever."

Sydney dropped onto the dressing table stool. Hadn't she just heard that adolescent phrase from Mark Bradford? She hadn't heard it from Arielle in at least five years. It didn't go with her new image.

"I assumed he might have called you by now," Arielle went on. "He said he was going to."

"When?" Sydney narrowed her eyes at her reflection.

"About an hour ago, at the castle."

"No, and I just got the strangest phone call from Mark Bradford," Sydney said.

"Ugh. Look, I'm coming over. I'll be there in about fifteen minutes."

"Not tonight," Sydney protested. "I've got a lot of work to do." At least, she was pretty sure she still had work to do. Mr. Bradford told her to complete the estimate.

"Ten minutes," Arielle said. "I'll see you then."

Philip's phone went to voicemail after six rings.

"Hi, it's Sydney. I just had a strange phone call from your friend Mark." Sydney scratched her nose. It didn't feel like something she could leave a message about. "Give me a call when you get a chance, please. Thanks!"

She opened her portfolio and spread papers on the bed. If she had her own apartment, she'd have room to work at a real table or desk instead of on her bed. The dressing table was worthless for anything but makeup, and she seldom wore any. Maybe she could replace it with a desk. Maybe she should just move out.

Arielle knocked even as she pushed the door open. "Sorry. I got stuck talking to your mom. She thinks you're overdoing it. Working too hard. You'll get circles under your pretty eyes, and then how will you catch a man?"

"She did not say that!"

"Not in those exact words," Arielle said, "but that's what she meant. You'd think this was Regency England and she had a whole flock of daughters to marry off. Or the 1950's. Mom says she was always like this, even as a little girl. All her Barbies had white gloves, pumps, and pillbox hats."

Sydney grinned. "I think she passed them all down to me, but I don't know what I did with them. I wasn't much into dolls."

"Anyhow." Arielle slashed a hand through the air, signaling an end to their small talk. "Philip was supposed to call you."

"About what? I got a call from Mark Bradford, telling me I'm not fired, and then you called, and Philip isn't answering his phone." She heard her voice rising and took a deep breath. "What's going on?"

Arielle sat on the stool. "I drove up to the castle, looking for you. Your mom said you were working out there today."

"No, I was trimming topiary trees at the nursing home," Sydney said. "A sort of pro bono job. The residents like to come out and give me advice while I work."

"Well, I drove up there, and I encountered the king of the castle. The emperor. The ogre." Arielle scowled. "Rude! He lit into me about being negligent and irresponsible and damage to the basement, without giving me a chance to introduce myself. He seemed to think I was you!"

"Oh, no."

"Yes, even though I was wearing my new white lace skirt and a coral sweater! And matching coral sandals too, so I don't know how he could think I was a landscaper." She tucked loose coils of curls behind her ear. "Did you really flood the basement?"

Sydney nodded. "Philip and I left a hose running while we were gone. We didn't know it leaked, of course. I just wanted to fill a dry creek bed and pond."

"The ogre thinks it was criminal negligence," Arielle said, "and he said I was fired. I said he couldn't fire me because I quit!"

"Arielle!" Sydney sat up straight and pulled a pillow across her lap. "So, did you tell him who you are?"

"He didn't give me a chance! He just said not to come back and don't bother submitting a bill because he won't pay it. You're supposed to be lucky he doesn't sue you." Arielle bit her thumbnail and looked at Sydney through her lashes. "I'm sorry. I ran into Philip on the way out, and he said he'd smooth things over."

"I haven't heard from Philip," Sydney said, "but Mr. Bradford called and said to continue with the proposal. He said I'm un-fired."

"Oh, good." Arielle blew out a long breath. "Maybe he's just not very bright. You know... able to live on his own, but a little slow."

Very likely, if he'd thought Arielle, with her short skirt and yellow Volkswagen bug, was the gardener. Sydney looked at her stacks of drawings and photographs. "I hope he's not too mad. The estimate keeps getting bigger. I've been trying to use low-maintenance plants because Philip said he doesn't think Mr. Bradford would hire a gardener.

"Poison ivy is low-maintenance," Arielle said. "What's that plant that attracts feral cats? Catnip? I know... you could use creeping charlie for a ground over. Stinkweed. Or turn all of his hedges into topiary animals – bunny rabbits or something."

"Thanks," Sydney said drily. "I'll keep your suggestions in mind, but I want this to be a centerpiece of my portfolio. If you don't mind, I really do have a lot to do tonight, and I want to be out there by seven tomorrow."

"Okay." Arielle jumped to her feet. She turned back at the bedroom door. "I've got it! Plant box elder trees, so the castle fills up with box elder bugs. Those things are indestructible!"

Perspiration ran down his temples and back in rivulets, but Philip pressed on, sweeping the last of the basement mess into a pile to be scooped and dumped before sending out the dove from the egress window. The flood was over. Pipes fixed, and Mark had even smiled that morning. Barely, but for Mark it was nearly equivalent to a grin.

Not only that, but Mark had even admitted that if they hadn't found out about the leak when they did, it could have damaged expensive landscaping. That comment had kept Philip going when he wanted to quit sweeping and scooping. Now that it was done, he had a call to make.

Pulling out his phone, he hesitated between an actual call and a text. Maybe a text would be better. What if she were in the middle of something? He opened his messaging app just as his brain kicked into gear. Duh. She'd just ignore the call until she had time. This wasn't high school when the idea of missing a call or text sent panic through— That thought died when he saw Sunday's text to her sitting there. Unsent.

No doubt about it. Time to call. He tapped the screen.

As if lured in by the promise of a chance to slobber all over her, Murphy galloped down the stairs and nearly tumbled to a heap at the bottom when his paw missed a step. Clumsy old thing. "Hey boy..."

"I didn't know I'd put in for a gender reassignment, but okay then!"

"Sydney! Philip here."

"That's what the screen says... everything okay?"

Translation: why haven't you responded to my texts?

"I hope it will be after an apology. I just found my unsent text from Sunday. Sorry. Didn't mean to leave you hanging. I was trying to get the leak fixed and the basement cleaned out. It worked out to our advantage too." As he spoke, he hefted the push broom and carried it up the stairs and out to the shed. The basement had seemed smothering while he'd been working, but the sauna masquerading as the castle grounds proved him wrong.

"Our advantage?"

"Talked to Mark..." Murphy barked, drowning out some response she'd made, and took off toward a copse of trees a few yards beyond his apartment. Philip just kept going. "If you have the proposal done, this is a great time to bring it—while he's in a landscaping mood."

As Philip hung the broom on the wall of the shed, he waited for some response. He got nothing. "Really sorry about disappearing. I thought I'd sent that text... Here. I'll hit send."

"It's not that. Things happen. I just... well, I'd decided he only said to keep going because you guilted him into it. You think he'll actually go for it?"

"Yeah." Did he? He did. "I really do. Hurry out, though. Mark's... difficult sometimes. Get him to sign whatever he needs to while he's in a good mood."

Laughter filled his ear. She had a great laugh. "I should've known you were joking."

"Not joking... but hurry. These moods rarely last." Then, before he could second-guess himself, he added, "Besides... It's been too long since I've seen you."

"On my way."

The east "wing" of the castle still needed all new wiring, and Philip's time was growing short. He'd be on his way to Columbia any day now (why did a two-hour drive feel so long now?), so while he waited to hear the outcome of Sydney's consultation with Mark, he worked on making the next room on his list a safe place to flip a light switch. A few of his buddies said he was wasting his skills on a simple rewiring job, but they didn't get it. This castle was part of St. Louis history. A guy didn't leave something like it to the hands of a day jobber with no license or education. And that's who Mark would hire.

Though he heard Sydney's truck drive up, Philip kept working, trying to gauge the amount of time to allow for pointing out all the plans. Then there'd be time to hash out materials, expenses, overages— all that fun stuff that comes with reno and installation projects. He'd give 'em another half hour and then go barge in.

Sydney found him inside ten minutes. It was definitely a go. It had to be with that grin. "Get it all squared away?"

"He's letting me do it all." She tugged her ponytail a bit tighter before adding, "Of course, he wants it all..." She dropped her voice to a low growl. "...low maintenance."

Uh, oh.

"Can you do that?"

"Sure. It won't be hanging plants here and fussy bushes there. It'll be great to show clients that a no-manicured landscaping plan doesn't have to mean it has to look neglected." She sagged against the wall nearest him. "I really thought he'd say no." Her gaze swept the room before landing on him again. "This is such a cool place."

"Yeah." Time to throw out his idea.

But before he could, Sydney pumped her fist with the power of Travolta's "Stayin' Alive" dance moves, if not the grace. "He said *yes!*"

So maybe she sounded like a guy who had proposed to a girl on a whim. So what? That couldn't have been a more perfect opening. "Time to celebrate."

Sydney moved closer and dropped to the floor. Sitting cross-legged, she pointed at where he kept pulling Romex through the wall. "So, what are you doing?"

Flirting time? Sure, why not? "Weeping, wailing, and gnashing teeth over your rejection of my flawless date suggestion." He shot her a grin before adding, "And pulling new wire through by pulling out the old knob and tube stuff."

"You can just pull it through the house like that? No breaking through walls?"

"I wish. No, some walls you have to get into. Others you can just pull. It's all about where they may connect—and where they often shouldn't."

She scooted closer, watching. Philip kept working as he tried to figure out how to bring up the date—that's what it would be, after all—again. He knew she enjoyed the last one. She'd sent all the right signals... right up to his suggestion of a celebration. Then everything shut down. Why?

"So... about this celebration."

"You had me nervous."

Sydney nudged his knee with the toe of her work boots. "That was the idea." As she leaned back on her hands and studied him, she asked, "So what'd you have in mind?"

The first thing that came to mind he went for. It had everything you could want. Romance, her favorite things, and food. Because a guy who's been working hard all day needs food.

"How about a picnic out by the fountain back where Mark wants to play paintball? We can do sandwiches, or I have frozen fried chicken we could pop in the oven."

"Kind of hot for that..."

A girl after his own heart... but he went for it. "Yeah, but we'll be out in the sauna out there instead."

"It's not too bad under the river birch and silver maples. Yeah. Let's do it."

He abandoned the Romex and stood, offering her a hand up as well. He didn't let go. In a Disney movie, she'd probably start singing about feelings and the golden glow in the air or something. He'd probably have his own part—a nasty tenor with his luck—about just knowing she was the one for him. That part? Totally true as far as Philip could see. She probably wasn't truly perfect, but she was perfect enough.

Baking fried chicken in an oven in late August should not be fun. It shouldn't be bearable. Regardless, they had a blast arguing over whether iceberg lettuce counted as salad material and if using a cold baked potato to eke out some potato salad would even work. For the curious—it did. And it didn't. It all depended on who you asked. She said yes. He was a decided no. Still, when they carried their "basket" (it was an Amazon box, but Sydney agreed it could do for a basket in a pinch) and "blanket" (a sheet, okay?) down to the fountain by the little woodland area, he ate the improvised potato "salad" mush and didn't complain. Who would with her sitting beside him?

"Isn't this place amazing?"

Philip looked at trees needing some serious pruning, overgrown grasses and... were they native bushes or some kind of shrub? He'd never admit it to her, but he didn't know his plants. "It might be when you're done with it. Right now, it's a mess."

"But look at the scope of this property! There's so much here and so close to the city. It should have been knocked down and turned into homes for people with more money than sense." Did he hear right? Did she really mutter, "And I know how that goes"?

"True..." What else did you say to something like that?

"I just can't believe he's not selling out."

She turned to him, awfully close now, and kept rambling about something—something about the expense of maintaining the castle, wasn't it? Philip couldn't keep up. Not with the idea of kissing her overriding all other rational thought.

"—so glad he isn't."

The grace of God kept him from saying, "Glad he isn't, what? I was distracted by your lips." A guy just didn't admit things like that. "Um... yeah." His brain kicked in gear when he looked away. "I've enjoyed making sure the knob and tube is eradicated."

"Philip?"

Okay he had to look back, but the moment he did...

"I saw it. I get it. Go for it."

If she only knew how that sounded to where his mind had been. But then he caught her gaze and realized, she really did. "Yeah...?" With an invitation like that, who wouldn't brush the hair away from her eyes, touch her cheek, kiss her until his back screamed in protest. It wasn't that he'd never kissed a woman. He had. But why had he ever considered those kisses anything special? This...

"Hey, let's walk a bit." At least if they were standing, he could work in an encore without sending him to the chiropractor. That thought had just marked him as "over thirty."

The bemused expression Sydney gave him told him she'd felt it too. "Yeah."

Instead of moving closer to the house, he led her deeper into Mark's beloved paintball wilderness. An obliging tree without the addition of ants allowed for a perfect repeat, back-pain-free performance. This time Sydney found it, scanned it, leaned against it, and gripped his shirt, pulling him closer. "Dare you to leave that last kiss in the dust."

"Sydney..." He dropped his forehead to hers. "How am I ever going to go off to this job in Columbia?"

Her lips drew closer... and closer... "We'll call... text... visit. It's only two hours away." They practically brushed his as she added, "But only if you prove that you can pull off another world-dizzying kiss."

What else could Philip do but oblige? Definitely an improvement— and not just because his back wasn't contorted in ways that constituted torture. Oh, yeah. He'd make the trip back every week for a reward like that.

Six

Putting the garden to bed.

Sydney had always loved that expression, but bedtime was coming too fast this year. She really should have started the castle gardens last fall, made preparations over winter, planted early, and worked on it all summer. She'd rushed the planning and proposal, but she hadn't accomplished much of the actual work this year.

That's how this business operated. Real landscaping wasn't a short-term project like planting a vegetable garden. Sydney turned in a circle, trying to envision the grounds as they'd look next summer. It would take years to truly develop the plan, and she'd normally be fine with that.

Unfortunately, Mark Bradford was less than enthusiastic about making it an ongoing project. He didn't seem to understand that a garden was a living thing. She couldn't just stick plants in the ground and be done with it; the castle grounds would require care and nurturing.

Sydney kicked at a rock. If Mark refused to invest in ongoing maintenance, this whole project would be a colossal waste of time and money. It was pointless to do any work at all if he was just going to let it all go wild again next spring. Every time she tried to talk to him about it, he reminded her that she'd assured him it would be low maintenance. What he really wanted was "no maintenance." If Philip were here...

She inhaled. She was a big girl... an adult woman, a professional landscape architect, and a small business owner. She refused to start thinking like her mother, believing that she needed a man to be successful. Sydney could manage difficult clients on her own, and this wasn't junior high school. As much as she'd love to see Philip, she wouldn't use his pigheaded friend as an excuse.

She'd love to see Philip, period. Not just for short dates, but... Sydney pulled off her gloves and shoved them into the pocket of her hoodie. They exchanged texts daily and talked on the phone nearly as often, but the easy camaraderie and breath-stealing kisses of the summer had become awkward after his move to Columbia. No, not awkward. Just different. She'd felt so bold and flirtatious back then. Now, they seemed to start from scratch every time they met, and by the time she relaxed and felt comfortable, it was time to leave.

They did better on the phone than in person. Philip seemed to enjoy hearing about her work at the castle and the adventures of Murphy. She hadn't acquired many new clients, but that would pick up in the spring. Philip's job seemed to consume his time and attention, but she didn't understand the complexities of it. She'd assumed that an electrical engineer was a sort of glorified electrician, but apparently not... Sydney just listened and made what she hoped were sensible responses.

Mark Bradford avoided her, and Arielle kept busy with her wedding planning—no, her events management—business. Sydney was beginning to be grateful for Murphy's company, and the big dog wasn't the most discerning of friends.

Sydney shook off the melancholy reflections. She had no business feeling sorry for herself. Her life was good. She'd make more friends here eventually, and in the meantime, her mother was always wanting to spend time together shopping, getting their hair done, visiting friends, doing lunch, and going to concerts and fundraisers.

Fundraisers like the country club's gala ball on Saturday night. This Saturday, and Sydney hadn't yet provided herself with an excuse to skip it. Maybe Arielle would like to do something. Anything. Sydney pulled her phone from her pocket, dropping the gloves in the process. Even as she stooped to retrieve them, the phone trilled out the familiar Disney melody. Perfect.

"Arielle! I was just about to call you!"

"Great. Listen. I have an idea, and I need your coopera- er, your help."

Instantly wary, Sydney dropped onto a stone bench. "What kind of help? On Saturday night?"

"What? No! Pay attention!" Even bossier than usual. "We're doing a fundraiser for the children's hospital, and I need you to convince your boss to let us use the castle grounds."

"He's not my boss." That might not be the pertinent point, but it mattered to Sydney. "He's the client. And you're dreaming."

"Oh, come on... I'm sure you can talk him into it. Tell him about the poor sick kids."

"No! Tell him yourself!" Sydney rose and started for the truck. She was done for the day, and she had no intention of talking to Mark. Not about this, anyway.

"No way," Arielle said. "He doesn't like me."

"Well, I'm not doing it. He'd just say no, anyhow—to whatever you have in mind, no matter who asks him. It doesn't even matter what it is. He'll just reject it." Did she sound bitter? Sydney opened the door and pulled herself up into the truck. "Hold your event somewhere else."

"We really need the castle! Just the grounds," Arielle said. "no one has to go inside. We want to do a parade of Christmas lights, starting in town and ending in a traditional European Christmas market."

"At the castle?" Sydney asked. She snorted. "Do let me know when you come up to talk to Mark, so I can be there to watch. I'd hate to miss that conversation."

"Please, Sydney? This is important to me."

Sydney steeled her heart against the cajoling voice. "No. You've met him. There's no way. A Christmas market... who came up with that bright idea?"

"Well," Arielle said, "It's an auxiliary project."

"The Children's Hospital auxiliary?" Sydney stopped in the act of pushing the start button. "They're always taking on overly ambitious projects. Mom's the worst of the bunch." She paused. "Um... are you telling me this was my mother's idea?"

"I'm not telling you anything," Arielle said, "but I agree with her. The castle would be the perfect venue."

Sydney rolled her eyes. "Yeah, good luck with that."

"But it would be good for you too," Arielle said. "You could use Christmas lights in your portfolio pictures, to show a garden in winter."

"Oh." She mulled over the idea. "It's not a bad idea, but I'm one hundred and ten percent sure Mark Bradford will say no."

"Ask him!"

Sydney started the truck and fastened her seatbelt. "Not happening. At least... I'm not doing it. And since when are you involved with the auxiliary?"

"I'm not. But they said that if I could set this up, they'd put my company in charge of managing it!"

Sydney heard the faint squeal of excitement in her cousin's voice and knew she was sunk. Arielle needed a project like this.

"But he really doesn't like me, Syd, and he'd be more likely to say yes to you. Oh! You know what? You should get Philip to ask him! Philip talked him into letting you submit a proposal and then got you un-fired later, even after you flooded the castle. If anyone can convince Mark Bradford to let us do this, it will be Philip."

Philip. Maybe he could get Mark to agree, and then she and Philip could put up the lights together. She couldn't see the auxiliary ladies doing that. It would all fall on her. And Philip. Putting up Christmas lights might be very romantic. They'd be working together in the castle gardens, just as they had done before. Yes.

"Okay, Arielle. I won't ask him myself, but send me a text with all the details, and I'll call Philip and see if he'll do it. No promises! Meanwhile, your job is to pray."

Somehow, having a valid excuse for calling him made it more important —a formal call instead of just to chat. The familiar anticipation of hearing his voice and making a date zinged through her. Sooner or later, if this relationship were going to progress, one of them would have to move. In the meantime—

"Sydney!"

There it was. She hadn't noticed what a warm and attractive voice he had until he'd moved away, and she only heard it on the phone.

"Hi, Philip. Is this a good time?"

"Any time is a good time for you."

She smiled. "You are such a charmer. Or a flatterer, and you know what the Bible says about flatterers."

"It's not flattery if it's true. So, what's up with you?"

Sydney scooted up to the head of the bed and propped pillows behind her. "Are you feeling like a knight in shining armor? I have an impossible task to set before you. It's really a favor for Arielle, but if you can make it happen—and it seems unlikely to me—it would be really fun for the two of us to do together."

There were a few seconds of silence—probably for him to untangle that sentence—before he said, "I want to say, 'at your service, my lady,' or something equally gallant, but you're making me a little nervous."

Sydney tucked her legs up underneath her and snuggled into the pillows. "Well, here's the deal..."

The first fall leaves swooped and swirled in the breeze as he walked from his meeting to his truck, his phone tethering him to the castle and Sydney's impossible request. Philip had started to make the call half a dozen times, but she'd be expecting a reply soon, so he'd given up and dialed, ending the second round of persuasion with, "And come on. It's for charity."

"No."

Though Philip tried not to wince, it wasn't easy. Still, it was better than Mark's first response of, "Not on your life!" He'd already weakened a little.

"You wouldn't have to do anything. It wouldn't cost you anything, but maybe if you actually let them do something there, they'd leave you alone for a while. You gave them a coup—a chance to do something no one else would ever do. Maybe that would drive away others from trying to be the first. And with Sydney and me doing all the work of setting up the lights—"

"You're coming back to help?"

Uh, oh. That could be really good or really bad. Philip didn't know which to hope for anymore. "Um... yeah. I mean, it's a two-man job, and I figured you wouldn't want Arielle out there."

"No. You keep her away."

He'd just agreed and hadn't even realized it yet. "She'll probably have to be there for the actual event, but you can be gone that day. Just lock the house and let them go."

"I don't have to make bathrooms available?"

As much as Philip wanted to point out that they really should, he didn't. Instead, he said he'd insist on port-a-potties. "That'll keep people from hanging around too long. Most won't want to use something like that at all, much less in the cold."

"Fine. Whatever. Just make sure you guys take those lights down by New Year's."

After assuring Mark that all would be well, again, Philip made the call. "I'll be there Friday night."

"Can I just say—for the record and all—that putting up Christmas lights before Halloween is just wrong? I think Arielle owes us funnel cakes or whatever they're selling at this thing."

"Agreed—on both counts." Philip hesitated before adding, "Hey, Sydney?"

"Hmm...?" She sounded awfully distracted already—just as she had for the past couple of months. Great. Maybe she really wasn't as into a "them" as he was.

"I'm *really* looking forward to spending time with you. I think I've learned something from all this separation."

That caught her interest. He could almost *hear* her snap to attention, sit up straighter, lean into the call. "Oh, yeah?"

"Yeah. It stinks. I need to make coming down every weekend a thing."

"You won't get any complaints from me." A bark preceded a squeal followed by an "oof!" Murphy must be at it again. "Murph agrees as well, for what it's worth."

Several thousand-foot reels of white Christmas lights lay spread out on Sydney's tailgate when Philip finally pulled in. He jumped from the cab, dodged a charging Murphy, and scooped her up in a hug. Yes, he swung her in an arc as if they were on a photoshoot for some weird romance book. Who wouldn't have? She looked amazing, and he hadn't seen her in three weeks.

"Missed you." Before he chickened out, Philip kissed her and murmured, "How can I have only known you for a few short months? You've become indispensable to me." There. Talk about putting your heart on the line. If she freaked out...

But she didn't. Instead, she slid her hand up behind his head, gazed at him until he felt certain he'd lost his mind, and dared him to kiss her again—really knock her socks off. Who could resist a dare like that, and why would he want to even if he could?

This time, she broke the kiss, sighed, gave him one more peck as if unwilling to be parted, and stepped away. "We really do have to get to work on this light design."

Murphy barked his approval, and although Philip couldn't argue that, he wanted to. "What about a compromise?"

As she pulled the first reel off her truck, Sydney shot him a suspicious glance. "Oh, yeah? What's that?"

"A ten-minute date break at the end of every reel finished."

That earned him a grin, another quick peck to his cheek, and... abandonment. She dashed to the left side of the castle and began applying clips and stringing wires. When she saw him staring at her, she called back, "Get a move on. First one done decides how we spend those dates."

The poor girl. She really thought she could beat him. Maybe he should let her win... It only took a minute of watching to realize that would be a colossal mistake. She'd never forgive him. Right now, anything that could jeopardize their relationship was a no-go.

Underestimating her diabolical schemes was his first mistake. Sure, she started on the left side of the building, but only long enough to leave something to attach another string of lights to—and to fake him out. By the time he'd clipped a design a third of the way up the wall, she'd created a lattice on shrubs and bushes around the whole left side of the door!

"Time!"

Philip couldn't resist ribbing her. "Do they work?"

Grabbing an extension cord from the jumble of things on her tailgate, Sydney attached it to the plug end and stormed the citadel—or at least the front castle doors. A moment later, the front glowed in fairy lights. From inside she called out, "Well?"

"Come see if it's what you're looking for." When Sydney jogged back outside, he burst out in a rendition of "You Light Up My Life" that would make Debbie Boone proud if he did say so himself. Murphy danced around him as if he'd serenaded the dog instead of the love of his life.

Whoa... that came out of nowhere. He couldn't deny it even if he wanted to. And he didn't. Not at all.

Though she shook her head and muttered, "Silly," Sydney also glowed. Or maybe it was the reflection of the lights, but Philip preferred to think it was his obvious admiration. Before he knew what hit him, she'd grabbed his hand and pulled him toward the side of the house. Murphy loped alongside them.

"Where are we going?"

"We're going on a romantic walk through the..." She made air quotes, still holding his hand. "'Forest.' We'll kick leaves and try to keep Murphy from ruining the mind-boggling kiss you'll give me before we head back. Deal?"

As his hand squeezed hers, Philip murmured, "You had me at mind-boggling kiss. Might need to rehearse that before we get there."

Sydney stopped, slid her free arm up around his neck, and said, "Great idea."

He could get used to a life full of invitations to kiss this woman. *So* used to it.

Seven

It had come back. The joy—the daring, newly-discovered flirtatious side of her personality—had come back as soon as Philip emerged from the truck. None of their other recent weekends had felt like this one. But now, after that phone call and his talk of coming every weekend, and especially after his exuberant greeting on Friday, she felt alive and... and sparkling from her fingertips to her toes. Sydney tossed her gloves onto the seat, grinning at the idea. She'd never sparkled before, not even when she was a little girl. When her friends were into glitter, bubbles, and unicorns, Sydney's pretty pink dresses were always filthy, and as for the dirt under her fingernails... her mother had hated that more than anything. Sydney submitted to the scrubbing and the concealing nail polish in exchange for the freedom to play in the dirt. Her mom should have had a daughter like Arielle, who cared about all that stuff. Instead, free-spirited Aunt Millicent had produced the Type-A daughter. Life was weird. She'd done almost as much light-stringing today, without the distraction of the tall, dark, and handsome electrician, as they'd accomplished over the weekend, interrupted by ten-minute dates and nine-minute kisses. If she worked hard for the next four days, they might be able to take fifteen-minute breaks next time. Sydney flipped down the sun visor to examine her face. Not entirely clean, but good enough for Culver's with Arielle, to assure her that everything was on schedule for her grand event. Arielle would enjoy hearing about her weekend with Philip too. And if she didn't... well, too bad. Sydney wanted to talk about him. She started the truck, still smiling, enjoying the deep sound of the engine. She'd feel ridiculous in her cousin's little bug. It was cute but totally useless. Kind of like Murphy. The dog had followed her around all morning, even resting a heavy paw on the ladder when she was running lights along the branches until Mark came out of the castle and whistled for him. Murphy bounded toward him, and Mark caught his collar. "I hope you have insurance. I'm not going to be responsible for you breaking your neck when you encourage the dog to jump on you." She didn't have time to respond to the unjust accusation before he reentered the castle, dragging Murphy and slamming the door behind him. Mark Bradford really was the most infuriating man she'd ever met. He'd paid for the landscape plans and initial work but wouldn't even look at her maintenance contract.

Sydney's smile faded. That was unjust too. She'd pushed him into the landscaping project. He'd have lived quite happily in the overgrown mess forever, mowing occasionally and using the whole property as his personal playground. Philip raved about the games of capture the flag, laser tag, paintball or whatever else he and Mark and their buddies played out there—even at night, in the dark. It sounded scary and dangerous to her.

At least Philip appreciated the landscaped parts of the grounds too. Philip. Sydney turned the car and headed down the driveway. Their relationship didn't depend on Mark Bradford or this castle project. They'd be good even if Mark fired her tomorrow, but Sydney couldn't let that happen. She'd invested too much time and money into this project. She needed a good portfolio to get the kind of jobs that would justify her recent purchases of equipment. Mark Bradford was getting spectacular castle grounds whether he liked it or not.

The mechanical voice announced she had an incoming call, and Sydney leaned forward to read the number. Not that it mattered... as a businesswoman, she didn't get to ignore phone calls.

"Hey, Arielle. I hope you're not calling to cancel our date. I'm starving."

"Something came up. I'm sorry. I'd rather go out to lunch, but there's an emergency meeting of the Christmas at Castlebourne committee. That committee has more emergencies than a hospital, and as their event manager, I have to calm everyone down and fix the problem. It's usually something minor, but it sounds like this one involves zoning, and that's always complicated."

"Christmas at Castlebourne? Mark will hate that."

"I thought so too."

Sydney grinned at the undercurrent of smug complacency, clear even through the truck's speaker system. "He's been growling at me all week."

"Like a dog?"

"Oh, no. Murphy is all too friendly." Sydney braked at the sight of flashing lights. "Shoot. There's a train coming. I was stuck here for fifteen minutes last time. Anyhow, you wouldn't believe what that dog did yesterday."

"I love a good Murphy story," Arielle said.

Sydney put the truck in neutral and settled back against the seat. "Well, I'd been working there all morning, and Mark pulled up in that old flatbed truck of his. Murphy had his head hanging out the window, barking as soon as he saw me." She had to raise her voice to be heard over the whistle of the train. "I'll text you."

"What?" her cousin shouted. "I can't hear you!"

Sydney disconnected the blue tooth and shifted into park before digging her phone out of her purse and opening a text window.

Sorry about that. Too hard to yell into the phone over the sound of the train. Anyhow, as soon as the truck stopped, he jumped out and ran right to me. I mean, it had been a few days, but he always acts like it's been years. Like one of those 'soldiers coming home' videos.

He loves you!

Sidney rolled her eyes at the multi-colored row of heart emojis.

Well, I don't love him. He's cute, in a scruffy kind of way, but way too friendly. He's always trying to kiss my face, and then I feel guilty for pushing him away, because he gets this hurt, puppy-dog look on his face. I get enough manipulation from my mother.

She'd say his behavior is the result of inferior breeding.

She might be right about that.

And a product of his environment. Just look at Mark. When your best friend is a rude, grouchy jerk... it's a miracle he has any social skills at all.

He has potential. It's just really hidden and under-developed. I only have to put up with him for a few more weeks.

You're going to miss him when this job is over.

Maybe a little. Still... I owe him! I'm pretty sure I wouldn't have got this job if it hadn't been for that skunk incident. I think Philip guilted Mark into hiring me after Murphy smeared skunk juice all over me.

That Philip is nice to have around. He talked Mark into the Christmas event too.

Yeah. I wonder if I could get him to talk to Mark about the maintenance.

Sydney looked up as the end of the train swept past. With a sigh of relief, she switched back to the Bluetooth phone.

Arielle answered on the first ring, speaking as if they hadn't been interrupted. "Before you get back to your puppy love, I thought I'd better ask you about this new guy your mom is trying to set you up with."

"Billingsley Hartford-Spooner." The syllables didn't roll off the tongue. One had to enunciate each one. "And don't call him Bill. I made that mistake, and Mom corrected me, right there in front of him."

"What does he like to be called?" Arielle asked.

"Billingsly Hartford-Spooner, according to Mom, and when he called me later, that's how he introduced himself."

"He called you? Did your mom give him your number?"

Sydney signaled her turn and waited for the light to change. "How did you guess? He's in real estate, and she told him I was a landscape architect looking for an office in the city—and also that I was single. I don't even want to know what else she told him, but he seemed to think we have a lot in common."

"Your mom set you up with a realtor?"

Sydney grinned at the skepticism in her cousin's voice. "Oh, no. He owns office buildings in the city. Buys them, sells them, leases them out... whatever. Nothing I could afford even if I wanted to."

"She probably told him about your inheritance," Arielle said, "and he's a fortune hunter in need of capital for his investments. She's probably telling everyone. You're close to being on the shelf, you know. A spinster of a certain age…"

"Been reading your mom's books again?"

"You do seem to be attracting suitors since you came home," Arielle pointed out, "and while you are a lovely young woman from a good family, modern young men don't go out of their way to… well, woo women through their mothers. Your mother approves of this one."

"I know," Sydney sighed. "And she hasn't stopped reminding me that I let the last one get away. I think I'm going to have to tell her about Philip." She should have started mentioning him months ago, instead of staying quiet, but her budding relationship with Philip had seemed so… well, fragile. Now, it was different. They were exclusive now. Her mother still wouldn't understand or approve, but Sydney could stand firm and use the relationship as a shield against her mother's schemes.

"Yeah, you should," Arielle said. "It sounds like things are getting serious there. Exclusivity is a big deal. Almost a commitment. I'm just glad he's up there at the castle, because it means you're getting more work done in preparation for the Christmas event. You're lighting up the castle in more ways than one. Between kisses, of course."

Time to change the subject. "Speaking of Christmas lights," Sydney said, "I got an email from an old college friend yesterday, inviting me to do the Christmas landscapes at a resort in Branson. It would be a great addition to my portfolio, and the income would be nice too."

"You have to do the castle!"

"I could do Branson afterward, but I'm going to turn it down. It's short notice, and I have a few local jobs. It's just a short-term project…" Sydney trailed off. She didn't want to leave Philip for six weeks. Not at this point, when they were just getting serious. So much for being a professional, ambitious businesswoman.

"That girlfriend of yours is a scam artist."

Philip's hand froze, the pizza slicer ready to take off his fingers. "Sydney?"

"Yeah." Mark held out his plate in a silent demand for sustenance. "She set all this landscaping up just to get me to sign a long-term contract to maintain it."

All right, that wasn't fair. Defend his girl—he rather liked the thought of her as "his girl"—he would. "What she's done so far is worth several thousand dollars and took up most of her summer," Philip reminded him. "I doubt she'd go to that much trouble for a maintenance contract worth a couple hundred bucks a month."

"That adds up. It all adds up." Mark stared meaningfully at his empty plate before adding, "You wouldn't believe the property taxes on this place."

Philip slid three pieces of pizza onto the plate. "You said your uncle left you enough money to maintain it. You know... like *maintain the grounds.*"

Mark's scowl said he hadn't changed his mind yet. "Maintain it, yes, but property taxes have gone up a lot since then. Seriously... I don't know how long I'll be able to keep it."

This wasn't good. Not good at all. He had to do something fast, or forget the maintenance contract. Mark could demand they kill the Christmas project too. "Maybe this Christmas project," he began, working up steam for new ideas, "will get people excited about the castle. They might pay to do events here." Mark's face clouded over twice as dark as before. Better divert him. "Just enough to pay taxes so you're not strapped. People pay a lot to host charity balls at places like this. You can just be absent or locked away in a tower while they... revel? Yeah, if it's a night of revelry, then they... revel. Right?"

"How should I know? I know reveil*le*, not revel."

At least Mark was making jokes now. That was good. For now.

Just as he reached for another slice, Mark shoved his empty plate away and chugged the rest of his root beer. As if a scowl had become muscle memory for his face, it contorted into all the frowns and furrows again. "I was thinking about telling her to forget it. But you have a point. If things keep going this way, I might have to. But first... grants.

Someone suggested grants to help preserve a historical house and all that jazz. If they fail, though…"

Philip wanted to say so many things, but he'd managed to stop the cancellation of the Christmas thing. He'd work on the other idea after the new year. For now, just a lazy lunch before Mark took off for a few days. Sydney would arrive soon, and maybe they could talk about his probable return to St. Louis (and her) in the spring. The Columbia project—or rather, his part on it—would be done, and corporate wanted him on a new aerospace project in the city. He'd only known her five months, but fast or not, it was enough for him.

He wanted Sydney in his life…eventually for life. But for now, he had to figure out how to let her know he was looking for exclusivity without going retro high school and asking her to "go steady." Then again, that kind of forthrightness, while cheesy, did have the appeal of a socially acceptable "claim" on someone. These days, he'd be likely to have her go off on him or something for admitting he liked the idea of "claiming" a person as his. Why was it so bad? He could be hers. He was fine with that.

Granddad had it good after all.

Mark broke through his thoughts with another observation. "Actually, your girlfriend has lots of connections to charity things, doesn't she? I mean, she was at some gala the other night with her parents—that Night of Dreams thing where they help terminal patients' families to pay bills and everything, so they don't have to worry about food when the breadwinner is dying or something."

The words grated. "Mark, you're getting too cynical and heartless. That's a serious concern. Picture a single mom being told she has six months to live. She has to spend half in the hospital or working like a dog, so her kids don't get taken away prematurely. C'mon!"

At least Mark had the decency to look chagrined for a moment. "You're right." He fumbled with his phone. "But see… if I did need to rent out the place, maybe having her on my side wouldn't hurt. She obviously moves in the right circles."

Philip had known about the gala. Sydney had even strongly hinted at wishing he were there so her mother would quit pushing her off on "suitable men." A glance at his own worn-out work boots and stained work jeans hinted that her mother wouldn't consider him "suitable."

A phone blurred his view of his boots. "See."

He did see. Sydney in a gown that had to have been expensive enough to provide a month's expenses for some family or other next to a woman who oozed "I get my way—always" from every perfect pore.

"She cleans up nice. You'd never know she was out there sweating and digging in my dirt."

"Yeah." *And I could have been there with her. I wonder who her mother tried to push her off on that time...*

"Then again," Mark continued without bothering to hide his disgust, "the castle is probably a perfect setting for Sydney the princess. Imagine her taking up with the serfs. Bet the Queen Mother there doesn't approve."

Did Sydney's mother even know about him? Somehow, he doubted it.

Philip glanced at his watch when Mark started making moves to get going and saw he had a little time. Google to the rescue. After a few botched search terms (searching "going steady in the 21st Century" only served to prove his point), he landed on a couple of articles that said to just do it—talk about being ready for exclusivity.

Just ask. Be prepared for a no. *Are you ever ready for rejection? That seems dumb.*

Murphy began to dance around the living room, a sure sign that Sydney had arrived. Perfect. Time to take the plunge... or should it be out to dinner? In a public place so she has to be civil if it's too soon?

No, he decided as he bolted from the room, just steps behind Murphy. Bring it up casually while stringing lights. That way if either of them was embarrassed, they'd have a way to hide it. Save face—for her as much as him. Right... that would be perfect.

The way she lit up when she saw him bolstered his courage... right up to the moment he realized she'd actually been looking at Murphy. Courage faltered. Then again, she did not allow Murphy to kiss her, but she did slip her arms around his neck in an obvious invitation. *Take that, Murph.*

"Missed you."

Her laughter—soft, almost melodic... when had he ever noticed anything like that? His own thoughts now sounded like some cheesy line from a romance novel or maybe a Hallmark movie. Melodic laughter.

She laughed again.

Philip caved. Okay, fine. It was melodic. With someone as full of life as Sydney, how could it not be? At least it didn't sound like Murphy's bark. He'd dated someone for three weeks who had a bark like a seal instead of a laugh.

"Same terms?"

Sydney's question jerked him from his (admittedly irrelevant) thoughts. "Sure."

"Readysetgo!"

She sprinted back to her truck and pulled out four rolls of lights— four perfectly wound rolls. She'd obviously set herself up for success. "Doing the gate!"

He'd have to work on the shrubs in front to be able to talk to her. Philip grabbed a few factory-wrapped (read: tangled mess of) Christmas lights and started after her. She'd already wrapped half the gate by the time he found the right end.

Better now than never. Wrapping the top around a curlicue near the hinge, Philip forced himself to sound relaxed. "So... I've been thinking."

"Yeah? I hear that's dangerous."

So far, so good. Banter was a good way to start off. "I've never tried it before, so I'll let you know how it goes."

Sydney shot him a grin. "You do that." Before he could muster up courage, she called back, "So... what were you thinking about?"

Here goes... maybe everything. "Um..." A stroke of genius hit. "Us."

"I like where this is going." Sydney moved closer to the center of the gate.

Taking that as a good sign, Philip mirrored her movements in a weird sort of light dance without music. "I realized that we're pretty important to me—we as in you and me." Perspiration beaded on his upper lip as he waited for her reply.

"I didn't think you and Murphy, so at least we're on the same page."

He must have looked as uncertain as he felt because she laughed. "We're important to me too."

Buoyed by her agreeability, Philip laid it out there—in the most noncommittal terms possible and with sweat dampening... everything. Good thing he was wearing a coat and she couldn't see. "I just thought that if you got to the place where you were comfortable in an exclusive relationship... well, you should know I'd... like that."

By this point, he doubted his coat was dry anymore.

Sydney dropped the lights she held and stared at him. Philip's throat went dry. She hesitated and then closed the short distance between them, took his face in her hands, and kissed him. It took too long for him to remember to drop his own lights, but he got up to speed eventually.

Murphy broke it up, of course. That dog really was a menace. Sydney shuffled her feet and let herself be pushed back, but she never took her eyes off him. "You owe me a do-over. I wasn't finished."

"Me either." *C'mon, Ward. You can do better than that.*

But Sydney turned away and picked up her lights. "Better get these up so I choose our date break." She'd looped her first bit before adding, "And I'm all for exclusivity. I don't think I'd handle seeing you with someone else well at all."

Yes!

Working double time, determined to beat her, Philip had to dash for more lights when he ran out of his sooner than he'd expected. When he reached the truck, Sydney called back, "Hey, Philip?"

"Yeah?"

"Can you check my notes on my phone. I need to check my plan. Four or five along this part?"

"Sure." As he tapped in the password she called back for him, a text message from Arielle arrived. He went to swipe it away for Sydney to read later and opened it instead. Philip started to swipe out, but a few words jumped out at him. *When your best friend is a rude, grouchy jerk...* Talking about Mark that way wasn't nice, but... His throat constricted. *Inferior breeding?* He'd always taken Sydney's description of her mother as an exaggeration. Now he wasn't so sure. Then... he saw the rest and his heart thudded, skittered, and dropped.

But she said she didn't want to see me with someone else. She's all for exclusivity. Maybe I missed context or something.

He found the notes app and saw "or 5" added to the "4 bundles on each side of the gate" note. Grabbing two more, he hurried back to the gate and handed her the phone. "A text from Arielle came in while I was unlocking it."

As she tapped and swiped, he watched her. She read, smiled, and pocketed the phone. "Looks like this Christmas thing is turning out to be a big deal. Arielle is thrilled." She shot him a smile. "Thanks for helping with it."

Just as he decided to admit he'd seen it and ask, he decided he had to have missed the context. He could always ask later if he saw a reason. Exclusivity also meant trust. Didn't it?

Sydney's voice broke through his thoughts. While she wasn't shouting, she did seem to be trying to keep the conversation quiet. Still, Philip strained to listen. "—another of Mom's stupid fortune hunters." A few seconds later, a snort appeared. "No, Philip is exactly opposite what Mom sees for me. Another of his many charms." She turned to look at him and grinned.

Though Philip smiled back before turning to attach a new string of lights, he couldn't help but wonder if that's all she wanted him for—to irritate Mommy dearest.

Eight

The air chilled further as darkness descended on Castlebourne. Already fall had burst onto the scene with record lows. Philip had pulled a jacket on and off more times in one day than he could ever remember. Physically strenuous work had the advantage of keeping you warm enough, but no one would consider stringing lights "physically strenuous."

While Sydney drove into town for burgers and shakes, Philip pulled his jacket back on and went to test the lights to see where they might need to fill in. A car pulled in through the gates just as he returned. The Audi screamed "I have money. Notice me."

A woman stepped from it in heels, ivory slacks, and... were those pearls? If her nose went any higher into the air, she might need a chiropractor for her neck, but despite the haughty attitude that dripped from the tips of each perfectly manicured fingernail, she wore a self-satisfied smile. If you could call the microscopic upturn of her lips a smile, that is.

Philip hurried forward. "Um, can I help you?"

As if she hadn't seen him (and he knew she had), the woman leveled a pointed look at him. "Are you Mark Bradford?"

"I get that a lot, but no."

The joke fell flatter than a Texas beauty pageant's hair in eighty percent-humidity.

"I'd like to speak with Mr. Bradford if he's available."

"Sorry," Philip said before he realized it was a lie. "Mark's not around."

The woman might have *said* she was sorry to have missed him, but he also caught a calculating look in her eye, even in the dim lights. "I see that the Elliott Landscapes crew has already begun work on the lighting for the 'Christmas affair.'" That nose rose. It had to have, but this time Philip could have sworn it was in an attempt to avoid the stench of... what? Plebeian society such as himself? "Are you part of Sydney's crew?"

He laughed. "Not hardly." The expression she shot him was so like one of Sydney's that everything clicked. "Oh! You must be Mrs. Elliott!" Philip thrust out a hand. "Philip Ward. Nice to meet you."

"And... who might you be if you are not one of Sydney's crew? Do you work for Mr. Bradford?" The air of superiority she wrapped around her stank to high heaven.

"No... just help him out when I can."

"Oh, right. The *electrician.*"

Okay, the constant misunderstanding about what electrical engineers do was bad enough, but the fact that he'd started out as an electrician to pay for college to *become* said engineer only made it worse. Maybe doing the extra work to become a master electrician had been overkill. But with so many years on the job, he'd had the hours... so why not?

Philip realized she was waiting for a reply. He wanted to give her one that would fill that snooty nose with just how foul his mood had gone, but this was Sydney's mother. He needed to keep things civil—for her sake. "Electrical engineer, actually."

"They do like to give people puffed-up titles these days, don't they?" The condescension rolled off in waves. "I heard someone calling a garbage man a *sanitation* engineer only the other day."

She took a step toward the side Sydney had been working on and nodded at it with evident approval. "Though you do string up lights well, so your training has served you."

"I'd love to say thank you, but Sydney did those."

The icy glare she shot him sent shivers down to his toes. *I should not be bothered by a woman who looks like she's terrified she'll scuff the bottoms of her shoes.*

"Sydney is a designer. She does not fiddle with light strings."

"Or dig holes, plant bushes, rig sprinkler systems... stuff like that?"

"Certainly not!"

He shook his head. "You really should come out in the daytime and see all the trees she didn't plant, the irrigation systems she didn't install, paths she didn't lay... though she did. She created wonderful land-scaping here... all with her own two hands, although I think I helped unload a fountain once." Philip threw up his hands. "She installed it, though. She's a genius with dirt—a veritable fairy yard-mother."

Maybe he'd gone too far, but who could blame him? What kind of idiot mother thought a landscaper didn't sully her pretty little hands with something as *common* as actual manual labor?

"Do not presume to know my daughter, Mr. Ward."

At least she remembered his name.

"Just because she was likely forced to show some slackard how to properly install a plant, doesn't mean she's part of the help."

Slackard? "Install a plant"? "The help"? Philip hadn't taken Sydney's complaints about her mother seriously, but he did now. Time to do a bit of fence mending.

"Mrs. Elliott, I'm sorry that you didn't know about Sydney's hands-on work here. She's an excellent designer who is probably a bit too much of a perfectionist to trust her work to a crew."

"You admit to doing shoddy work then, Mr. Ward?"

What is with this "Mr. Ward" business? Philip just shook his head.

"Well then why else would she be out here doing *your* job if what you say about those lights is true?"

"It isn't my job. I work in Columbia—just came down to help her and spend time with her." He couldn't help but add, "We've become close in the past few months... exclusive as of..." Tonight was probably not the best word. "Quite recently."

All hauteur became icy darts. "You presume to claim a... *friendship* with my daughter?"

"It's called dating, ma'am. Been dating for months now."

Laughter—or its fake equivalent, anyway—cut the air between them. "If a pathetic fortune hunter like you thinks he can connive his way into *my* daughter's affections... And months? Strange that she never mentioned you while she was out with several *eligible* men... isn't it?" After watching him for a moment, she gave a sad little shake of her head and returned to the car. Just before climbing in, she said, "You poor, pathetic boy."

He should have laughed. The woman was so over-the-top not, even a British period drama would have endured that performance, but slow, creeping doubts sprouted vines more invasive than kudzu wrapped around his thoughts and invaded every corner of his mind. Conversations about dates, her mother's obsession with "society," the text exchange with Arielle... *"Inferior breeding."* What did that even mean? And she had mentioned fortune hunters herself—said he was an improvement because her mother wouldn't like it.

The rational side of him said to talk to her—find out what it all meant. But the pictures of a lifetime of snide remarks from Mrs. Elliott every time he was in her presence, holidays ruined, their *children* subjected to such indoctrination, and the reality of how often people became just like their parents despite their best efforts overrode rationale until he began packing his truck for the trip back for Columbia.

Sydney drove in and climbed out of her truck with their bag of food and a drink carrier. "I have dinner, but you owe me for it..."

Standing before him, she cocked her head and shook the bag as if to say, "Kiss me while it's hot," but the smile faded when he pulled his wallet out and removed a twenty.

"I'll take my burger and shake..." He tucked the twenty into an empty hole of the drink carrier and removed his shake. She was stunned enough not to protest when he grabbed the bag, removed the burger with "no onions" scrawled on top of the box, and stepped back.

"I'd like to say it's been nice knowing you, Sydney, but I'm not there yet. For the record, I'm no fortune hunter, I don't consider myself guilty of 'inferior breeding,' and I'm not here for you to use to get back at your mother. So don't worry. I won't try to hold you to that 'exclusivity' agreement. We both know it wouldn't have happened anyway."

It really should have felt better when he drove away, leaving her standing there with a bag in one hand, a drink carrier in another, and mouth agape. It really should have... but it didn't.

Branson, Missouri

She'd never had a crew before, and Sydney couldn't decide if she loved it or not. Their perfectly reasonable disrespect for Gary had worked to her advantage—they all hoped she'd stay and replace him permanently. On the other hand, they seemed to regard his absence as something to celebrate with a holiday. She hadn't yet learned the art of supervising, and they could tell.

The astonishingly high budget had delighted her, and she'd enjoyed using the more technical skills she'd learned for her landscape architecture degree, but her rosy dreams of putting together the most spectacular Christmas display ever were fading under the reality of working with a crew. Why hadn't they covered this kind of management in school? Because the degree program was designed for office-bound architects who didn't get their hands dirty.

Sydney grunted as she shoved another urn into place. She should have taken courses that would help her as a general landscaper and small business owner. "Hey, Syd. There's an electrician here to see you."

Sydney spun around, startling the young woman who held a cell phone in one hand and a pair of loppers in the other. "The front desk clerk called me because you didn't answer your phone."

Sydney ignored the rebuke. "Where is he?"

"In the hotel, I guess. Probably at the front desk."

The girl thrust her phone into her cargo pockets. "And I'd appreciate it if you don't use me as your personal secretary."

"Sorry." Where was her phone, anyhow? She'd meant to keep it with her today, after missing two calls from sick crew members yesterday. In the truck?

Sydney brushed her hair back. She couldn't go inside like this. Her face was probably dirty, and her hair... She curled back her fingers and groaned at the sight of her broken nails. What would her mother say? It didn't matter what her mother said.

Sydney drew a deep breath and let it out slowly. Philip didn't care about her nails. If he'd come all this way to see her, knowing that she was working, he'd expect her to look like this. Except for her hands, he'd seen her in worse condition plenty of times, and he'd still found her attractive.

But then he hadn't. No word of explanation, other than his dramatic statement that he wasn't a fortune hunter, and no goodbyes. He'd just left. He didn't answer her calls or her emails or her texts… and after a week, her self-esteem demanded she quit trying. He didn't want to talk to her.

"Stop dithering. Have some self-respect, girl." Sydney muttered the words to herself as she pulled out her braid and ran her fingers through her hair. "Don't you dare rush right in there and fall into his arms."

The image of herself running into Philip's embrace in a scene straight from a Hallmark movie made her frantic. "Greet him cordially and ask him why he's here. Wait for his apology. His explanation. Don't throw yourself at him."

She kept up the mantra as she walked toward the hotel. No running. Still, she was as out of breath as if she'd sprinted the distance by the time she opened the door, and no amount of internal lecturing helped.

The lobby was empty except for the desk clerk and a woman waiting for the elevator. Had he changed his mind? Irritation came to Sydney's aid, enabling her to speak with a modicum of composure. "I'm sorry I didn't get your phone call, Marcy. Is someone looking for me?"

The receptionist tipped her head toward the elevators. "Someone from the Branson Electric Co-op is here to inspect the power for your display. She says she has an appointment, but it must have been with Gary, and he didn't tell me about it."

The electrician stepped forward. Sydney stood still, not breathing. Her chin started to quiver uncontrollably at the very moment the first fat tear rolled down her cheek. Another followed. She tried to speak, but her throat wouldn't cooperate. A tear slid into the corner of her mouth, and she reached up to wipe it away before remembering the state of her hands. Now she'd have mud smeared on her face. That was okay. The tears would wash it away.

She tried to swallow, but it was too late. An audible sob escaped, and she fled. She'd deal with the fallout later, making some kind of excuse, but for now, she just fled.

Nine

The restaurant pulsed with laughter and conversation as Philip entered. Over the heads of sitting diners, he saw his friends at one end of the long tables that characterized Juniper. Dave and Piper sat with... oh no. Not them too. Ever since breaking up with Sydney, his friends had, one by one, begun the process of "setting him up" with another "great girl" who he'd "love."

Not true—not yet, anyway. He'd made the right decision. Of that, he had no doubt. But his heart still hurt when he stopped moving and working long enough to notice. Sydney had meant more to him than he'd realized. *Another reason ending it before it went further was the right decision.*

And if he kept telling himself that, he'd eventually believe it.

Piper saw him hesitating and instead of waving him over, dug her phone from her purse. A text arrived. It's not a set up. She was here with friends and stopped at our table for a bit. She'll be leaving soon. Deep breath and come on over.

Great. Now he'd become *that* guy.

Piper rose and hugged him and gestured to the seat next to the woman. "Hana, this is our friend Philip." She left off the other half of the introduction, and something about that smoothed his ruffled nerves.

He pulled off his jacket and seated himself while attempting a pleasant, "Nice to meet you." To Dave he said, "How're the ones and zeroes treating you?"

"Well enough, but we were getting ANSI over here..."

Piper allowed her head to drop to the table. "And the jokes begin."

"I think I'll take that as my cue to get going." Hana rose, said goodbye to all, begged him not to torment Piper with too many puns and jokes, and strolled out.

Dave looked ticked. "C'mon, Philip. She's great. Why did you have to run her off like that?"

Piper jabbed him in the elbow and said, "Stop it. Leave the guy alone."

"It's been weeks! He'll get over her faster if he has someone else—"

A glass of water appeared in his peripheral vision. "No thanks—"

"Give me one good reason not to pour this over your head."

He looked up to see Arielle standing there... *seething*.

"Because assault is assault—even with something as simple as water?"

"You broke my cousin's heart, and you think I care about an *assault charge!*"

The restaurant quieted. Piper looked panicked. Dave looked around as if trying to find a bowl of popcorn. Knowing him, he probably was.

Against every instinct, Philip rose and gestured to the door. "Would you mind if we took this outside?" He dropped his gaze to the glass she still held. "Bring that if you feel you need protection."

"I will. Let's go." And without waiting to see if he followed, she marched right out the door.

The brisk evening air bit through his shirtsleeves as he stepped outside, but maybe it would keep him alert enough to dodge flying ice water. "What do you want?"

"What happened?"

Philip ached to play stupid and say, "with what?" but their server would probably like his order and— That thought stopped him. "Hang on. Need to let Piper know what I want so they don't have to wait."

"Get the blackened catfish—*Sydney's* favorite."

He hated admitting it but said, "Mine too."

"Figures."

With the message sent and his phone stowed in his pocket again, Philip crossed his arms over his chest and said, "I decided I was done being her convenience."

With a huff and a puff of air to blow a curl out of her face, Arielle matched his cross-armed stance and said, "I don't know what that even means. I get an ecstatic call saying you guys have gone exclusive—it's the most girly I've ever heard her—and less than an hour later, she's sobbing and saying you dumped her and drove off. She still doesn't get what happened."

"She should ask her mother."

The retort Arielle had been loading and ready to fire after his response never launched. A flicker in her eyes hinted she understood. "No... Aunt Clara came out there?"

"Yep." Maybe it was madness, but he had to get back in, and Arielle still held the glass of water. Pretty impressive how she did that with those arms crossed. He'd have poured it down the front of him. "Look, she came out, mistook me for 'the help'—her words, not mine."

"Oh, I believe you. Sounds just like her."

"Told me I did shoddy workmanship if Sydney had to come out and sully her perfectly manicured nails—how did she manage that?"

"Almost daily manicures to keep Aunt Clara from harping. Let's just say it was the lesser of two evils. Go on. I can almost finish for you, but in case you missed some of the possible insults, I don't want to add them to the pile."

A large party arrived and made talking impossible for a moment. Once the door closed behind them, Philip said the rest in a rush. "Um... electrical engineer is a glorified term for electrician, Sydney never mentioned me—"

"Lie."

"I figured." He scrubbed his jaw and closed his eyes. "Look, from all that to being called a fortune hunter after I overheard her talking about me being a great way to irritate her mother and the message I accidentally read where you guys talked about my inferior breeding..."

"Oh, no..." Arielle shook her head. "You—"

"Look. I saw her at that gala with that guy that her mother obviously prefers. I don't know why Sydney agreed to exclusivity, but it was obviously a *bad* idea."

Through the last few words, she shook her head. "No... no it wasn't. You were so good for her, and I see it here. You miss her."

"I miss who I thought she was."

She must have heard the catch in his voice because Arielle set the glass on the ground by the door, threaded her arm through his, and tugged at him. "C'mon. We need to talk. You need to learn a little bit about Aunt Clara and a lot more about Sydney. Or..." She gazed up at him. "More like, learn that she's just who you think she is. She doesn't play games with anyone but her mom, and that was only a survival technique. Now she's pretty much not speaking to Aunt Clara, although I'm not sure why." She smiled at him. "Although now I wonder just what she *hasn't* told me."

They walked down Laclede Avenue, past the post office, all the way to Intramural Field and back to Juniper. The picture Arielle painted was one he'd never have believed if he hadn't seen Mrs. Elliott's colors flying high and proud—oh, so very proud—that night. And she painted a broken, hurt Sydney. Still, his concerns had been valid, hadn't they?

"I wish I'd talked to her. It might not have changed much, but at least—"

"What do you mean not changed much? It would have changed *everything*."

No... her mother. As much as he cared about her—yes, still—a lifetime of her interference with him, with Sydney, with their kids... no. "Her mother would have torn us apart. Maybe not right away, but we'd have ended up fighting over—"

"No, you wouldn't. Because she's done with Aunt Clara. I told you."

"But for how long? How—?"

Arielle cut in again. "As long as her mother won't back off." The flames of fury settled into a smolder when she looked at him again. "I know you don't believe she can do it, but there's only one person more strong-willed than Aunt Clara. That's Sydney. She keeps the peace where she can, but only because there's no reason not to. If she had a *reason*, she'd stand up to her mother in a heartbeat."

Philip had to concede... something. "Look, I'll go see her. Talk to her. Maybe—"

"You can't, you big idiot. She took that stupid job in Branson covering Gary's butt."

"Do I want to know who Gary is and why he's walking around exposed?"

Arielle glared at him.

"Fine. Okay... So, let's say I thought and prayed about this—"

"Maybe if you'd *prayed* about it before you went off on her, we wouldn't be freezing out here trying to fix your mistake."

Okay, she had a point, but he hadn't been totally irrational. He'd just been... precipitous. "Anyway... So, assuming I get the go ahead from the Lord... what would you suggest?"

The grin that spread across Arielle's face would shame the Cheshire cat. He twitched just as she said, "Grand gesture, Philip. Do something big—huge. *Show* her you're sorry. And make it romantic. Sydney's not her mother's toy and she's more than a killer gardener—"

"I think I called her a 'fairy yard-mother' when Mrs. Elliott irked me."

That got him a grin. "Well, as I was *saying...*" she continued. "Syd does love romance—real, authentic, make-her-toes-curl romance. Show her you know how."

As if I do. But with those eyes glaring at him, all Philip could do was nod. "I'll have plenty of time to think up something. I'm down here to take down the lights now that the Christmas thing is over. Mark made me promise, so while I..." He froze.

Arielle nodded, that grin making her previous one look like a warmup. "Yeah..."

"'I'm sorry' in lights across the gate?"

"Do better than 'I'm sorry,' or I'll beat you up myself." As if to emphasize her point, she retrieved the ice water. The cubes still clinked in the glass.

"I love you?"

After an eloquent roll of the eyes, Arielle patted his arm. "*Say* that but use other words. It's called subtext. It's romantic."

Five hours later, Philip sent a photo of his final display to her. The words, *Come Back to Me,* glowed against the tree break near the paintball "wilderness" Mark had insisted on.

In seconds, she replied. Perfect. She'll love it. I'll plan the fastest wedding ever executed and have it ready for the weekend.

It was a joke, and he knew it. He also knew Sydney would never agree. But... Eyes closed, heart pounding... it would be subtext like nobody had ever sub-texted before. She'd see how sorry he was. She'd feel how important she was to him. She'd *know* what he hoped for... someday.

Arielle would kill him when Sydney said, "Not yet" (or worse, "not on your life"), but Philip texted back, Do it.

The hotel owner flipped the oversized switch, lighting the grounds. Elation—and relief—flared in Sydney when the crowd gasped in delight. A spattering of applause grew in enthusiasm, and when the glossy red ribbon was cut, the guests surged forward to explore the illuminated garden display. Her work. Her achievement.

Sydney smiled happily, enjoying a warmth that had nothing to do with the overcrowded space or patio heaters. She'd been a little nervous at first. The grounds looked great in the daytime, but she and the crew had only seen it all lit up once, late at night, just to check it over. Mr. Seaton hadn't wanted to spoil the surprise for his guests at the hotel's winter gala.

And now, the formally dressed guests and the live music provided the perfect finishing touch. It had needed life in it. Sydney walked up the steps to the broad patio and leaned over the railing to survey her work, considering the idea. God had put people into His garden. He'd made the world, lit it up, gave it water, planted things, and filled it with living creatures. Interesting.

What would the castle gardens look like for their big event? Those gardens had plenty of life already, with Murphy bouncing around. They'd be illuminated, thanks to... She brushed away the memory. Her mother's event—no, Arielle's event—wouldn't be as formal as this one. Arielle's menu featured hot chocolate and apple cider rather than champagne.

Sydney ran a hand over the smooth railing, admiring the gleam of the lights reflecting on her gold bracelet. Her nails—clean but not manicured—were a silly, private symbol of her independence. The dress too.... she hadn't brought an evening gown to Branson with her, and she'd taken great delight in finding an outfit at a consignment shop rather than one of the many expensive boutiques. Another small, significant shift.

She looked up at the sound of an all-too-familiar, slightly pompous voice and saw Gary Pritchard lounging by a refreshment table, talking to a tall blond man. Would Gary congratulate her on her achievement and thank her for coming to his rescue? Not a chance. At least she'd gotten good pictures for her portfolio and been paid generously for her work.

Sydney started to step away—in the opposite direction of her old classmate—but a lifetime of social training blocked her exit. She needed to say hello and goodbye. Really, she ought to thank him. The opportunity to escape St. Louis had been a gift. It would be rude and unprofessional to just go away without acknowledging him.

She drew closer, hoping for a break in their conversation, and Gary's words caught her attention.

"There's nothing so satisfying as taking a barren landscape and turning it into a beautiful living space. I especially enjoy these seasonal projects, where the challenge is to create a magnificent garden display..." Gary spread out his hands to encompass their surroundings. "...in a short period of time. At the end of the season, it goes away. Poof! I return it to its former glory." He took a champagne glass from a passing waiter and raised it in an apparent toast to the garden. Or maybe it was a toast to his own genius. "And the next year, I make something wonderful and new all over again."

Did he really just say "poof?" In the act of rolling her eyes, Sydney caught sight of the badge on the other man's lapel. Press. A reporter. Gary was taking credit for the Christmas display, to a reporter. The man said something she couldn't hear, and Gary went on. "Yes, I was away for a while, but my crew is well-trained, and they were able to carry out my instructions. Everyone is working virtually now, you know." He chuckled. "At least, those of us who do the designing."

Unbelievable. Entirely believable. Enough. She strode toward them, outrage giving her the assertiveness she needed.

"Hello, Gary." She smiled at him, using all of her expensively aligned teeth.

He blinked. "Um... hi, Syd. How are you?"

"I'm good, Gary. Are you going to introduce me to your friend?"

"Uh..."

She didn't give him time to decide. "I just wanted to say thank you for the opportunity to design the Christmas display this year. I think it turned out well, don't you? Mr. Seaton said it's the best one they've ever had here." She turned to the reporter and extended her hand. "I didn't catch your name. I'm Sydney Elliott, of Elliott Landscapes. I'm normally based in St. Louis, but when my old friend Gary needed help here... well, I made room in my schedule.

The man looked at Gary, who stuck out his jaw in something very like a pout. Sydney beamed. "That's Elliott with two T's."

It had been all the best parts of what she'd learned from her mother, with only a teensy bit of malice toward Gary. She'd stood up for herself. Sydney pulled the bobby pins from her hair and shook her head.

Her mother would have set the reporter straight, but she'd have annihilated Gary in the process. She would have made sure Mr. Seaton knew that Gary had tried to take credit for the job and done her best to get Gary fired.

Sydney dropped onto the bed and kicked off her heels before rolling to her back. When she went home tomorrow, she'd be going to stay with Arielle. Arielle would help her stand firm against her mother's efforts to bring her back under her thumb.

As if summoned, the mermaid song trilled from the phone on the nightstand. Sydney answered it without sitting up. "I was just thinking about you!"

"Good. I like it when people think about me. As long as it's good thoughts, of course."

"Of course. How's everything going there? Are you still willing to have me for a roommate until I get a place of my own?"

"Definitely," Arielle said. "I don't think it will be for very long, though."

Sydney hoped not. She loved her cousin, but Arielle's high-energy lifestyle was almost as exhausting as her mother's—in a much nicer way.

"I saw Philip last night."

Sydney sat up. "You didn't talk to him, did you?" She could just imagine how that conversation would have gone. Arielle was still incensed at Philip's unexplained departure.

"Well..."

Sydney could imagine her cousin settling deeper into her chair, preparing for a nice cozy gossip. "What did he say?"

"You're not going to like this," Arielle warned. "It's not exactly a shocker, but... well... your mother found Philip at the castle and proceeded to tell him what a no-good loser he is. He's just a manual laborer. A peasant not fit to lick your Gucci boots. Furthermore, he's deluded, since he claimed that you actually planted things with your own dainty hands."

Sydney gasped and jerked upright. "Seriously?"

"Things really got ugly when he told her you had a personal and exclusive relationship. That's when she called him a liar and fortune hunter."

"Oh no. That's why he said..."

"The thing is," Arielle began, "he might not have believed her, but apparently, he saw part of that text message about Murphy. The one where you said he had inferior breeding and you'd be glad to never see him again after you finished the job at the castle. Except that you didn't make it clear who you were talking about. I found the text, and it's really pretty funny out of context."

Sydney felt sick, not amused. A chime sounded in her ear, and she jerked the phone back to look at the text. Philip. She tapped on the icon and a picture filled her screen. She squinted at it, unable to identify the image.

Arielle continued talking, and Sydney interrupted. "I have to go." She disconnected the call without ceremony and used her finger and thumb to zoom in on the picture. Lights. He'd sent her a picture of Christmas lights? She zoomed out again and held the phone at arm's length. Words? It crystallized suddenly, and she caught her breath.

Come back to me.

Yes. Sydney jumped up and pulled the suitcase from the closet. She was going back to Philip.

Ten

Murphy's crazed dancing and barking could only mean one thing. Someone had arrived. Philip pulled out his phone and checked the security camera app. That thing had proven worth the battle with Mark to install the thing. He'd avoided Arielle and Mrs. Elliott, a reporter, and some committee member, and even Mark a couple of times.

This time his heart hammered in his chest as he saw the familiar truck pull through the gates. He had seconds... and a half-crazed dog to make this work. *Thank you for showing up at all, but especially for arriving after dark!*

He scrawled a quick note and ripped duct tape from the roll. Wrangling excitable dogs one handed might not do much for his resume, but if he ever needed it... Philip jumped back and jerked open the door.

While Murphy raced to greet Sydney—bowl her over and lick her half to death was more like it—he took off in the opposite direction. There, panting from the exertion of dog wrestling and racing to position, Philip waited. Twice he half-tested his plan and unless something had gone terribly wrong, it would be perfect.

You should've gone out to meet her. What kind of jerk asks a woman to come back and then tells her to keep coming while you stand around like an idiot? Maybe he should have thought this through more. *What do You think, Lord?* But Arielle had mentioned grand gestures, and this was the grandest he could think of—that still had meaning. Yes, it was pathetic, but he wasn't a grand kind of guy.

That's when the full truth of who Sydney was hit him full force. *She's not a "grand" kind of woman. That's* Arielle, *not Sydney. What've I done?*

Spurred to action, Philip took off. He'd meet her in the middle at least—show that he figured out his stupidity before it was too late. What he didn't think of was turning on the flashlight app on his phone. The minute he entered a curve in the path, Murphy bounded around the corner and connected with his legs.

Philip stumbled, shifted, and promptly fell face-forward. The ground—no, *legs*—rushed up to meet him. Arms reached out and half-caught him, and only the grace of God turned a face plant into a stumbling two-times-two-times-two step there on the path.

He wrapped his arms tight around her and held her. "I'm sorry, Sydney. I should've trusted you." Did her holding on tighter mean anything? Anything good? Philip held his breath—or maybe she just squeezed it out of him.

"Yes," she said at last. "You probably should have, but my mother is enough to make the most rational person on the planet do the most irrational things." She released him and Philip nearly coughed as he sucked in air. Her wobbly smile hinted she might be near tears, and if he knew her like he thought he did, Sydney didn't do tears often. "Maybe I should apologize for not being more forthcoming about things. I tried to give hints and mild warnings, but I didn't want to scare you off, and look where that got us."

His vocal cords went on strike. After several failed attempts to say *something*, it occurred to him, in a very Hallmarky sort of way, that his lips would still work just fine. Should he have taken a moment to really look at her? Possibly. Should he have met and held her gaze, letting his eyes say what he otherwise couldn't? Probably. Should he have touched her face, stroked her hair, done *something* a little more romantic than crush his lips to hers? Definitely.

But he didn't. And mid kiss that went from what could only be described as an attack of lips to a sweeter, gentler, *I missed you*, Philip kicked on the switch and waited for her to notice. Sydney didn't. She went right on kissing him until why clicked. And he chuckled.

She leaned back, gazing at him. "What's so—?" Her gaze slid sideways. Philip prayed they were far enough away for her to be able to *read* the lights. "I buo yu-u?"

A glance at the lights lengthened into a stare. Philip dashed behind them and fixed the o and v in love. She'd have to figure out the rest. "It was stupid," he said as he grinned at her laughter. "But I wanted to make some effort." She took a step closer, shoulders still shaking. "But I mean it," he continued. "I do love you. It's fast and crazy and I'll totally understand if you need lots more time, but on the off chance you're feeling daring..."

Philip let the lights fall and raced around the display. He'd planned to drop to one knee, but whatever had sent Murphy off on a wild goose (one could only hope not skunk) chase had failed to hold his attention and the pooch now wove around their legs, trying to decide who to attack first. No knees. He'd have a face full of Murphy slobber, and then how could he expect another kiss?

Instead, he grabbed both her hands and moved closer. Pressing his forehead to hers, he said, "Arielle has been tasked with setting up everything for a wedding on Saturday. I'll be there in whatever get up she's ordered... if you tell me, you will."

Sydney pulled back, staring at him as if he'd lost his mind. And hadn't he? The day a woman drove into Castlebourne and his (or as good as his) dog attacked her, and she mistook him for someone else. "Married? *This* Saturday? Are you nuts?"

"About you?" He shrugged at her "did you really just say that?" look and added, "I didn't have much to work with, but it's true."

"And you let *Arielle* plan this thing? You really are nuts! She'll spend a fortune on something that is way too soon to happen." She hesitated. "Don't you think?"

The panic that had risen leveled and slowly dropped as he saw what he needed most. Desire. She'd say no, and that was okay, but she *wanted* to say yes. "I knew you'd probably say no, but I needed you to know that nothing—not your crazy cousin, your even crazier mother, or my stupidity would change the fact that I want this. Whenever you're ready for it. And... *that* is worth every penny that Arielle has probably drained from my account. I'll just start saving again."

It must have been the right thing to say, because her next kiss lasted until they couldn't stop laughing at Murphy's howls. "That dog," he growled.

"Wonder if Mark would let us have him..."

Us? What? He searched her face, looking for some hint that maybe she'd agreed to more than a "we'll give this another shot." He wouldn't hold out for a premature wedding (it really was, but he wanted it anyway). But maybe an agreement to become engaged... soonish?

"You want Mark's dog?"

"Only if I get you in the bargain."

Shouldn't that be the other way around? Philip decided he hadn't earned the right to say that. Instead he said, "I've heard dogs make great ring bearers."

Sydney cocked her head and eyed him. "I wonder if Arielle could get him a bow tie in time..."

Epilogue

December 24th

Too bad more brides didn't let her pick out the wedding attire. Arielle twisted to inspect her back in the mirror. The vintage Gunne Sax dress—flounces and ruffles and all—was the polar opposite of her usual style, but it worked. She looked feminine and almost sweet.

She settled the wreath of flowers into her curls. The retro hippie boho look wouldn't suit every bride—or bridesmaid—but Arielle hadn't been able to resist the princess theme, with the castle all decked out for Christmas. And was it decked! Sydney had only decorated the grounds, so Arielle had hired a florist to adorn the great hall with boughs of holly and ornaments, lights and flowers, and anything else the woman thought would look good.

She'd also hired a caterer, a photographer, a couple of musicians, and a baker for the cake. It had been harder to find someone willing to rent and deliver the tables and chairs all the way out here, especially for such a small wedding and at such short notice. And then they'd needed a clean-up crew. She certainly wasn't going to do it, and...well, Mark Bradford wouldn't do it, and he'd be furious if they left a mess.

The man already snarled and stomped around his castle as if he'd taken lessons from "Beast" in the Disney version of that fairy tale. He even glared at the women she'd hired to clean the place up (maybe he was just offended that none of them looked like a teapot). Arielle had to inform him that Halloween was over, and it was time to dispose of the cobwebs festooning the castle. Apparently, he liked the dust. He said it had deflective properties, warding off unwelcome invaders.

Arielle had never thought of herself as a violent person, but the urge to punch Mark Bradford in the nose swelled to a nearly irresistible level before Philip intervened.

Keeping the wedding simple took more self-control than she'd expected. If not for the resident ogre, Castlebourne would be the perfect wedding venue. She could create fabulous events here—much more appropriate to the setting than paintball tournaments. Big events. Expensive, lavish weddings. This one would be nice and romantic and elegant, in a quiet kind of way, but she could do so much more if only…

She scowled at herself in the mirror and then sighed. It would be a very nice wedding, and Arielle was glad everything had turned out so well. She should be grateful that Sydney had actually shocked everyone by saying "yes" at the eleventh hour. Still… planning a small, intimate wedding was proving to be more difficult than the big extravaganza she'd done for that bridezilla in St. Louis. Everything had to be kept low-key, with no fuss.

No entrance down the magnificent staircase or orchestral wedding march for this bride. She was getting—and glad for—a short aisle entrance on the arm of her father, to a simple worship song. A wild-flower bride with simple tastes, who would only care that she was marrying the man she loved.

Arielle twirled like a four-year-old, enjoying the flare of her dress. It might be childish, but half the pleasure of this wedding lay in thwarting her aunt's dreams of a high society wedding for her only daughter. If Sydney didn't have such an irritating habit of extending grace, Aunt Clara wouldn't even be here today. She really should take lessons in Christian charity from Sydney—maybe next year. As a resolution or something. In the meantime, Arielle had assigned the "if you utter so much as one peep…" threats to her own mother, who had a way with words and no illusions about her sister.

This place... it must cost a fortune to maintain. The taxes... Arielle stopped dancing and sat on the edge of the sheet-covered bed. How could a retired soldier afford this place? Unless Mark Bradford had independent means—a lot of them—it must be draining his reserves. He seemed attached to the place too, if only as a giant playground. He wouldn't want to lose it.

He probably had no idea what the castle was worth in the right hands. Arielle's hands. He'd object strenuously, of course. She felt a grin growing but was unable to contain it. Mark Bradford would definitely dislike it, but when she showed him how much money he could make renting out the castle as a wedding venue... priceless. If it proved a constant irritant to him, well... that would be icing on the wedding cake. The five-tiered cake that cost more than most kids first cars.

She'd have to give him a few days to recover from the... er... excitement of this small and modest wedding before she approached him. And then she'd have to persuade him that by making her the exclusive provider of Castlebourne weddings, he'd avoid having to work with a dozen different women. It would give him the illusion of control. He'd like that.

Arielle took a deep breath, rose to her feet, and turned in time to see Sydney emerge from the bathroom. Her cousin looked breathtakingly beautiful in creamy lace and ribbons, a tribute to Arielle's artistic vision, and she was just the first of the many brides Arielle intended to see at Castlebourne.

This was going to be fun.

Dear Reader

A few years ago, Cathe and Chautona hashed out an idea—a castle set in St. Louis along the Mississippi River. One of those "summer playground" places that the wealthiest of America's wealthy built between the 1880s and the 1920s. We'd have a guy who inherited it and couldn't quite afford to keep it going. We gave him an arch nemesis—an *event* planner who loved to torment him by turning his "home" into a venue for fabulous weddings.

Mark would be the kind of guy who hated words like "venue."

When the *Keeping Christmas Collection* came up, we knew it was time. We'd introduce the castle and the original state in a prequel novella to the Castlebourne Series. We'd offer glimpses of Mark and Arielle, but we wanted the story to be about another couple.

Cathe created Sydney—a woman who never got over her love for playing in the dirt and the daughter of a woman who preferred to think of dirt as something eradicated back in the dark ages. Chautona created Philip—an average guy who worked his way through his electrical engineering degree by becoming a master electrician. That one little personality trait made writing Sydney's mother a whole lot of fun for both of us.

But the real story will be about Arielle and the people she will curate to create the best wedding planning—um, I mean *event planning*—business St. Louis, Missouri has ever seen. Oh, and Mark. He'll insist on having a say in things, too. It's just his grumpy way.

About Chautona Havig

Chautona Havig lives in an oxymoron, escapes into imaginary worlds that look startlingly similar to ours and writes the stories that emerge. An irrepressible optimist, Chautona sees everything through a kaleidoscope of It's a Wonderful Life sprinkled with fairy tales. Find her on the web and say howdy—if you can remember how to spell her name.

Learn more about Chautona's books at: http://www. celebratelitpublishing.com/chautona-havig/

facebook.com/chautonahavig

instagram.com/ChautonaHavig

amazon.com/author/chautonahavig

bookbub.com/authors/chautona-havig

goodreads.com/Chautona

pinterest.com/chautonahavig

About Cathe Swason

Cathe writes books with creative plots and engaging characters of all ages, to glorify God and entertain and bless readers. Her heartwarming stories will make you laugh and make you cry – and then make you laugh again.

Learn more about Cathe's books at: http://www.celebratelitpublishing. com/cathe-swanson/

facebook.com/CatheSwanson

instagram.com/CatheSwanson

pinterest.com/catheswanson

bookbub.com/authors/cathe-swanson

amazon.com/author/catheswanson

goodreads.com/CatheSwanson

The Girl From Dalarna

OLIVIA TALBOTT

One

Stockholm, Sweden. 1833

She didn't know she was beautiful. Even if she had, she wouldn't have cared. One cannot live off of beauty.

Linnéa walked onto the cobblestone streets, gripping her small bag of belongings in white hands. She dipped her chin. Her scarf tied tightly over her blonde hair kept her unruly curls in place. No one seemed to notice the young woman as she walked down the bustling street by the docks.

Men yelled and cursed, navigating the channel teeming with life. Towering boats with massive sails and minuscule oars made their way through the dark water like they were in some kind of mystic parade. The smell of salt and the stench of rotting fish blew into her face, Resolved to this life, she drank it in like a bitter draught of ale.

Following the directions she was given, she came to a door punched into the side of a leaning brick building. The sign swinging above read "Spanish Grape." She had rehearsed the words she intended to say the whole way there, trying to ensure that they came out smoothly. Her hands shook as she struggled to open the latch.

Clunk! It slid open begrudgingly, gliding from her hands and slamming against the inside wall. Reluctantly, Linnéa stepped into the darkness. As her eyes adjusted to the dimly lit room, she caught the sudden whiff of men and body odor. The room held five men, now all staring at her.

"What have we got here?" one man asked. But he soon seemed to forget her as he resumed staring at his boots.

The others grumbled and turned back to their drinks or cards.

"If you're looking for someone, you're likely lookin' for me." The gruff voice came from the left corner of the room.

Linnéa nodded, relieved not to have to speak.

The big man's eyes took her in, and he let out a quiet "humph," before disappearing into the adjoining room.

"I n-need a j-job, s-sir." Linnéa followed him, trying to calm the quaking in her voice. She entered a room with a desk, a bookcase, and a faded picture of the channels of Stockholm hanging on the wall. She knew she was in the right place.

"Are ye needing a job then?" The man inspected his greatly worn heel, but wouldn't make eye contact.

"Y-yes and I m-must have o-one." Linnéa replied, the urgency behind her reluctant words propelling them out of her. She tried to ignore her hitching voice, because if she focused on it, her stutter would worsen.

"Where ye hail from?" His eyes met hers. They were disapproving.

"I'm from the d-dales," she spoke quickly.

"Ahh, a Dalarna girl."

"I can w-work hard a-and..." She was growing agitated, her stuttering speech causing tears to prick her eyes. She had not come all the way from Dalarna to be sneered at.

"I'm just going to spare ye the trouble," he interrupted. "We're not going to hire ye."

"W-why n-not?" Linnéa squeaked. She could feel her face heating.

"You're a waif!"

"I m-may be small, b-but..."

"Small? Huh! The channel would eat you alive!"

Linnéa dipped her head, clenching her fingernails into her palms and stepping forward into the thin light coming from the window.

"I am c-capable of anything a-another w-woman can do!"

Through her tears, Linnéa noticed the man's expression change from indifference to wonder. This stung her worse than his words, as she despised her beauty and delicate build. "I've w-worked on a f-farm my whole life. I'm s-strong. I can outwork a-any other woman. You just h-hire me, you will s-see!"

The man stood with his mouth agape, before remembering himself and swallowing.

"Like I said, we cannot be hiring ye as a rower woman."

Linnéa opened her mouth to protest again.

"There's no sense in taking your frustration out on me!" His tone softened. "With a slight figure like yours and a face that looks like an angel herself, we cannot not be hiring ye to work in one of the hardest and most unforgiving jobs in Stockholm. I'm sorry, miss."

Linnéa had heard it her whole life, but this time, it stung differently. She was delicate and beautiful. That unforgivable quality had closed more doors in her life than it had opened. "If I had been b-big and b-brawny, would you have hired me then?" Her voice squeaked.

"It would help the possibility along," the man chuckled.

"Y-you don't understand, Sir." Her words were barely a whisper. "I have no other p-prospects for e-employment in a new city. There i-isn't work at h-home and my m-mama sent me to work here, because my p-papa is dead, from s-smallpox." She thought she should perhaps use the term "deceased" or "left this earth," but it wasn't the truth. Linnéa's Papa had died unexpectedly, abandoning her, her mama, and her five other sisters to scrape and grovel to live. She wasn't going to mince her words and try to make them sting less. She needed this man's pity, for pity's sake.

"A lot of folks from the country have it hard. I'm not saying I don't care. I'm saying we will not and cannot hire ye! We've had several other brawny women fill rowing positions, and you don't stand a chance against them."

"Thank you for your t-time." Her words cut through the clenching feeling in her throat. She turned to leave.

"Wait..." the man paused. "I have an idea of something more suit-able for ye."

Linnéa paused, but didn't turn around, her fragile pride dangling by a thread.

"Do you really want a job?" He prodded her from a place of silence.

"Yes, s-sir. I-if it's r-respectable."

The man chuckled, but his tone wasn't overly reassuring.

"You should know that it might not be the kind of work you came to the city for. But I can't think of anything else that would suit you and that is needing someone with your, ummm, qualifications."

Linnéa was uneasy.

"How old did you say you were?"

Linnéa shifted, searching the cracks in the floor.

"Do you want a job or don't ye, girl?

"I d-do." Linnéa concluded. "I'll be t-twenty in March."

"Then meet me at the doorstep at 6 a.m. tomorrow." He waved his hand, turning his attention back to his heel. "My name is Anders, by the way. Yours be?"

"L-Linnéa."

Linnéa was released and moved towards the door. Her mind whirled with curiosity, but also a prickling feeling she couldn't identify. Could she trust this man?

"Face like an absolute angel, that one has."

Dust swirled in the light coming from beneath the door, and she stomped it out along with Anders' musing, turning to leave. She feared that her face and every passerby's opinion of it would plague her until her dying day.

Two

Linnéa stood on the cobblestone in front of the door she'd entered the day before. She clutched her shawl around her tightly, though it did little to ward off the gusts of wind coming from the harbor. Her teeth chattered and her eyes darted into the shadows of the street. "Let this not be a mistake, Lord, help me to be wise."

The man had assured her the work she would be doing was respectable. But standing out in the frost in the early hours of the morning, awaiting her new employer already felt a bit uncouth. She had arrived early, but Linnéa liked to be early as it gave her the advantage against her own deficiencies.

Her mind wandered to her restless night. She had spent it at cheap accommodations above one of the local pubs. Initially, she was put off by the location, but there seemed to be few other options. The bed had been stiff, but that was nothing new. The sights, smells, and surroundings of Stockholm were what plagued her dreams. In the early morning mist, she despised this new world.

If returning home was an option, she would turn and run as fast as she could. But her mama had taken great care to secure transportation for her and had seen her off with regret and relief shining in her tired eyes.

"Go with God, my dear." The hurried words were whispered into her hair, like a whisper sent into the wind. They were both a plea and a prayer, but most of all, a warning.

Although Linnéa was young, she knew the world was a treacherous place, full of traps for a young woman. Traps set by starving men. She knew she was fresh meat to the appetite of those who slunk in the darkness. Of this she was determined to be wary.

"Well, I see ye've come." Anders emerged from the door as he shrugged on his coat.

Linnéa nodded, her demeanor still icy.

"Yer a hard one to crack, aren't ye?" he glanced sideways at her as they began to walk.

"To be h-honest, sir, I'm not sure if I will take this o-offer of employment a-after all."

The man looked taken aback. "I assure you, you won't receive any other means of employment, and of that I can be absolutely certain."

"You have n-not given me any a-assurances."

"I'm not sure how else to assure you than to show you there myself."

Was she being a fool? A blasted fool? Linnéa continued walking in stride with the man down the cobblestone streets. They watched as the rower women rowed their cargo and passengers into the harbor. Even beneath their woolen coats, Linnéa could see their large arms and bulky frames. They wore massive hooded hats to keep out the rain and splashing of the oars.

"Like I said, they would eat ye alive."

Linnéa glanced at him, her words jamming in her throat.

"We have been known to hire other dale girls like yourself," he said. "But they're all brawny and brash, very unlike yourself miss, no disrespect intended to ye."

She didn't even bother to form a retort, knowing full well that he would not hire her, and there was no need to humiliate herself further.

"The trade's changed considerably over the years and managers like myself are new to the occupation. It's a lot easier to get into now than it was, thanks to the workers guilds. It used to be that the only way you were a rower woman was if you knew someone retiring and bought yer boat, or inherited a boat from ye mother. Very desirable business, that it is. It's the easiest way to get around the various islands, to Lake Malaren, and ports in Stockholm. It takes strong arms and a back, as some boats carry up to 25 passengers."

He chuckled. "Some of the old sort aren't too keen on the prospect, though as they keep to the old ways and see all the upstarts as greenhorn competition. They weren't in favor of the old ways being abolished as it gave nearly everyone an entry into the trade."

"Not e-everyone." Linnéa muttered.

"Yer a feisty one." Anders laughed, slapping his thigh. "Even beneath that hitching tongue."

They continued onward in silence, walking toward the outskirts of town. The city bustled with life. The clomping of men rolling barrels across the cobblestone filled the air. Horses pulling carts piled with goods cut across their path, and people moving in a hundred different directions crowded the wide cobblestone street. The grime and smoke gave way to graveled lanes, which cut through rolling fields of green. The air was clear and stung Linnéa's lungs. Sheep grazed, their dewy bodies glowing in the early morning sunlight. The rolling green hills of the countryside tumbled into the bay, with ships gliding through the luminous water. Looking over her shoulder, Linnéa lingered, overwhelmed by what she saw.

"It's a sight, isn't it?" Anders paused in his stride.

Linnéa gazed at the landscape, hardly able to take it all in.

"A sight." He repeated the words, barely audible over the sound of the gulls.

Linnéa could feel Anders' eyes on her. He wasn't watching the ships any longer, which made her want to shrink into the grassy ground.

After a moment, he shook his head, turning to continue up the road, whistling a melancholy tune.

Linnéa lost herself in the view once again, free to enjoy it at last.

"Best be hurryin'!" he called over his shoulder.

As if pulled from a trance, Linnéa hurried after him as they descended into a dale. A red house surrounded by several outbuildings was nestled in the countryside. The chimney puffed smoke that curled around the thatched roofs like a shroud. Sheep, cows, and chickens scuttled the farmyard, with a black and white collie trying to keep them all in line. Linnéa relaxed into the breeze as they descended into the barnyard. It felt familiar and comforting.

"Hallo!" Anders called into the misty morning air.

The collie came running with a smile spread across her face, but soon resumed her crouched position as she stalked the loose geese.

A woman emerged from the house, carrying a bucket and a baby. "What brings you out, Anders?" She continued towards one of the outbuildings, barely pausing in her stride.

"I've brought ye help, Edla! Before you start huffing and puffing about how you don't need help, your husband was just in the pub last week saying that you've been needing it with the cows."

The woman stopped mid stride and turned to assess Linnéa, not bothering to contradict Anders. Her grey eyes flashed as she repositioned her baby.

"Have you milked before?"

"Of course she has! She's a Dalarna girl!" Anders exclaimed before Linnéa could open her mouth.

Edla softened, like warmed butter. "My kin are from the dales." A smile cracked across her drawn features.

"Yes m-ma'am, I've lived there m-my whole life, but came to S-Stockholm for employment."

"Employment as a rower woman," Anders interjected. "But I told her she would be much more suitable for this type of work."

"I'll give you a chance to prove you can work hard." Edla turned to resume her mission, which Linnéa assumed was milking.

"You can start now if you like!"

Anders winked and turned to go, whistling as he made his way back to Stockholm.

"T-Thank you!" Linnéa's voice trailed after him, but only the dog remained, still keeping a wary eye on the stray goose.

The excitement of the city, if even for one night, made this regained sense of normalcy and the familiar smells of animals, a welcomed one. She could talk to cows without fear of her hitching speech. Tying her shawl around her waist, she followed her new employer into the barn.

"Nothing is more respectable than cows."

Three

Her head swam with dreams of the night before, but the coldness in her hands snapped her back to reality. Linnéa's head rested against the cow's stomach, feeling her rhythmic breathing as she chewed her cud. Bellows of steam rolled up around the beast's head buried in a mound of hay. Sucking in her breath, Linnéa nuzzled her own nose deeper into her scratchy red scarf. The rhythmic sound of milk hitting the frothy pool almost lulled her to sleep, if it weren't for the coldness in her hands that ached past her skin and sank into her bones. "You're giving a lot today, aren't you, Aslög?"

The cow just continued to chew.

Linnéa wiped her hand on her apron, the froth coating each finger, before continuing the task. She pulled one side down, then the other, feeling the surge of milk as it was released from Aslög's udder.

Aslög was the easiest to milk of all the cows, so Linnéa started the day with her rather than the more temperamental Sigge.

The herd was made up of Aslög, Sigge, Wilma, Tindra, Ebba, Ludda, and Bamse. Each was milked twice a day, and each one had a different personality. The one thing they all had in common though, was their massive doe eyes rimmed in long eyelashes. This made them especially endearing.

Patting Aslög's rump, Linnéa stood, being careful not to slosh the white, frothy liquid that reached the top of the wooden bucket. "I'm glad you didn't have even one more o-ounce in ya, old girl."

Releasing her head from the station, Linnéa let Aslög make her own way. She knew the way back to the field without her help. Linnéa merely opened the gates for her. It was a wet, cold morning, very unlike the one when she had made her way to the farm with Anders. Thick fog clung to the outbuildings and danced above the ground.

"Let's see, there's Wilma, Tindra, Ebba, Ludda and Bamse," Linnéa counted the cows. The cows gave her blank stares, eagerly waiting for the bursting sensation in their udders to be relieved.

"Where are ya, Sigge?" The fog was even thicker in the dales of the field. Linnéa called the cow's name. Nothing. "Come Letty!"

The collie came running and Linnéa climbed the fence in search of the missing cow.

The farther she walked, the denser the fog became as she dipped into the lowlands. Pulling her thick wool shawl tighter around her, she continued onward, Letty at her heels. The scene was ethereal and enchanting, and if she hadn't been searching for a cow, Linnéa would have stood, watching the landscape change around her.

Remembering the ancient cow call she had used since childhood, Linnéa sang into the churning air. Her tone sounded flat, so she cleared her throat. She had only spoken a few words to the cows so far that day. She called again, the melody of her song cutting through the fog in clear, distinct tones. Even out of her lips, the song was enchanting, hinting at ancient languages and heritage buried in her own. It rippled from her lips, like underground water bubbling up from some place inside, pure and icy. When she sang, her words came unhindered.

Linnéa had struggled with hitching speech since she could remember. Her mama had tried to cure her time and time again, giving up at last. When she was with the cows or children though, her words came easily with hardly an error in pronunciation. When she was nervous or intimidated, her words were like mud, clinging to her dry mouth, refusing to flow easily. Nothing made her angrier than her rebellious words. She sang her frustration, her words mounting and swelling like the fog.

Cling! Clang! The sound of a cow bell. She stopped to listen. The sound came closer.

Linnéa called out one last melody for good measure to ensure the rebellious cow was returning. Relief trickled down her spine. She had been worried that the cow was gone for good. Although her new employers were kind, the loss of a cow under her keeping would surely have ended her employment.

Sigge emerged, at first thickly shrouded, but becoming clearer with each step.

"There you..." Linnéa's words died in her throat.

A tall man emerged from behind Sigge, carrying a long stick.

"I found her with my bull this morning," he said, his lucid blue eyes laughing. "Even your *Kulning* wouldn't tear her away."

Linnéa was stunned, her words refusing to come.

"I'm Rane, I own the farm just..."

His words faded into silence as his eyes settled on her, reflecting both surprise and curiosity. Her hem sunk knee-deep in mud, and she could feel her hair curling around her face from the dampness in the air. She shrank beneath his gaze, wishing she could retreat into obscurity again rather than standing in the cow pasture so exposed.

"You must be the new milkmaid." Recovering, Rane smiled boldly.

Silence settled between them with the fog.

"I thought you were an *älva*, but your—" he motioned to her hem "—gave you away."

Warmth crept across Linnéa's face, but words wouldn't come.

"What's your name?" He closed the distance between them.

She smiled tensely, before turning to follow Sigge, who desperately wanted to be milked after her morning misadventure. "I-I'm L-Linnéa," she called over her shoulder. Her face flushed, because no matter how hard she tried, she couldn't help her stutter. "T-thank you for b-bringing her b-back!"

"Anytime!" Rane called, disappointment clinging to his words the way the mist clung to her face.

Four

"Are ya sure ye got it?" Edla's brow furrowed as she eyed Linnéa's slight frame.

"I'm sure."

"Ye know how precious your cargo is, so I'll leave you to it."

Linnéa shouldered her yoke, balancing the canisters of milk- one on each side. The strain pulled at her shoulders and the hard wood pushed on her vertebra, but she had grown used to this burden. Somehow, her slight body was made for carrying buckets of milk, being deceptive in its hidden strength. Climbing from the dale onto the ridge overlooking the ocean took every ounce of her strength and steadiness though. Reaching the top, she allowed herself a moment to take in the beauty. It was still dawn. The slow sun tarried longer than normal as winter approached. Darkness was something every Swede was accustomed to, but Linnéa hated to see the sunlight dwindle. It was as if the world pulled inside itself, boarding up against the harsh reality of the winter ahead, while Linnéa desperately wanted to hold on to the last warmth of fall.

Turning her mind to her job, she rehearsed the lists of customers expecting milk in Stockholm. She didn't relish this part of the job, as conversing with strangers—or really anyone for that matter—didn't come naturally to her. Yet, like the pain in her back, the discomfort was a part of the job.

Linnéa's breath came in hot bursts as she entered the already crowded streets of Stockholm. Unable to take another step, she lowered the canisters onto the cobblestone street twice before spotting her first stop.

Creaking open the door of the shop, she entered, cringing at the sound of her feet dragging across the rough floorboards.

"I h-have m-milk for ya, sir," Linnéa choked the words out.

Without looking up, the shopkeeper mumbled his thanks and slid a pail across the counter, in which Linnéa carefully ladled his allotted amount. He then tossed the payment, and it clinked across the wooden slab.

Gathering up the payment and canisters, Linnéa turned to go.

"Ye shorted me, a cup girl!" An empty bottle scraped towards her once again.

"My apologies, s-sir." Linnéa felt her face flush as she fumbled with the lid. Looking up, she caught the man's disapproving scowl, but much to her surprise, the look of frustration quickly evaporated into a look of admiration, making her even more uncomfortable. "I'll get it r-right, next t-time." She tried to shake the man from the spell he seemed to be in.

"Nothing's amiss." He closed his mouth after remembering himself. "Nothing's amiss in the least." He continued to stand and stare at her as she turned to leave, not attempting to quiet her scraping feet across the rough floorboards as she scrambled to get out of the gaping man's presence.

"Hey, Aalf, get in here, quick!" Linnéa heard the man call, as she exited the shop.

Before she left the street, she felt as if she were being watched. She kept her eyes plastered ahead.

"Ain't she something, Aalf?"

Linnéa breathed a sigh of relief to have the first stop behind her as she continued with the rest of her deliveries.

❄

The next day, as Linnéa strode into the streets of Stockholm, she was pensive. She dreaded not only the conversations, but the undesired attention she received.

Why did this feel so difficult? Anyone else would appreciate the adoration and the unsolicited compliments. *What's wrong with me*? Would she feel differently if she didn't dread conversing so much? As her worn shoes scuffed across the cobblestone streets, she kept her eyes down, hoping to avoid detection. Upon rounding the corner, voices and the sound of shuffling feet made her want to slink into the shadows. Stopping to rest, she caught her breath before carrying her burden the rest of the way to her first stop: the dreaded gawking shopkeeper and his son who had made such a fuss about her the day before.

"It's her!" someone called. The weight of the milk felt as if they might push her to the ground. She took a reluctant step forward, refusing to lift her head.

"Why're you being so shy?" another voice called and several laughed. "We want to get a good look at you!"

Heat pressed against her temples. She could feel the stares of the couple dozen men lining the streets.

"Leave the poor girl alone," A female voice came through the crowd. Linnéa escaped into the dark shop as fast as she could, but to her dismay, it bustled with activity.

"At last!" The shopkeeper hailed her, sliding several pails across the table with a grin. "We'll take your whole supply today, as we have an unexpected uptick in demand." His meaty face beamed with pleasure.

Someone chuckled. "Lift your head, sweetheart."

Her eyes burned, but she lifted her gaze, blinking back the tears.

Her face warmed. She could feel the whole room staring at her, every eye scrutinizing her face, her clothes, and her hair. Had she smoothed her hair before starting the trek? Her hem was wet with mud. In spite of the fire raging in her body, she held her head high and poured the entire contents of her load into the pails the man provided.

"What's your name, Dalarna girl?" Several curious voices echoed in unison.

Linnéa swallowed and wiped her eyes as a tear escaped. "L-L-Linnéa." She propelled the words out of her.

"What girl?"

"L-L-Linnéa!" She choked the words out.

Someone chuckled. "Don't be shy, girl!"

Shouldering her milk canisters as fast as she could, Linnéa stumbled for the door, unable to stop the tears from sliding down her cheeks.

"Heavens! She's even angelic when she's worked up!"

Linnéa ran past the men still congregated outside.

"Angel, don't run! You're famous!"

"We just want a good look at you!"

"Hey, everyone, it's the milkmaid!"

The crowd grew as the narrow alley filled with people, like a bottle filling with water. Linnéa tried not to look at them, but their presence pushed and shoved around her and she felt like she might drown. Someone grabbed at her arm. She ripped it away, but one of her canisters clattered to the cobblestone. She left it and continued to push forward. Her mind screamed for God's help, but no words escaped her lips.

"Poor girl, leave her be!" Someone called, but Linnéa could see nothing through the tears clouding her vision.

The alley was bustling with people. It stretched out endlessly, lined with drab buildings that had their shutters thrown open to the bleak morning sun.

"Behold, the most beautiful woman in Sweden!" Another voice called. "The Dalarna girl!"

Was this a nightmare? *Someone please wake me*!

"What's your name?" Several people called as she pushed through the crowd.

"Linnéa," she heard a faintly familiar voice, but she couldn't remember to whom it belonged. "Linnéa!"

She caught a glimpse of a face she recognized through the throng. Who was it? Heads were in the way as people shoved and crowded around her, preventing a second glance.

"We've got to know your name!"

"Don't answer the hecklers, girl!" Someone yelled.

A whistle blew through the crowd, shrill and splitting. "What's happening here?"

The throng parted, letting an officer through.

"Who's the Dalarna girl?" he huffed into his mustache and frowned. "They're chanting her name in the streets!"

"Her!" Several people nodded towards Linnéa.

"What is the meaning of this?" He spat, eyeing her and her single milk canister. "This is not the way to sell more milk!"

Linnéa swallowed, her throat clenching around her words, refusing to let them pass.

"Best come with me." Grabbing Linnéa's arm, he propelled her through the crowd. They eyed her like a captured bird, getting to gawk at her at last.

"Nah, don't break up the fun!" Someone called.

"You all get about your day!" The officer spat back, some of the spittle landing on her face, as his hands still pinched her arm.

"Linnéa!" The familiar voice called again, as if lost in the throng. "Get out of my blasted way!"

The crowd dispersed as the officer yanked Linnéa down the alley. He stopped at a dimly lit building. The throng of people dispersing through the streets like poured out water, their fun spoiled.

Trembling, Linnéa was shoved in front of a desk with a stern looking man peering back at her.

"This was the one causing the riot in the street!" The man with the mustache spat. "The crowd completely blocked the southeast alley, stopping all through traffic. They chanted and she just..." The stern man stood, silencing the man with the mustache.

"What's the meaning of this?" he asked. His form towered over her as he rose.

"I-I-I d-d-d—" Linnéa swallowed, her words choked her. Even her tears deserted her, leaving her exposed and vulnerable to assumption.

"One can only assume what caused such an outburst! Her 'milk peddling' couldn't have been the cause. She's probably not even a milkmaid, but a common seller of 'her goods,' if you catch my meaning!"

Linnéa shook her head, opening her mouth once again. She didn't intend for any of this! Were they blaming her for inciting a riot? How could they assume such gross accusations?

"I-It's n-n-n—" Linnéa tried again, clenching her soiled skirt, as if to squeeze the reluctant words out of her.

"Let me through!" A voice called. The same voice she'd heard in the street. "I know this woman!"

Rane entered the room, his blue eyes icy and his jaw clenched. Those startling eyes were clapped on her. "Are you all right?" He asked, his eyes not moving from hers.

"Of course he knows her," the man with a mustache murmured. "It seems every man from Stockholm to the dales knows her!"

"What's your meaning?" Rane asked, his words sharp and hot like embers. "What is Linnéa being held for?"

"Inciting a riot!" The man with the mustache sneered. "One can assume many things."

Rane stepped forward, the muscles in his neck straining.

"There is nothing to assume." His words were steady and calculated. "She was harassed and surrounded as she was making milk deliveries. She works at my neighbor's farm and was hired just last week."

The man with the mustache shrunk in Rane's shadow, clearly beaten.

"Aalf told everyone across Stockholm about the 'most beautiful woman in Sweden' to monopolize his father's business and cause trouble. Linnéa is not responsible."

"Likely story," the mustache man interjected.

"Does she appear to be enjoying herself?" Rane yanked his hat off his head and ran his hands through his sandy blonde hair. "How can you be so insolent?"

"You have no..." the mustached man began.

"That's enough!" The stern man barked. "It's not a crime to be beautiful, and the girl is not at fault."

"I'd rather hand out fines for ugliness." He chuckled. "Take your beautiful neighbor home!" He motioned to Rane. "Just make sure there aren't any more riots of this kind in my streets ever again!"

Rane shoved his hat back on his head and took Linnéa's arm gently, leading her to the street.

"Wait a minute." He disappeared into a nearby alley to retrieve the canisters she'd left behind.

Linnéa's hand shook as she reached to retrieve her forgotten task.

Rane shook his head and sauntered forward, leading the way through the maze of streets towards the farm. He walked quickly, his hands still clenched and his hat still cockeyed on his head.

Linnéa stumbled after him.

"Oh, sorry." Rane slowed his pace but didn't say another word.

Linnéa was thankful, because if someone asked her one more question, she wouldn't be able to stop the torrent of hot tears and searing humiliation pent up inside her. They walked in silence until the air seemed cleaner, the gulls called overhead, and it became easier to breathe.

"What a day." His tone wasn't sarcastic, nor was it making light of the situation. He seemed to be voicing his thoughts as he glanced down at her.

Linnéa nodded and opened her mouth to speak. *Don't cry. Do not cry.* But the tears came despite her pleading. She wiped them quickly.

Rane didn't look at her again, and for this she was thankful. He also didn't say another word, but continued onward, leading the way through the narrowing path, still carrying her yoke over one shoulder and the empty canisters clenched in his other hand.

Approaching the farmyard, he didn't stop his steady stride until he reached the door of the house and deposited Linnéa there. He then tipped his hat and turned to leave, abruptly.

"Thank y-you!" Linnéa's voice squeaked.

Rane turned and faced her. "I'm just sorry it happened at all." His eyes sparked.

Linnéa cast her gaze downwards and heard his boots crunch in the gravel as he walked away. How could she ever face him again?

Five

"P-Please, d-don't make me g-go there again."

"I'm sorry, Linnéa, but this is the job. I cannot take the milk myself because of the baby, the butter, the washing, and everything else. This is what you were hired to do."

"You d-don't understand." Linnéa choked the words out. "T-they laughed and crowded m-me—"

"This is the job. If you can't do it, we'll find someone else."

Linnéa shouldered her burden and began her journey to Stockholm, her mind clouded with worry. "Use your w-words. Use your words," she repeated louder and with more force.

Someone whistled from behind, but Linnéa hurried up the path, dreading an encounter. At the rate the oncomer moved, he was about to overtake her. Linnéa kept her eyes on her feet, as if ignoring the person would cause them to cease to exist.

"Goot morning!"

It was Rane. At the sound of his voice, warmth crept up her neck.

She nodded her greeting. Could he tell how embarrassed she was?

He carried a load of firewood slung across his shoulders. "Beautiful day, isn't it?"

Linnéa smiled, tucking her chin. It wasn't a beautiful day being blustery and grey.

He continued to whistle.

Use your words. Linnéa cleared her throat.

Rane stopped whistling, waiting for her to speak.

"T-Thank y-you f-for t-this," she whispered the words.

His gaze remained forward, as if he didn't hear her. They were able to walk abreast at this place in the path. "That looks heavy." He broke the silence.

"S-So does that!" Linnéa smiled, motioning to his own burden.

"You kinda get used to it, I suppose." He laughed.

Linnéa nodded, the warmth in her cheeks cooling.

They walked in silence again until the path narrowed forcing them to walk single file. Her milk canisters clanked against his legs as she stumbled forward.

"You all right?"

She nodded, her face flushing once again. *Am I to be a boiling kettle this whole way?* Trying to regain her composure, she continued onward.

They entered Stockholm, the cobblestone streets curling in fog.

"W-Where are you delivering the w-wood?"

"So happens Aalf has a sudden need!"

Linnéa hung her head. "I d-don't want y-you to feel obligated t-to w-walk with m-me."

"No, I'm serious when I say that Aalf be needing wood."

How'd he arrange that? She imagined Rane threatening Aalf into buying the wood to make up for his stunt. Rane seemed like that type. Not a bully, but someone who was capable of getting others to bend to his will—especially those like Aalf.

"T-Thank you."

"No need, really, Aalf is paying a price that is more than fair."

As they strode through the streets, a few passersby stopped to gawk at Linnéa and several called "Dalarna girl!" But with Rane beside her, they didn't seem a threat beyond a few calls and unwarranted looks. Linnéa felt her face warm with each encounter. Her desire to slink into the shadows and scurry through the streets like a mouse grew ever stronger. If it weren't for the milk canisters hanging from either side, it would be much easier to remain anonymous. Much to her dismay, it seemed that everyone they passed knew who she was and the notorious stir she had caused. They approached the shop, each relieved to be laying their burdens down for a moment.

Aalf was nowhere to be seen, but his father stood behind the counter which was littered with bags of goods. "Goot morning to ya!" He called, his face hidden by sacks of flour.

Linnéa looked to Rane to announce their presence, but he was oddly silent.

"M-milk delivery, s-sir," Linnéa whispered.

"Ahhh!" The man slid the largest bag out of his way. "There's our famous little milkmaid!" His eyes devoured her hungrily.

"And wood," Rane growled.

"We didn't order wood..." the man began.

"Aalf did."

The man studied Rane's face, before seeming to slink back into himself. "He didn't mean no harm."

Rane said nothing, but stood planted behind Linnéa. A shadow passed in the doorway behind the counter.

Linnéa measured the milk out into the provided milk jars.

"Not as much as last week," the man muttered, his eyes not leaving Rane. "Thanks to you." The shopkeeper nodded in Rane's direction, his eyes dark and glowering.

What did he mean? What had Rane done? The thought of him having a confrontation on her behalf made her feel sick. She never intended for him to feel personally obligated to carry out the officer's command that "nothing of the sort would ever happen again," because he was the only one there to stick up for her. He shouldn't have to be punished on her behalf!

"Aalf, I'm here with the wood!" Rane's voice split through the air unexpectedly.

Like a rat, Aalf slunk out of the back room, as if waiting for Rane to leave before resuming his day.

With a grumble, Aalf handed over several coins and Rane dropped the wood at Aalf's scuffed boots.

Linnéa and Rane turned to leave.

"Face like an angel," Aalf's voice slithered after them, "But a voice like the devil."

Rane's jaw worked in and out and Linnéa could feel the rage exuding from his body, like heat from a fire.

"P-Please, don't." Linnéa grabbed his arm.

Much to her relief, Rane kept walking, but his jaw remained clenched.

"You shouldn't have any more trouble on the rest of your route." Rane turned down an alley, heading back to his farm and his waiting mill.

"T-Thank you." Linnéa called after him, frightened by the storm in Rane's eyes.

Six

"I'm here t-to deliver milk, M-Mrs. Felecia."

A regal woman looked over her spectacles as Linnéa approached. She sat reading a newspaper in her kitchen as a maid set tea before her. She had never met this woman, but caught a glimpse of her through the laced curtains as she made her deliveries.

Linnéa had heard that she had been the daughter of a baron, but due to marrying someone below her station, she had lost her standing in society. Yet, despite her misfortune, she continued to carry herself with dignity and distinction. Why was she here in the common kitchen? Her attention to Linnéa caused a cold sweat to gather around her temples.

"Are you the girl they wrote about?" The woman thumped the newspaper before her.

Linnéa dropped her gaze as she ladled milk into the bottle the maid produced. She had heard about the news article from Anders, but she dared not read it, rather pretending that it didn't exist.

The woman stared at her, awaiting a response. Linnéa could feel her cool blue eyes boring into her soul. "Y-Yes, it is."

"Are you ashamed of the attention?"

Linnéa reflected for a moment, studying the milk flowing from her hand. "I'm a-ashamed it's k-kept me from m-my w-work."

The woman nodded, as if satisfied with her answer. "I have a proposition for you. I know you resent the attention, but this publicity could be an excellent start to your career, and one I believe you will excel in under my tutelage. Work that could far exceed your current income capabilities."

Linnéa's mind whirled, like the pearly liquid swirling before her. What in heaven's name did this strange woman mean?

"I'm n-not sure I u-understand."

"You are beautiful and young. You have a chance to improve your prospects considerably. Am I correct in assuming you came to Stockholm to help earn a better way for yourself as well as your family back in Dalarna?"

Linnéa nodded.

"Then this is the opportunity that you have come for, I assure you."

"May I-I s-still continue my work as a m-milkmaid?"

"Most definitely, it helps your visibility, and it is working for you thus far."

"Then w-what, may I a-ask, d-do you n-need me for?"

"You will be paid and admired for your beauty, and I assure you, the compensation you will receive will be worth your time. Additionally, you will receive guidance in proper etiquette and an education from me in exchange for a percentage of your income."

Linnéa stared blankly, her mind floundering in the woman's words. Paid for her beauty? Given an education?

"I'm s-sorry, but I d-don't fully understand."

"No matter, speak to your employer and secure her permission first. I require a few hours each afternoon, as well as the evenings that I request, after your work is completed of course."

Silence filled the room.

"Do you agree to this?"

Linnéa stared dumfounded before nodding reluctantly. Although she was not entirely sure what she was agreeing to.

"Good. You may now go, please return tomorrow with your employer's consent."

Shouldering her yoke, Linnéa plodded her way home, with one question berating her. What would Edla say?

Linnéa waited to talk to her employer until she had finished milking all the cows that evening, fed the animals, and entered the galley kitchen to help Edla with the butter.

Linnéa's hands moved rhythmically like a dance, gripping the oar of the butter churn. She could feel the cream slogging around in the basin, slowly turning from a rich liquid to a thick, creamy substance. Her hands worked, but her mind was elsewhere, struggling with the impending conversation.

"Might as well just spit it out, daft girl!" Edla kneaded dough on the roughly hewn table, beating it into submission. "I can tell something is eating at ya!"

"I-I'm n-not quite sure how to say..." Linnéa peeked inside the butter churn, thankful to see that the cream had fully turned. She stared blankly, trying to find the words. "I was d-delivering milk to the w-widow Mrs. Felicia in Stockholm today, when she m-made me the s-strangest offer."

Dumping the butter into a bowl, Linnéa added water and washed it to remove the buttermilk. Her spoon smoothing and cutting it repeatedly until the liquid ran clear.

"What offer?" Edla's words didn't hint at curiosity as much as they prodded Linnéa from her silence.

"She said the p-publicity I received from the n-newspaper a-article could h-help me s-start a c-career. Something about being p-paid to be admired. She w-wants to give me an education in e-etiquette and s-schooling." The words came out flat, uncertainty lurking between each one.

"A career to be admired and schooling to boot, huh?"

"I p-promise to wake up as early as needed to get all m-my work d-done," Linnéa blurted. "She said a few hours in the a-afternoon and some e-evenings."

Edla chuckled, thumping her fist into the dough ball.

Linnéa remained silent, working the last of the buttermilk out of the yellow lump before her. Why was Edla being withholding, unlike her usual self? "D-Do I have your p-permission, ma'am?"

"Yes, girl, I won't be standing in your way of bettering yourself. I know Felecia, and she's an honorable woman, she will keep good care of ya."

Linnéa was stunned into silence, surprised that Edla took so little convincing. She had half hoped that she would be denied and that would be the end of the strange proposition.

"I'm still not sure if it's the r-right t-thing though..."

"Do you have any idea what other girls would do to be in your shoes? What a privilege it is to be able to live off of beauty? You've been dealt a mighty fine set of cards, that's for certain."

"At what cost t-though?" Linnéa mumbled.

"To be adored and admired, groomed and educated, petted and praised," Edla prattled on, "mark my words, it's the dream of any country girl, Linnéa, any red-blooded girl from any time and any place."

Linnéa stared at the buttermilk left in the bowl, as if she wished it would speak and tell her what to do. In the back of her mind though, she knew the possibility of making more money to send to her mama was an opportunity she couldn't refuse. The opportunity her mama no doubt prayed for while kneeling on the cold floor every evening. Her only wish was that it would be something that would cause her to have less visibility, not more.

Seven

"I think you're about ready to make your first appearance!" Mrs. Felicia beamed.

"W-What?"

"Did you forget this part of the bargain, my dear? What do you think we have been preparing for?"

Linnéa swallowed, staring down at the books that littered the table in front. Her mind was seeped in world history, culture, and she had even learned some French for the past month. The most difficult task however, were the hours Felecia spent making her repeat words and phrases in hopes that her speech impediment would improve. She had given herself to the study, enjoying the new world it opened to her but dreading the price. "I confess, I had forgotten." Linnéa measured each word, speaking with precision, as Mrs. Felicia had taught her.

"Yes, as the yuletide season approaches, I have already spoken to several in the aristocratic circles who wish to present you at their various salons and banquets. Your first will be tomorrow evening."

"So s-soon?" Linnéa's voice faltered.

Mrs. Felicia's piercing eyes surveyed Linnéa. "What are you afraid of, my dear? Your speech has come along considerably, and you're becoming quite distinguished if I do say so myself."

"The attention."

"As I have stated before, look at this as an avenue for income. Just as there are things about farm life that you do not enjoy, this part will be endured with grace and fortitude."

Linnéa knew this, but it didn't make the prospect of being admired and surveyed like a statue in a museum any less intimidating.

"We must be moving along. You have a dress fitting and then we have an errand with Anders. Do you know that he is a lawyer as well as a dock manager?"

Linnéa nodded, not feeling like conversing.

The two women walked through the streets of Stockholm, arm in arm. Mrs. Felicia would typically have taken her carriage, but like each time they went out, she insisted Linnéa remain visible to the public. "They must see you as a mascot, my dear, and for that you must be visible."

Linnéa much preferred walking with Rane, as his presence diverted eyes rather than welcomed them as Mrs. Felicia's presence seemed to.

The door glided open to a femininely adorned waiting room filled with magazines and photos of elegantly dressed women.

"Ahh Madam Felicia and our beautiful Dalarna girl! How wonderful to see you again!" A petite woman with dark hair piled high on her head, who spoke in a French accent, escorted them to a seat.

"Wonderful to see you Marie!"

"I've very much enjoyed making the pieces you suggested, Madam Felicia, and I believe they will be exquisite on Linnéa." Taking Linnéa's hand, she whisked her into a dressing room where a maid stood holding various undergarments. The air smelled of rose petals and tea making Linnéa's stomach groan. Vibrant colors and sateen textures caught her attention as a rack of gowns stood nearby.

"These are e-exquisite!" Linnéa breathed, her senses overcome. Her eyes wandered over the oceans of color which rippled and curled beneath her touch.

"Just wait until they are on!" Marie's eyes sparkled as she closed the curtain with a flourish.

The maid helped her don the corset over her undergarments, bloomers, and silk stockings before she helped her slide into one of the gowns. It was frosty blue with tiny flowers across the bodice and delicate lace trim around her wrist and collar.

"Oh, my..."

The maid nodded, reassuring Linnéa. Opening the curtain, she stood aside to let Linnéa pass. Soft exclamations sounded from the two women, who sat with looks of great expectation on their faces as they waited for Linnéa to emerge.

"She's beyond my expectations, Marie! This gown is angelically inspired, I'm certain of it!"

"Sweet Linnéa was born to wear it! Look at that fit! Look at that face!"

The two women petted and praised, circling Linnéa like bees do a flower. They brought jewelry, rouge for her face, and furs to try with it, exclaiming that each one surpassed the first. She tried on seven gowns, but lost track of the shoes and endless accessories that Marie produced to be paired with them.

Linnéa felt her reluctance, like spring ice, melt in the warmth of the praise. Perhaps being admired was not as terrible as she had once thought.

"I will have it all delivered this afternoon!" Marie waved as the two women left the shop.

Linnéa felt flushed, as if she'd engorged on the most delicious feast and that it had not been entirely good for her.

"One last errand!" Mrs. Felicia led the way through the merchant district towards the docks and the "Spanish Grape." Rapping gently on the door, Mrs. Felicia didn't wait for a reply before pushing it open.

"Good afternoon to ya, Mrs. Felicia and Linnéa!" Anders called, still seeming a little groggy.

"We are needing a contract that stipulates certain, let's just say para-meters around what Linnéa is employed to do. You see, she has her first viewing tomorrow!" Mrs. Felecia beamed.

Anders nodded, clearly intrigued.

"Something that states that her presence is the sole reason for her employment, not leaving any room for misunderstandings of the unsa-vory sort."

"Ye want to make sure people aren't assuming...things," Anders interjected, leaning forward. "Because of the money you will receive?"

"Exactly."

"Well this is an interesting, and let's just say, delicate matter we've got here." Anders rose and paced about the room.

"We need to establish a clear contract outlining what you're about."

Mrs. Felicia nodded.

"Some type of document or certificate that ensures those in attendance, of say any party that you attend, understand the limits of the arrangement."

Mrs. Felicia nodded again.

Anders picked up his pace, his words coming faster as if he awakened fully due to the arousal of his legal mind. "I think securing the signatures of people of authority or prestige will be sufficient." He paused, deep in thought. "Whether it be a baron, baroness, lord, or lady." He looked directly at Linnéa for the first time. "You know, this will be completely blown to Hades if, God forbid, you be transgressing the terms that such a contract would stipulate."

Linnéa dropped her head, sickened at the thought. "N-Never."

"All right then, come by tomorrow and I'll have something drafted for ye."

Eight

Linnéa forced herself upright, knowing it was early morning as the silvery light crept through her window. She slumped on the edge of her bed, allowing herself a moment before going out into the cold. Pulling the thick wool blanket around her, she wished she could sink into it, but today she had much to do. She couldn't shirk her milkmaid duties for the more frivolous ones.

Blinking, she studied the small room which was situated off the kitchen. Her eyes took in her meager belongings she had brought with her from Dalarna. Her three worn dresses, her apron with the delicate flowers her mama had embroidered for her, and an old pair of boots. They starkly contrasted the finery that awaited her at Mrs. Felicia's home. *Am I living a double life?* She felt as if she had one foot in one world, the world she knew and loved, while stepping into another. Did she want to leave this one? The allure of beauty beckoned her, but the wholesomeness of her current existence wasn't lost on her.

Wrapping her thickest shawl around herself, Linnéa headed toward the barn. Her lantern cast long shadows across the ground as the day sluggishly awoke.

"Goot morning, girls." Linnéa opened the latch, letting the first cow to bolt through the gate receive the honors of being milked first. The others stood demurely, waiting their turn.

Linnéa slowly lowered herself to her three-legged stool. She had learned the hard way and knew that Sigge was not someone who liked to be startled or approached as a means to an end. She was sensitive and had an attitude the size of a mule. Her milk needed to be coaxed out of her.

"Easy there, Sigge." Linnéa patted her brown-and-white splotched side. Linnéa blamed the cantankerous nature on the Guernsey-Jersey cross breeding. Blowing into her hands, Linnéa warmed them because Sigge didn't enjoy cold hands on her warm udder.

Sigge tensed, her tail flicking although there were no flies.

Swap! Sigge's tail smacked Linnéa in the face, the manure clinging to it slipping between her teeth.

"You blasted bag of bones, good-for-nothing nag!" Linnéa spat, the insults flowing from her tongue smoothly. She grabbed the bucket away, expecting Sigge to kick it over as she had done the first day, baptizing Linnéa in the warm, frothy liquid. Knowing better than to keep yelling at her, Linnéa calmed down, lightly patting Sigge's side.

"You worthless, beast, you," Linnéa cooed softly. "Time to let down your milk, you old ogre."

Sigge burrowed her head in the hay at the head of her stanchion, yet her body remained tense and rigid.

Linnéa rolled her eyes and sang a familiar ballad in soft soothing tones.

"In our pasture grows blue berries,
Come joy from the heart,
If you need me for something, we will meet there!"

Sigge relaxed, chewing her cud contentedly.

Linnéa began to milk. The sound of the milk hitting the pail making the rhythm she sang to.

"Come lilies and aquilegia, come roses and Salvia.
Come sweet crisp-leafed mint, come joy from the heart!
Fair little flowers will ask for a dance.
Come joy from the heart!

If you want, I can make a crown of flowers."

The barn cats gathered around, waiting for a squirt or two. The pigeons from the rafters cooed, and the mice scurried in the sweet-smelling hay. Even Letty gave up her vigilance for herding the goose for a moment as she rested her head on her paws. The melody swelled, and Linnéa lingered over the sweet sound of the lyrics on her tongue, the melancholy notes lurking.

"The crown of flowers
I will put in your hair
Come joy from the heart!
The sun goes up and down,
but hope stays strong."

Feeling someone's presence, Linnéa glanced over her shoulder to find Rane ducking into the barn.

"Don't stop on account of me." He smiled. "I just came to deliver some wood for Edla." Disappearing into the adjoining room, she could hear the wood plunking to the ground. Despite the cold, Linnéa could feel warmth filling her chest. She hadn't seen Rane for a few days, and she had missed him.

"Can I help?"

Linnéa looked up surprised, but grateful due to all she had to get done today.

"I'm sure you have much to do!"

"Nothing that can't wait a bit."

Smiling, Linnéa turned her attention back to the milking as she heard Rane retrieving another cow. Soon Ludda barreled her way into the barn, heading straight for the vacant stanchion.

Rane pulled up a low bucket and blew on his hands.

"I see it's not your first time."

He chuckled. "I wish it were."

"There are worse things than milking."

Sigge's tail twitched threateningly, as if to warn Linnéa.

"Grumpy beast, she doesn't like the interruption to her morning ritual."

Rane smiled, nodding for her to continue her song.

Linnéa began the song again. The lantern light flickered across the floor, making the typically mundane task into almost a mystical one. The rhythmic sound of milk splashing into the bucket swelled with Linnéa's voice as she gained confidence.

Glancing around Ludda's hindquarters, Rane caught Linnéa's eye. His eyes reflected the light; the eyes that said so much more than he ever did. For once, Linnéa didn't skirt his gaze, but lost herself in it.

"It's a big day for you." Rane broke the spell first, the rhythm of the milk squirting into the bucket picking up speed.

"It is," Linnéa sighed, wishing the rest of the day wouldn't come, so they could stay like this.

"I hear there will be quite a turn out at your viewing event."

Discomfort pricked her spine.

"I greatly hope not."

Rane remained silent, as if struggling to find the right words.

"I just...want you to be careful." His words came at last, but she could tell it was only a glimpse into the internal dialogue he was having with himself.

"There, I beat you!" Linnéa stood, trying to lighten the mood.

Rane stood too, finished as well. By the look on his face, Linnéa could tell he hadn't shaken free from his stormy thoughts.

"I understand this is an exciting opportunity for you, and I'm happy for that, but I can't help but feel that you're playing with fire. Just because it's beautiful and inviting doesn't mean that it won't burn you in the end. It doesn't mean that it's truly good for you."

"Don't worry about me, Rane! Mrs. Felecia is like a mother hen and has taken great care to arrange that all is well and proper."

"Yes, but even people with good intentions can be blinded by their own hopes." Rane released Ludda's head from the stanchion, and she and Sigge ambled back to the pasture.

Linnéa grabbed Rane's arm as he brushed past. "Thank you for your concern, Rane, you've been so good to look after me. I feel so safe when you're around." To her surprise, her words flowed smoothly from her tongue. She liked to think that it was due to the intense phonetic regiment that Mrs. Felicia had her on, but she knew better. She knew it was Rane who put her at ease.

"I can't always protect you though, Linnéa. Especially at these gatherings you're set to attend."

Edla emerged from the house, carrying a basket of bread and cheese. The unfinished conversation blew like snowflakes to the sea.

Nine

"Malla Silfverstople is a distinguished member of society and is our hostess this evening." Mrs. Felicia looked intently into Linnéa face. the severity of her gaze hinted at the situation that lay before her. "She is not only a writer, but also an avid traveler, and she was inspired by her recent visit to Paris to open a salon."

"What's a salon?" Linnéa endeavored to keep her voice steady, resisting the urge to bolt from the carriage.

"It's an elegant gathering to provide stimulating and enlightening conversation. Madam Malla is a vital connection to your success, and if her salon goes as expected this evening, we will secure many other engagements. Just remember to smile and stand up straight," Mrs. Felicia whispered the words in Linnéa's ear as she stepped from the carriage and entered the dim building.

Her gown swished through the narrow doorway, and her eyes adjusted to the light. The scent of mahogany and wine greeted her senses as she beheld a room with dozens of well-dressed ladies and gentlemen.

"Ahh, our guest of honor! Please, come this way!" A woman of slight stature and dark piercing eyes beckoned Linnéa.

"Ladies and gentlemen, this is the Dalarna girl whom we've all heard so much about! She has caused quite a stir in the streets due to her unflawed beauty, and we've invited her here today to discuss beauty and its prominence to the needs of humanity."

Linnéa sat in an elegant chair that was provided for her on an elevated platform. Warmth flushed her face as she was surveyed like a painting, every detail of her appearance and clothing scrutinized. Whispered conversation behind gloved hands and knowing nods circulated the room. What could they be saying? What were they thinking? For the first time, Linnéa was self conscious about her appearance and was uncertain if she measured up to the expected standard. Gripping her skirt, she tried to still her trembling hands.

"Beauty is a universal language, it need not be expressed in words, but is purely ornamental and speaks to the language of the heart. It disarms and stupefies the critic, satisfies the romantic, and even intrigues the enlightened mind. It's been the subject of countless sonnets, poems, and paintings since the dawn of time, being a worthy subject of our contemplation. I welcome each of you to discuss amongst yourselves the importance that beauty holds in your life. Is it celebrated as we celebrate it today? Or do you find it lacks importance? What do you find to be the most beautiful things in your life, whether intellectually stimulating or visually stimulating? Please, ladies and gentlemen, discuss, discuss!" Madam Malla clapped her hands, and the room erupted in murmurs and the light tinkling of glass.

Linnéa noticed a large man entering the room but remaining at a distance. He kept to himself, sipping a glass of wine, but not engaging in conversation with anyone else. He wore a wide-brimmed hat pulled low over his face, but she caught his eyes surveying her hungrily.

Linnéa squirmed in her chair. Did he like what he saw? Why was he staring at her so? Allowing herself a quick glance at her hands, she distracted herself with the emerald ring Mrs. Felicia had stuck on her finger moments before they had departed her home.

When she looked up, the man had disappeared. Had he come just to see her? Questions swirled in her mind, crowding out the sound of Madam Malla's voice as she recited poetry and read from several texts before concluding the evening.

"You were magnificent, darling!"

Linnéa's eyes focused, landing on the woman before her, who squeezed her hands. "We're so fortunate to have you gracing the streets of Stockholm."

"Your company has been most enlightening this evening," an elderly man said, bowing low.

"If I had known beforehand, I would have brought several others along. So many want to meet you after that newspaper article!" A third lady, with glimmering jewelry gushed.

"You're going to put Stockholm on the map, miss!" Another voice called.

Madam Malla rescued her from the adoring crowd, pulling her aside to where Mrs. Felicia stood nodding in approval. "This was the best turnout we've had in weeks, and several joined from the street because they heard that Linnéa was in attendance!"

"I'm so glad that we could be of service to you!" Mrs. Felicia beamed, patting Linnéa's shoulder gently. "Your discussion on beauty was perfectly enlightening!"

"You should expect several invitations from the fashionable and aristocratic circle, as I heard several commenting on hoping to secure Linnéa to adorn their festive parties approaching Christmas!" Madam Malla leaned in, as if to disclose a secret. "I wouldn't be surprised if several proposals came your way, dear girl."

Linnéa was stunned. How could someone want to marry her without a single conversation? The absurdity of the possibility haunted Linnéa as they drove back to Mrs. Felicia's home, while the moon cast eerie shadows across the cobblestone streets. The reality that her life was changing rapidly seemed out of her control. She felt as if she were stuck in water, freezing at an alarming rate, yet she was unable to flee its numbness.

Linnéa shivered against the frosty night air, pulling her shawl tighter around her shoulders. What began as a seemingly harmless experiment was turning into something much bigger than she had ever anticipated. As the shadows danced past, it seemed that the only place to go was forward.

Just as Madam Malla had predicted, invitations to salons, parties, and banquets poured in, along with extravagantly generous sums of *riksdaler.*

She feared this other life, the one where she wore fine gowns and sipped champagne, was causing a coldness to grow between her and Rane. He had been supportive of her, but the unfinished conversation they'd had the week prior left her with questions. Dozens of "viewings," as Rane called them, were scheduled and the extra income she'd been promised was becoming a shocking reality before her eyes. Despite the frills and glamor, Linnéa still felt hesitant to engage in such a vain pursuit, her conscience feeling like a burr beneath her stocking each time. Shoving the sensation aside for the thousandth time, she walked forward into her life of glamor.

Ten

"The candles symbolize the light of Christ coming into the darkness of the world," Linnéa paused, hearing her mama's words repeating in her soul like a familiar song.

"In Him was life, and the life was the light of men," Linnéa whispered, completing her mama's imagined unfinished words. Her breath caused the candles to shudder. "And the light shines in the darkness, and the darkness did not comprehend it."

Lifting the garland of holly, Linnéa placed it on her head, being careful not to topple the unlit candles nestled in the greenery. St. Lucia day was her favorite holiday, not because it began the yuletide celebrations, but because the picture of Christ's light coming into the world, into the darkest places of humanity and during the physically darkest time of the year, was an image unlike any other. It was the image of hope, of the promise of a future, and the assurance that no matter the depth of the darkness God's love would ever be farther reaching.

Linnéa slipped into the simple, yet elegant white dress she was instructed to wear and tied the red sash around her waist. It felt good to wear something less elaborate for a change. Did she look like the Saint Lucia? The virgin martyr who smuggled food and goods to the persecuted Christians, hiding in the Roman catacombs? Her eyes fell.

"I hope I can have half the faith and courage that she had." Linnéa breathed the prayer, shame prickling her skin as she looked at her reflection in the mirror. She felt very short on courage. Lost in the tantalizing glow of the candlelight, Linnéa ignored the reality of the next "viewing party," like it was an impending storm.

"It's time to leave, dear." Mrs. Felicia's voice sounded muffled through the door.

Retreating from her place of solace, Linnéa followed Mrs. Felicia into the carriage and toward Stockholm's city hall. The red brick building with striking green shutters thrown open came into view sooner than she had hoped.

As she climbed out of the carriage, Linnéa noted several other young ladies who were also adorned in St. Lucia attire. Relief welled within her, quelling the dread. She could have hugged each one, overjoyed that she was not alone, but due to Mrs. Felicia's nearness, she remained austere. None greeted her with warmth, however. She fell into ranks with them, being thankful that she didn't have to enter the great room alone, to be the only one who was ogled and stared at. The shaking in her hands subsided.

"And now, for the procession of the most beautiful women to be found! It is up to you to decide who deserves the title of the most beautiful woman in Sweden!" An orator's voice boomed from within the lively ballroom.

What? Mrs. Felicia had said nothing about a contest of beauty. Linnéa searched Mrs. Felicia's face. Had she known? From the stern expression she wore, she gave Linnéa no look of sympathy or way out.

Her face flushed, and she fought back tears. Had the others been told?

As if on cue, she caught the steel-blue eyes of the girl in front of her. From the way her jaw was set, and the haughtiness in her stride, it appeared that she knew exactly what was expected of her, and she had long awaited this moment.

"Entering first, is the exquisite Mariana."

The procession of girls dwindled until it was only Linnéa and one other. Faint exclamations and applause from gloved hands sounded within the room, as the orchestra played an elaborate flourish of strings.

"Next, is Dota, the sailor's daughter!"

A similar response echoed off the walls.

"In closing, Linnéa, the magnificent milkmaid from Dalarna!"

Linnéa forced a small step forward, her pulse quickening as the darkness of the night clung to her from behind. She wanted to recoil into its depths, away from the sound of applause and flickering lights.

"You must go inside, dear." Mrs. Felicia propelled her forward, her arm resting firmly on her back.

Linnéa shook her head, but was unable to utter a word. With a gentle push, she was released into the room. The light was suffocating, the sound of the orchestra deafening, and she felt as if she were walking directly into the sun, searing in its heat.

"The magnificent milkmaid of Dalarna!" The orator repeated, his volume mounting. The applause swirled around her, and the room exploded in an uproar of murmurs and exclamations.

Linnéa couldn't make out any faces, just grotesque costumes in garish colors. They swirled around her, like bubbles in an ocean, as she drowned in the relentless waves.

"This way!"

Linnéa took her place next to the other girls on a platform, which appeared to be contrived for this reason.

"Behold! The most beautiful women to be found in all of Sweden!"

The room erupted in the most deafening applause, as the orchestra played in time. Linnéa's eyes glistened as she held her head erect, refusing to topple the headdress. She would not concede to this mob by crying. Her eyes scanned the crowd, willing to see Rane amongst the monsters. But he wasn't there because he hadn't been invited. The questions pounded in Linnéa's skull, like the sounds crashing around her.

"Who is found to be the most beautiful, the most magnificent, the most exquisite?" The orator boomed, his voice causing another frenzy of clapping and tinkling of glass.

A chorus of voices called out, making the din louder. A single tear escaped down Linnéa's cheek, but she couldn't stop it, nor did she try.

"A raise of hands will suffice!" The orator raised his gloved hands in mock offense.

"Who votes for the beautiful Mariana?" Several hands went up, mostly the elegant hands of women.

"Please Father God, let it not be me, please let them choose another!" Linnéa pleaded the prayer, which escaped with her labored breath. As each name was called, panic mounted.

"Now, who for Dota the sailor's daughter?" Two-dozen hands went up.

"Finally, who of you see the Dalarna milkmaid as the victor of them all?"

Frenzied hands shot into the air in an overwhelming number. Each one stole the breath from Linnéa's heaving lungs. How could this be? She didn't want this!

"Behold! The most beautiful woman in all of Sweden!"

The room felt hot and lights swirled around her. Lowering herself to a chair that was provided for her, Linnéa sipped on the drink someone had offered. Eyes looked at her from all directions, and people nodded their affirmation. Did no one truly see her? Did no one see that she was screaming on the inside, begging to be let out of this charade?

The feeling of being utterly betrayed stung in her gut like a poker. How could they think anyone would enjoy being such a spectacle? She caught the disappointed glance of Mariana, her rival, and the tilt of her head gave her disappointment away.

Linnéa studied her shoes, shame creeping into her face.

Eleven

At last, Linnéa climbed into the carriage as the silvery morning light dawned across the chimneys and roofs. Their smoke trails puffed into the sky as the stars gave way to the churning of daylight. Linnéa wanted to be in bed with the rest of the working world and be waking up from this dream. As her forehead rested against the window of the carriage, she closed her eyes, disappearing into oblivion.

"Wasn't that the most magnificent food that you had ever tasted?" Mrs. Felicia's words felt like cold water splashing over her shivering body.

"I-I didn't have any of it."

"Oh, my dear, why not? The roasted pig, the herring, the soups, and the desserts exceed anything I have had in years!" She patted Linnéa's arm. "It's no wonder that you are feeling peaked, after such an eventful night!"

Linnéa stared out the window, her eyes not seeing what passed before her. "D-Did you know...did you know about the contest?" She turned to look at Mrs. Felicia, who squirmed in her seat.

"My dear, let's just put all that behind us and be thankful..."

"Did you know?" Linnéa's words came out like ice.

Mrs. Felicia dropped her eyes, staring at her hands, which were primly clasped in her lap. "The invitation mentioned something about a contest now that I recall, but I didn't know it would be quite this grand!"

"Did you conceal it from me because you knew I wouldn't consent to going?"

Mrs. Felicia grew silent, as if internally debating her next move. "Darling, it was for the best, can't you see that?" She gripped Linnéa's hand gently. "You're famous because of it!"

"For the best? It was a m-mockery to why we celebrate this day!" Linnéa sputtered, turning back to the window, surprised at the conviction that boiled within her.

"It was a beautiful tribute to St. Lucia! What a turnout!"

"T-Tribute? St. Lucia day is about h-honoring sacrifice, faith and c-courage, not vanity! It's about remembering that Christ came into this world destroying the d-darkness with His light and truth."

Mrs. Felicia fell silent.

Hot tears fell down Linnéa's face. "I appreciate all that you've done, really I do, but I'm afraid I'm unable to continue this c-charade. I am not the one suited to this job, you will have to find a-another."

"Don't you see? Linnéa, there is no one else! You have been declared the most beautiful in all of Sweden! Your destiny is established, and your path paved before you!"

"That may be so, but I cannot continue with the v-viewing parties and the v-vanity. No amount of m-money could make up for feeling that I am betraying who I a-am."

Mrs. Felicia lowered her head as she dabbed at her eyes. "I don't want to force you, my dear, I just want to offer you a different life! I want you to enjoy the opportunities that I wasn't given. Harming you or your dignity was never my intention. I will not force you to continue, if you do not wish."

"Thank you, Mrs. Felicia. I truly appreciate your intention of k-kindness. I am v-very thankful for the French, history, and p-phonetic lessons that you have given me. You have opened up a n-new world to me, and for t-that I will b-be forever grateful."

The carriage approached Mrs. Felicia's home and stopped with a jolt.

"Please keep the remainder of the m-money you receive f-from tonight to pay off any outstanding debts f-for the fine things you bought for me and the lessons. I hope y-you can find someone else to w-wear the gowns." Linnéa stepped out of the carriage.

"Allow my coachman to drive you home at least!" Mrs. Felicia's words grabbed at her back.

"I don't mind the w-walk, thank you!" Linnéa stole through the streets, pulling her cloak hood low over her face. She nearly ran, knowing it was growing late, and the cows waited to be milked.

Not bothering to change out of her gown, she bent down and hugged Letty, thankful that the dog didn't see her any differently. Sigge let out a bellow. She stood and opened the gate to begin a chore she welcomed more than ever before.

"Oh, thank heavens for cows!" Linnéa ran her hand over Sigge's side as she jogged toward the milk parlor, her bag bulging from side to side.

Grabbing an apron from a peg, she pulled it over her gown and eased herself onto the stool.

"So much useless fabric!" Linnéa grumbled, smoothing the poof that occurred as she sat. "Do you like my dress, Sigge? Do you think I'm beautiful?" Linnéa cooed, her eyes feeling heavy. Resting her head against the cow's stomach, she tried to keep from nodding off. "I got all dressed up, especially for you..."

Linnéa awoke with a jerk, her senses reeling. What had happened? Rubbing her pounding head, she felt her hair in a tangle of curls and ribbons and straw. Her mind raced back to reality as she raised herself from the hay mound she was laying in, her cloak draped over her like a blanket. Confused, she glanced around, trying to make sense of the situation. Poor Sigge! Had she fallen asleep while milking her? Going to where she had left the cow, she was surprised to find Tindra standing there instead, chewing her cud happily as her milk squirted into a bucket.

"Edla, I'm so sorry! I..."

Moving around the cow, she discovered Rane hunched over milking, not her disgruntled employer!

"Rane! What are you doing?"

"Finishing your job." His eyes laughed, when he didn't. "When I came in to see what had become of ya, I found you asleep against the cow you were milking. You looked like you needed a bit more sleep before your deliveries, as I'm sure your customers wouldn't appreciate me instead of you."

"I'm sorry! But you didn't have to let me sleep!" Linnéa squirmed.

"I figured by your attire that you hadn't gotten much sleep last night."

Glancing down at her clothes, she realized the odd spectacle she must be, milking a cow in her white evening gown! Warmth flooded her face.

"This is the last one, if you want to go and change or something."

"Thank you, Rane," Linnéa mumbled as she ran from the barn, scattering a flock of chickens congregated in the barnyard.

Letty flew about, frantically trying to gather them.

"Sorry, Letty!" Throwing on an old white dress and her flower-hemmed apron that laced up the front, she ran back towards the barn.

Rane was just finishing up, as he poured the contents of his bucket into the large canisters. "Ready to go?" He beamed at her.

Twelve

~~~

Rane and Linnéa walked in silence for several minutes, the biting December air stealing their breath. Snowdrifts gathered along the path, while other places remained bare. The countryside that had once been covered in swaying grass and wildflowers remained but a memory. Sunshine and its warmth had all but vanished too, but today a beautiful pink hue was cast across the sky. Linnéa steadied herself, trying not to slip with her yoke and canisters and spill her precious cargo.

"You all right?" Rane stopped, shaking his tattered scarf from his face.

Nodding, Linnéa walked in stride with him.

He carried a load of wood, one of the many loads he would haul to town due to the cold. Linnéa glanced sideways at him, shaking her head in amazement at the amount he could carry in a day.

"How was your St. Lucia event?"

Linnéa burrowed her head deeper into her scarf, hoping the question might blow into the sea.

"Rather not talk about it?"

"I guess you could say that, but I will tell you." She paused again, trying to come up with the right words before telling him of the previous night. Struggling, she made it through, relieved when the humiliating tale had ended.

Rane was quiet, like usual, but he didn't seem surprised or disappointed in her.

"I've told Mrs. Felicia that I won't be taking anymore 'viewing parties' or anything of the like. I think I had the wrong motive from the beginning because the money wasn't worth the way it made me feel."

"How did it make you feel?" Rane's eyes searched hers.

"Ashamed."

"Being praised for your beauty did that?"

"No, making such a profit off of being stared at. It was a celebration of vanity and all that is wrong with the world."

Rane nodded, knowingly.

"I think you were right. You tried to warn me while we milked in the barn weeks ago, but I wasn't ready to accept it then. I couldn't get the money out of my head and what it could do for my family." Linnéa fell silent again, pondering her mama and sisters and how difficult it was for them when the cold and darkness came. She could almost picture them, huddled together enjoying warm *Ärtsoppa*. Growing up as the eldest of her six sisters cemented in her the difficulties of raising such a large family. It was difficult even before her papa died of smallpox a year before. Now that she helped her mama share the burden, the weight of it felt suffocating sometimes. It was her sole motive in migrating to Stockholm. It was the driving force that made toting the milk each day a doable and welcomed chore if it helped distance her and her family from absolute poverty. "Do you think I'm selfish for not continuing because the money could help them so much?"

"No, I don't that. I think your mama would much prefer that you not sacrifice your conscience for money's sake. If I were her, I would be proud of you."

Linnéa burrowed her head in her scarf, the chill biting at her cheeks.

Rane mumbled, but his scarf muffled his words.

"Sorry, couldn't hear you."

He shook her scarf away and swallowed. "I'm proud of you."

His unexpected praise warmed her to her core, like a draught of

Christmas glogg, rich and sweet. The warmth carried her all the way to the frozen streets of Stockholm.

"Sometimes we have to do the next right thing and trust God with the rest." Rane's words gave her comfort, helping her find her footing when she felt like slipping back into Mrs. Felicia's eager tutelage and easy pay.

"It's the milkmaid, the most beautiful woman in all of Sweden!" A voice called, stopping Linnéa in her tracks.

"Three cheers for the Dalarna girl!"

"Congratulations, you deserve the honor!"

As they approached Stortorget, the town square, dozens of people were congregated around the old well. They appeared to have been waiting for her.

"It's her mommy, it's her! Can we say goot morning?"

Linnéa searched the crowd, trying to find the owner of the little voice.

A girl who appeared to be about the age of eight, pointed and pulled on her mother's sleeve, pleading with her to look.

Walking towards her, Linnéa bent down and looked into the girl's rosy-cheeked face. "Goot morning to you! What's your name?"

"It's Lisebet." The girl beamed back. "I've been excited to meet you!"

Linnéa grinned. "I've been excited to meet you, too!"

People gathered around, smiling their encouragement, offering their congratulations.

As much as Linnéa wanted to run and hide, something Mrs. Felicia had said the night before chimed in her soul, like a bell from the nearby church tower.

Your destiny has already been established, and your road already paved.

She knew that running and hiding wouldn't get her far. Looking into the little girl's eyes for courage, she stood allowing the yoke to remain on the cobblestone where she left it. She felt Rane beside her, his strength infusing her with her own.

"Goot morning, everyone!" Linnéa's voice came crisp and clear, as she waved. "Thank you all for your kindness!"

The crowd broke into cheers and several men came forward to lift Linnéa onto their shoulders and parade her through the streets.

"Allow me." Rane's eyes searched Linnéa's, questioningly.

She smiled in response, nodding her consent. He lifted her in a single motion and she balanced on his broad shoulder, before another came to assist.

The crowd erupted in cheers as hats and flowers were tossed into the air, dancing with the falling snow.

Thirteen

"This is more than normal, ma'am," Linnéa assessed her weekly earnings. It typically wasn't much, as she received free room and board, but there were extra *riksdaler* staring at her from her open palm. "How can you afford this?"

"Oh, we ain't payin' that extra, girl." Edla laughed. "Let's just say someone left it for you to be 'included in your weekly pay.' Didn't want me naming names."

Mrs. Felicia, it had to have been! Although she wanted to return it, Linnéa knew that poor girls couldn't afford such vanities. Her mama would be overjoyed in receiving the extra income, especially considering the amount had dwindled significantly as of late. With a grateful heart, she continued on her way.

Rane had always announced himself with a whistle, cresting the hill in the early morning fog. If he didn't meet her at the gate, she would tarry, watching the boats through the haze in the harbor. She didn't necessarily do this intentionally, or even consciously, but the trek to Stockholm was lonely without him. She no longer feared the stares, the calls, and the constant attention, but she felt so much more confident with Rane beside her.

But today, he was nowhere to be seen. Linnéa waited for him as long as she could justify, but knowing that the morning was growing late, she forced herself onward. What could have happened? Maybe she had mistaken his kindness for something more. The inclination that he thought more of her than the mere moral obligation he held, had accompanied her on their many walks to Stockholm. It made its presence known like a faithful dog, trailing behind. It never presented itself in conversation, but if she stopped and turned to look behind her, it was always there smiling at her. Without meaning to, Linnéa picked up her pace, nearly stumbling over the rocks that littered the path.

She made her deliveries quickly, barely paying heed to Aalf and his gawking father, with their snide jokes and overt praise. Without Rane, she noticed things about Stockholm that she hadn't before. The colorful buildings, the way they all sloped west, as if they were old men, leaning against the wind that blew in from the harbor. Her feet clattered on the cobblestone as she walked in silence, alone. She made her next stop and left the tired looking woman with her six children huddled around her skirt before making her way back toward the farm, her load lightened at last.

"Linnéa! Linnéa!"

Looking up from the cobblestones, Linnéa peered around her, trying to discover who was calling her name.

Eva, Mrs. Felicia's maid, ran toward her down one of the alleys. Her face was red despite the cold, and she panted from the exertion. "There ye are!" She called. "I've been tracking ye down for what seems like ever so long!"

"W-What's the matter..."

"Mrs. Felicia sent me."

"B-But my deliveries!" Linnéa protested.

"She sent me urgently, miss."

Linnéa did her best to keep up with Eva as she wove through alleys and back streets, navigating the confusing city confidently. As they approached Mrs. Felicia's home, a soldier in Royal uniform stood outside.

Mrs. Felicia stood nearby with pursed lips and a helpless expression. "He insisted he deliver the contents of the letter to you, dear. He would not be deterred."

Linnéa felt her face drain of warmth. What could be happening? She wished Rane were here to help her make sense of it!

The man's stern expression, vibrant blue attire, and tall fuzzy hat made her wither. She wanted to disappear into the cracks of the cobblestone, like a speck of dust.

The man stepped forward, his heels clicking, as he completed the stride.

"Madam, I have formal correspondence from the Royal Highness." Bowing, he handed her a large envelope on elegant paper.

Linnéa felt as if everyone in Stockholm were staring at her, their whispers tickling her back.

"What in heaven's name?" She heard one woman say as she hurried past with her children.

"It's the Dalarna girl!" someone else said.

As if following some internal, secret command, the soldier turned and climbed back onto his horse. As if she were a fixture of the street, Linnéa watched as he road away into the dim distance. The sound of horse's hooves echoing off the walls around him.

"What does it say?" The sound of Mrs. Felicia's voice made her remember to breathe.

Uncurling the letter, Linnéa gazed at its scrawling script.

Fourteen

～

His whistle kissed her ears the way the mist kissed her cheeks. Keeping her head low, she trudged over the muddy ground, struggling against the canisters dangling from either side of her. She felt him nearing, hearing his sure steps and his heavy breathing. Soon she felt it on the back of her neck.

"Goot morning!"

Linnéa nodded, but didn't reply. They walked in silence.

"Have I done something to anger ye, Linnéa?

Linnéa shook her head but didn't reply.

"Would you please talk to me?"

Linnéa sighed, then bit her lip. They continued in silence. "It's just...just that you didn't come yesterday."

"Ahh." He came in stride with her once again.

"I don't understand why," Linnéa continued, not getting a response. "I thought you cared what h-happened to me. I thought you made a promise to the officer the day I was a-arrested to look after me."

Still silence. Was he even hearing her? She couldn't decide if the feeling of being forgotten was worse than feeling like a fool. "I was just silly." Linnéa buried her nose in her scarf. She wouldn't look at him. Had she said all that? How could she? He didn't owe her anything! What a stupid girl she was to presume that he cared at all for her.

His silence taunted her, whispering through the grass. He opened his mouth to speak, but closed it again, walking a while more. "I didn't want you to think you needed to hide behind me." His words came at last, his breath showing like smoke in the air. He paused again, struggling with his words. "I didn't want to...what's the word? Oh, I didn't want to cripple you by making you feel like you're incapable of handling yourself. I didn't want you to stop using your words because you expected me to speak for you. I didn't want you to feel unable to tell the blokes who harassed you to go and jump in the ocean, yerself." He stopped and turned to face her. "You have more strength inside you than you want to allow room to grow. If I always fight your battles, it won't grow."

Linnéa was stunned. Rane had never spoken to her in this way, and she didn't know what to feel. She wanted to be angry for his presumption, but she also wanted to push through the sting of his words and explore for herself if there was any truth on the other side of them. She sighed. "I really just want to be invisible." She looked into his eyes and saw deep pools of ocean water.

"You want to be invisible, but Linnéa, you are not and you never will be. Don't wish ye were."

"No, Rane, you don't understand. It's not that I wish to be invisible. I...I just wish to be far less seen. I feel like some sort of strange and mystical creature that everyone wants to observe. It's humiliating, it's violating, it's..." She stopped and let the canisters rest on the ground. She reached into the pocket of her apron and pulled out the letter and thrust it at him.

Setting down his wood, he took the delicate paper in his windchapped hands and opened it carefully.

She could see his pulse quickening, beating in the soft spot of his temple.

"They want you to attend the royal masquerade ball on Christmas Eve?" He paused. "By invitation of his Royal Highness? To be an accessory?" His eyes continued to scan the page. "Holy Mother! They promised an outrageous sum of money!"

"At least I will be a well paid accessory." Linnéa chuckled, trying to calm the storm she saw in his eyes, a storm like water crashing against the rocks. Linnéa reached her hand out to retrieve the letter because it looked as if Rane might toss it over the cliff's edge. They continued to walk, but in a deafening silence.

Rane's hands and jaw remained clenched the remainder of the way to Stockholm.

"Please...please don't be angry at me, no matter what I choose."

Rane didn't reply.

"How could I ever refuse the King's invitation? It just can't be done!"

Just before they reached the bustling city, Rane glanced down at her, and for a moment, his eyes seemed less daunting. "You haven't stuttered once this whole conversation." He grinned, sauntering down a side street, clearly delivering wood to a legitimate customer. "You do what you think is best and I won't badger you about it." The words came with the wind, blowing over Rane's shoulder.

Fifteen

Linnéa stood outside Mrs. Felicia's home, staring at the beautiful mahogany door. She hadn't wanted to come here again, especially under these circumstances. The struggle within her to be grateful for the opportunity to be requested by the King, yet the insatiable desire to run for the countryside played tug-of-war within her. At last, she swallowed the lump in her throat and knocked on the door.

"Linnéa, it's wonderful to see you! Mrs. Felicia has been expecting you, please come this way." Eva escorted her into the sitting room, before hurrying off to bring tea.

The tick of the clock was relentless as Linnéa looked around the grand room. The maroon drapes, although drawn, made the room dark against the sparse sunlight. A grand piano sat austerely before a bookcase bursting with luxury. She found herself studying the names of the books, smiling over the ones that Mrs. Felicia had made her pour over. They had transported her to another time and place, opening the world of history, language, and culture to her. Never had she imagined she might be called upon to mingle with royalty!

"Ahh Linnéa, it's lovely to see you!" Mrs. Felicia swept into the room, her elegant day dress trailing after her.

"I'm sorry to come like this after our l-last conversation." Linnéa struggled to get out the words she'd rehearsed all the way there. "I fully i-intended not to continue anything of this sort but..."

"No need to explain, my dear. The invitation changes everything."

Linnéa nodded, staring blindly out the window. "Is there any way that I can p-politely decline?" Even as she uttered the words, Linnéa knew the answer, but she owed it to herself to ask anyway.

Mrs. Felicia was grave. "Not only would it be a great insult, but it would also disgrace you and your good name forever. You absolutely must accept. I am not saying this as your advisor, but as your friend."

Linnéa swallowed, staring at the teacup in her lap.

"Might I add, that this is an outcome that far exceeds any expectation that I could ever have for you. I knew that you would be loved and heralded in Stockholm, but I never dreamed that you would garner the interest of the King himself! Linnéa, I want you to fully understand that this is an honor above every other honor. Relish it, lean into it, and don't wish it away."

"What must I do to be ready?"

Mrs. Felicia's posture slumped slightly, her relief being evident. "With only two weeks to prepare, the time is growing late. There is no way that you will be able to maintain your current job, as well as prepare adequately for an audience with the King. You must polish your French, become intimately acquainted with the Royal lineage, etiquette, and of course, dancing! You must dedicate all your time to the task that lies before you, for it is a great task indeed."

"I can't leave Edla like this! They just bought another milk cow who is about to freshen any day! I haven't given her any notice!"

"I'm sorry, but there is no other way. In fact, we must head to the seamstress immediately so she can take your measurements and begin your the gown for the grand masquerade!" Mrs. Felicia excitement showed, her grey eyes flashing.

Reluctantly, Linnéa followed her out the door, glancing at the discarded yoke and emptied canisters that lay idly by the steps. She hoped that Edla would understand.

"Come along, dear! We can't waste any time dawdling!

❄

Linnéa, placed the bucket of milk into the great farm sink, while dreading the conversation that lay before her.

Edla peeled potatoes, oblivious to her presence, as she sang a lullaby to Helvi who slept in a basket near her.

Linnéa smiled at the chubby baby, who slumbered peacefully, bundled till only her little round face showed. Linnéa had grown to love this family, and she knew that they relied on her, especially with Edla's husband being gone so frequently. She hated the thought of letting them down or leaving Edla with even more work than she already had.

"Ahh, Linnéa there ye are! Could you hand me the garlic and sage?"

Reaching into the roughly hewn rafters, Linnéa broke a clove of garlic that hung from the slanted ceiling. She breathed in the smell of drying herbs as she snipped a few leaves from the bundles. Linnéa handed the produce to Edla.

"How's the new cow looking?"

"She's looking like she might give birth any day!"

"Good! I hope she's worth the pretty penny we paid for her! She is a looker ain't she?"

Linnéa smiled. "She's the sweetest little jersey that I've ever seen! I'm sure she'll be a good milker."

"You've earned us a few extra pennies yerself, Linnéa." Edla continued. "Demand for milk from the 'most beautiful woman in Sweden' has increased our prices! We're even selling more cheese and butter as well."

The feeling of dread deepened into the pit of Linnéa's stomach. "I'm happy to be hearing dat! Would you like me to start the cheese?"

The two worked side by side in silence, as Linnéa worked up the courage to ask Edla for the time off. Linnéa strained the milk and warmed it over the stove until it almost reached the boiling point to begin the cheese process. "There's something that I'm needin' to talk to ya about."

Edla didn't respond, as she stirred her stew.

"I can't tell ya how much I hate to be askin' it, but Mrs. Felicia says there is no other way. It's so unfair right before the new cow..."

"Ahh ya funny girl, I already know. News is all over town about it! Don't look so aghast!" Edla laughed, shaking out a cheesecloth. "I didn't figure you could be going to meet the king as well as keep up your chores around here!"

"Oh, thank you ever so much, Edla!" Linnéa slumped into a chair, relief swelling in her. "It will only be for two weeks and then I'll be back."

"Whoever said beauty doesn't pay, never met you! Anders is pleased as a pickled herring because he discovered ya! Heavens, all of Stockholm is proud!"

Linnéa stared at the herringbone, brick floor, her mind whirling in Edla's words. "I didn't intend for any of this to happen. I would have been so happy to be a simple milkmaid for the rest of my life!"

Edla looked at Linnéa, surprising her with her intensity. "Don't be despising your gift, Linnéa. You've been given beauty, don't be ashamed of it."

Sixteen

She began her journey to Stockholm, but the yoke was not hanging from her shoulders. Despite the lessened burden, her steps still did not come easily. Rane leaned against the rock wall that adjoined the two farms. He stared unflinching as Linnéa approached, but she couldn't hold his gaze, dropping her eyes to her worn boots. "I didn't think you'd come."

"Can I take your bag?" Rane came in stride with her.

Should she refuse? No, that was petty as neither of them had a physical burden to bear that day. Linnéa nodded, relinquishing her tattered bag. They walked in silence, which wasn't unusual for them. But unlike all the other times it was a type of silence that blew like the icy wind from the ocean below. Shivering, Linnéa burrowed herself deeper into her thoughts. Snow scattered the ground, tossed around in patterns, barely a skiff in some places but a heaping pile under the pines. The wind breathed through the trees, murmuring like a pining sailor calling to his lost love from the sea.

Linnéa glanced sideways at Rane without moving her head. He was bundled against the cold, his nose barely showing. "Please don't be upset with me for this."

"I'm not upset with you, Linnéa. I understand why you must go," he replied, but he didn't look Linnéa in the eyes.

"You don't think I'm weak for this?"

Rane shook his head. "I just wish…wish there were some other way for you."

"You and I both, but as everyone keeps telling me, this is the most glorious thing to ever happen to a person—let alone a milkmaid of no importance. I think I'm just too idealistic, too selfish to see it. After all, it's just one night."

They continued on, strolling along the harbor, tasting the salt of so many words left unsaid. Boat whistles blew and men heaved their burdens onto their waiting boats, dories, and ships. For once, no one seemed to notice Linnéa as the chill in the air didn't afford anyone such luxuries of stopping to stare. It was as if everyone was in danger of freezing slowly, like water in a barrel, if they stopped for long.

They approached Mrs. Felicia's house, and Linnéa's knees began to shake. "Thank you for w-walking with me these past months." Her voice hitched.

"Breathe easy, just pretend that everyone you encounter is me, and your words will flow like a river." Rane winked, but his eyes lacked their typical appearance of sunlight on the ocean.

"Sincerely, t-thank y-you f-for your kindness to m-me. I don't know what I would have done without your h-help, and you so faithfully keeping your promise to the officer a-after my a-arrest," she rambled, her thoughts jumbled in her uneasiness. She reached for her bag, only to find Rane staring unabashedly at her, his hat in his hands and his blonde hair flicking in the frigid air.

"I've not been walking with ya to town all these weeks because of the promise I made to the officer. I think ya should know dat. I wanted to be with you, Linnéa."

No words came. Linnéa stared back at him, as she accepted the bag into her trembling hands. Their hands lingered together for a moment on the worn handle before he released it to her. "Merry Christmas Eve, Linnéa." He leaned close to her ear and placed a gentle kiss on her cheek.

She wanted to lean into him and the smell of cedar, retreating away from the daunting task before her. But he straightened and turned to go, leaving her trembling at Mrs. Felicia's mistletoe-adorned door.

In the sluggish sunrise and morning shadows, Linnéa cursed her beauty and what it required of her.

Dazed, she knocked on the door and was whisked inside to find Mrs. Felicia surrounded by a posse of women.

"Let us begin." Her words were stern, matching her thinly drawn lips, but she wore an elaborate wine colored gown trimmed with black lace. The seriousness of the situation haunted the room, like the smell of cloves that wafted through the house.

The next several hours were spent in meticulous preparations. First Linnéa soaked in a rose petal bath, scrubbing herself until her skin ached. She was slathered in rose scented lotion and donned her crisp, lace-trimmed undergarments. Her face was powdered, and her cheeks and lips were rouged. Even her eyelashes were tipped with a liquid coal dust, making them starkly contrast her golden hair. Woven throughout the preparations, Linnéa repeated phrases of French, rehearsed the names of kings and queens, and practiced snippets of conversation until her words flowed smoothly and without error. Her waist-length hair was crimped and curled with a hot poker before being braided around her head. Her corset strings were drawn around her thin frame to help her posture and disperse the great weight of the gown. Then three women carried Linnéa's gown into the room, being careful not to wrinkle its yards of exquisite fabric. The gown curled around her body in rich and voluptuous blush-colored fabric. It had a floor-length cream skirt with a half-skirt that made an upside down v at her waist. The flared sleeves and square neckline were trimmed with delicate lace, and the bodice was woven with gold lace and flowers.

Mrs. Felicia lifted a delicate lace mask to Linnéa's face, refusing the more elaborate and bulky accessories she had been offered. A dainty pair of shoes were then placed on her feet and, at last, a simple pearl necklace was clasped around her pale neck. "She is complete." Mrs. Felicia's words sounded breathless, but satisfied.

To her relief, Linnéa was left alone for the few moments before the royal coach arrived. Lowering the mask from her face, she stared at the woman behind it, not recognizing her. Did she like this woman she had become? This woman who was famous for her appearance? Linnéa dropped her gaze, glancing at the pathetic carpetbag that sat slumped in the corner holding her own hairbrush, soap and discarded clothes, reminding her from where she had come. She wished to retreat back there, to celebrate the eve of Christ's birth with her mama and sisters. Smiling, she reminisced on the memories of making candied almonds and constructing the comical *Julebock,* laughing over their own creations. Looking at the ceiling, she tried not to cry, fearing what Mrs. Felicia would say if she messed up the coal powder on her eyelashes. "Please Father, help me endure tonight graciously and help it not...not change who I truly am." She prayed the words, struggling over her emotions and fears.

"It is time!" The voice came from outside her door.

Seeing the waiting carriage outside her frosted window, Linnéa slunk into the shadows of the room. The Swedish coat of arms was plastered on its side, causing the feeling of curdled milk in Linnéa's stomach to intensify. She knew they didn't have to travel far, as the Drottningholm Castle was a mere 9 miles from the banks of Stockholm on the island of Lovön, but the distance was still daunting.

"Come, Linnéa dear, we must be going!" Mrs. Felicia's voice pulled her back to reality like a gust of icy wind.

Seventeen

"Let me help you, madam."

Linnéa allowed the footman to assist her out of the carriage. Although she knew Stockholm lay in the distance through the fog, she had entered a new world. She stepped onto a finely grated pathway lined with immaculately manicured shrubs and glowing torches. A light dusting of snow made the whole scene almost impossible to believe.

"Mind your gown, dear."

She looked from her feet to see the castle looming on the horizon like great, rolling storm clouds. It was growing late, and the night sky was completely eclipsed by the castle, which cast long shadows across the ground. An icy feeling crept up her spine.

"Right this way."

Linnéa and Mrs. Felicia followed, their breath showing like billows of smoke in the frigid air. Dozens of ladies and gentlemen approached the castle from various directions, the sound of horses whinnying and the clop of their feet filling the air. What had she agreed to? She knew that royalty had summoned her, but she hadn't been prepared for the grandeur. As she approached the massive structure, her pulse quickened and her palms grew sweaty as she gripped her gown, so as not to tread on its fabric. The sound of her feet on the gravel was deafening, and she seemed to shrink as she approached the structure growing larger with each step. Its cream-colored walls and rounded green-domed roof made a striking spectacle with the immaculate Swedish flag flapping above it.

She placed her foot on the first step. What would meet her inside?

Another step.

Did she look all right? She felt ridiculous with her mask already in place.

Another step.

Why had she agreed to this? She didn't belong in a place like this!

Another step.

She wished Rane had come, and then all of this would be a grand adventure. Pushing her thoughts aside, she walked up the remaining steps. She counted seventeen in all. The massive front doors stood before her, draped in lush evergreen interwoven with holly. Two ferocious lions guarded the entrance on either side, their stone manes curling like fire down their backs, their mouths open, and their front paws resting on a coat of arms. Torches cast dancing shadows across their faces. Two more steps and she was beneath the vestibule.

A servant opened the large wooden door as it clanged on its hinges. He stood like an object, rather than a person.

Linnéa continued past, up two more steps, and into the foyer.

The outside grandeur had not prepared her for what lay inside. The interior was lit by candles hanging from chandeliers and flickering from sconces on the walls. There were stairs to her left and right. They were marble and untarnished by the years. The floor to ceiling reflected the same salmon tones of polished marble, swirling with hints of cream, like smoke. Scrawling ribbons and coats of arms clung to the walls and melted into the cream ceiling, which soon gave way to majestic scenes of angels and clouds. Dozens of white marble statues stood at different places along the stairway, their flowing garments frozen forever in the immortal trap of stone. No space was untouched by adornment. No space was left bare of elaborate garlands of greenery and red ribbon.

Linnéa's mind whirled. What she saw was dizzying. She had never conceived what it was like to glimpse a place where only the lovely was allowed to exist, gilded in gold. They followed the crowd up one flight of stairs, past one landing, and onto another. Fine busts of ancient kings stared unblinking back at her as their faces changed eerily in the candle-light. The stairs opened up to a grand room with massive windows showing the starless night sky.

"Miss Linnéa Ersdotter, the 'most beautiful woman in Sweden,' and Madam Felicia Karlsson."

Linnéa blushed, thankful for the mask to hide behind as they ascended the stairs.

"Mind your posture and glide...glide."

Linnéa had trouble focusing on Mrs. Felicia, being completely taken aback by a massive pine tree erected in the center of the room. Vibrant fruits, ribbons, and lit candles decorated its limbs, making it the most peculiar spectacle that Linnéa had ever seen.

"It's quite a sight, isn't it?" A young man gave a slight bow, making his presence known to Linnéa. His face was hidden by a comical looking mask with a long nose and a large hat.

"Y-Yes! I've never seen anything like it!"

"Ah yes, the royal and wealthy families of Sweden have imported the idea from Germany. Do you think it will become a tradition?"

"It's doubtful." Linnéa chuckled, bewildered by the beautiful yet odd spectacle.

"May I reserve a dance with you this evening?"

Linnéa nodded demurely as she had been instructed.

"The king and queen will be entering soon," Mrs. Felicia whispered the words. "Position yourself over here."

Swallowing a retort of protest because she didn't want to "position" herself anywhere, Linnéa did as she was instructed. Sobriety and an air of expectation blanketed the room, as everyone looked around antici-pating where the royal hosts might arrive from. Two doors swung open at the end of the great room near Linnéa.

"All stand for King Karl Johan Baptist Julius the 14th and Queen Eugenia Bernhardina Desideria."

All conversation and movement subsided as every eye was clasped on the royal couple, who emerged into view slowly walking through the crowd.

The king wore an extravagant military coat, adorned with gold tassels and filigrees. He wore a simple black cloth mask and feathered hat, starkly contrasting his solemnity.

The queen paraded in an exquisite black gown, trimmed with lace and an enormous train. Massive red feathers adorned her hair, and an elaborately jeweled mask disguised her face.

Linnéa wished to disappear into the background, but as Mrs. Felicia had predicted, she was perfectly positioned at the front row. Catching her eye, Linnéa's heart quickened as the queen inspected her from head to toe. The moments stood still, trapped in an eternity of doubt. At last, the queen nodded approvingly. Sucking in her relief, Linnéa waited until the queen was several paces away before daring to breathe.

Once they reached the center of the room, the orchestra began to play and the king and queen began to dance. The room morphed into an oval as they watched the elaborate fabric of the queen's gown swish and sway in the twinkling light. The scene was mesmerizing, and soon everyone was welcomed to join. A young gentleman bowed, taking her hand and inviting her to the dance floor. After a quick glance at Mrs. Felicia, Linnéa consented as the music sped up and became staccato in tempo.

"Are you familiar with the polka?"

Linnéa nodded, relieved to be performing the steps of a more traditional Swedish dance rather than the more elaborate imported ones that she had been instructed in. Linnéa all but heard Mrs. Felicia's words playing in her mind, "Keep your head up, mind your gown, and float!" But after a few turns, Linnéa fell into stride and began to lose herself in the movement, gliding about the floor gracefully and effortlessly. Soon another gentleman took her partner's place, and she continued to twirl and glide, until the room became a mirage of greenery, satin, and twinkling lights.

Dance after dance passed and Linnéa grew winded, when another man approached.

"Excuse me, but I'll take this one." He was large and wore a grotesque looking black mask. He abruptly replaced her partner, who relented with little protest, clearly not wanting to make a scene. "My name is Count Borgar. You look exquisite, my darling."

She smiled demurely in response, knowing that nothing else was truly needed, but his words made her uneasy. The men she had previously danced with rarely spoke to her, but instead gazed unabashedly at her, as if she were some exotic bird in a cage whose sole purpose was to be surveyed.

"I've often hoped that I would run into you again."

What did he mean? She didn't recognize this man! Why was he acting so familiar with her? "Excuse me...I'm feeling a little t-tired." Despite her best effort, she faltered.

"Oh, just a few more turns and the song will be done, I assure you. Hardly enough time, my dear, hardly enough."

Feeling like a butterfly trapped by a pin, she swirled about the floor. She didn't like the firm grip Count Borgar had on her waist or the way he pressed himself nearer than the dance required. Just a few more minutes and she would be free.

"You're a natural, even among royalty. Every man wants you tonight."

Linnéa cringed, recoiling from him, but his hands remained clasped around her free hand and waist. Should she cry out? Not wanting to draw any attention to herself, she prayed for the song to end. As if on cue, the orchestra finished with a flourish.

"Ladies and Gentlemen, the King and Queen welcome you to the grand Christmas Eve *Julbord*! Come and feast!"

The throng around them clapped, and the man loosened his grasp. Pulling free, Linnéa backed away, losing herself in the crowd. Trembling, she rejoined Mrs. Felicia, who seemed very distracted with the announcement of food, although midnight seemed to be a very late hour for such a feast.

"The first course is served," a servant boomed as he opened two doors leading to the banquet hall.

"The *julboard*!" Mrs. Felicia droned, admiring the tables. "Remember to peck at your food, dear, just a small portion."

There were over a hundred dishes spread as far as she could see, but Linnéa's stomach churned at the sight of it. A pig's head sat at the center, surrounded by dishes of fish, liver pate, pickled vegetables, soups, meatballs, cheeses, and sweet breads. Looking around, she feared to see the man pursuing her, but he appeared to be nowhere in sight.

Eighteen

"Can we retire early?" Linnéa whispered the question over the din of those enjoying their food and drink.

"Heavens no, dear, that would be unthinkable! A few more hours and the footmen will bring the carriages around, but there's no hope that I could track them down this early! You'll get a second wind, I'm sure of it."

Should she insist? How could she make her realize that she felt unsafe with the presence of Count Borgar lurking somewhere behind her?

Brushing the thought away, Linnéa tried to enjoy herself, but she managed to eat only a few bites of food.

After what felt like hours of feasting, the orchestra began again, and the throng of people migrated towards the dance floor once again. Reluctant, Linnéa stood beside Mrs. Felicia as if she were a shadow.

"Dear girl, you mustn't blend into the drapery! No one will ask you to dance!"

"That's quite all right, I've had enough for tonight, I think."

Mrs. Felicia clucked her tongue disapprovingly and began to protest when a regal looking gentleman approached.

"Would you care to dance, madam?"

Mrs. Felicia stepped aside, to allow Linnéa a clear path forward, but the man lifted his gloved hand.

"Your companion is charming I'm sure, but the invitation was directed at you."

Mrs. Felicia bowed elegantly and followed the man to the floor, hardly able to hide the twinkle in her eye and the lightness of her step.

Linnéa felt a hand grab her waist and hot words whisper into her hair. "I was hoping for one more dance, fair one."

Linnéa froze, the glass she held quaking in her hand.

"I know you said you're tired, so let's just talk instead. Somewhere more private perhaps?"

He opened a side door and pulled her into a cramped servant's hallway, his hand clasping around her mouth as she opened it to scream.

"No, please..."

"No need for alarm! You're quite safe with me."

Unease prickled her skin as he pulled her past several doors. No one seemed to notice their departure, and Linnéa watched as the light from the banquet hall disappeared behind them. They entered a deserted sitting room and Linnéa quickly collapsed on a chair, putting as much distance between herself and Borgar as she could. A scream lodged in her throat, but as if the wind had been knocked out of her, she couldn't breathe.

Borgar pulled Linnéa up from her seated position and directed her to the couch that could fit both of them, barely. As Borgar lowered himself beside her, she felt his thigh press against her own.

Linnéa recoiled to the farthest distance she could maintain.

"I've thought of your fair face constantly since our last encounter. You captivate my dreams. You are the most beautiful woman I have ever seen."

His breath made the candles behind them flicker.

Linnéa trembled. "P-Please, let m-me g-go..."

"I'm not finished, my pet." He put his finger to her lips and pressed.

Could she flee? Every fiber within her screamed for her to lunge for the door, but she felt pinned like a bug beneath his hand. God help her out of this nightmare!

Borgar unstrapped his mask, letting it fall to the floor. He then reached for hers, ripping it from her face in a single movement. "Since the first moment that I saw you at the salon, I knew that I had to have you."

Linnéa's mind whirled back to the last time she had seen his face. He had worn a hat, but he had stared at her the same way he was now.

"Then again at your St. Lucia debut, where you were declared the most beautiful woman in all of Sweden. You really have a way of capturing a man's attention."

Shuddering, Linnéa stood, grasping for something to cling to, but he stood too, pursuing her.

"My desire is to fulfill your every desire and every wish. You will be the most adored woman that ever lived, which is well deserved because you are the most lovely."

He moved closer, closing the slight gap that Linnéa had managed between them.

She could feel his breath on her face and smell the glogg on his breath. He grabbed her by the waist and pulled her towards him, wrenching her gown off of her shoulder.

"I won't stop until I have what I want. I can be a persistent man, you know."

Linnéa tried to pry his hands free, but one clamped on her waist like a vice and the other groped around her neck.

"S-Sir, p-please l-let go!"

"I finally have you, at last..."

Light and the sound of music flooded the room, along with a maid who carried several coats and furs. "Pardon me, I'm sorry to disturb you both." Bowing she quickly exited the room.

In the moment of surprise, Linnéa freed herself from Count Borgar's grasp and lunged across the room toward the opened door. "Could you s-show me b-back to the b-banquet hall?"

But the maid was already gone. Linnéa sprang after her, hearing Count Borgar pursuing her from behind.

"I'm not done with you Dalarna girl. You can't just walk away from me! I'm giving you the universe and all the stars. Don't be ungrateful, you..."

Linnéa stumbled down the hallway, tripping over her fine gown and crashing into a vase of flowers, as she ran towards the light and the music. Panic and tears streamed down her face as Borgar's words pounded in her brain, like trampled flowers and shattered glass. She lunged for the door and imagined Rane standing on the other side of it, waiting for her. But he was barred from this world of monsters and men.

Nineteen

"Why won't you tell me what happened, Linnéa?" Mrs. Felicia pressed her for answers for the hundredth time.

But Linnéa remained unmoving, staring out the carriage window, losing herself in the deepest darkness of the misty Christmas morning.

"After the dance had finished, I came back to find that you had completely disappeared! Only to reemerge without your mask, disheveled, and in tears! I should have never let you out of my sight! I'm just happy that I whisked you away before either of the Royal Highnesses could see you in such a state! Please, tell me what happened to you!"

Closing her eyes, Linnéa tried to shut out the memory that felt like a burning ember in her soul. No doubt remained in her mind what would have occurred had the maid not come in. Linnéa shuddered, wrapping the luxurious shawl around her shoulders, trying to pretend that it had been merely a nightmare.

"Other than the mishaps at the end, you were magnificent my girl, absolutely magnificent." Mrs. Felicia patted her back. "Here, dear, I know you're exhausted." Scooting aside, she cleared a space for Linnéa to lie beside her on the bench. Stretching out, she lost herself in sleep almost instantly.

She awoke to the smell of bread and cinnamon wafting into her room next to Edla's kitchen. Her stomach grumbled, prodding her from her warm cocoon. What time was it? Glancing around her tiny room, she saw her gown draped across a rickety chair as if a ghost from the night before, still haunting her. Linnéa pulled her wool covers back over her head, retreating into their warmth once again. Why had she ever agreed to be a mere accessory? Accessories were meant to be used, as any object was. Had she set herself up for Count Borgar's unwanted advances? Should she have expected this? Shame smarted inside her, bitter and suffocating like smoke from burning tar.

"And through city and country tonight
The joyful message of Christmas is now being carried
That born is the Lord Jesus Christ
Our Savior and God."

Edla's voice crept under her door, reminding her that it was Christmas morning. She wanted to stay in bed all day, but she knew that the cows needed to be milked and that Edla would need her help. Her feet rested on the stone floor and despite the thickly knitted socks, the cold slithered through. Standing on shaky legs, she donned her simple chore attire and pulled on her worn leather boots. The stitching was beginning to come apart at the seams and she knew that she would have to purchase another pair soon. Cracking the door open, she watched the happy scene before her numbly.

Mother sang to her daughter, whose chubby hands waved in delight.

Linnéa wanted to smile, but it refused to come.

"Ahh, Merry Christmas, Sleeping Beauty!"

Linnéa knew she meant no harm, but Edla's words stung. She wanted to reject the title and everything that had come with it. She wanted to erase herself in the process. "I'm sorry I slept so late. Why didn't you wake me?"

"You came in at the wee hours of the morning and slept like the dead when I crept in to check on ya." Edla chuckled. "You must have had quite an evening dining and dancing with the king and court."

Linnéa glanced at her shoes, wanting to change the subject. "I'm sure the cows are desperate to be milked, I best be going."

"Daft girl! They were milked hours ago! It's nearly 2 o'clock!"

"Oh, I'm sorry!"

Edla waved her hand as if to swat the apology away. "Hans is home and is taking care of everything."

Linnéa's stomach growled.

Laughing, Edla handed her a plate of hard cheese, smoked salmon, dried berries, crisp bread, and a warm glass of milk sprinkled with cinnamon. She savored each bite, losing herself in the flavors and tastes.

"We've got a bit of time before the evening milking, can you run these cardamom rolls over to Rane?"

Linnéa's stomach dropped. She didn't want to see him today and feel his eyes on her—the eyes that always saw into her soul. "Would you like me to watch Helvi for you? I'm sure a walk would be nice!"

"Hush girl, I think our young neighbor would much prefer you delivering his Christmas morning rolls rather than me."

Linnéa ignored her implied meaning and drank down the rest of her milk.

"That poor boy lost his parents much too young, and with only sisters for kin who've married and moved away, he is quite alone." Edla bustled around the kitchen, grabbing a basket and linen cloth to wrap Rane's warm rolls in. Helvi started crying, so Linnéa hoisted her to her hip, bouncing and cooing to her.

"You know, I'm shocked that some wealthy count or some such hasn't snapped you up for their own!"

Linnéa turned her back to Edla so her employer couldn't see the sudden paleness of her face.

"Although you could do far worse than Rane, mind you. You wouldn't live in luxury, but you would have a respectable life at least."

"A simple life is all I've ever wanted." Linnéa muttered the words more to herself than to Edla.

"What's that?"

"Oh, n-nothing."

"Here you are!" Edla thumped the basket's handle. "Mind you don't dally, they're best warm!"

Setting the now happy Helvi back in her basket, Linnéa retreated to her room and grabbed a parcel wrapped in brown paper. Stuffing it in her coat, she buttoned it up to avoid Edla's nosy gaze.

The air was crisp and tasted of snow as Linnéa trudged over the powdery ground. The smell of the cardamom rolls wafted from the basket she carried. Letty walked at her heels, smiling up at her reassuringly whenever she looked down. Pulling her scarf down, she breathed in the air, allowing it to bite as it filled her lungs. Closing her eyes she focused on the rhythm of the crunching snow beneath her feet and the sound of the wind in the pines.

"Linnéa!" Rane emerged from the tree line, an axe slung over his shoulder. "I thought I heard someone coming up the road."

"Edla sent her cardamom buns!" Linnéa held out the basket, hoping to finish the errand quickly.

Rane closed the distance between them. His nose was red from the cold, but his jaw was covered in a week's unshaved stubble. Snow draped his shoulders, and he wore mostly furs, making him look like a wild thing of the forest. Bending down, he petted Letty, who wiggled with excitement at his approach. "How are ya?" He stood, his unsettling eyes meeting hers.

Avoiding them, she bent to stroke Letty. Why couldn't he talk about the weather or about how tantalizing the buns smelled?

Stooping, he met Linnéa's eyes.

"Care for a bun? Edla insisted you eat them warm!" Thrusting the basket at him again, her eyes pleaded.

Consenting, Rane walked over to a felled tree and sat down.

Shivering Linnéa walked over and sat beside him, placing the basket between them in the snow. Removing his mittens, he reached inside and pulled out a steaming bun, handing it to her first. "I hope I'm not going to eat these alone." He grinned.

Linnéa took it and bit into it, marveling at the sweet and piney warmth on her tongue.

"Has the new heifer calved yet?" Rane's voice interrupted her thoughts.

"Yes! She did a week ago. I haven't gotten to milk her yet, but Edla says she's easy to handle."

Nodding, Rane continued to chew, staring at Linnéa.

"She had the sweetest calf. Pure jersey. Her eyelashes are as long as her legs!"

Rane laughed, throwing his head back.

Linnéa smiled, feeling the numbness in her chest warming slightly.

They continued to chew in silence, listening to the sound of the snow falling from the limbs of the trees as they shook off their weight. The continual dusk that settled over the landscape gave the forest a mystical feeling, as if it rested drowsily in the darkest part of the winter, conserving its energy for when the sun breathed life into it once again. Linnéa retreated into the feeling of nothingness, wishing to crawl beneath a felled tree, content to retreat from the living and breathing world. Feeling Rane's presence beside her prodded her into the light though, even if there didn't seem to be any on the horizon. She wanted to tell him about Count Borgar and how it had made her feel. She wanted to cry. She wanted to scream. Why had the previous night upset her so? She wanted to shake off the weight of it, like a tree does the snow, but instead she felt as if she were sinking into the darkness. Shaking her head, she stood, not bothering to brush the snow from her thick skirt.

"I have something for you, but it's not with me," Rane began. "We could..."

"Oh! I have something for you, too..." Linnéa reached inside her thick coat and pulled out a wrinkled parcel and thrust it at him. "Merry Christmas."

Turning to leave abruptly, she trudged back to the path, succumbing to the feeling that iced over her veins despite the warmth and the desire for transparency that had begun to fester in her heart.

"Could you wait while I retrieve your gift?"

"I better get back, I've already left Edla with much work for far too long!"

"Thank you for this!" His voice echoed through the quiet forest.

Waving, she turned her back on Rane who stood planted, like a tree, watching her leave.

He let the paper fall to the snow as he wrapped his newly knitted scarf around his neck and burrowed his cold nose into the emerald yarn.

Twenty

Sighing Linnéa heaved the yoke onto her shoulders, her muscles twitching from the strain after her absence. It was delivery day, and she set her face towards Stockholm.

"Goot Morning!" Rane called. He had been waiting for her, his cords of wood bundled at his feet.

"I'm sorry, I must be a bit late this morning!"

"You're not late. I just wanted to catch ya to give ya this."

He produced a lumpy package from behind his back. A lump rose in her throat. She had left so abruptly yesterday; she didn't deserve his constant kindness.

Fumbling with the stiff paper, she pulled at the strings when a pair of leather boots fell out.

"Rane, this is too much!" Linnéa tried handing them back, but he shook his head, gathering up the firewood.

"T-Thank you," The words scratched their way out of her throat.

"Do they fit?"

Bending down Linnéa untied her old boots and slipped her woolen clad feet into the new ones. "Yes, they do. Perfectly." Linnéa stared at her feet, reluctant to meet Rane's eyes.

They walked in silence most of the way, but it wasn't a silence of mutuality. Rane wanted to speak, with a million questions burning on his tongue.

Linnéa wanted to speak, too. She truly wanted to tell him everything so that she could lay down the burden of shame and regret she carried, but she didn't know where to begin—even to Rane.

She struggled with the words until her new boots scraped across the cobblestone streets. The usual bustle of the city was already stirring, as docksmen and laborers pulled carts and rolled barrels to the waiting ships. She had long become accustomed to people staring and praising her, as she was often greeted in the streets of Stockholm with children giving her flowers and salutations from the passers by. The feeling of humiliation had given way to gratitude as she was constantly warmed by the kindness that complete strangers showed her on a daily basis. It was a certain kinship with the people who lived there, a rarity in such an expansive city.

But as she moved through the already bustling street, she felt a chill that wasn't just from the cold. She was met with narrowed eyes and whispered conversations. Even a mother grabbed the hand of a waving child, pulling her away. Did she have mud on her face from Aslog's tail? She paused briefly to view her reflection in the shop window, before making her first delivery. She did not miss the gawking shopkeeper, but she knew there was no avoiding him. She and Rane entered the dimly lit building.

"Ahh! If it isn't the Dalarna girl, returning from her life of toil!" The shopkeeper emerged from behind the counter, taking his pipe out of his tar-teethed mouth. "Did you have a grand time with the king and all his men? I heard it was a grand and very profitable time! Was it very difficult to return to more...*honest* toil?" The shopkeeper slid his coins across the counter slowly, his face jeering.

The words sunk into Linnéa's gut like a lump of coal. What did he mean by honest toil? She searched Rane's face for answers, but the storm in his eyes gave little clarity. She knew she had better get him out of there quickly, before he erupted. Uneasiness fluttered inside her chest. Measuring out the allotted portion of milk, Linnéa quickly donned her yoke to leave.

"You've earned yourself quite the reputation!" The shopkeeper's words nipped at her back, like a yapping dog's bark.

Linnéa steadied herself, endeavoring to keep a firm foot as she exited. What reputation? What had changed? How could they know about the compensation that Mrs. Felicia collected?

"What reputation might that be?" Rane growled, as he turned around.

Linnéa touched his sleeve, pleading with him to leave the conversation as it lay. "No, Rane, I'm leaving." Swallowing the burning sensation in her throat, Linnéa began to descend the steps, but something caught her ankle and she crumbled to the cobblestones, her milk canisters clattering after her.

Hot tears burned her eyes as she glanced over her shoulder to see a broom handle quickly disappear beneath the steps. Rane bounded to her side and helped her up, before searching the shadows.

"Did something bite ya, miss?" The shopkeeper laughed, stomping in the doorway as he held his swollen abdomen. "You best be watchin' yer step!"

Milk frothed around her as she stood, attempting to save what she could from spilling. People gathered around her, their unsympathetic eyes boring holes in her back. Why were they treating her this way? Confusion pooled like the spilt milk mixing with the dirt and smearing the cobblestone street.

"Have you grown weary of honest work?" A female voice called through the gathering crowd. Several voices chimed their agreement.

"What was it like bringing yuletide pleasure?" Someone else asked, followed by a chorus of laughter.

"I hear ye were more than fairly compensated for your work!"

Linnéa stumbled her way through them, her vision blurring and her heart pounding. Feeling something pelt her back, she turned to see a rotten cabbage smashed on the cobblestone, lying at her feet.

"That's what the likes of you deserves!" An old woman called. "Get off with ye!"

"Oh leave her alone!" Rane called, running up behind her, his eyes darting wildly around the crowd, his fists clenched as if he couldn't decide whom to fight.

"Could I be acquiring your services at my ball?" A masculine voice called, followed by peals of laughter.

The realization dawned on her, like the smell of death on a hot day. It sunk past her skin and into the pit of her stomach, making her want to wretch. They believed she had prostituted herself for profit.

No! This could not be! How could such a devastating rumor have begun?

Barely feeling her feet hit the frozen ground, Linnéa ran towards Mrs. Felicia's, her shattered honor flying behind her like scattered snowflakes in the seaside wind.

Twenty-One

With shaking hands, she pounded on the door, not minding the earliness of the hour. A maid whom she didn't recognize quickly opened it and Linnéa burst inside.

"I need to speak to Mrs. Felicia."

"I'm here, Linnéa, I'm here." Mrs. Felicia stood in an overcoat with tired eyes and a simple braid dangling over her shoulder.

Linnéa had hoped the regal, confident woman would reassure her by her presence alone, but in the morning shadows, she looked like a tired old woman who was as scared as she was. "Have you heard the rumors?"

Mrs. Felicia lowered herself to a chair. Nodding, she rested her forehead in her palm.

"Please, you have to help me. Didn't you have a plan if this happened?"

"Yes, but a servant from the castle said she saw you and Count Borger alone in a room together and that you weren't...decent. It's already all over town, being whispered about in every pub and back alley. My own maid, Eva, has also been spreading rumors about the generous compensation that you have been receiving. She must have overheard conversations between you and me or saw the letters I've received."

Linnéa sank to a chair, numbness drifting through her, like the smoke from the fire the maid stoked in the fireplace. "He forced me down the servants' hallway." Linnéa's words were flat, lacking the emotion she had felt boiling in her since the incident. "He intended to have his way with me and ripped at my gown, but a servant came in just in time. It must have been the same servant who has been spreading the rumors. She did see me and Count Borger, but I was dragged there against my will."

Mrs. Felicia rose and came to Linnéa, placing her hand gently on her trembling shoulder. "This is my fault, and I'm so sorry that I forced you to do something that you did not want to do. I'm so sorry I didn't protect you."

Linnéa shook her head, but no words came to her aid.

"No, Linnéa, I must." Silent tears fell down the woman's face; the same woman who had had all the answers and all the plans since Linnéa had first met her. "I saw you as a way to rewrite my past. You see, I married a man of low standing, and by marrying him instead of a baron as my father had been, I lost my place in society. We were happy and in love, but he died in the factory he worked at, leaving me alone and desolate. All this—this was my father's!" Mrs. Felicia circled her hands in the air, before they landed back at her sides helplessly. "When I heard about a poor Dalarna girl who had an opportunity to move upwards, instead of downwards as I had done, I thought that it would give my dismal life something of a legacy!

"Ha!" Her laugh was sarcastic, lacking all humor. She slumped back into her chair. "Not only have I forced you into a role you didn't want, but I have brought you lower than you ever would have been before my meddling. No respectable man will marry you, no one will employ you except a brothel, and you will be shunned from society. Linnéa, I'm so sorry."

Linnéa was at a loss for words, but sat staring at the fire as it consumed the log. She stared in silence, grappling with her feelings for what felt like hours. "You are not responsible for the lies, dear Mrs. Felicia," the words were barely a whisper. "I don't blame you; I blame myself for engaging in something I knew was not right for mere money. I'm so thankful for everything that I've learned beneath your care, and nothing could ever change that." Silence fell between the teacher and student, except for the sound of the crackling fire. "I know your intentions are good, but could you please stop supplementing the pay I receive from Edla? I want these rumors to stop, and I am not owed anything."

Mrs. Felicia looked up, her eyes dewy with tears. "I have respected your wishes and have not accepted any more compensation on your behalf. You have already received everything that we had discussed weeks ago."

Linnéa was shocked, as her mind rummaged through every person that might possibly be adding to her earned wages. "This is not the end of the story, Mrs. Felicia." Standing Linnéa walked from the room and into an uncertain future.

Twenty-Two

"You won't be taking the milk tomorrow, Linnéa."

Linnéa placed her bucket on the kitchen floor.

"I'm s-sorry about what happened Edla, but I promise I won't trip again."

"Girl, I know you didn't trip, but you aren't going."

Linnéa searched the leathered face, worn before its time.

"Are you d-dismissing me?"

"I'm so sorry, really I am, but we can't keep you on as we're losing customers by the day, and the rest have made it clear that you're...no longer welcome."

Linnéa sank onto a nearby stool, her words an unbearable blow. "How could this be? I've tried everything to clear my name."

Edla patted her shoulder, the warmth melting into Linnéa's trembling frame.

"I wish I could take all this unfairness and make it not our ever-breathing reality, but I can't. One of the neighbor girls who helped me when you were away preparing for the ball has agreed to help me starting next week."

Tears stung Linnéa's eyes, but she didn't want Edla to feel guilty for her decision, so she hung her head. "Are you taking the milk to town in the morning?"

Edla scoffed. "I wouldn't make it half the trip, and Hans won't be home for a few more days."

"I won't let you be ruined because of me, Edla!"

"You will remedy it, my dear, don't fret. Run over to Rane and see if he can spare the time, just this once."

"No...I can't do that."

Edla's expression hardened. "You can and you will!" She swatted after her with a dishcloth.

Linnéa approached Rane's door reluctantly. She had never been to his home before and felt awkward standing on the roughly hued boards without an invitation, especially since she had been avoiding him for the past few weeks. He had tried to break through her icy demeanor, but she hadn't allowed him in.

"Rane, are ye home?" The only sound she heard was the wind in the trees. Linnéa knocked. She knew it wasn't likely that he was home at this time of the day, but she didn't feel right poking around his place without trying the door first. Going around to where she knew the sawmill would be, she breathed in the smell of freshly cut wood. It smelled like Rane.

Letty barked, wagging her tail as he emerged.

"I saw you coming," his words came out flat and uncertain. His eyes looked shadowy, like a forest in a windstorm.

"Yes, I'm sorry to be coming over like this, but Edla insisted."

"She can be pretty insistent." He attempted a chuckle, but failed.

"I...well I don't know where to begin." Linnéa searched the sky, willing herself not to cry in front of the only man who seemed to see right through her.

He took a step closer, his fist clenching. "Why have you been shutting me out?"

Linnéa stared at her muddy shoes.

"Linnéa, please look at me."

Lifting her head, she dared a quick glance into his eyes, scared at what she might find there. Suspicion? Anger? Disgust?

"If y-you talk to Mrs. Felicia, she could give you proof..."

"I don't need to talk to her. I want to talk to you."

She was silent.

"Linnéa, please look at me."

"I w-was such a f-fool to start the whole ridiculous thing. I should have listened to you from the beginning!"

"Linnéa, please look at me."

She allowed herself a glance into his eyes, but she didn't see any of the things she feared she might. They were piercing, but not angry. "What happened to you Christmas Eve?" His question surprised Linnéa, and she stepped back into the shadows of overhanging limbs.

"I know t-that's where the r-rumors began, but..."

"I don't care about the rumors, I care about you." His directness was unsettling. Something about his demeanor and the intensity of his being would not relent until all stones were left unturned.

"I-I d-don't want to t-talk about it," she said the words, but she didn't believe them. The truth was, she wanted to tell him. She wanted to tell him everything, about Borgar's brutishness and the emptiness of wealth and prestige. But she couldn't wring the words out, because she had given herself to that life for money. Money she now despised and admiration that had turned into a prison. There in the shadow of the pines, Linnéa unraveled inside, the events of the past months parading before her eyes like a waterfall into oblivion. She felt helplessly trapped, plummeting into the depths. "Edla sent me to a-ask if you would b-be so kind to d-deliver the m-milk tomorrow morning, I a-am no l-longer welcome." She recoiled farther into the shadows. "I'm leaving for Dalarna tomorrow." Linnéa wished the earth would swallow her and wished for once that Rane would just help her finish the words that were hard for her to say, but he didn't and he never had. He always stood, with a measured expression, not showing the pain of listening to her labored words. As if he hung on every one. "I'm returning your *riks-daler*. You shouldn't have d-done it." She tossed the bundle into his unsuspecting hands.

"Linnéa, don't you see, I want to give you everything I have!" Rane tossed the bundle at his feet, grabbing her hands and pulling her from the shadows. "I know you could do so much better than me and that you probably think I'm blunt and bullheaded and..." He tore at his hair, staring into the forest. "Well, I'll never be wealthy and give you the life you've now tasted."

Linnéa raised her eyes, the realization of his words dawning on her, warm and sweet, like the sunrise hovering just below the horizon. "Good enough for me? Rane, it is I who am ruined! You should find someone not so...so tainted!"

Rane's gaze settled on Linnéa again, but she wouldn't meet it. "That's not what I think." He lifted her chin, forcing her to look him in the eyes. "I think you're resilient. I think you have a voice that sounds like a summer brook. I think you seek to live by the narrow path, not the way that is wide and easy." Rane's voice began to build momentum, his words coming faster and with more confidence. "I think you see people as they should be, not as they are. I think you're wise, perceiving more in a glance than most do in a million lifetimes. I think your humility makes you beautiful. I think that anyone who questions your virtue hasn't spent one second in your presence..." He reached out his hand, touching a stray curl that danced across her lips.

"And I love you with everything that I am."

Linnéa closed her eyes, feeling the warmth of his touch, her soul letting the sunlight in.

Looking up into his eyes, she lost herself in them, not wanting to shy from them any longer.

"Linnéa, would you be my wife?"

"Yes, forever, yes." She pressed her answer against his lips.

"Then yes, I will deliver the milk for you in the morning and forevermore, if need be!"

Epilogue

Linnéa tucked her arms around Akoo, her three-week-old infant, drinking in his fresh baby scent. The fire in the hearth blazed, warding off the chill creeping through the walls. Her other four children were busy around her, as they made their *Julbocks* and compared whose was the best.

"The cow gave almost three gallons today!" Her oldest daughter's words sung through the chorus of happy voices as she entered the room carrying two buckets of frothy milk.

"What a Christmas blessing that is! How's the new calf getting on?" Linnéa looked up from her suckling infant, as she watched Ella strain the milk.

"She's a bit wobbly, but she's eager for milk. She has the prettiest eyes and long eyelashes too, Mama!"

"Jersey's always do!" Linnéa smiled, her memories parading over the many cows she had milked over the years, with the dainty Jersey's remaining her favorite. "Where's your Papa?"

"I'm here," Rane's voice came gruff and strained as he dropped a load of firewood onto the pine floor. The floor he had felled and built himself when they outgrew the cabin he and Linnéa had lived in when first married. "Merry Christmas," he whispered the words into

Linnéa's hair, kissing her on the forehead. "How's our little Akoo, today? I didn't even hear him in the night!" Rane bent to stroke the baby's foot protruding from the blanket, before tucking it back into the warmth.

"He's a good sleeper. I think he'll take after you!" Linnéa teased, her words hinting at the loud snores that she had endured for the past decade and a half of her life, while sharing Rane's bed.

Rane smiled, looking into her eyes, which Linnéa knew were rimmed in smile lines and fine wrinkles. She knew that she wasn't the beautiful and youthful girl that she once had been, as years marked by childbirth wore on, and her grandeur faded. Although she still walked through the streets of Stockholm from time to time on errands, no one called her name or seemed to notice the woman who was once so lauded in their streets. Linnéa didn't mind, happily resorting to the quiet and humble life—the life she'd always wanted. The scorn and cruelty she once had received from the townspeople had long waned, becoming markedly better after Rane took her for his wife. The love and admiration of the man who commanded respect due to his character alone, was all that was needed to quiet their flapping tongues, until eventually it faded all together.

"What are you thinking?" Rane's voice brought her back.

"Oh, just that I'm thankful for you and this life—our life." Linnéa looked into his eyes again, seeing his earnest love reflected there, as clear and transparent as ever it was like the brook that cackled out their front door during the spring. Linnéa reached up and stroked his beard, now flecked with grey, the pressure inside her chest needing a release.

Rane wasn't much for her elaborate words of affection, so she settled for something simple.

"I love you, Rane.

"I love you, my Linnéa." He had never once called her "the most beautiful woman in Sweden," or anything of the sort, but always called her simply "his Linnéa." He never alluded to the so-called title or distinction of her early days, as if refusing to tarnish his love by evoking memories of regret and heartache which she had shared with him in full.

She didn't need to be beautiful in all of Sweden's eyes, because she only cared about his.

"Does anyone want a cardamom bun and a glass of cinnamon milk?"

A chorus of happy voices chimed, and Linnéa handed Akoo to Rane so she could pull the warm rolls from the oven. Her children gathered around eagerly, their youthful faces shining.

The warmth that filled her heart now, as her family gathered around her bursting with Christmas cheer, had long eclipsed any memories of good or ill. All that remained was a simple life filled with loving her family and those around her, well. Those beautiful and ordinary things that no one strives for, but makes life grand indeed. Linnéa relished the thought that nothing else was truly needed in the end. That reality sung through her life, like the sound of a cowbell, constant and clear.

About Olivia Talbott

Olivia Talbott is a word-addicted author who has a BA in Creative Writing and English. Her debut novel will release in September of 2023, being historical fiction based on the true story of a survivor of the Cambodian genocide, who finds redemption. Her passion is telling stories that the world needs to hear: stories based on actual events where Jesus intersects the narrative. Outside of reading and writing she enjoys gardening, farm life, homeschooling and co-running a tee-shirt printing company. Her life is wrapped around her three children and an incredibly supportive husband named Steven, all who reside on a small farm in central Kentucky. Scribbled between the lines of her life is the constant love of God, which breathes beauty and purpose into the otherwise mundane. If you're interested in learning more, her website can be accessed here: oliviatalbott.com facebook.com/authoroliviatalbott

instagram.com/olivia_talbott_writer

The Cross at Morioka Castle

KATHLEEN J. ROBISON

To my sons, David and Jonathan Robison,
and their faithful wives, Tomo and Maki.
JEM's Missionaries to Japan

One

Ariko walked along the outside perimeter of the castle ruins. The black granite blocks mirroring the darkness within. They rose up, shrouding the moonlight, and she contemplated discontinuing her walk. Glancing over her shoulder, she squinted at the glaring lights from touristy Odori Street. Their brightness assured her she was safe.

She shrugged off her body's false warning. She was in Japan now, not the United States. Crime was practically non-existent here. She'd spent too much time in America. The guilty thought returned along with the pain of her father's recent funeral.

Morioka Castle ruins stretched in front of her, but rapid footsteps tapped behind. Forgetting once again that she was in Japan and not America, she contemplated running, but instead, she spun around.

A body ran smack into her, almost toppling her to the ground. He grabbed her in a full embrace as if protecting her from the fall. Still, she struggled to free herself.

"Let me go," she yelled.

"*Suimasen*," the man who held her said, and he gently let her go while bowing repeatedly. "I'm sorry. I was in a hurry." He continued speaking in Japanese but ran a hand through his dark hair. "Are you all right? I didn't expect you to turn so suddenly."

Ariko twisted her purse strap. This stranger spoke perfect Japanese, but his mannerisms were western. "Don't worry about it. I'm fine."

"Are you sure? I'm so sorry. I was trying to cross the street before the light changed back there." He jerked his thumb behind him. "That Odori Street gets pretty busy." He grinned a beautiful smile.

He is a dichotomy. "Are you from America?" she had to know.

"No. I am Japanese, but I attended university in the U.S. I did graduate study there, and now I travel back and forth for work."

Work. She was ashamed that she'd just lost her job in Los Angeles when she had to return home after her father's death. Tears welled in her eyes, and she was thankful for the night's covering. She looked down before swiping a tear, hoping he wouldn't see it. She lifted her gaze.

His brows raised, and she wondered at the expression of concern on his face. So unlike a Japanese man to show emotion. A slight smile crossed his lips, and he drew an audible breath. Waiting. He should be moving along.

"*Sayonara*," Ariko said.

"*Sayonara*," he said bowing deeply, but never taking his eyes off her.

Ariko turned and continued her walk. He followed, and more annoyed than frightened, she spun around again.

"Why are you following me?"

The stranger wore a sheepish grin. "It sure looks like that doesn't it? I just happen to be going in the same direction."

That grin again, and this time she noticed his straight white teeth. They gleamed. "I promise, I'm not a stalker. I love walking around the castle. The walls fascinate me."

"At nighttime?"

"I'm not in Morioka for long, and business keeps me busy during the day. I came back from the U.S. for the holidays."

He rambled a bit more this time, still speaking Japanese, but she didn't hear the rest after he commented about the holidays. *Holidays?* What Japanese person returns home for Christmas? It wasn't like the country gave days off to celebrate the birth of Christ. Ariko glanced back at Odori Street. Although, with all the decorations and lights, you'd wonder. Santas, snowmen, and Christmas trees adorned stores everywhere. But not a manger or nativity in sight. At least not yet. Ariko had plans to find a Christian church while here.

Her cell buzzed. "Suimasen," she said as she turned to check her phone. Just as quickly, she turned back. "Excuse me. I must go."

"May I walk with you?"

Ariko frowned, and she shook her head.

"Too forward, right? I guess I've been in the states too long." He bowed once more, his white neck scarf blowing in the breeze, and his leathered gloves rested perfectly on his knees. When he stood, his black hair had fallen across his forehead, and he brushed it back. His dark eyes lingered.

Ariko bowed and turned to leave.

"Merry Christmas!" he called out.

She chuckled but continued to walk without turning back. She was sure he wasn't following, and her mind retreated to the reason she was here. It was to tidy up her father's business. But would she stay? Scattered thoughts rambled through her brain, and she rubbed her temples. Stuffing her gloved hands into her coat pockets, she trudged home.

She approached a tiny soba restaurant and stopped. It had more windows than her father's store, allowing her to peek in. It was much the same. A few small wooden tables, and a counter with four stools, all occupied, with hunched customers slurping soba.

Behind the counter in the small kitchen, the cook wearing a white head scarf scooped up the noodles and broth.

A young girl, the lone server rushed about.

Ariko watched. Her father and mother had owned a shop like this. But her father had also used it for his ministerial outreach. She wrapped her arms around herself and darted away, apologizing to people as she bumped along. Turning the corner, she ran up a dark street but slowed at the incline. Her great-grandmother's substantially large home sat atop the hill.

Simple, dignified, and beautiful. The traditional architecture of the Edo period pervaded the design with an all-wood structure that was well preserved. The imposing wide roofs cast shadows, but at the same time lent a protective presence. Ariko let out a loud sigh and leaned forward as she trudged to the top of the cobbled street. Cold air filled her lungs, and she wished she'd taken up running in America like her roommates. Though thin and healthy, she wasn't in shape for strenuous exercise, physically or mentally.

Reaching for the door, it opened, and Ariko gasped.

A man glared back at her. He had the face of her father, but his eyes were hard, and he appeared older. His bow was not deep, merely a head nod, as if she didn't deserve his respect.

"I am Shio Hiroshi. Your father's younger brother. *Obaachan* has been waiting for you. Follow me." He left the door open and walked to the stairs.

Ariko removed her shoes and hung her jacket and purse behind the door as quickly as she could. She shivered at his impatience. As is the nature of the Japanese, he hid all outward display of annoyance.

Hiroshi led her up the stairs to a large room and opened the shoji doors. "*Dozo*," he said as he gestured her to enter. His mask of politeness did not fool her.

The earthy aroma of rice straw permeated the room. Tatami floors made of the natural fibers, compressed and tightly fastened, soothed Ariko's stockinged feet as she bowed and stepped in.

Obaachan, Ariko's great-grandmother, sat hunched on the floor behind the large square kotatsu. It had been years since Ariko sat around the low table that emitted heat from underneath the thick drapes hanging over each edge. She blew out a breath, and a wispy cloud hung in front of her before disappearing. She shivered and wished she'd kept her coat. A kerosene heater made rushing sounds close by, and she wanted badly to stand next to it, but instead, bowed low towards her Obaachan.

"Dozo." Obaachan waved a palm, motioning for her to sit.

Ariko glanced at Hiroshi, wondering if he would sit too. He didn't, so she complied.

"You will stay in Japan, now?" said Obaachan.

Though it sounded more like a command, Ariko hesitated to answer. The truth was, between the sudden death of her father, and losing her job in the states with her abrupt departure, she didn't know what she would do. There was definitely more potential for livelihood there than in Japan. But she was torn. Japan was where she grew up. Where her father and mother had always lived and where she felt closest to them, but she'd stayed away too long.

"Suimasen, Obaachan," *Excuse me, Grandmother,* "I will assess my father's business here, but I still have an apartment in America. I am not sure yet what I'm going to do."

Hiroshi grunted but remained by the door. "Your father's business is nothing. He didn't even own the building."

"Yes, we lived in the apartment above the shop. I grew up there."

"If your father had not been so stubborn, you might have inherited some of this." Obaachan waved around the room.

"Obaachan, we have not discussed this." Hiroshi cleared his throat.

"Hiroshi, we have talked of it, but you have not listened." Obaachan coughed into her sleeve.

Ariko's head swiveled, as she tried to follow their conversation, which was not to her, but about her. She bristled and turned around to face her great-grandmother, wondering what Obaachan meant regarding an inheritance. Reverence cautioned Ariko to remain quiet.

"Ariko-chan, I am old, and I would like the company of my great-granddaughter. You will stay with me."

"But you have me, and my family. We will take good care of you." Hiroshi stepped forward.

"Hiroshi, please leave us. You and I will talk soon," said Obaachan.

Expecting him to argue, Ariko waited, but Hiroshi bowed. The doors clapped as he slid them shut and exited the room.

Ariko's pulse quickened and being alone with her great-grandmother caused a shiver. Her eyes riveted on a large, lacquered three-sided box behind Obaachan. Much like an oversized, jewelry case, but instead of silver and gems, it contained orange *mican,* and a small bowl of gleaming, white *gohan.* The food rested beside burning incense inside the box. Small red envelopes graced the beautiful scene. But it wasn't just a decoration, and there was no hint of Christmas. It was the family shrine.

"As I said, you will stay here."

"*Arigato.* But I cannot impose on you. I'm staying at my father's shop for now."

"You will not. Your father had no business raising you in such a poor neighborhood."

"It was not so bad. I enjoyed working with my mother and father."

"Enjoyed? Working hard to make ends meet. Preparing, cooking, and serving all day and night? Your father did not have to live in poverty. He chose to subject you and your mother to that."

Ariko's lips drew taught. True. There were times she'd wished they hadn't been so poor. Yet, as she recalled the sweet times at Ajiwau, her father's soba shop, warmth arose. She recalled happier times with her parents, remembering how she'd sit at the restaurant tables, listening to her father teach. Her smile faded. Obaachan had no right to criticize him like this. Still Ariko remained respectfully quiet, choosing to relish the memory.

"I am right," Obaachan chuckled, and a cough followed.

Before Ariko could rebut, her great-grandmother coughed again, and again.

Ariko slid on her knees across the smooth tatami floor and handed a cup of green tea to her obaachan.

She took the hot tea, sipping it in small bits. Obaachan nodded. "Arigato. Now enough. I am tired. You may leave."

"Suimasen," Ariko dipped her head. "How do I call a taxi?"

"Taxi? What for? You will stay here from now on." Obaachan turned her head towards the shoji doors. "Hatsuko!" she called, but her voice cracked as she hacked repeatedly.

The doors slid open, and a middle-aged woman walked in. She wore a dark dress, covered by a plain white apron-like jumper. "Hai, Shio-san."

Ariko smiled at the sweet woman she'd met earlier.

"Show my great-granddaughter to the guest room." She closed her eyes. "Any one of the rooms will do. Then come assist me."

"May I help you?" Ariko asked.

"No, but tomorrow we will make whatever arrangements you need to stay here."

Two

Hatsuko helped Ariko settle into a small but comfortable room. She pulled two thick futons from the closet and stretched one out across the floor. The second folded on top of the first. She backed from the room, closing the doors behind her.

Ariko's heart warmed as she admired the beautiful futon. A fabric of white cranes soared in blue skies with pink, red, and orange flowers filling the foreground. Never had she had covers such as these. She kneeled and scrunched the thickness between her fingers. A deep breath released a tear, then more. How could father be gone? Ariko felt so alone. Having lost her mother to cancer years before, her father had been all she had left. Then he sent her to university in the United States and waited for her graduation and return, but she never did.

Ariko gulped. She had always planned to return, but when she was offered a job as a translator at a Japanese owned corporation, the salary was too tempting. Speaking Japanese in America was a much sought-after skill. And the Japanese companies in America wanted Japanese nationals who were proficient in both English and Japanese. She was the ideal candidate. Having gone to university and graduate school, Ariko had adapted well. But was it the right decision? With her father gone, she wasn't so sure. Ariko clutched her stomach as she fought to control her emotion.

The doors slid open, and Hatsuko bowed as she stepped in. Folded in her arms was a thick, padded kimono. She instructed Ariko to dress in it for sleeping and left.

Ariko's stomach churned as she sat on the plain futon, contemplating her fate. *Should she stay? Did she have an obligation for loyalty to her family?* She changed her clothes, and drawing the colorful futon over her, she laid down and hoped that sleep would come. It was not to be.

Lord, what shall I do? After funeral and travel expenses, Ariko's savings were dwindling, and her mind toiled thinking of her great-grandmother's offering of family and home. *But at what price?* The price her father had turned down, and all to do the Lord's calling and work. Father had never spoken poorly of his family, only that they were not interested in hearing about Jesus. Ariko recalled always praying for them. Suddenly, a faintly familiar sound arose.

Silent Night
Holy Night
All is Calm ...

She listened, and it came from outside and grew louder. It was singing. Christmas carols in Japanese words, but the same familiar tune.

Ariko cinched the kimono sash tightly around her waist and ran from her room. She fled down the stairs and snuck to the front door. She peeked out, and her heart soared. Walking up the street with candles in hand were carolers. Not in Dickens costumes like she'd seen in America, but carolers just the same. She hummed along. "Silent Night." It had been a long time since she sang the songs in Japanese as she had when her father held Christmas Eve services in his soba shop. He had handed out booklets, and mother baked sweets, wrapping them perfectly for each person who joined them.

As they drew close, she waved, and they stopped at her door, singing, "The First Noel." Ariko sang along, and her heart swelled. Before they finished, she heard a floorboard creak, and she slowly turned.

Hatsuko approached with a tray of *dorayaki*. Ariko's mouth

watered just looking at the little pancake like sandwiches filled with sweet red beans. Hatsuko bowed and handed the lacquered tray to Ariko, who offered it to the carolers.

They politely took one each and bowed. Ariko asked what church they attended, and they eagerly told her where. She promised to join them, thus sealing the fact that she would not be leaving soon. Perhaps God had made it clear that here was where she belonged. When the carolers left, she eased the door shut and turned.

Hatsuko stood behind, her eyes sparkled as her hands grasped a tiny gold cross around her neck that had previously been hidden.

Ariko awoke refreshed. Surprisingly, the nighttime carolers had soothed her spirit. That and the cross she spied in Hatsuko's hand. Her great-grandmother's house servant had informed her that Obaachan would meet her later in the day, so Ariko left the house early. She had a longing to visit Morioka Castle. It was as if the grounds drew her.

Morioka Castle's maintained stone walls rose 12 meters high, nearly forty feet. The wet granite sparkled in the morning sunlight. Colorful waving flags lined the way. After sending a parting glance at the souvenir stand filled with castle relics, mini-torii, red gates, and iconic treasures, Ariko entered the grounds. She sucked in a breath and the icy air smelled clean but ancient.

Wide stone steps and stairways laced with moss in-between climbed in every direction. Ariko turned slowly around, taking in the stark beauty of the ruins and thankful for the quiet. The steady dripping of snow from tree branches deafened the whispers of the few people who were present.

Ariko perused the ruins until she noticed a somewhat enclosed structure. Like the rest of the castle, there were no roofs, just broken-down walls. Still, she could imagine the former rooms.

The signage of this particular section indicated that she was inside the personal kitchen to the Shogun. She chuckled thinking if she had been alive centuries ago, this would probably be where her family would have spent time if they had been so lucky to be part of the Shogun's inner circle.

She laughed. A cook being in the inner circle? She read the sign more closely, and it told the story that this was where a private chef had cooked for the Shogun, and soba was the specialty. Ariko's eyes widened but quickly narrowed as they focused on the back wall. She stepped closer. There, carved into the stone wall, was a cross. The surrounding foliage and traditional designs almost obscured it, but a cross was carved into the stone.

"Incredible, isn't it?"

Ariko turned, and when she saw who spoke, her eyes widened and a gasp escaped, but her voice caught in her throat. The tall stranger from last evening stood in front of her.

He drew his shoulders back, and grinned. "Oh, it's you." That amazing smile flashed. "Wow! This is a nice surprise." The man was culturally so bold.

"What are you doing here?" Ariko pulled off her felt beret and loosened the thick knit scarf around her neck. "Are you following me?"

He pulled back his shoulders. "Suimasen? No, of course not."

Ariko doubted him and couldn't help but wonder why he was here. Her mind flashed to her uncle's annoyance at her being in Japan, and how he bristled when Obaachan mentioned the word *inherit*. Could this stranger have something to do with her family? It was a stretch, but this couldn't be a coincidence.

"Then why are you here?"

His brow furrowed, and he looked at her like she was crazy. "I could ask you the same."

"Do you live here?" Ariko asked.

He chuckled. "For a Japanese girl, you ask a lot of questions. No. I'm staying in Tokyo, but I had a few free days, and I always try to hit this castle." He scratched his head. "Déjà vu. I think I said that last night. Anyway, there's just something about it." He pointed to the wall.

The wall? Ariko wondered if he meant the cross.

"What about you? What brings you here?" he asked.

"I'm just sight-seeing... I guess." Her shoulders drooped, and for the moment, she let go the anxiety she'd felt from the evening before.

"Well, Morioka Castle is my favorite spot in Iwate," he said.

"Really? Why?"

He pointed to the cross. "Every time I come, I wonder about that cross. I've done a little research but haven't found much. I'm guessing the cook, or the architect of the castle was a Catholic. With the Jesuit priests coming here way back then and all."

"But Christianity was outlawed. Keeping the faith was a death sentence."

He nodded. "Yes, but God has his ways, doesn't he?"

All red flags flew away, and Ariko grinned. "Are you a Chrisitan?"

He nodded again but lifted a finger to his lips. "Shhh. There aren't many of us around here."

Ariko thought of the carolers last night. Then of Hatsuko's cross necklace. "Oh, I'm not so sure about that."

His eyes sparkled. "You've had some strange encounters, have you?"

She studied his face and wondered why she suspected him of anything. His kindness shined, and she felt some kind of bond. It was foolish to deduce that so quickly, but she had a hunch. A feeling. A spirit-led ease.

A cold wind blew reminding her that she was devoid of her gloves, hat, and scarf. Quickly she tried assembling herself in warmth, but her trembling hands fumbled, dropping everything.

He motioned her to stop and knelt and retrieved her white beret, scarf, and gloves. "May I?" he said while holding the items and taking a step closer.

Heat crept up her neck despite the cool air, but she nodded.

He gently wrapped the scarf around her neck and handed her the gloves. He placed the knit beret over her hair, gently brushing back loose sleek strands that framed her face. His hands lingered for a moment on her cheek, but just as quickly, he dropped them and stepped back.

"Arigato." She bowed, still marveling at his mannerisms.

They stood as frozen as the air around them when snowflakes drifted to the ground. Ariko wondered if she'd ever seen a more beautiful sight as the light fall of white sparkles floating through the stark tree branches. She pulled her beret down tightly and rubbed her hands together. "Just in time."

Snowflakes dotted his sleek black hair, and he shook his head. Gazing at her, he took in a breath, and blurted, "Can I buy you a cup of tea or coffee?"

Ariko liked his American-like boldness but wasn't sure she should accept his invitation. She didn't know anything about him, and her narrowed eyes expressed her concern.

"Did you have someplace to be?"

She paused a moment and smiled. "No, not really."

"Good. Let's go then." He offered his hand, and she hesitated.

Once again, he placed both hands on his knees and bowed deeply. "*Watashi no namae wa Kai desu.*"

His formal introduction loosened the rising tension in Ariko's shoulders. "Ariko, desu," she responded, pointing to herself, and bowed in return. "It's nice to meet you, Kai."

"Hello, Ariko. Shall we?" He offered his hand again. "The steps are getting pretty slippery. I might need some help." He chuckled.

Ariko took his hand. Although she could feel no warmth through their gloves, a tingle coursed through her body.

He led her carefully from the grounds, giving her a little history of the castle and what he knew about the kitchen, which wasn't much. He stopped at the souvenir stand, but the attendant was unfurling tarps, ready to protect his treasures from the snowfall. Kai stepped over to help.

Fastening the cover over one booth, he quickly pulled Ariko over to the furthest corner of another section and rummaged through a basket. He pulled out a small stone item. It was granite, like the castle walls, and about an inch tall. A cross.

Ariko's eyes widened as her heart warmed.

He spoke to the attendant and offered a few coins. The attendant bowed, then deposited the money in the register. The light smattering of snow quickly turned into a flurry, and Kai handed the cross to Ariko. He took her hand once more, guiding her down the street. With her head down, she followed.

He passed a large chain establishment, slipping into a smaller café next door. The counter and four tables were full.

Ariko gasped. It was the image of the soba shop her mother and father had run. Like the one she grew up bussing tables for, before cooking with her mother in the kitchen. All the while, her father had greeted and served customers with a heart to share Jesus if the opportunity arose. So un-Japanese, but so disciple-like. Her eyes welled with tears, and she pressed herself into the back wall.

"Are you all right? Is it too warm in here?" He asked.

Typically, all the stores were overly warm in the winter, but it wasn't the blast of hot air. The shop was alive and bustling, not quiet and empty. The reminiscence of what used to be and might never be again seared her heart. "I'm fine," she managed.

Ariko was thankful when a couple paid their bill and exited, leaving an empty table. But before Kai and Ariko made their way over, an older woman entered crowding in against the wall next to them. She bowed low, hunched over a cane.

"Dozo," Kai helped the woman to the empty table.

Returning, he asked Ariko, "I hope you don't mind waiting a little longer?"

"Not at all," she said with a smile. *A gentleman, too.* She removed her hat, gloves, and scarf once more.

When a table opened up, they sat. A young girl, scarf on her head, notepad in hand took their order.

"Have you ever eaten at Shio Soba?" Ariko asked.

"The chain?" Kai nodded and waved his hand. "No. I like the little family-owned ones better. How about you? Is it good?"

Ariko shrugged. "I've never eaten there either." She didn't want to go any further into the complications of her Obaachan's family business. She slipped her hand into her pocket and found the cross. Drawing it out, she asked, "So, what's the story?"

Her question went unanswered as their order came. The steaming bowls sat in front of them, and Ariko waited, as did Kai. An awkward silence permeated the space between them.

Kai spoke first. "Dozo," he said, signaling for her to begin eating.

She took a breath, "Do you mind if I pray, first?"

Kai's mouth gaped. "Suimasen. Of course. I'm not used to asking God's blessing out loud, in public. At least not in Japan." He offered a hand and said, "Dozo, I'd be honored."

Ariko gave thanks quietly, and Kai nodded.

"Thanks, Ariko." He smiled and picked up the ohashi, *chopsticks,* and slurped the noodles, as was the custom when eating soba. Yet, he did so in a gentlemanly manner.

Ariko laid the cross on the table before tasting the noodles and broth. The soba was good but not as good as her parents'. What they served was more than just delicious soup.

Kai pointed to the cross. "Shocking, right? I was surprised when I found them last year at Christmas. I think that's the only time they're sold there. Anything to get the word out, right?"

"Do you think the owner of the souvenir stand is a Christian?"

"I don't know. But I should probably ask. I'm guessing it's more of a commercialized thing, but I shouldn't judge. You never know." He winked. "So, how did a nice Japanese girl like you become a Christian?"

Ariko brushed a finger over the cross. "You first."

Kai gave her a sly, sideways glance. "Mine's easy."

"Easy?" Converting to the Christian faith in Japan was never easy. A profession of faith was serious. The Japanese viewed it as turning your back on your ancestors. Her father had always told those he taught to count the cost.

"Suimasen. I only meant I come from a Christian background. My grandfather received Christ right after the war. A U.S. soldier was walking in the bombed-out ruins in Yokohama, and he found the people were starving, and some needed medical care. He offered to help, but they wouldn't receive him at first."

"I'm not surprised. That was pretty bold of the soldier."

Kai nodded. "He hung around, picking up and discarding debris. Making scrap wood piles. Finally, my grandfather was the first to accept his help. The soldier made some repairs on his house, and with his encouragement, a few more townspeople, welcomed him."

Ariko's eyes widened and her heart swelled. "He had a big heart, huh?"

"Well, he helped as much as he could, and my grandparents kept inviting him in, so he kept going back. Eventually, he earned their trust, and he shared the gospel with them before being transported back to the states."

"Was he a missionary?"

"I wouldn't be surprised. But the Holy Spirit was definitely at work."

The waitress came and took their finished bowls and frowned at the wall of people waiting.

Kai followed her gaze. "We better go." He stood.

Ariko longed to stay and hear more, but she was mindful of the waiting crowd.

Three

After arguing over the bill, Kai insisted on paying it, but Ariko pulled out yen to leave on the table. He tapped her ungloved hand, and the delight she experienced at his touch surprised her as warmth ran through her arm.

"You're in Japan, now. No tips, remember?" He picked up the money and handed it back to her.

Ariko giggled. "I forgot."

They scooted past waiting customers and stepped outside.

"So, you were saying?" Ariko wanted to hear more.

"About what?"

"Your grandfather."

"Oh yes. So, my grandfather raised my father in the faith, and sent him to America for education. It was there that he got involved in church, and met my mom, and that was it."

"So is your mother, American? You don't look half, but you act it."

Kai laughed. "Mother is a Japanese American. Her mother spent time in internment camps and was also a Christian."

She loved this encounter. Another believer, in her hometown. Ariko peered back at the handsome face. And how unlikely to meet a Japanese man that was a believer in Christ. Her heart warmed. Ariko couldn't help staring but shook herself. "So, they married, and what?"

"They did, and my father was in the right place at the right time. He was gifted in electronics, then later computers. He started a tech company, and it blew up. I mean, it took off."

"So, you're techy? A nerd?" Ariko teased.

"I am. It's the only part of the business I like. Now, your turn." Crossing his arms, he smiled back at her. He seemed to be studying every inch of her face.

She couldn't help but look back. His hair was not as stick straight as most Japanese men. It held more fullness and wave, and the cut was perfect. Yet, like many young businessmen, he was well dressed, and the white shirt and dark tie accentuated his chiseled features. The nicely tailored overcoat smacked of an actor in a New York setting.

Buzz...Ring...

Kai laughed. "Saved by the bell." He reached for his phone.

Ariko did the same, for hers rang simultaneously as his buzzed.

When they finished their respective calls, Kai said, "Listen, I know this is sudden, but could we meet again? In all the years I've been in Japan, I've never met another Christian girl, and you're a nice one at that." He shrugged. "May I call you sometime?"

She would have thought it was a line, and it could have been, but there was truth to it. Japanese Christians were scarce. Other than her father's Bible studies and church services, she'd never met another Christian on the street.

She hesitated.

"There's just something different about you." He tilted his head back and rolled his eyes. "Come on. You owe me your testimony, at least."

His flashy grin sent tingles through her once more. She nodded, and they exchanged numbers. She replaced her phone and slipped on her coat.

He helped her with the sleeve. "Listen, I'm only here one more day. Can I meet you back at the castle tomorrow?"

Ariko felt the heat rise again. "Yes. I'd like that, but I need to check with my obaachan. She may want us to have breakfast together. How about we meet at noon, and I'll text you if things change?"

"Your obaachan is blessed to have you. But okay, noon it is." He pointed to his phone. "I have to run. I must take care of business. So much for a short getaway." He sighed and raised a hand to hail a cab. "I'll see you tomorrow, Ariko."

Ariko stopped him. "Chotto-matte-kudasai." She held up a finger signaling for him to wait.

A souvenir stand stood right next door and she spotted something flashy. Ariko chuckled, noticing everyone's dark, monochromatic clothing bustling down on the street. She grabbed a bright red and green plaid scarf. Ariko paid for it and handed it to Kai. "Thank you for soba, and Merry Christmas."

Kai laughed and tied the flashy scarf around his neck. "I guess it could be worse. At least it's not Santa and his elves."

Ariko covered her mouth, hiding a giggle. She was shocked that a serious businessman would wear such a thing. She'd meant it as a joke.

He took both hands in hers and squeezed. "Arigato, Ari-chan."

She flushed at the term of endearment and waved as he left. The heat from Kai's touch lingered. Waiting until he disappeared, she peered back, and a bittersweet joy warmed her. She was thankful for the sweet reminder of her blessed life with her mother and father. A smile crossed her lips, and she thought that her parents might have liked Kai. *Perhaps, me too.*

"Oh, Lord, please guide me," Ariko whispered.

Ariko flapped her arms. With the temperature dropping, she hailed a cab instead of walking to Obaachan's home. The snow had stopped falling, but the air chilled even more. Thoughts of Kai heated her all the way to the house.

The cab driver pulled up to the house at the top of the hill, and Ariko reached in her purse to pay. Inadvertently, she spilled the contents and scrambled to retrieve everything off the floor. Opening her wallet, she paid the man, and thanked him.

Once inside, Ariko removed her shoes, as Hatsuko approached. Worry wrinkles framed her face. Pointing up the stairs, she motioned for

Ariko to follow. She slid the doors open to the room where Ariko had met with Obaachan the night before.

"Where have you been?" A gravelly voice called.

Ariko's cheeks flushed, and she bowed as she stepped in.

Hatsuko slid the doors closed behind her.

"I'm sorry, I arose early and went for a walk. The castle is so beautiful."

"Old ruins for tourists. Did you eat breakfast?"

Ariko frowned at the comment and her great-grandmother's abruptness. She dared not confess that she'd already eaten breakfast and lunch. Miso soup for breakfast was her favorite, and the soba at lunch filled her quite nicely. "I did, thank you. Hatsuko's miso soup is so good." She tried to sound cheery, hoping to infuse joy into her great-grandmother's sour demeanor.

Obaachan waved a hand. "We have business to attend to." She bid Ariko to join her around the kotatsu.

Ariko welcomed the invitation and padded over and kneeled. Lifting the heavy, thick cloth that hung over the low table, she covered her knees, relishing the warmth that emanated from under the table.

"Ariko-chan, I would like you to stay here and help me. Forget your father's business. He was a foolish man."

The sharpness of Obaachan's words strengthened Ariko's courage. "I loved my father, and he was greatly loved by all in our small prefecture. I was happy there."

"Then why did you not return?"

These words cut her. She had visited Japan over her years away, but never stayed. Now it was too late. Still, what right had her great-grandmother to attack her like this. Ariko swallowed hard, struggling to hold back tears.

Obaachan closed her eyes, and when she opened them, her eyes too glistened. "Ariko-chan, gomenasai," she whispered. "I loved your father, too."

Ariko shook her head and wanted to scream. *Loved him? Then why did you throw him out? Never to let him return?* The thought brought back a harsh memory.

She'd only met her great-grandmother one other time, when she was a little girl. Her parents had dressed her up in her finest kimono and brought her to this house. It was Obaachan's seventy-fifth birthday, and the first time either of them had seen each other. She remembered the immediate joy in her great-grandmother's face upon seeing little Ariko at the door, holding her father and mother's hands. But Obaachan's joy waned, and she had turned her back and walked away. She instructed her servant, to close the door on the young family. Whispering gomenasai, sweet Hatsuko did as she was told.

It wasn't until her father's funeral that Ariko saw her great-grandmother once again. She had recognized the stranger in black, with a cane who hung back from the small band of guests. It was Obaachan. Before Ariko could greet her, Hatsuko had helped the old woman to a black automobile. A day later, Hatsuko arrived at Ajiwau, expressing that her great-grandmother requested her presence.

Obaachan swiped at her eyes. "Your father is gone. Domo, you will stay here now." She cleared her throat. "Now, what do you know of the Shio Soba Shops?"

"I know there are many here in Morioka."

"Not just Morioka. At one time, we were in all of Iwate, and your father was responsible."

Ariko's brows furrowed. "But my father's soba shop was just—"

"I don't want to hear of his paltry business." Wrinkles lined her brow.

Obaachan had hardened as quickly as she had previously softened. "Your father was a shrewd businessman who threw away his gift."

Ariko fisted her hands under the kotatsu.

"He took our one Shio store and grew it to twenty before he shamed our family by turning to Christianity and marrying your mother." Obaachan's lips drew a taught line. "All this would have been yours today if not for his throwing away his heritage. But I am willing to give you a chance to see if you are deserving."

Ariko wrung her hands together. This was news to her. For all she knew, her parents were poor business owners who ran a local soba shop, which drew a poorer clientele because of affordable but delicious noodles. Her father was a pastor who led Bible studies in the store.

"Hiroshi, your uncle, he was not gifted in business as your father.

He took charge when your father left and lost half the restaurants when he tried to modernize. His chefs altered our old family recipe, and he refused to go back. With everyone gone but me, I had no choice but to let him be."

"My father was a kind and generous man. Why didn't you call him back to help?"

"That is exactly why I didn't call him back. Generosity has no place in business. Kindness, yes, that's what your uncle is missing. Greed took him over." Obaachan's eyes watered. "I see kindness in your eyes, my child. I missed that when your father left."

"But he didn't leave. You said you...you banished him."

"It was his choice. He chose your god over his ancestors."

Ariko's brain toiled over the mixed messages. Who left who? Obaachan credited her father with kindness, but also with shrewdness.

"But you also said he was shrewd. I don't understand."

"Shrewd is not bad."

That was almost scriptural. Ariko hid a smile.

"He had a good mind for business, but once he became a Christian, he didn't care for growing the family shops. He only wanted to talk about Jesus' love."

Ariko drew a breath. *It was now or never.* "I would do the same," she said softly.

Obaachan grunted. "Speak up. I am an old lady."

Ariko sat up straight and said a silent prayer for courage. "I would do the same. It is my desire to continue with my mother and father's tradition, but I would use the shop to tell others of Jesus as well."

Four

Ariko blinked, waiting. Obaachan's face displayed neither shock nor anger. The rise and fall of her great-grandmother's chest was slow and rhythmic and seemed to last forever.

Finally, Obaachan placed her hands on the kotatsu. She leaned forward. "Then you are as foolish as he. But you are young, and I will teach you otherwise. You will stay with me and learn."

The coolness in the room overtook her, and Ariko shivered. "Learn what, Obaachan?" Her voice wavered.

"The business, of course. If I leave it all to your uncle, there will be nothing left before I die, and that is coming soon enough." As if on cue, she coughed, cleared her throat, and coughed again. Her annoyance turned into a spasm, and she reached for her teacup, sipping with quiet control. "You are your father's daughter. I admit my regret in breaking all relations with him. As you said, he was a kind man, and he was very good to me. Therefore, I would like your presence in my last days."

Ariko's heart wrenched. When she had heard the news of her father dying, the loss was significant, but coupled with the fact that it left her utterly alone in the world, she'd felt as if God had abandoned her. Yet, in the few days she'd been in Japan, the Lord had given her renewed hope. Family. Her great-grandmother reached out to her, but soon she would be gone. Ariko studied the stark wrinkled face, with little hair to soften it.

Obaachan wore her hair pulled back in a tight low bun and wore a traditional kimono. The dark fabric with discreetly patterned flowers graced the garment, but a chanko partially hid it. The short, thick kimono-like garment kept her warm.

Last days. How could that be? Obaachan appeared strong. She sounded strong. Ariko's great-grandmother sat proud and straight, unlike other elderly women in Japan who suffered from severe bent over postures. Ariko always wondered at the condition and often forced herself to sit up straight.

Obaachan cleared her throat. "Besides the fact that you are my family, you have been educated in America. This world is changing, and you are needed. Hiroshi has tried, but he does not have what we need to prosper again. Perhaps we were hasty in cutting your father out." Obaachan's lips drew a straight line, and Ariko watched as the skin on her face grew taught. Yet her eyes glistened with wetness, and she seemed to be blinking away tears. She pulled a handkerchief from the sleeve of her padded kimono.

"Respectfully, Obaachan, I don't think I can help. I'm trying to reestablish my father's business." Ariko twisted her hands together. "My job was terminated when I had to leave. My future in America is uncertain. The store is all I have right now."

The hand rose again. Palm out. "Nonsense. You have me. And I have many restaurants. Now, light incense for your father. I have chosen to honor him once more in our family shrine."

Ariko's eyes followed where Obaachan pointed. Her eyes widened, and a sickening feeling in her gut arose. She couldn't do that. She couldn't worship her father or any of her other ancestors. Her great-grandmother's dark eyes glistened blacker.

Still, Ariko hesitated. *Could she light the incense and pray instead to her only true God? Jesus, her Lord?* She bowed her head.

"Suimasen, Obaachan. I cannot do that. My God says I shall put no other gods before him."

Obaachan inhaled deeply. "He is a god like all...like all the ...." Obaachan choked. "Fine. Just leave. We will meet again, later, this evening."

Ariko wondered at the faltering and relenting of Obaachan's manner. She stood and bowed. "Obaachan, I will gladly say a prayer to Jesus, thanking Him for my father and mother and you. I am so grateful—"

"Do not tell me of your prayers. Leave." Obaachan shifted, pain furrowed her brow, and Ariko wondered how she could still sit on her knees at ninety-six years old.

"Ariko-chan, send Hatsuko in, please."

Ariko did as she was told, then wandered the halls of the cold, old house. The rooms were traditional, with shoji doors lining the long wooden hallways. She tiptoed down the stairs and noticed partially open doors and peeked into a small living area. An ornately carved low table surrounded by embroidery padded cushions graced the middle of the room. Along the back wall stood a glass case.

Ariko checked behind her, back down the hallway both ways before stepping fully into the room. Padding her way over, she moved toward the case. Behind the glass rested a sword. Two small gold grips, formed like cupped hands cradled it. She recognized it as a samurai sword, much like she'd seen in children's storybooks.

She pressed closer, her hands gripping the edge of the glass. Her eyes moved along every inch of the gleaming treasure. The stunning black sheath etched with gold covered the sword down to the hilt.

"Iye!"

Ariko jumped at the voice.

"Iye," Hatsuko repeated, shaking her head. "You must come away from there." Hatsuko waved Ariko out. "No one comes in here."

"But why?"

"Your great-grandmother is too old to make it down the stairs now, and this room is no longer for anyone's pleasure."

"Hatsuko? The sword?"

The kind woman shook her head, waving her hand in front of her face. "She will tell you if you are to know. It is an old family treasure, but we must not talk of it." She turned and beckoned Ariko to follow. But her thoughts lingered on the ancient heirloom.

Hatsuko led her to the somewhat modern kitchen. The room

seemed to be an add-on but had a small stove, refrigerator, and sink. The rich aroma caused Ariko to smile. Ariko could recognize that broth anywhere. "That smells like my mother's recipe."

Hatsuko's wide grin made her eyes disappear. "It is your father's."

"But I thought—"

"Your mother was an excellent cook, but she kept to the traditional Shio soup base. It cannot be improved upon."

Ariko walked over to the stove. "Did you know my mother?"

Hatsuko sniffed and turned to face Ariko. "I did. She was a kind, sweet woman."

"How did you know her?" Ariko's heart soared at the prospect of learning more. Anything to bring back the closeness of family that she so desperately needed.

Hatsuko took both Ariko's hands in hers and squeezed. "Someday, we will talk, I promise."

"Ariko-chan!"

She spun around at the harshness of her name and faced her uncle.

"You will accompany me to a meeting."

The anger in her uncle's eyes flashed and his face reddened. Ariko wondered why he would want her. His animosity toward her hung in the air.

"Suimasen, where uncle?

"Here in Morioka. I need a translator."

"For what?" She winced at her lack of respect.

"I am meeting investors. They are American."

She bowed and for an instance wondered why he had never learned to speak English. It was apparent how desperately he desired to be a successful businessman and learning English could only benefit him. "Of course, I'll do what I can to help. When?"

"Tomorrow. I will pick you up here at noon."

Ariko shook her head. She was meeting Kai at noon. "I'm sorry. I have an appointment."

"You will change it," said Hiroshi

Ariko reached into her coat pocket, searching for her phone. It wasn't there. Thinking she left it in her purse, she nodded to her uncle. "I'll try."

"You will."

"Could we make it one o'clock?"

"No."

Ariko nodded again. She was torn between her desire to see the handsome stranger she'd met and her obligation to her new family. Kai would understand, and she hoped he wasn't leaving to return to Tokyo right away.

After her uncle left, Ariko turned to Hatsuko and shrugged. Hatsuko grunted and mumbled words that Ariko couldn't make out and figured she didn't need to know. She struggled with trying to love her uncle as it was.

"You don't have to listen to him," said Hatsuko.

"But if he needs my help...."

"He is selfish." Hatsuko lifted a spoon to Ariko's lips.

She sipped. "Oiishi," Ariko said, and nodded. "This is exactly like my mother...I mean my father's."

"Yes, but Hiroshi changed it. Your uncle added many new types of soup bases. He ruined everything. That's why you must keep Ajiwau open."

"I'll try, Hatsuko. I've always wanted to come back and help."

"I will assist you."

"But how? You're needed here."

A sly grin crossed her face. "I can get away. Afterall, I must go for fresh produce every day. I will come help you whenever I can."

Ariko took a clean ladle. "May I?"

"Dozo."

She filled a small bowl with broth and noodles and let the liquid warm her throat as she sipped.

"Especially the Bible studies." Hatsuko winked.

Ariko smiled, and it wasn't just the broth warming her insides. "Bible studies? Did you attend, Hatsuko-san?"

"Of course. Ariko-chan that is what kept the place going. Many people loved your father. But it's been a month, and the people are hungry."

"But how will I find them?"

"I will round them up for you. But first, we need to go clean. I'll find the landlord and see what needs to be negotiated."

Ariko put down the bowl and enveloped Hatsuko in a hug.

Hatsuko stiffened, then laughed. "You have been in America too long." Pulling away, Hatsuko bowed low. "With God's help, we can continue your father's legacy in Morioka."

Ring, ring. Ring, ring.

Bells rang on the kitchen wall. The old calling system for servants made Hatsuko jump. She excused herself, explaining that Ariko's obaachan was calling her.

Ariko sat at the kitchen table. Not on the floor but on a simple wooden stool. She missed the warmth of the kotatsu, but the heat from the stove and the news of the Lord's work through her father's shop kept the cold at bay. Things in Japan were looking up. She thought of Kai and stood to look for her phone.

Five

~

Ariko searched everywhere, but her cell phone was nowhere to be found. She had to give up the hunt when Obaachan summoned her to make the arrangements necessary to reside in Japan. She spent the rest of the day filling out forms, running to the post office with Hatsuko, and taking care of loose ends. She was exhausted by the end of the day. After dinner with her Obaachan, she bathed, changed, and climbed into the futons. So much was happening, and her mind toiled throughout the night. Her restless sleep came to an end with the frigid morning.

Cold hung in the air, and Ariko clutched the futon tightly around her. She thought to throw the cover off and run for her clothes but abandoned the idea at the first attempt. Instead, she reached for her cell phone, but her eyes focused on the tatami flooring. The phone wasn't there. She'd forgotten she'd lost it, unable to call Kai and change their meeting at the castle. Her stomach knotted.

It will turn up. Ariko rose from the floor and threw on her clothes. Knowing the meeting was important to her uncle, she decided to call a cab to take her to the apartment above Ajiwau where she'd left her suitcase. She hadn't expected to be at Obaachan's for any length of time, and after two nights, she needed a change of clothes.

Hatsuko secured transportation for Ariko, and she promised to be back before her uncle arrived. When the cab delivered her to her father's shop, the familiarity of her old neighborhood flooded her. She bowed at the neighbor sweeping up next door. Ariko waved, but the woman didn't recognize her. Ariko had been eighteen when she left for the states, and except for a few short visits, she hadn't been back in quite a while, since before her mother died.

Raising a metal plank that barred the front wooden door, she slid the rough panel aside and retrieved her keys. Etched on the clouded glass on the front door, was the word, Ajiwau, *savor*. Her father hoped his customers would learn to savor the love of Jesus, as well as the soba.

The little shop was sandwiched between small houses and other tiny businesses. The narrow road provided room for only one car at a time to pass by. Although it wasn't a one-way street, creative driving maneuvers challenged all pedestrians. Shallow ditches ran along each side of the street, and small, rectangular, concrete slabs covered them. Spaces between each slab allowed rain to flow into the gutter basins, but waste and stagnant water left a foul odor.

As Ariko opened the door, another neighbor ventured close.

"Who are you? Why are you opening Shio-san's shop?"

"I am Ariko. His daughter." Ariko bowed.

He bowed back. "Ah-so desu-ka. I'm so sorry for his passing. He was a good man."

"Arigato. He was a good father as well."

"Are you from America?"

"No. I am from Japan, but I was working over there," Ariko said.

"Will you be re-opening Ajiwau? We miss his soba." The man grinned showing his stained crooked teeth.

"I hope so." Ariko tried to decide whether she should prod him into answering some of her inquiries. So many questions about her family rattled her brain. "I'm glad you enjoyed his soba. Did you know my father well?"

He nodded, and his eyes glistened. "Well, enough. I started coming to his Bible Study a few months ago. Very interesting. I had peace whenever I came, and I miss that."

His words confirmed she was needed, and here was where she

should stay. "Well, if all goes well, Ajiwau will open once more, and the Bible Study will commence again."

"Will the soba be as good?" The man laughed.

"Of course. I am my father's daughter." She bowed and opened the door, offering him to join her.

He waved a hand. "Ieye. It is too soon. He only just died." The man backed away.

"Yes, I understand. Arigato." Ariko bowed, and the man departed.

She stepped out of her shoes and into the entryway. Removing slippers from a drawstring bag she carried, she slipped them on and closed the door behind her.

Ariko squinted. The dark eeriness of the tiny shop sent shivers of sadness up her arms. As her eyes adjusted and her ears picked up familiar creaks and whistles from the outside, the glow inside assured her this was home. But the warmth rising inside her wasn't enough for her to remove her coat. Still, sweet memories flooded her as she breathed the imaginary aroma of the rich daishi broth filling the room. Her memory slurped the buckwheat noodles that had drawn the customers lining the walls and sometimes the street as they waited for a seat.

Pulling out a chair, Ariko sat. Four small tables, each with two chairs, squeezed into the small space. The counter stretched out in front of the kitchen, with a few tall stools pushed underneath. She envisioned her mother cooking, herself serving, and her father greeting. Her eyes welled, and tears threatened. Shoving her gloved hands into her coat pocket, her fingers wrapped around the cross. It was still there. She looked at the wall behind the stove. It was still there too—her father's cross.

Knock-knock.

Startled, Ariko turned toward the door. Hatsuko bowed. "Suimasen, Ariko-chan. You must come. Your uncle came looking for you. He wanted to make sure you didn't forget. He's very anxious to make a good impression."

"Hai. Let me get my suitcase."

Ariko ran up the wooden staircase nestled in the back of the kitchen. The two sleeping rooms and toilet were clean but a bit dusty. It was as if her father had just cleaned the small apartment. She grabbed her luggage and joined Hatsuko.

Back at Obaachan's, Hatsuko drew a hot bath for her, but she had little time to relish a good soak. She sat on the small stool washing herself and rinsing off before stepping into the deep tub. She sighed. *Just a few minutes.* She closed her eyes and lost track of time. A quiet knock at the door jolted her. "Coming, Hatsuko!" Ariko toweled down, dressed, and joined her uncle downstairs.

"I came early to apprise you of our meeting."

He muttered details that Ariko couldn't understand, and she didn't want to, but she listened as he finished. "I am meeting an American investor. He is considering helping me to expand the Shio shops."

"Where did you meet him?"

"None of your concern. You will tell him exactly what I say, and no more. If he asks of our history, you will tell him only what I tell you."

"Yes, Uncle."

Driving through the streets of Morioka, they passed the castle. Courage arose, and she asked, "Uncle, do you know the history of the cross in the castle kitchen?"

He stiffened. "Fairy tales. Glorified samurai babble."

"Do the stories have anything to do with the sword in Obaachan's house?"

Hiroshi glared at her. "Did you enter that room?"

"I... I didn't know. Gomenasai," *I'm sorry.*

"Never go in there again, and do not mention it to anyone."

Six

With one last glance at the castle, Ariko wondered if Kai was there, waiting for her. She pushed the thought out of her head. "Uncle, I've misplaced my phone. May I purchase another today?"

He ignored her.

Ariko stared out the window. The cold condensation on her window matched the icy demeanor of the man sitting next to her. *Why did he hate her so?* Her father hadn't spoken much of his brother, only boyhood memories. Fun stories of a competitive nature, but also close and loving. Yet she had never seen or met him before. The first time was at Obaachan's home after the funeral. Hiroshi had made her uncomfortable from their first encounter.

The cab stopped in front of a high-rise hotel, and the sun blinded Ariko as it bounced off the glass and gold structure, sandwiched between smaller buildings. This was a part of Morioka that Ariko knew nothing about.

Her uncle ushered her inside.

Club chairs in the lobby were taken by men and women on their phones. A man with blonde hair lifted his gaze and stood as they approached. He smiled when he saw Ariko. He towered over her, but not over Hiroshi. Like her father, he wasn't a short man.

Ariko had gotten her small stature from her mother.

"Hello, Shio-san." The man bowed.

Hiroshi bowed and told Ariko to respond in English.

"Hello, I'm Ariko. Hiroshi Shio is my uncle."

The man smiled. His perfect white teeth sparkled behind his tanned face.

Ariko thought how much he resembled a California beach boy.

"So, you speak English. Well, this should be much easier than our last meeting. I'm Benjamin Trudell. Nice to meet you, Ariko." He glanced at his watch. "I'm sorry, I don't have much time. I have to catch a train back to Tokyo soon." He motioned to the coffee café. "Shall we?"

The meeting was quite revealing. Ariko learned that her uncle needed this man's investment capital. The man was kind but firm about what he expected in the expansion of the Shio Soba Shops. Ariko's stomach fluttered when she thought of her Obaachan. *Is this what she wanted?*

Trudell had done his homework and drilled Hiroshi on why he hadn't expanded. And worse yet, why he'd lost half the restaurants in the last twenty years.

Hiroshi grew red with embarrassment and glared at Ariko as if it was all her fault. His clipped Japanese excused himself of all blame.

She translated. "My uncle expresses his consternation over the situation. He says family interference is to blame, but the dynamics have changed. He assures you that he is the one in total control of the business."

"Is this true?" Mr. Trudell asked Ariko.

She lowered her eyes.

"No matter right now," Trudell waved a hand in the air. "We can't do too much with the holidays approaching, but I'm attending a Christmas Party at Watanabe Enterprises next week. I'd like you both to join me." Benjamin Trudell explained that the corporation was currently equal to a Fortune 500 company here in Japan. He was seriously considering hiring them to bring the Shio Soba shops up to the new millennium in every area, from the production of their noodles and soup bases and possibly ready-made soba for mass production.

Ariko's stomach churned. She knew this wasn't what Obaachan wanted. She couldn't help but ask. "What about the taste? Shio Soba is all about broth. You won't change that, will you?"

Mr. Trudell chuckled. "I assure you. I consult with a biochemical flavoring company. The formula will undergo massive testing, and we'll get it right. Better than ever."

"But the recipe is ancient. It's been handed down for hundreds of years." Ariko pleaded.

"Nanni itteno?" Hiroshi asked.

Ariko explained to her uncle, and he cut her off, blurting a string of Japanese sentences that silenced her. His last words were a reprimand.

Ariko lowered her eyes once more and nodded.

Her uncle commanded her to apologize.

"Suimasen. I spoke out of turn."

Mr. Trudell reached across and touched her hand. "Not to worry, Ariko. We'll keep the essence of the ancient flavor. You'll see." He stood and pulled a large card from his coat pocket. "Here's an invitation to the Watanabe Christmas Party. It's black tie. Formal. I'll see you there." He shook hands and left.

Hiroshi turned to Ariko. "Never do that again. How dare you speak for me. If this deal does not go through, you are responsible."

"But–"

"I said never. Your boldness brings shame. You are a mere translator, that's all. Never speak out of turn again." He stormed from the building.

For an instance, she hung her head, but straightened and drew back her shoulders. No matter, she didn't belong in that world. Though sorry for her Obaachan, what could she do? Ariko stepped out onto the busy business district. Her uncle was nowhere in sight. She walked the streets until the fancy buildings gave way to older parts of the city. A few more blocks, and she strode into familiar territory again. Not recognizable in that she'd been here before, but comfortable with the old, wooden stores. Small, family-run businesses, much like Ajiwau.

Although the sun was shining, a chilly wind blew. Ariko pushed her hands into her coat pockets. Her fingers found the cross, and her eyes widened. Morioka Castle! Perhaps it wasn't too late. Ariko checked her watch. The meeting hadn't taken that long, maybe Kai would still be there. She ran back toward the business district, hoping to hail a cab.

The cab driver pulled up to the castle's front entrance.

Ariko paid him and ran up the ramp, turning toward the broad steps, leading to the grounds. From there, she couldn't remember which way to go. The granite walls rose everywhere, and the stark, leafless trees all stood in unison. Old and gnarled but strangely beautiful. So many of them. Too many to remember any as a landmark.

If she were in America, she'd stop and ask someone for directions. Not in Japan. Instead, she ran back to the front entrance and grabbed a map, searching for the kitchen. Even on the map, she found it challenging to locate. She lowered the folded paper and peered at the street.

A tall man in an overcoat, wearing a bright red and green scarf scurried away from the castle.

Ariko rushed after him, but by the time she was close enough to call out, the man had hailed a cab. Everything in her told her to call out Kai's name. Once again, had she been in America, she may have done so. Not so, in Japan. She watched as the yellow car drove him away. The red taillights blended with the twinkling Christmas lights, illuminating the busy holiday bustle of downtown Morioka. They did nothing to ignite her darkened heart. Kai was lost forever.

Seven

A week later, Ariko's uncle argued with Obaachan on what Ariko should wear to the Christmas party. He insisted she buy a new gown. It was imperative that she make a stunning impression. But Obaachan had instructed Hatsuko to retrieve an exquisite white and gold furiosode, a kimono exclusively for a single young woman going to a formal event. The woven silk depicted an elaborate array of chrysanthemums across the body of the garment. Graceful, white cranes embellished the sleeves and back. The hemline rippled to the floor.

Ariko had never seen anything so beautiful in all her life. The light sheen sparkled, and the crisp smell of sandalwood and cedar permeated the room. Hatsuko's face beamed as she held up the garment.

"It's the most exquisite kimono I have ever seen." Ariko stared wide-eyed.

"But you will not wear it. There is no place for the archaic traditions." He bowed to Obaachan. "Ariko will wear a gown. I will take her shopping. This is my meeting, and my concern."

Ariko's back went rigid, and she recalled his scolding after their meeting with Trudell.

Bowing utmost respect towards Obaachan, Ariko waited to be dismissed, defying her uncle.

Obaachan nodded, then waved her off. She instructed Hatsuko to take away the kimono.

Ariko watched as Hatsuko carefully folded the treasured garment.

"Ariko-chan, come now," said her uncle.

"Hai."

The car ride to a large department store downtown was quiet. Her uncle said not a word.

When they arrived on the uppermost floor, Ariko was overwhelmed at the gorgeous mannequins and racks of formal wear. The garishness of holiday decorations gave way to perfectly coordinated racks of elegant dresses, bags, and shoes. She'd seen such in America but had never visited the department stores in Japan.

Hiroshi spoke to the clerk, handed her a card, and left Ariko to try on gowns she'd never dreamt of wearing.

She hadn't tried too many on before settling on a fitted white chiffon dress, reminiscent of the forties movies she'd watched back in the states. She'd fallen in love with the flowing styles of Ginger Rogers, and apparently so had the designers in Japan. The sweetheart neckline with flowing sleeves accentuated Ariko's petite frame. The swirling hemline floated with every turn.

The store clerk nodded her approval. She offered Ariko a white woolen cape with a faux fur collar, but Ariko opted to wear her long white coat. It would suffice.

When the day arrived for their trip, they took the Shinkansen to Tokyo. Ariko had never ridden the bullet train, and fortunately, Morioka train station was a direct route to the busy capital. They checked into a modest hotel, and Ariko rested before the big event.

Hours later, after dressing, she met her uncle in the lobby, and he said nothing when he saw her, but his widened eyes seemed to express his approval at her appearance. He ushered her to the big event by taxi.

Ariko gasped when they arrived. She held up her gown as she stepped from the cab, the valet offering a gloved white hand.

"Yokaso," he said, bowing low and gesturing a welcomed hand. "Yokaso to the Grand Nikko Tokyo Daiba Hotel."

Her eyes travelled up the massive high-rise, and she marveled at the gorgeous, lush grounds surrounded by the waterfront. Ariko had never heard of the hotel, but one couldn't miss seeing the buildings and surroundings if they'd flown into Haneda Airport in Tokyo. Dusk settled over the capital city and the shimmering lights highlighted a spectacular view.

As the glass elevator rose, the city spread out before them. A bell dinged, and the doors opened to the Penthouse. The sparkle of holiday cheer almost blinded Ariko as she stepped into the sea of black tuxedos. Ladies wearing gowns of every color swirled around the room.

Her uncle stepped behind Ariko and proceeded to help remove her coat.

She patted her loose chignon and pushed back a few tendrils. Her stomach fluttered. Never had she felt so out of place. Excusing herself, she found the ladies' room and hid in an alcove with a private mirror. Her image stared back. *What was she doing here?* She swept a hand across the marble counter, took a deep breath, and exited.

Straightening her shoulders, she headed for the ballroom but froze. At the end of the hallway, one man's gaze stopped her. His smile set her stomach fluttering. She couldn't make her feet move.

No matter, because he moved toward her. His black tuxedo and white shirt framed his beautiful face, and heat flooded her neck.

"Ariko? What are you doing here?" Kai took her hands and squeezed.

She lowered her eyes.

Dropping her hands, he stepped back. His brows furrowed. "I waited as long as I could at the castle. I thought you might call."

"I'm so sorry. My uncle made me come with him to a meeting, and I lost my phone."

Kai grinned. "Well, that changes everything. Except, I'm wondering how you landed up here."

"I might ask you the same thing. I thought you were returning to America?" Ariko took a deep breath and slowly let it out.

He did the same and wouldn't remove his gaze from her. "You're so beautiful." He offered a hand but quickly dropped it. "I did return to the states, but I had to come back." He bowed and motioned. "Domo," *please*, "Come, let's get something to drink, and you can apologize for standing me up at the castle." He grinned. Kai led the way before she had a chance to respond.

She wanted him to take her hand, but they'd only met once, and in Japan, it wasn't the custom in a crowded, private setting. When they entered the ballroom, Ariko again felt the flutters churning inside. They turned sour when Benjamin Trudell stepped in front of her.

He took her hand and kissed it.

She pulled it away and peered around him.

Kai had stopped a few feet ahead and looked back. His brows furrowed.

"Well, Ariko, I must say, you look every bit as engaging as a red-carpet Hollywood celebrity." Mr. Trudell grinned.

"Arigato...I mean, thank you," said Ariko switching to English.

He turned. "So, how do you know Kai Watanabe?"

Kai stepped forward and bowed but said nothing. His eyes darkened.

"Well, this is interesting." Mr. Trudell grinned. "And fortunate."

"Do you know Trudell-san?" Ariko addressed Kai.

Her uncle suddenly intruded on the circle. He whipped his head between the three who conversed in English. Finally, he whispered to Ariko, asking for an explanation.

She answered but withheld anything about her missed encounter with Kai.

Mr. Trudell interrupted. "I know now is not the time to discuss business, but perhaps we can arrange a meeting soon, Mr. Watanabe."

Ariko's brows furrowed. Suddenly her eyes widened. "Watanabe? You are the Watanabe corporation?"

Kai sighed. "No. My father is."

"Mr. Watanabe is being modest. The rumor is he'll soon be CEO. His technology is the driving force behind helping small businesses expand into franchises and corporations. Shio Soba being one of them."

"Shio Soba?" Both Ariko and Kai spoke simultaneously.

"Perhaps I can explain. Ariko is the niece of Hiroshi Shio here, and he is seeking to expand his restaurants. I've had preliminary talks with your company and was hoping to get your input." Trudell rocked back on his heels.

Ariko narrowed her eyes at Kai and spoke quietly. "But I thought you were interested in helping small businesses?" Her mind drifted back to their lunch the other day and how interested Kai seemed in the tiny cafe. How disinterested he was in the franchises, the chains.

"I am. All this," he waved around the room, "this is my family, not me."

Mr. Trudell laughed. "Humility is indeed a Japanese trait, but come on now, Kai, you were schooled in the U.S. You know what it takes to advance in this world."

"This world? Not just in Japan?" Ariko asked.

Hiroshi again interrupted.

"My uncle would like to know when your business talks can commence."

"Slow down there, buddy. This is a party. We're just getting to know Mr. Watanabe. It's not a coincidence that we've met so early in the evening. Can we meet, say next week?"

Before Kai could answer, an older couple stepped to a large platform. They bowed and spoke first in Japanese, then in English. They called Kai up to the stage.

Ariko listened as Mr. and Mrs. Watanabe thanked their clients and business associates. They expressed their appreciation for those investing in the future of Japan and ended by introducing Kai as the future of Watanabe Corporation.

Ariko heard all she wanted to hear. He wasn't who she thought he was. Other than Hatsuko, she felt as though she'd lost the only friend she had in Japan. The song, Rocking Around the Christmas Tree sung in Japanese blared from speakers around the room. A twenty-foot Christmas tree with changing lights sparkled and the bulbs glittered with each exchange. It was the perfect display of a western, commercialized Christmas.

Ariko had to leave and excused herself, much to the mutterings of her uncle. She located her coat and ran for the elevator. Fortunately, with all the festivities, she was the only one leaving at that particular moment. She stepped into the elevator.

A large hand stopped the closing doors. "Ariko. We have to talk."

She pulled her coat tight around her. "No. I don't think so. We're worlds apart, Kai. You're everything my father gave up."

"Because my father owns Watanabe Corporation? I'm not taking the CEO position. My father knows that. That announcement was just a big ploy to pressure me to accept."

"How do you know Mr. Trudell and my uncle?"

"I don't really. I met Mr. Trudell in passing at our corporate offices once, but I've never even seen your uncle before."

"Why didn't you tell me who you were?" Ariko asked.

"Looks like both of us are guilty of hiding things. I didn't know you were heir to Shio Soba."

"I'm not. But apparently, you thought I was, or you wouldn't have—"

Two couples slipped past Kai and joined Ariko.

"Sayonara," said Ariko.

She left him standing outside the closing elevator doors. Her heart hurt, and her eyes burned. The couples giggled and spoke in whispered tones. Jingle bells rang over the loudspeaker, and Ariko sighed.

When she stepped into the lobby, her shoulders sagged. She'd forgotten she was in downtown Tokyo and not Morioka. It was late, and she must wait for her uncle. Finally, she sat. The lobby was packed with cheery partygoers coming and going, Much more festive than anything she'd attended in America. She'd never participated in big office parties that celebrated everything but the birth of Jesus. Her Christmas memories had been filled with sweet advent ceremonies and church services.

Ariko opened her purse. The little granite cross stared back at her. She pulled it out and held it up to the bright chandelier overhead.

An elegantly dressed, uniformed bellman approached her. "Miss, may I call you a cab?"

"Oh, no, thank you. I'm waiting for someone," Ariko said, still holding the stone figurine.

He pointed to the cross. "Did you get that from Morioka Castle?"

"I did. How did you know?"

The short man grinned and clasped his white-gloved hands in front of him, and his brass buttons shined brightly. He leaned forward and reached into his pocket, pulling out a similar cross.

Ariko felt a stir in her spirit, and the companionship of yet another fellow Christian made her smile.

Ariko reached out, "May I?" Taking it into her hands, she rolled it over in her palm, comparing it to the cross. "It feels very ancient, not like this one."

"Do you know the legend of the cross in the castle kitchen?"

"I heard a bit of the story," said Ariko.

"It is no story. It is truth." The bellman swung his hands behind his back and clasped them. "A truth buried before it had a chance to thrive."

Ariko nodded. She knew too well the persecution of the Japanese Christians and the stigma that persisted today. Though it wasn't overt, and freedom of religion held no restrictions in Japan, Christianity had failed to thrive here.

A flurry of people rushed through the revolving glass doors. A flash of sparkle shot round the metallic and marble lobby, and the bellman backed away.

"God bless you," he whispered as he rushed to help the visitors.

Ariko turned her cross over in her hand. She was anxious now to return to the castle and uncover the mystery of the kitchen cross.

Eight

Visitors checked in, and their quiet, festive mood and elegant style reminded Ariko of a Christmas movie with guests checking into the Waldorf Astoria in New York. The chiffon swirls of her gown peeked out beneath her long white coat. Pocketing the cross, she pulled out her gloves and put them on. Her stomach churned as her uncle approached.

"Ariko-chan? That was rude of you to leave."

Ariko faced her uncle. "Gomenasai, Uncle." She bowed. "I felt a little lost up there. And it did not seem that you needed me."

"Well, I will. We have a meeting set up for tomorrow afternoon."

"With whom?" She clutched the buttons on her coat, stopping herself from twisting them so tightly they might pop off. She'd hoped Kai wouldn't be there.

"Trudell-san desires it, and we will meet him here in the lobby tomorrow morning."

A pleasant dinging sounded across the lobby, and Ariko turned to see the elevator doors open. Her shoulders dropped.

Kai walked out with a beautiful woman clinging to his arm. But his eyes froze on Ariko.

The woman released his arm and walked down a corridor.

With long strides, Kai approached Ariko. "Ariko, please. I don't know what the mix-up was. But let me explain." He spoke in English.

"There's no mix-up. You're in the business of...well, big business, and I'm not."

"But I had no idea you were in the Shio family. I had no idea about the soba shops. You never told me."

"I'm not in the business. But if I had been and had I told you, maybe I would have seen past your façade."

"I'm not sure what you're referring to, but perhaps I should be the one a little annoyed. You never came to the castle, remember?"

"I told you. I lost my phone, and I couldn't call you. It was my uncle. He needed my help."

Kai nodded at Hiroshi who bowed low returning the nod. "Ariko, I think I understand. Your family means a lot to you, don't they? Young people aren't as respectful or loyal here anymore."

Hiroshi cleared his throat, but Kai's dark eyes pierced Ariko's whole being. It was as if he was examining or admiring her. She didn't know which, but she wondered why the situation had to be so difficult. Staring back at him, she swallowed hard. She could use a friend here and they connected. *But now?*

"Watanabe-san. It was a pleasure meeting you tonight. Thank you for allowing my niece Ariko and I to attend your wonderful party." Hiroshi broke the moment.

Kai bowed. "The pleasure is all mine. But it's my parents who hosted this event." He shrugged. "I'm not one for such extravagance."

Ariko looked away.

"I hope to be doing business with you soon. Trudell-san has great plans."

"Yes, so I've heard," said Kai. "Be cautious. I understand Trudell-san to be very ambitious."

"Oh, and you are not?"

The beautiful woman who arrived on Kai's arm returned. Her sleek black hair hung long down her back. High cheekbones accentuated her lovely dark eyes.

"Everyone, this is Lily," Kai said.

The beautiful woman flitted her fingers in the air. "Hello. Oh, Kai, you're so modest." Lily patted his arm. "Why, if it hadn't been for Kai, the Watanabe Corporation wouldn't be the conglomerate it is today."

"Lily, please," Kai said.

She laughed. "Lily. He calls me by my American name. I'm Yuri." She spoke perfect English.

Hiroshi gaped at her.

"Shio-san, you flatter me," she said in Japanese.

Like Kai, this Lily's mannerisms were very western. So uncharacteristically friendly. She was dialoguing flirty lines like an American movie star.

Her uncle's slack jaw and widened eyes caused Ariko to stifle a giggle. Kai caught it. When their eyes met, the brief lightness relieved her bitterness toward him. For an instant, the camaraderie she'd felt with Kai a week ago returned.

He raised his brows and grinned.

Ariko nodded.

"But as I was saying, Kai's expert IT skills brought the Watanabe Corporation to a new height. They are in the Fortune 500, you know?" Lily grinned, and her bragging continued.

Ariko felt the brief closeness with Kai disappear. Her mind drifted as Lily droned on, and Ariko's adoring gaze toward Kai turned hard.

Finally, Kai interrupted. "I need to get Lily home. Ariko, did you find your phone? May I call you?"

Lily slapped Kai's arm playfully. "Kai? How dare you flirt with another woman while we're together."

He rolled his eyes and quickly shifted his gaze back to Ariko. He shook his head, but she merely shrugged.

Hiroshi interrupted again. "Watanabe-san, I look forward to meeting with you again soon." He bowed deeply.

"Ariko?" Kai pleaded.

"Yes, she will join us." Hiroshi seemed to misinterpret.

Ariko shook her head and turned her gaze on Lily. "It was nice to meet you, Lily. Merry Christmas."

Lily bowed elegantly. "Happy Holidays to you, too. Come, Kai. I need my beauty sleep. Your mother has a hectic day planned for me tomorrow."

Ariko winced but managed a smile.

Lily dragged Kai away as he glanced over his shoulder.

"Well, how do you like that?" Her uncle raised his brows. "Everything may work out. Perhaps I can work with the Watanabes without the American." He grinned. "Thanks to you, I guess."

Although Ariko thought anything without Mr. Trudell would be better, she wasn't sure her uncle had the capital or the business sense to implement whatever systems Kai might offer. Her heart dropped at the thought. He seemed so sincere when he took her into a small soba shop. His kindness and respect for the meager establishment and the modest customers appeared genuine.

Yet, she knew nothing about him. Not really. Her guard went up when she squinted out the window. The beautiful Lily hung on Kai's arm.

Ariko's uncle, no longer discouraged, sounded as jolly as the atmosphere in the lobby, as he prattled on and on about the possibilities of Shio Soba Shops. He made no effort to leave.

Ariko turned to her uncle. "Are we staying here?"

"Of course not." He wagged a finger. "But one day. If all goes well, we may be living like the Watanabes." He walked to the bellman, and Ariko followed.

A cab arrived and took them to their hotel, a two-story building housing tiny, sparsely furnished rooms with hospitality ever-present. Cartons of green tea were presented on a tray and a package of rice cookies lay against the pillows. The welcoming gesture somehow comforted Ariko.

She hadn't brought her Bible but pulled out the new phone and scrolled. Remembering that there was no Bible App, she laid down her phone and walked to the window. There was no view, just another building rising high. *Would that be the fate of Shio Soba? Just another big corporation?*

Ariko searched the streets and watched the sea of pedestrians traverse the sidewalks and crosswalks of Tokyo. There were so many people all bundled up in fine clothing. As a flurry of snow wisped through the air, the people scurried.

Her eyes caught a glimpse of an old woman bent over, wearing a plain kimono. She appeared so out of place here in Tokyo, but she wouldn't have in Morioka. Ariko had seen such women at the castle. A twinge pinched her heart, and she longed for Morioka, but it wasn't Morioka. It was a longing for the people. The simpleness, and still, it was more than that. It was her father.

Nine

The following day Ariko stepped out of the hotel and gazed upwards. The busy streets of Tokyo shined clean and impressive in the bright sunshine. One couldn't help but be amazed at the high-rise structures all around. The sweet-smelling air filled her lungs, but she longed for the old, earthy aromas of her childhood. Nothing reminiscent of that surrounded her.

That afternoon, Ariko entered the meeting room releasing a heavy sigh. Kai wasn't there. She didn't want to see him again, but her nod of affirmation did nothing to quell her disappointment.

Mr. Trudell led the meeting, but his friendly manner seemed somewhat harsh and directed when Hiroshi gave his input and expressed his concerns.

The numbers they discussed flew around Ariko's head. She stuttered as she translated.

Many times, Hiroshi's eyes widened so that Mr. Trudell laughed. Hiroshi could not hide the redness rising. Her uncle was clearly not in Trudell's league.

"Get with the new millennium, Mr. Shio. We're taking the Shio Soba to the next level, and hopefully, with the help of Watanabe Corporation." He sipped his tea and set the cup down with a loud clink. "I plan on opening up a few in the states. With or without you."

Ariko's head swiveled back and forth between her uncle and the American. *Was Kai a part of this?*

"Uncle, can you trust this man?" she whispered in Japanese.

Hiroshi's face flushed brighter. He silenced her and instructed her to speak politely. He wished to know if Mr. Trudell planned to invest in Shio Soba and how much.

Sweat beaded on her uncle's forehead, and Ariko's heart shrank for him. As courteously as she could, she posed the question.

The American's eyes narrowed. "That all depends on...percentages."

Ariko wasn't entirely sure what he meant, but she translated.

Her uncle's brow furrowed in confusion.

Mr. Trudell continued to stare at Hiroshi but removed a pen from his pocket. He searched the table and frowned. "Why you people don't put napkins on the table baffles me." He raised his fingers, clicking them in the air.

A waitress rushed over, and Ariko asked for paper.

Mr. Trudell clicked his pen two, three, four times. Finally, looking down, he scribbled and passed the paper over.

"Explain to your uncle here that the first number is the amount I agree to invest. If he complies with the second number, which is what I require as controlling interest, we have a deal." He placed the pen down.

"Where does the Watanabe Corporation come into all this?" She knew she spoke out of turn as her uncle's lips tightened.

Trudell laughed. "Perhaps you are the businessman in your family." He rolled his eyes disrespectfully at her uncle. "Leave that to me. We opened the doors last night." He winked. "Thanks to you, it may go quite favorably."

Ariko reddened as she glimpsed the figures written on the napkin, but her uncle slid it out of her reach.

His eyes widened, and he darted a glance at her.

She whispered, repeating precisely what Mr. Trudell had expressed. With a slight shake of her head, she continued. "Uncle, please. This is not fair."

His clenched jaw silenced her.

Mr. Trudell stood. "You're fortunate that I am a patient man. In the spirit of the holidays, take the week to dwell on it. I'm headed for Aspen tomorrow. I'll be in touch." He winked at her. "Tell your uncle not to wait too long."

Ariko nodded and stood. "Mr. Trudell, why go to Aspen when our Nagano has the finest skiing in the world?" She straightened her shoulders even as her knees shook. Ariko spoke out of turn, and had her uncle known how she'd challenged Mr. Trudell, she didn't know what he would do.

"Ariko, are you offering to take me?" Mr. Trudell laughed out loud, causing those in the restaurant to gawk. He nodded and waved rudely as the customers turned back to their meals.

Her uncle blurted out a string of questions, and Ariko managed to subdue him with nods. "I'm sorry, no. I don't ski, but I have been to Colorado, and I dare say, I believe Nagano is even more beautiful."

"You got me there, girl. I've never been to Nagano. Maybe next time. But you have to promise to be my guide." He extended a hand.

Before Ariko could take it, her uncle stood and shook instead.

He straightened but didn't look the American in the eye. He bowed and expressed his thanks for the generous offer. He instructed Ariko to convey his anticipation of Mr. Trudell's return trip.

"Make it worth my while, Shio-san." Mr. Trudell bowed and left. He never bothered to pay for their lunch.

"Rude American," Hiroshi grunted.

"Uncle, please do not accept this offer. It would kill Obaachan."

"My grandmother is already dying. It will kill her if I continue to let the business decline." He dropped into the chair.

"What can I do to help?" Ariko asked.

"Help? It was your father who destroyed the business. He never let me in on the dealings. He never trained me for what he did."

"Gomenasai."

"Never mind. He had a sharp mind for business, and he threw it all away. For what?" He glared at Ariko. "For your mother, for your...for that God of yours."

Here was the opening. Ariko wrapped her hands around the teacup and said a quick prayer. "Uncle, that God, He is my God."

"Then you are as stupid as your father. What did it get him? A dead wife, a rented shop in the worst parts of Morioka. He could have been as big as Trudell-san. Shio Soba could have been a big corporation like the Watanabe's."

"Is that what you want?"

"Want? I want Obaachan to respect me! It was your father she mourns for still, and yet he left. He left her. He left the business. What was I supposed to do?"

"Did you ask him to help?"

"Of course not. He was too wrapped up in his new religion. He ignored our shrines, our ancestors."

Ariko thought of the sword with the cross carved in the hilt. "Uncle, about our ancestors...were there any who were Christians?"

"Who told you such nonsense?"

Hope flooded through Ariko. Her heart floated, giving courage to her words. "There was, wasn't there? Is that why the sword—"

"I told you that sword is none of your business."

"Please, Uncle."

"Only Obaachan can share that tale."

"Did my father know?"

Hiroshi shook his head. "None of us did. Not until your father left the family did I hear Obaachan ranting about the castle kitchen cross. It haunted her. No matter how your father built our business. No matter how prestigious we became with Shio Soba in the community, she was not happy. But when he left, something inside her relented."

"But she made him leave."

"Yes. She pushed him out, but there was something besides the restaurants that she wanted from him. Yet, she could not bring herself to ask."

"What was it?"

"If I knew, I would have asked him myself."

"Did he know?"

"I think maybe he did. He spoke to me of your Jesus. Obaachan overheard him, and that was when she made him leave. She never spoke to him again, but she made me tell her everything he said to me."

"And what did he say?" A breath caught in Ariko's throat. She dared not breathe out.

Her uncle's face softened. The lines in his forehead smoothed, as the muscles in his jaw relaxed. For a brief moment, his sad eyes searched her face. "That this Jesus came to redeem us from our life of brokenness." Suddenly a quiet laugh erupted. "Imagine. A life of brokenness. We had more money at that time than the Shio family has ever attained."

"Were you happy? Was Obaachan happy?"

"What is happiness?"

"Joy?"

"Joy. Your father spoke of joy. I think that's what he wanted for our family. Something we lacked. So, no. We were not happy."

"You were broken. Like all of us. That's why Jesus—"

"Enough. It was your father that broke our family. Obaachan mourned his loss when he left, and now even more that he is dead."

Ariko's heart hurt, but it swelled with courage. "But she doesn't need to. He's not dead, but alive in heaven."

"I said, enough." He stood. "I have much on my mind. I must consider this offer from Trudell-san."

As if a pin had popped her inflating heart, Ariko blew out a breath. She must talk to Obaachan.

Ten

Ajiwau needed a good cleaning. Hunching over on hands and feet, Ariko scrubbed the floors and walls of Ajiwau. She was saving the stovetops for last. Although they weren't filled with grease and grit, they needed a good cleaning. She was thankful. It took her mind off the disturbing plans that her uncle had for Shio Soba.

Ariko pushed her hair off her face and read the sign on the window. "Ajiwau." The glass was dull, and the Japanese Kanji needed repainting. A board had loosened, which made the glass wobble whenever she slid the door open. Ariko blew out a breath and closed her eyes. *"Oh God, please help me."*

"Ariko-chan?" A voice came from the doorway.

That was fast. Ariko chuckled, attributing the greeting to an answer to prayer. "Hai." She jumped to her feet and bowed.

It was the friendly neighbor from the last time she'd been here. "So, you are planning on reopening? I thought the landlord was tearing this place down."

Involuntarily, Ariko's fist gripped the wet sponge. The icy water dripping through her fingers made her shiver. She lowered it into a bucket. "What are you talking about? Did he come by?"

"Hai," *yes*, "He brought a man, and I listened. I'm sure they were speaking of rebuilding a bigger structure."

Ariko wiped her hands down the apron. She straightened the scarf holding back her hair. "When did they come?"

"Just yesterday."

He couldn't answer her continued questions, so she asked if he had the owner's name and number. No luck.

"What will you do? Many are waiting for you to reopen Sensei's shop."

Sensei. A respectful recognition for teacher. Ariko smiled. *Not Shio-san, but Sensei*. A warmth spread through Ariko, and she rubbed her hands together. "We shall pray and ask God to reopen Ajiwau."

The neighbor stepped back. Though he'd not walked through the threshold, he was now on the curb, holding his hands up. "Not me. I told you, I did not embrace Sensei's teachings." His eyes lowered, and he wrung his hands together. "I came for the soba."

"But you said you enjoyed being here. That something—"

"No, I did not say that." He looked up and around as if a lightning bolt might strike him.

"You're like a frightened rabbit." A schoolgirl in uniform called behind him. "Boo!"

The girl jumped as he faced her.

"Now, look who is the rabbit. Be respectful of your elders." The man scowled as he ran across the narrow street.

"Never mind him. He came to the meetings. Maybe just for the free meal, but he always came," said the young girl.

"I am Ariko. Shio-san's daughter." Ariko bowed.

Below the fringe of thick, black bangs, the schoolgirl's eyes widened. "A so desu ka. He mentioned you. Talked about your job in the states, but how you'd soon be back to help him." She nodded in a less formal bow. "I'm Emiko. You can call me Emi." She pointed to her nose as she hiked a heavy backpack onto her shoulders. Dangling key chains covered the straps. Pokémon and other plastic characters jingled.

"Yes, I had planned to return. But..." Ariko's voice trailed.

"Your life got crazy, eh? I wish I had a life." Emi's appearance exuded sweetness. Her short plaid skirt barely peeked out below a heavy jacket, similar to a navy peacoat. Her knees held a blue hue in contrast to the high white knee socks.

"You're so young. Your life is just beginning."

"I'm thirteen already, and my life is boring." Emi shrugged.

Ariko beckoned her in and reached for the sliding wooden door behind her.

Emi stepped in, removing her shoes.

Before sliding the door shut, Ariko peeked out. A few people milled about, staring and pointing. Ariko bowed, and the few bowed back, smiling.

"They all loved Sensei, you know." Emi's tone softened as her backpack slid to the floor.

"Please sit. I'll make tea."

Ariko put on the teapot and lit the flame. She took teacups from a cabinet and wiped them inside, setting them on the table. A grocery bag sat on the counter, and she pulled out dorayaki, a pancake filled with sweet beans.

Emi's eyes widened. "Oh! I'm so hungry. I forgot my after-school snack today, so I was headed to a coffee café. Sensei always let me come here after school. No one is ever home at my house. Both my parents work, so he used to help me with my homework."

Ariko pressed a hand to her chest at the picture of her father with Emiko. She placed the dorayaki on a plate. They were for Obaachan, but she decided Emi needed them more and moved the plate in front of the girl.

"Arigato." Emi took a bite of the dorayaki but quickly lowered it. "Gomenasai. Sensei always prayed before we ate." Her eyes watered.

Ariko wanted to ask what else he taught her but listened instead.

"If no customers were here, he'd sit next to me and work on his studies."

"What study?"

"Oh, you know, his Bible. That's one reason all the people came. That and his guitar. Did you know he played well?"

Ariko nodded and reached over, clasping Emi's hand. Again, a very

American gesture, but Emi didn't pull away. Ariko said a short prayer asking for the Lord's blessing and giving thanks for Emi. "Amen," she said.

Emi repeated, "Ah-men." She wiped her eyes on her sleeve, but the tears kept coming. Like a faucet bursting, she couldn't seem to contain the water flooding down her cheeks. Throwing her arms on the table, she buried her head. "Why? Why did God have to take him? I have no one else."

Ariko clutched her chest. Emiko had family. Ariko didn't.

"I understand."

"But you left him, and he was the most wonderful man."

"Yes, he was. My father sent me to school in America. But I didn't leave. I just didn't make it back as planned."

"Why not?"

Ariko shook her head. "I'm not sure. I always wanted to come back and help, but finances were so tight. I felt I could help more by sending money."

"But he said he didn't care about the business. All he cared about were the people. The people that came almost every night."

Ariko's eyes widened. "Every night?"

Emi took a bite of the bean cake and nodded. "Hai," *yes*. "He'd put out the closed sign at eight o'clock every night, and anyone who didn't leave got a lesson." Emiko giggled. "He locked us in."

"Wait, and you were here then?"

"Not every night. But my parents both work late, so I was here a lot."

Ariko wondered about her friends. *Did the girl have none?*

"It was mostly single people. Not like me, but in college. Neighbors too." Emi shrugged. "When he told the Bible stories, they were so interesting. But when he played his guitar and sang everyone really listened."

"What kind of songs?"

Emi began to sing so quietly that Ariko leaned forward. Emi's sweet soprano wavered at first but grew stronger as she closed her eyes and sang.

My Jesus, I love you, I know thou art mine…

When she finished, she giggled and clapped her hands together. "The hymns were my favorite."

"Mine too." Ariko recalled how her father would play the guitar every evening after dinner. And she too, like Emi, would take part in the worship before and after the shop's Bible study. But when she was little, it was only once a week. The other days, her father stayed open until eleven o'clock at night. Sometimes to midnight. It was their only means of support. "So my father had Bible study every night?"

"He did. Sometimes he had only one or two people here, but if they listened, he would preach. It was funny, though. Some people would bang on the door. He invited them in, but all they wanted was soba, and since he always kept a pot cooking, he would give them a takeout order.

Knock-Knock.

Emi's eyes darted to the door.

Ariko greeted a woman dressed in a uniformed skirt and top. A white scarf covered her hair. They bowed, and the woman politely introduced herself and apologized for the intrusion while Emi glared until she interrupted.

"Mother, what are you doing here?"

"Suimasen, Emiko. You must come with me. Your father is in the hospital. I had to leave work early."

Emi sat frozen. Her lips pursed. Moments passed, and she said nothing.

"Emi? I can call a taxi," offered Ariko.

"Kekko desu." Emiko's mother shook her head. "We will ride the bus. Please, Emiko. Your father needs us."

"What for? He's always at the pachinko parlor. That's why you work two jobs. He gambles all the time, and he never comes home after work. That's why I come here."

The mother lowered her head.

"Emi?" Ariko whispered. "If you remember anything my father taught you, you must go with your mother. She needs the peace of Jesus right now."

"That's what Sensei always said. That we all need that." Emi stood and bowed. "Yes, Mother. Let's go."

They exited quickly, and as Emiko glanced back, Ariko motioned praying hands and nodded. *Oh Lord, Jesus, soften hearts, please.*

Warmth enveloped her as she thought of how her father had laid the groundwork on the hearts of fertile soil. She perused the four walls, and her eyes rested on the cross on the wall above the stove. Feeling a pull toward Morioka Castle, Ariko locked up and left.

Eleven

Ariko arrived at Morioka Castle, and it was still daylight. Her first inclination was to go straight to the castle kitchen. But something inside her made her want to explore the rest of the grounds first. She said hello to the souvenir stand attendant and chose to look around some more.

She found some small samurai swords with a cross etched on the hilt. She held it up to the attendant, who shrugged. Ariko searched some more and found plastic, lacquer-looking soba bowls, and right next to them was a booklet entitled "Wanko Soba." Wanko Soba was Morioka's claim to fame, though she didn't know why. She perused a few pages and found that historically, it was believed that the shogun of the Nanbu Clan of the Morioka Castle invented Wanko Soba. Ari chuckled and wondered if the expert cook had something to do with the invention. She purchased the booklet and a sword and left to explore.

Walking the castle ruins, Ariko recalled the tragic history of Christianity in Japan. She took notice of stone statues that added to the starkness of the trees. It painted a sad picture against the gray skies. When she approached the kitchen area, a small group was there. She hung back and listened to the tour guide. He was partly Asian, and Ariko concluded he must be half. She went in closer and listened.

He explained the castle's kitchen history, but his emphasis was on the cross. "The Castle Kitchen Cross, as I call it on my blog, is where an ex-samurai and his wife practiced their faith and shared it secretly with those who came to the kitchen. The cross carved in the stone, although obscured, was hidden behind pots and pans hanging on the wall."

Ariko's ears perked when he mentioned ex-samurai.

He rubbed his hand over the stone carving and welcomed others to do the same. A guard walked by and shook his head sternly.

"Oh, right. Better not touch. Anyway, the legend says that this banished ex-samurai fled Edo, now Tokyo, and settled in Morioka. He and his wife had no means of support. But she was an excellent cook, and soba was her specialty. Most important was her broth that no one could copy. The ex-samurai constructed a cart, and he and his wife began selling soba bowls to the samurai and noble people going in and out of the castle. Some would stop and wolf down many bowls at a time. One day the ex-samurai heard of a plot to overthrow the Nambu clan by assassinating the shogun."

A young blond boy with two swords strapped across his back raised a hand and spoke. "The Nambu Clan was loyal to Tokugawa in Edo. Was he the shogun that banned the samurai?"

The blogger sighed, then patted the boy's head. "Uh, I'm not sure about that. Maybe send me an email, and I'll look into it." He turned to the crowd. "So, the ex-samurai told the loyal Nambu samurai of the plan, but they scoffed at him. Afterall, he was just a noodle maker. So, he took it upon himself to thwart the evil scheme. As a trained warrior, he donned his armor and sword one night. And rumor has it that he carved a cross into the hilt but covered it with leather straps."

The boy raised a hand again. "If straps of leather covered it, how did they know a cross was carved in it?"

Ariko chuckled but had the same question.

The blogger chewed his lip. "Well, someone must have seen it, kid… Anyway, when the ex-samurai successfully defeated the ninja hired to assassinate the shogun, the failed attempt caused an investigation, and it was discovered that ex-samurai was responsible. Nanbu Shogun called him and offered him a samurai position and lord over lands. He refused and confided at the risk of death that he was a banished ex-samurai due to his Christian faith. But the shogun was so grateful he hushed him and made him his personal bodyguard instead. The shogun had also eaten many bowls of his wife's soba that were brought to him, so he hired her as his personal chef."

"When she offered the soba from the cart outside the kitchen, she served them in little bowls. The shogun named the noodles, Wanko soba, Wanko meaning little bowls, and took credit for her delicious noodles and broth. The shogun became famous for the Wanko Soba, but it was really the ex-samurai's wife who created it." The blogger took a swig of water.

Ariko frowned. Soba, Christianity, a sword? So many similarities.

The blogger continued. "So Wanko Soba blossomed from the castle kitchen, but Christianity did not. Though they practiced their faith in secret, it spread within the ex-samurai and his soba cooking wife's family and secretly passed down to each generation. But when Imperial Westernization in the 19th century began, the samurai class and shoguns were dismissed as warriors. Castles were dismantled ... destroyed was more like it, and the castle cooks and other servants were turned out to the streets."

"And some of the samurai became poor merchants and farmers. The lucky ones joined the imperial court as politicians." The blond boy smiled proudly.

"Right," said the blogger while rolling his eyes. "So, with no further loyalty to the local dismantled shogunate, Wanko Soba popped up everywhere." He clapped his hands. "And that's the history of the Castle Kitchen Cross. Now, how about we all go across the street and enjoy some Wanko Soba!" The blogger received a round of applause as he passed out his business card.

Ariko stepped forward and took one. "I have a question," Ariko asked in Japanese, although his talk had been in English.

"I'm sorry, I wish I understood. I'm ashamed to say I don't speak the language."

"I was just wondering what happened to the family that cooked in the kitchen." Ariko shifted into speaking English.

He raised both palms upward. "That's a good question. My next blog will be all about the Wanko Soba, but maybe I should do one on the family. Although that may be more history than cultural entertainment, which is what I write."

Ariko pulled the souvenir sword from her pocket. "And what happened to the sword?" She pointed to the cross.

"Is that a cross or a scratch?" He squinted, then ran a finger across the etching. "Interesting. Nope, I never heard what happened to the sword. If there really was one." Handing it back, he waved the group out of the kitchen area. "Come on, people, follow me."

Ariko rushed home. "Hatsuko!" She called.

Twelve

"Ariko-chan, I'm so glad you are here. Hurry, please. Obaachan is ill. She wants to see you." Hatsuko called from the top of the stairs.

Removing her shoes, Ariko started up the stairs, but her uncle came round the corner. He scowled at her, but she brushed past him in a hurry to join Hatsuko. At the sound of footsteps behind her, she turned to see her uncle was also following her.

"Please, she's waiting." Hatsuko opened the shoji door to Obaachan's room and ushered Ariko in.

Her great-grandmother lay on a futon instead of sitting at the kotatsu. A kerosene heater hummed by her side. She rolled over and coughed into a tissue, crumpled in her hand.

Hatsuko quickly scooped up the soiled tissues on the tatami and left the room.

When the coughing stopped, Obaachan sat up on one elbow.

Ariko wondered how her thin arms could support her body, although there wasn't much to her slender frame. "Ariko-chan, I must know. What are your plans? Will you stay here in Japan?"

Ariko shivered. The kerosene heater did nothing to warm the room, but it was more than the physical cold. She noted the old house. If

Obaachan had moved to a modern house, perhaps her sickness wouldn't have overtaken her. Yet, she knew that old families stayed in their old homes. "I would like to stay in Japan and restore my father's shop."

Obaachan grew rigid, then struggled to sit up.

Ariko reached forward but was waved off. "Stop this nonsense, Ariko-chan. If a restaurant is what you want, I need help with the Shio Soba. Hiroshi cannot handle it alone, and you may have some of your father's business sense."

"No. I do not. I think I can reopen Ajiwau with the help of some of the neighbors, but—"

A gnarled, wrinkled hand stopped her. "You have family. There is no need to enlist strangers. If you stay and help with the family business, I will write you into the will. You will own not just one store, but many— half of what we own. Hiroshi will retain the other half. Right now, that is five stores for each of you."

A clattering sounded outside the room. They stopped and Obaachan waved Ariko to investigate.

When she reached the doors, she slid them open and peered out. Her uncle was just descending the stairs with heavy footsteps.

Ariko didn't know why, but she felt obligated to protect him. Returning to her great-grandmother, she shrugged, but Obaachan was an astute woman.

"It was probably my grandson. If he heard about the will, you must be careful."

Ariko's heart raced. This was not what she wanted. "Suimasen, Obaachan. I'm so very grateful, but I know little of running a business."

"What of this Watanabe Corporation?"

Ariko gasped. *How did Obaachan know about them?* Ariko thought of Benjamin Trudell and was sure her great-grandmother would have nothing to do with him.

"They can help, can't they? Hiroshi told me a little about them. He said they could make our restaurants run more efficiently. I'm not looking to expand. I don't think my grandson is capable of running more stores. I care for him, but he has failed the family business. I don't want to lose what we have." Her rheumy eyes stared back at Ariko. "If only I had not banished your father. He would have helped his brother, and he still could have promoted his religion. I think now I would have allowed him to do so."

"He didn't want to do that. Obaachan, you don't understand. Our faith is not one to be propagated, but to be shared because we have a wonderful loving God, who deserves our loyalty and devotion."

"Enough. You do not need to tell me who your God is. I know all about Him."

Obaachan knew about Jesus? How could that be? Ariko searched Obaachan's face. Her great-grandmother, the only family she had left. Her eyes glazed past her and rested on the family shrine behind. Ariko's brow furrowed, but a flicker of hope arose. A seed had been planted somewhere, and Ariko's heart leaped at the chance to find out. But now was not the time.

"Ariko?" Obaachan clapped her hands.

Snapping back to attention, Ariko bowed. "Gomenaisi. Hai."

"Tell me what you discussed at the meeting? I don't think Hiroshi told me everything."

"What did he tell you?"

"He told me he had an investor. But I want nothing to do with him."

"Yes, I met him. But without funding, you cannot afford Watanabe Corporation. Perhaps there are smaller businesses that can help if it's just streamlining some processes."

"Do you think I am poor? You talk with Watanabe, leave Hiroshi out. Find out the costs. Not for expanding. I only wish to see where we can save on the modernization process—perhaps ordering and keeping financial accounts. I don't want to cut anything having to do with the noodles or broth, but we shall return to the old recipe, regardless of cost. Shio noodles were the original Wanko soba. Did you know that?"

Ariko's eyes widened. She had just heard the story and recalled the booklet she'd bought at the castle. She nodded.

"Oh, so you know. Did your father tell you the legend of the Wanko Soba? Probably not. Things like that weren't important to him. All he cared about was his God. Never mind, we don't need the Wanko name. Shio Soba had quality, not cheap legends. And we must restore it."

Restore. Ariko liked her great-grandmother's choice of words.

Perhaps the planted seed would restore faith in Obaachan, and Ariko prayed it was there. It had to be. Each new day brought revelations from her Obaachan, and this surpassed them all. Her great-grandmother had said she knew all about God. *How?*

As old as she was, her mind was sharp. Perhaps this was where Ariko's father had inherited his shrewd business skills. But Ariko didn't care about that. And now, all she'd learned that afternoon with the blogger filled her mind as Obaachan mentioned Wanko Soba.

Obaachan went into a coughing fit. She grabbed the tissue box then pointed to a teapot on the coffee table.

Ariko poured hot tea into a cup and handed it to Obaachan.

Through short spans of breath, Obaachan instructed Ariko to leave and have Hatsuko bring up dinner in thirty minutes.

When Ariko entered the kitchen downstairs, Hatsuko stood at a frying pan. She sauteed tofu, cabbage, and other vegetables, coating them lightly in oil. She turned.

"Hatsuko, Obaachan would like dinner in thirty minutes. But I am worried about her. Shouldn't someone stay by her side?"

"Yes, but what she commands is what we must honor. I will do as she says."

"What do you know about Wanko Soba and the samurai sword with the cross on the hilt?" Ariko blurted.

Hatsuko placed a flat lid on the frying pan, turning the knob to reduce the flame. "What do you know?"

"I heard a legend today. About an ex-samurai and the cross in the kitchen at the castle. The shogun and the cook who concocted this Wanko soba that's so famous in Morioka. I'm so confused. Do we have anything to do with it? Hatsuko, the sword, the one in that room, does it have a cross on the—"

"That is for your great-grandmother to share," Hatsuko said.

Thirteen

Frustrated at the silence about the legend and her family, Ariko busied herself at Ajiwau. The landlord had come by and given her a ninety-day notice, and for that, she was grateful. Christmas was approaching, and she wanted to open it on Christmas Eve.

With hands on her hips, she nodded. It was just about ready. Her cell rang, and she fumbled through her purse. It was Emiko.

"My father is dying!" Emiko cried through the phone. Distraught, she didn't know what to do.

"Text me the address. I'm on my way."

Thankfully the bus system hadn't changed much since she'd lived there, and Ariko found her way to the hospital. As she rushed in and found the room, she stopped short.

Kai stood there, his back to her.

Ariko froze in the doorway.

Emiko ran over and pulled Ariko to the bedside where her mother sat sobbing while holding her husband's hand. Slowly, she raised her head and wiped her tears. "Shio-san, thank you for coming," said Mrs. Tanaka.

Kai turned, and his eyes widened. Before he could speak, Mrs. Tanaka continued.

"This is my employer, Watanabe-san."

Ariko bowed at the same time as Kai, but she couldn't take her eyes off him. "Employer?" she finally asked.

"Yes. I work office catering events at the Watanabe building, and Mr. Watanabe is always so kind to me."

Ariko's brow furrowed. *Did she work in Tokyo?* Emiko said that her mother worked two jobs, but that was crazy. Tokyo is six hours away. And she wondered what Kai was doing in Morioka again. Her heart raced, and she struggled to keep her attention on the need at hand. "How is Tanaka-san?"

Emiko whined, "Not good. He never took care of himself, and he suffered a great heart attack."

After four years in America, Ariko learned that hugging was a great comfort. In Japan, it was an intrusion, so instead, she placed a hand on Emiko's shoulder, but Emiko immediately wrapped her arms around Ariko and sobbed. *She is only thirteen years old, of course she'd hug.*

"Tanaka-san." Kai turned toward the mother, away from Ariko. "If there is anything you need, I will provide. Anything at all."

"Prayer," Emiko whispered. She wiped her nose on her sleeve and pulled away from Ariko, looking at her. Though she was young, they were at eye level, as Ariko was relatively small. Emiko took Ariko's hand. "Can you pray for my father? Please?"

Ariko's lips formed a tight line, and she asked, "Kai...Watanabe-san, will you pray?"

Emiko and her mother gasped.

"No. Suimasen, please forgive us. We could not ask you." Emiko's mother bowed.

Kai smiled at Ariko. "Yes, it would be an honor."

"Wait, do you know Jesus? Do you pray to our Christian God?" Emiko's brows furrowed.

"Emiko-chan. Silence." Her mother hissed.

Raising a hand, Kai nodded. "I do. I am Christian." He glanced down at Emiko's father. "Is your father?"

Shaking her head, Emiko spoke. "No, and neither is she." She pointed to her mother.

"Do you mind if I pray?" Kai directed his question to the mother.

She bowed deeply. "Domo."

"God, we ask for Tanaka-san's healing. Bring peace to the family and reveal your son to them all. Amen."

Emiko cried, and her mother wept, draping herself over her husband lying still in the bed.

Motioning Ariko to follow him, Kai pointed to the door. He led her to an empty waiting area where she found a window seat and walked over. The falling snow sparkled against the city's Christmas lights, and Ariko's heart warmed over Kai's prayers. *Had she misjudged him?* His eyes were kind, and he had shown such compassion coming here all the way from Tokyo for an employee. She didn't know anyone who would have done the same. Her gaze lingered, and she couldn't help but take a deep breath.

"Ariko, can we begin over?" He slapped black leather gloves in his hands. "I know we just met, and many things have transpired. Too many misunderstandings, but I would like to get to know you better. You are kind and loyal." He smiled. "And you are a Christian."

Thoughts jumbled in her brain, and Ariko blurted, "What are you doing in Morioka?"

"Looking for you. I leave for America tomorrow, and I couldn't leave without seeing you. But I got word that Tanaka-san's husband took ill, and since I was in Morioka, I rushed here. It looks like God brought us together...again...Neh?"

He swung his arms wide. "Besides, what are the chances that we'd meet here. Ariko, it had to be Him." He pointed up.

"Our faith? Are you talking about our faith?"

"Yes. Most importantly, that. I spend most of my time in America, and when I come here, that is what's lacking in my life. I know it now."

"Do you not attend church in Japan?"

He hung his head low, and his chin almost rested on his chest. "No, I'm sorry to say, I've never found a church home here. I'm always too busy with work and family commitments when I come back into town."

"So your home is not here." Ariko's stomach flipped. Japan was to be her home now.

"Not now, but I could change that. I'd seriously love to consider it." His dark eyes locked onto hers, and he lowered his body into the chair next to her. "Ariko, I'd like very much for us to think about a relationship, or at least..." He scooted to the edge of his seat. "At least spend some time together and see."

See? See what, she wanted to ask? But at that moment, spending time with him, being with him, was precisely what she wanted. Her body responded to his words, and Ariko felt as if a magnet pulled her to him.

His eyes explored her face, resting on her lips. Their faces drew close, and her heart pounded. Gently, his lips barely brushed hers. As his hands squeezed her shoulders, she felt as if her heart would burst.

A child screamed behind them. Ariko didn't know who pulled away first, but heat rose on her cheeks, and Kai stood. The mother struggled to calm the child while bowing again and again toward Kai and Ariko.

"Suimasen," *I'm sorry*, she said. The small child continued to throw a fit.

Kai politely excused the intrusion and turned back to Ariko. He drew a hand through his black hair. "Ariko, I must leave tonight for America. I have a late flight, but I'm serious about us."

Us? She'd just met the man, but she wanted there to be an *us*.

"May I please have your phone number again?" Kai asked.

Ariko removed her scarf and bristled at the sweat dripping down her neck. She wanted to discard her coat as well. She wished the hospital temperature wasn't so high, despite the snow falling outside. Thoughts swirled through her mind, not the least of which was Lily. *Who was the woman? Perhaps she should find out and give Kai a chance.* She searched his face. She thought of her great-grandmother, who wanted Ariko to pursue communications with the Watanabes. *Would this jeopardize or help?*

Ariko extended her hand. "Give me your phone. I'll insert my number." *Why not a second chance?* She liked Kai from the moment she met him. the chance of finding a Japanese Christian man...even as a friend in Japan, was pretty near impossible.

He handed her his phone with a smile, and she tapped in her number. When she handed back the phone, he wrapped his hands over hers. The electricity of his touch coursed through her fingertips.

Ariko closed her eyes, wondering how this could happen. It was not why she came back to Japan. She pulled her hand away.

Silence enveloped them, and moments later he spoke. "Please hear me out. I'm leaving tonight. Lily and I have some—"

"Lily?" Ariko's mouth gaped, and she stood. She grabbed her scarf, and her hardened eyes glared back. "Lily? You're asking for my phone number, and you're travelling with her to America?"

Kai pocketed the phone. "Please, you don't understand."

Ariko thrust her hand out. "May I please have your phone?"

"Can I please explain?"

Ariko wriggled her fingers at him.

He blew out an exasperated sigh and removed his cell phone from his coat pocket. His lips pursed. "You don't understand."

Don't understand? All Ariko's doubts returned. All her questions arose. She didn't have time for this. His life. Her life. They were too different. Their worlds would never unite. "There are many things I don't understand, and it's not just Lily. I don't understand why you have an interest in small businesses. Small noodle shops specifically. Yet your company takes them over."

"That's not completely accurate."

"And what a coincidence that you met me near my home, six hours away from Tokyo. Had my uncle contacted you about me?"

"I'd never met your uncle until the Christmas party."

"And what about Trudell-san?"

"I told you. I met him briefly after he met with our Acquisition's Director. It was in passing."

"Well, perhaps that's where we are, in passing. Don't bother to call my number. I won't answer."

Ariko grabbed her purse and left the waiting room. She checked in on the Tanakas but decided against disturbing them. As she turned, Kai stood behind her. She brushed past, but he didn't stop her. Reaching the elevator, she turned but he was no longer there.

Fourteen

Ariko's cell rang as she stepped from the elevator.

"It's your obaachan," Hatsuko's shrill voice cried.

Ariko gasped, hearing that Obaachan was in the ER at the same hospital. She rushed to find them.

"Hatsuko, what happened?" cried Ariko.

Hatsuko wrung her hands together. "I took her soba. She ate well then said she wanted to sleep. An hour later, I checked on her and couldn't wake her."

"What did the doctors say?"

"They ran tests, and we are waiting. It could be her diabetes."

Ariko's eyes widened. "Obaachan is diabetic?" She wanted to ask why soba noodles and rice were still in her diet, but she refrained.

Hatsuko's sweet face, contorted with sobs, nodded back at her.

Taking Hatsuko's hand, Ariko prayed, and Hatsuko agreed in asking for Obaachan's healing. Ariko added a prayer for salvation, and Obaachan's eyes fluttered open.

Hatsuko's eyes widened in fright, and Ariko caught a gasp in her throat as she said Amen.

Obaachan looked at Hatsuko, then at Ariko. She took her hand.

"Thank you, my great-granddaughter." Her lips turned up in what appeared to be a smile, but her eyes closed. "It's time I returned."

Ariko stole a glance at Hatsuko whose wide eyes no longer showed fright but joy.

Returned? Could she possibly be talking about faith? Ariko dared not ask as it seemed her great-grandmother had slipped into a light sleep.

A doctor rapped on the door and walked in. He reported that her diabetes numbers were way off, and they would admit her to a room and keep her overnight.

Hatsuko hugged Ariko, and she warmed at the natural bond between believers. Ariko slipped into the hallway and ran into her uncle.

He bowed but swept past her as she pointed to where Obaachan lay.

Ariko leaned against the wall and lowered her head as tears slipped down her face. She couldn't lose Obaachan now. Fear gripped her, and she recalled how just moments earlier Kai had comforted the Tanakas. She needed him. A feeling drew her, and she peered down the end of the long hallway. Kai stood there, and everything inside her melted.

She burst into tears, and he came to her, grasping her shoulders and pulling her close.

"It's my great-grandmother." Ariko's head cocked toward the ER. "I think she'll be all right, but I'm so scared. I just lost my father, and I have no one but her."

"What?" Kai's voice choked. "Ariko, you never told me that. When?"

"That's why I'm here. My great-grandmother summoned me after his funeral, and she wanted me to help run the business, but..." She remembered to whom she was talking and stiffened. She pulled away. "Everything happened so fast between us."

Hiroshi dashed from the room and skidded to a halt upon seeing Ariko and Kai. He bowed. "Watanabe-san. What are you doing here?" He didn't wait for an answer. "Ariko-chan, come quickly. Obaachan wants to see you."

Without a glance, Ariko left. "Obaachan. How are you feeling?"

Hatsuko sat in a corner chair, dabbing her eyes.

"I will be fine. They will stabilize me, and I'll return home tomorrow. But we must attend to business. Hiroshi? Where did he go?"

"Obaachan, please. It can wait."

"No, it cannot. Hiroshi?" She called again.

He entered, motioning behind him. Kai's tall frame filled the doorway.

"Obaachan, Watanabe-san is here."

Narrowing her eyes, Obaachan glared at her grandson. "I'm not even dead, and you are ready for a takeover?"

"No. Watanabe-san was visiting someone here," Ariko said.

Kai walked forward. "Shio-san. I apologize. I'm sorry you are ill."

"I'm fine. I don't know what's happening here but tell me what plans my grandson has for our restaurants."

Kai's eyes shifted from Ariko to her great-grandmother, but the doctor walked in silencing anything he might have said.

"Shio-san, respectfully, you must rest, and all these people must leave. Your room is ready, and we'll be transporting you."

"Leave us for one moment." She waved the doctor off, but he remained.

"Please, you must comply," said the doctor.

Kai nodded to the doctor but spoke to Ariko's great-grandmother. "Shio-san, you have my word. Nothing will transpire between our companies until I can meet with you." He glanced at Ariko. "I'll return just after the New Year, and we'll talk then."

New Year? Ariko couldn't help but think that meant he'd be spending it with Lily. Closing her eyes, she shook her head. Rising tall, she bowed to her great-grandmother. "We will all leave so that the doctor can take care of you. I will ready things at home." She turned. "Hatsuko, will you stay with Obaachan?"

"Of course."

Ariko, Kai, and Hiroshi left the room. Ariko couldn't exit fast enough, but Kai called her name.

"Ariko, I'll call you."

Her uncle frowned. "Call her? But I'm the one with whom you'll be discussing our plans. If you have a moment, perhaps we can have tea."

Ariko heard her uncle's words and kept walking. Tears streaked her cheeks as she left the hospital.

Fifteen

Obaachan returned home the next day, and over the next week she settled into her routine. With Hatsuko attending her, Ariko was free to spend her days readying Ajiwau. One morning before leaving, her great-grandmother summoned her.

When Ariko entered the chambers, she was surprised to see Obaachan with color in her cheeks. Layers of kimonos covered by a chanko padded her slight frame. She stood with a cane.

"You look well," Ariko said.

"I am well, and I want to go out."

Ariko frowned.

"Why are you making that face? Are you telling me, no? We will go to the castle."

"But it's Christmas Eve." Ariko's lips tightened. She had planned a small service with Emiko and the neighborhood people at her father's shop. An older man, a friend of her father's, had returned and offered to lead the small group in celebrating the Savior's birth. Ariko checked her watch. It was still early. Perhaps there was time.

"Precisely why I want to go to the castle. Call Hatsuko. She will help me down the stairs."

Ariko bowed and did as she was told, though hesitant. She'd never seen her great-grandmother descend the stairs. It was the emergency crew that had brought her down to take her to the hospital previously.

Hatsuko hurried in, shaking her head. She muttered that they had no choice but to do as they were told.

When the front door opened at the bottom of the stairwell, it startled Obaachan, who faltered.

"Obaachan!" Ariko's uncle yelled.

Obaachan dropped onto the bottom stair. Her eyes widened, but soon a smile, then a laugh broke out. "Hiroshi. Are you trying to be rid of me already?" She laughed as she clutched her chest.

"You should be in bed. You are ill. Let me help you."

"No, Hiroshi. What are you doing here?"

His face reddened and his head hung low, while he stared at the floor. "Hatsuko-san, Ariko-chan. Domo, *please,* may I have a word with Obaachan?"

Ariko glanced at Hatsuko whose wide-eyed expression mirrored Ariko's surprise at her uncle's respectful tone. They stepped outside, but before Ariko slid the door shut, she saw her uncle on his knees before Obaachan. Ariko called a cab and waited.

By the time the cab arrived, Hiroshi helped his grandmother out the door. They acknowledged one another and bowed.

Obaachan's eyes watered, and a slight smile raised on her face. "Thank you, grandson. We will make this work." She pinched his arm. "You will make this work, and Ariko will help."

Arriving at Morioka Castle, they moved slowly from the cab to the entrance. Christmas Eve was like any other winter day at the castle. Not a holiday, so schools were not out yet. The grounds were populated with a few tourists and local visitors but no crowds of children on field trips.

As they ambled past the souvenir stand, Obaachan turned and made her way over. Searching the baskets and shelves, she dug through the baskets that Ariko had found days before. The ones Kai had shown her. Obaachan picked up a stone cross, a tiny toy sword, and the booklet that read Wanko Soba. She paid for the items, tucked them into her shopping bag, and turned back to the entrance. The high granite walls seemed to guide them as they made their way up and around. Stopping so Obaachan could rest. The drip-drip of snow falling from the stark trees tapped out an unsynchronized yet melodious tune.

She stood and pointed with her cane. "Around that corner."

Ariko's eyes rounded. "The kitchen?"

Smiling, Obaachan nodded.

Looking at her great-grandmother's shaking hands, Ariko grasped them. *Did Obaachan know of the cross in the kitchen?* Ariko held back hopes that her great-grandmother might have believed at one time. She watched as Obaachan seemed to grow stronger as she approached the kitchen walls. The legend of many Japanese Christians turning apostate due to the persecution was well-known. More turned than were martyred. Yet, Obaachan wasn't ancient. The Christian faith was not persecuted in modern times, though certainly frowned upon.

Once inside the kitchen ruins, Obaachan made her way to the wall and brushed aside leafless branches snaking across the granite. Her shaking hand swept over the cross carving. Her legs faltered.

Hatsuko rushed over and led her to a stone bench close by.

Obaachan stared until tears ran down her cheeks. Her face wrinkled so that her eyes and lips disappeared. Her head dropped to her chest, and she mumbled, "I'm sorry. I'm so sorry. Jesus, I am sorry. Please take me back."

Ariko rushed to her side. Hatsuko's face was streaked as she mopped it with a crumpled tissue. Ariko waved her over. The huddle remained until Obaachan flung off the tight band of arms around her.

"Ariko-chan?" She pulled out the bought items.

Ariko remained silent, not disclosing that she had previously bought the same souvenirs.

"Let me tell you a story," said Obaachan.

She laid out the items on the bench between her and Hatsuko and began repeating the words that the blogger had shared with his crowd a week ago. Only the stories were more detailed. She went on at length and then dropped the bombshell. "This ex-samurai was my great, great, great grandfather. And his wife created Wanko soba. They spread Jesus' love to those who came to the kitchen, but sadly, I was the generation that stopped Christianity in our family." Obaachan's rheumy eyes stared at Ariko.

"I fell in love with a rich man. One who wanted to help expand our family soba business. We never called it Wanko Soba, but it was the same, and ours was the best." She sniffed and cleared her throat. "Perhaps, because of me, it is no longer. I blamed Hiroshi, and although your father built us up, my lack of faith, my apostasy, cost us too much."

Ariko didn't know what to say. Who was she to know the way God worked in the lives of believers and non-believers? She trusted that whatever he did, it was for good. And she knew he was a good God that had her best interests at heart. "It does not matter, Obaachan. All that matters is that you have returned."

Obaachan patted Ariko's hand. A softness that Ariko had not received from her, ever. "Oh, but it does matter. You see, I fell in love with a good Christian man. I wanted to marry him, but my father would disown me. My mother taught me the faith, but my father never embraced it, so I let the man I loved go." She sniffed but pulled herself straight. "And I married a rich unbeliever, and I left my faith. I was angry at God. So, my children and grandchildren, your father and uncle, knew nothing of Jesus. Not until your father went to an American Christian concert and met your mother."

"So he never knew the legend? His history?"

"Maybe. Maybe not. But I buried it. And when my husband died, and your grandparents died, all I had left was your father and uncle. I could not live with losing him to Jesus, so I pushed him away. I banished him." Obaachan dabbed at her eyes. "But God had other plans. Your father still found his way to Jesus." She took Ariko's chin in her palm. "And you, you will continue the faith in the Shio family. We will never leave Him again." Admiration held her eyes. "As he has never left or forsaken..." her voice cracked, "me."

Ariko enveloped her great-grandmother and Hatsuko. A few moments later, she pulled away.

"Wait a minute. The sword? Is that for real?" asked Ariko.

Obaachan's eyes sparkled. "Of course! And I have it. Perhaps we can display it at Ajiwau?"

"My father's shop. You'll allow me to..."

"Allow you? I will supply all you need. Although, with all the fine buildings we have, I don't know why you need to continue in that one."

"Well, I'm not sure that I can. The owner has only given me ninety days."

Obaachan waved a hand. "I will buy the building from him, and you will pray and ask God's guidance for Shio Soba."

Ariko gave her great-grandmother a slight nudge. "*You* will pray, Obaachan, and ask God's guidance. He will show *you*."

Obaachan patted Ariko's hand, then reached over to squeeze Hatsuko's. "Yes, *I* will pray. Now, I am hungry. Let's go have Wanko soba."

Sixteen

"There is a small cafe across the street, but they may be closing soon. It's Christmas Eve," Ariko said.

"That will not stop them. This is Japan. Let's go." Obaachan stomped her cane.

Hatsuko and Ariko helped Obaachan out of the castle grounds across the street to the Wanko Soba shop. So many people milled about, and a line formed outside. Pictures adorned the window of customers with bowls piled high.

"What's going on here?" Obaachan asked.

Some young people laughed and jostled one another. "Don't you know? They pay you a prize if you can eat the greatest number of soba bowls here."

Ariko frowned. *Gluttony? They pay for that?* She refrained from judging, but her great-grandmother didn't.

"Ah, so it must not be so good that you swallow noodles whole without tasting the broth. That you only come for the prize."

"It's all right. Better than that chain, Shio Soba. It's not very good," a young man quipped.

Ariko's mouth dropped, and she darted a glance at Obaachan. Her heart melted at her grandmother's saddened face.

An elderly man leaning over his cane piped up. "It used to be excellent. Many, many years ago, Shio Soba was the best. I don't know what happened."

Obaachan leaned against the building. Her shoulders sagged. "Suimasen, Ariko-chan, please take me home."

"Yes, Obaachan. Shall we stop somewhere else? You must eat."

Her great-grandmother rose up. "Yes, Take me to your Ajiwau. You will make me soba." She nudged her cane at Hatsuko. "Shall we stop at the market first?"

"Suimasen, but Ajiwau is not open for business."

Ariko had prepared just enough noodles and broth for the Christmas Eve service and the few people attending, but she hadn't counted on her great-grandmother coming. She darted a glance at Hatsuko, who smiled.

"Loaves and fishes," Hatsuko said. "God will provide."

Ariko examined her watch. "Yes, Obaachan. Let's go to Ajiwau."

Hatsuko hailed a cab, and they drove in happy silence to Ariko's father's shop. The lights were on, and the outer wooden door slid aside. Emiko and the others must have opened up for her. She had given Emiko a key. Tanaka-san's recovery was better than expected, and Emiko had been helping Ariko to prepare for Christmas Eve.

As Obaachan exited the taxi, she peered at the shop's shining glass window and read aloud. "Ajiwau," *savor*, she whispered. "Very appropriate. Now we shall see if it is true."

Ariko bowed and led her Obaachan across the steps covering the gutter. She half-expected her to cover her nose at the smell from the stale water that ran through the ditches outside this poorer section of town. But her great-grandmother did no such thing, simply stepping into the threshold.

An associate of Ariko's father greeted them. He was dressed in a dark suit, white shirt, and tie, and he gripped a Bible in one hand. He bowed deeply toward Obaachan and pulled out a chair for her and Hatsuko. Emiko and her mother stood behind the counter, waving. They wore white scarves on their heads, ready to serve soba.

Ariko peeked around the room and gasped when she saw Emiko's father sitting at a table too. He was pale and weak, but he bowed his head and nodded with a smile. Ariko said a quick prayer of thanks for his recovery. A few neighbors sat at tables, and the tiny café all but overflowed.

The man with the Bible waved a hand toward a guitar that stood in the corner. It was her father's, and Ariko walked over and picked it up. She began strumming "Silent Night," and a few voices around the room sang in Japanese. Her eyes locked with her great-grandmother's, whose mouth barely moved, but Ariko heard the shaky voice. In the last verse, the voice grew louder as she sang, *Christ the Savior is born*. Her eyes twinkled with wetness, and she bent a deep nod toward Ariko.

Laying aside the guitar, Ariko bowed toward her father's associate.

He explained to the small band of believers they would eat first, then worship after. Praying, he asked God's blessing over the food, and Ariko approached the counter to help serve.

Hatsuko joined Mrs. Tanaka in the kitchen and dished up the steaming savory soba.

Placing a bowl in front of her great-grandmother, Ariko held her breath.

Obaachan picked up her ohashi, *chopsticks*, and slurped a few noodles. Her eyes widened, and she nodded. "Oishi." *So tasty!*

The real test was the broth, and Ariko's brows arched as she clenched her hands together.

Obaachan picked up her bowl and blew on the hot soup, tipping it to her mouth. She pursed her lips and sipped the savory soup. Lowering the bowl, she removed her hands and clasped them together. Finally, she peered up at Ariko and nodded. "Pafekuto." *Perfect.*

Ariko swiped her eyes. She'd never seen her great-grandmother grin so broadly. More faces smiled, and she listened to the cheerful chatter. There were no Christmas decorations, but they weren't needed. The spirit of the Lord embellished all their hearts, and the small gathering was as eager to hear the Christmas story as they were to eat the Ajiwau Soba.

The door opened, and a whoosh of cold air flurried in. Ariko turned and stiffened.

Hiroshi and Kai Watanabe stood at the door. Her uncle bowed and humbly asked if they could join.

Obaachan waved him over.

Kai stayed by the door, staring at Ariko.

Emiko walked over. "Dozo, Watanabe-san. Come sit down. I'll get you a bowl."

"Arigato-gozimashta," *Thank you very much*. "But I won't be long."

Emiko frowned. "Oh, you won't stay for a bowl of soba and the service?"

"Well, that depends." Kai gazed at Ariko but nodded to the door.

"Ah. I see. Go, Ariko. We have this covered." Emiko winked and nudged Ariko to join Kai, who already had one foot out the door.

Ariko followed, and her insides felt like the soba noodles. As a blast of cold air hit her, she turned toward the shop.

Kai laid a hand on her arm. "Domo?"

Without looking at him, she said, "Kai. I'm very busy with my family. My Obaachan needs me, and I can't navigate a complicated relationship right now." She almost scowled at how American she sounded.

"I can't either. That's why I need to explain. Please listen to me. Lily's family and mine have a business relationship. I have no interest in her, and she has a boyfriend in the states. We were going back to explain to her parents that our relationship was not personal and never would be."

Butterflies floated in Ariko's stomach. "And what of my uncle and Trudell-san?"

Kai stuck his hands in his pockets, and his gaze hardened. "Ariko, did you really think I lied to you? When I said I loved the small shops, I meant it. My dream is to use my skills to help them come up to speed to run more efficiently, so they can sustain a small business in this crazy world of franchises. I'm leaving Watanabe Corporation to start my own company. I convinced your uncle to cut Trudell-san off, and Shio Soba is my first client."

Ariko swallowed hard, ashamed of how she misjudged Kai.

"Do you believe me?" Kai shook his head. "Because if you don't, I'm leaving right now. I'll work with your uncle, but I'll never bother you again." He pulled his hands from his pockets and threw them in the air. "My gosh, how that pains me to say that. I thought you were the one."

Ariko giggled inside. She wanted to laugh at his exasperation.

His dark eyes almost burned into her. "I meant it. I admire your honor and respect for your family. But most importantly, I love your faith. I haven't ever found anyone quite like you."

She couldn't believe how God was working things out. It couldn't be more...

"Pafekuto!" Ariko yelled but quickly covered her mouth, surprised at her own outburst.

"Suimasen?" *Excuse me?*

Ariko grabbed his hands and squeezed. "Gomenasai, Kai-chan." *I'm sorry.* "You're right. I think God brought you into my life, and I'd like..." A snow flurry swirled, and Ariko could barely see Kai in front of her.

He pulled her under the eaves of Ajiwau and wrapped his arms around her. He squeezed her tightly and gazed down. A current seemed to pull them closer.

His perfect hair and sparkling eyes mesmerized her, but it was his parted lips that drew her. She closed her eyes and felt the warmth of his mouth on hers. Her insides exploded like fireworks, and she wanted his sweet kiss to last forever.

He pulled away, and she gulped, breathless. Kai chuckled and searched her face. His hands moved to cup her cheeks, and the pressure of his soft lips melted onto hers.

The door whooshed open. Ariko tried to pull away, but Kai held her close.

"Ah! I caught you two. Come on in. Sensei is about to start the service. You can kiss later." Emiko laughed but closed the door behind her.

The lingering smell of delicious broth hung in the air, and Kai shivered. "I'd love to stay out here and kiss you all night, but that hot soba is calling my name." He laughed, then wrinkled his nose. "Besides, the smell out here is not so great."

Ariko punched his arm lightly.

Kai breathed deep. "I've been waiting a long time for someone like you, Ariko."

"Oh, it's probably just my soba you want."

"Well, if it's as good as everyone says, that's a big plus." A serious expression drew across his face. "I have no doubt that God brought us together at the castle." He kissed her forehead. "Say, I did a little digging about that castle where we met. More specifically, the kitchen. The legend is pretty amazing. There was a Christian samurai from centuries ago, and legend has it that he had a sword with a cross engraved on it. Can you imagine? But it's never been recovered. Anyway, like I said, we have a lot in common, the castle being one of them."

"Oh, you have no idea." Ariko squeezed Kai's arm. "Come on, let's have soba and talk about that legend."

He wrapped his arms around her once more and kissed the tip of her nose. "Merry Christmas, Ariko."

"Merry Christmas, Kai."

The End

Author's Note

I love it when I find out there is truth to a story. Although The Cross At Morioka Castle is fiction, some fascinating facts exist.

Years ago, my missionary sons took me to Morioka Castle ruins. And they are ruins. Massive granite walls, broken down blocks, and stone steps everywhere. Still, as I walked the quiet grounds, I couldn't help but think of what might have transpired there. My imagination took hold, and I wanted more. Sadly, I learned that many castles in Japan were destroyed at the end of the feudal age (1868), and others were lost in World War II.

The history of Morioka Castle is fact, and there is some truth to the bits of the narrative by the tour guide and the little boy tourist. But the accurate history ends with the Nambu Clan, and their loyalty to the Tokugawa shogunate during the Edo period.

Regarding the Christian Samurai element, a small minority of people, including samurai, embraced Christianity, and it was tolerated, but not as far back as the banished samurai in our story. He and his wife and their soba cooking are purely my imagination.

The quirky Wanko Soba is actually a legend with some truth. Which legend is debatable, so I chose the one I thought you might enjoy. And the restaurant that posts the winners who slurp the most bowls of soba? That's for real, in Morioka, and quite the tourist attraction.

I wish the cross in the kitchen was true, but that came as I remembered wandering the ruins years ago. The serene eeriness of the park made me stop at every statue, wall, step, and bridge. It made me wonder. Who were the people that lived here? Did any of them know Jesus? And if they did, what did it cost them? I knew the answer for many.

Centuries ago, persecution against Christians in Japan was so horrific that I often wonder if the stigma of turning away from Shinto or Buddhism remains. Though the Japanese have freedom of religion, less than 1% embrace Christianity in Japan. My sons and missionaries like them in Japan serve for years and years with little growth, but they plant seeds, trusting in our sovereign God who propels them to continue to the task they've been called. Like Isaiah said, *"And I heard the voice of the Lord saying, "Whom shall I send, and who will go for us?" Then I said, "Here I am! Send me."* I'm blessed and honored that my sons answered the call.

My mother was reached for Christ by missionaries who came to Okinawa (Japan) before WWII. As a young teen, she worked for the missionaries, cleaning, cooking, and helping with their children. She was one of the few of all her family and friends who received Christ as her savior. After the war, only one-third of the native Okinawans survived. My mother was one of them. Hallelujah for those missionaries and the Lord's protection over her. Her legacy of faith touches our entire family.

When I was asked to join the Keeping Christmas Novella collection, I knew Morioka Castle Ruins in Iwate, Japan would be my castle. The difficulty was Christmas and Christianity in Japan. But the hope of Jesus Christ reigns, whether in Japan or the darkest, most persecuted countries in the world. I prayed that the Lord would give me a story of faith. I hope you've enjoyed this novella about an unlikely Christmas romance in an unfamiliar setting, but most importantly, a story of God's redemptive work that crosses all boundaries. Merry Christmas, whenever and wherever you are!

Acknowledgments

First and foremost to the Lord God Almighty who gave me life and purpose. I'm eternally grateful for His Word. To Cathleen Armstrong for reading my manuscript and always encouraging me. She is my inspiration. To my sister Margaret and her husband Walter for correcting my Japanese, and to many others who have read, edited, critiqued, and spurred me on to love and good works in this manuscript. You are my support group. A special thanks to Sandra Barela, Celebrate Lit Publishing, and Chautona Having for inviting me to participate in this collection. I am truly honored and blessed. And always to my wonderful husband, Bruce. I wouldn't be here without him. To God be all the glory.

About Kathleen J. Robison

Kathleen J. Robison is an Okinawan-American. Born in Okinawa, raised in California, Florida, Mississippi, and Singapore. Her travels are the inspirational settings for her stories. She and her Pastor husband have eight adult children. Seven are married, blessing them with fourteen grandchildren and counting. The diversity of their 31 family members provide the inspiration for more lively characters than can be imagined. Her husband grew up in the streets of Los Angeles raised by a single working mom, and that life provides fodder for many of the conflicts of her characters.

Tackling difficult life's trials with God's strength are the central theme of Kathleen's stories. She hopes to inspire her readers to trust God and with His strength, weather through and rise above trials and tragedies. If you like suspenseful stories with a thread of romance, you will enjoy Kathleen's Bay Town Series!

Learn more about Kathleen's books at: http://www. celebratelitpublishing.com/kathleen-robison/

facebook.com/kathleenjrobisonauthor

instagram.com/kathleenjrobison

bookbub.com/profile/3794692396

The Ghost of Christmas...

DENISE L. BARELA

One

Abbigayl walked down the hall, the soft light surrounding her reflecting gently off the gold frames on the wall. Her biggest dream had finally come true.

Not only was this castle the inspiration for the staple piece at her favorite theme park, but it also held a dark history that she found fascinating. She couldn't help but hope she might encounter a lingering bit of the past.

Abbigayl shook her head. That wasn't possible. Ghosts weren't real, and encountering them wasn't a possibility. She adjusted the cloak around her shoulders. *Must be a draft in here.*

Further along the hallway, noise and music filtered through the air, beckoning her to join in on the festivities. The smell of apple cider curled around her and forced a shiver down her spine. *Ugh.* It was colder than she'd thought it would be. Maybe she should have put on all the era clothes they'd provided. *That underdress looked so uncomfortable, though.*

"Hello, are you here for the Christmas celebration?"

A gasp pushed itself from her as she turned to face the owner of the voice. A portly old woman stood behind her with a gentle smile on her face.

"Yes. Sorry, I was admiring the architecture. It's absolutely beautiful." Abbi looked up at the painting next to her.

From this close, she could see the strokes of the brush across the canvas. Each little ridge told the story of how this painting was put together.

"This castle has many an interesting history. It's nice to meet someone who appreciates what makes this place so special." The woman's smile was so wide the corners of her eyes crinkled.

"It's too beautiful to not stop and admire."

She gave Abbi's shoulder a soft squeeze. "Well, come on, my dear. Let's get you some food and drink."

Abbi nodded and followed her into the warm room. There was a spread across the table with groups of guests mingling as they picked the various offerings laid out on golden platters. The aroma of meat made her mouth water as she drew closer to the table.

Someone clapped their hands, and the room fell silent. A young dark-haired man stepped into the center of the room, standing tall over those who had gathered around him. The joy he exuded seemed to light up the room as he smiled wide at everyone there. His blue eyes almost seemed to twinkle as the light danced within them. *He's certainly got the personality for this job.*

"All right, everyone!" He waved his arms toward himself, beckoning the eager crowd closer.

Abbi stood toward the back of the group. She would rather not be drawn in and noticed. She was much more comfortable just blending in.

"Welcome one and all to our tenth-annual Christmases of the Past Celebration! We endeavor to make this experience as immersive as we can for you." He smiled down at those closest to him. "I see you've all found the costumes we've laid out for you. We ask that you remain in costume as much as possible."

Pulling at the waist of her dress, Abbi sighed. *I guess this isn't the worst thing.* The dirndl fit her perfectly, and the blue accented her raven hair and dark eyes. She couldn't help but stare at herself in the mirror earlier. She didn't look anything like herself. *Maybe that's for the best.* She could hear her mother now going on and on about what a waste of money this trip was and how she would never land a man this way.

"Christmas is meant to be spent with family."

How many times had she heard that in the last few months?

The man clapped his hands again and everyone dispersed. Had she missed anything important? The group all made their way over to the food tables once more, so naturally, Abbi followed. Her stomach rumbled, and the man next to her sneered at her.

Guess he woke up and chose snobbery this morning. Abbi chastised herself. That was rather un-Christlike, and these were the little moments she was working to fix. She piled food on her plate as she went along the length of the table. There were so many different options, and they all looked amazing.

Don't you think you've taken too much? How much weight is that going to add?

Abbi halted mid-reach for the next platter of food. Her mother's words swirled in her head. She couldn't afford to gain any more weight, not if she wanted to be around her mother in peace any time soon.

She tucked herself away in a corner and nibbled away at the food she had picked. Her appetite was rather small after her mother's reminder. People mingled throughout the room, and the noisy chatter filled her ears. *What I wouldn't give for a little peace and quiet.* Would anyone miss her if she snuck away now?

The group around her seemed so happy to be here and getting to know one another. Visiting this castle had always been Abbi's dream, so why wasn't she just as excited as they were? She sighed and moved food around her plate, not bothering to finish what was left. Handing her plate to a staff member, she made her way out the door and down the hallway to her room.

The interior of this place was just as beautiful as the outside. The murals on the walls, the style of the architecture, every piece of it mesmerized her. If only she could capture this feeling in her heart and experience it for the rest of her life. She would live here if they would permit her, but that was a silly dream. Her mother had always reminded her of that when she was little. No plain little girl ever grew up to live in a castle. Cinderella was a story parents told their daughters to make them feel special even though they weren't. But Abbi already knew she wasn't special. She didn't need her mom to remind her of that.

She took in the rooms of each open doorway she passed, admiring the views that greeted her. How amazing it must be to help restore this place to its former glory. If she had the talent, this job would've been at the top of her list. Regardless, she hoped the money from her admission would be well spent helping in the one way she could.

As she reached the end of the hall, she found herself staring into a room that had been closed off that morning. Paintings covered the walls of the room, and each piece was in pristine condition. *The restoration team has done an incredible job in here.* She took in each piece of artwork as roamed around the room. What she would have given to study art, but her mother was quick to put that idea out of her head.

"*Was machst du hier drin?*"

Abbi spun around and clutched at her heart. "I'm so sorry!" She didn't know what she was apologizing for, but the words were out of her mouth before she could stop them.

The man before her had dark brown hair and vivid green eyes, not so far off from the beautiful landscape she'd passed on the way here. His face was blocky, but his jaw and chin were chiseled, and the slight hint of stubble dusted them. He was wearing a German military uniform. Did the military here provide security for this event? Maybe this room was off limits, and trouble was the last thing she wanted to be in.

"I-I didn't mean to intrude, it's just, the door was open. I thought it was okay to enter." She tucked a piece of stray ginger hair behind her ear. "I really am sorry."

His brows furrowed as he stared at her. "You don't speak German?" he asked, his accent thick.

"Um, no, I'm sorry. I don't really know German, but I did take some Japanese and Spanish classes in high school." Abbi stammered.

He tilted his head. "Spain and Japan? You don't sound like you're from either country."

Abbi laughed, scratching at her cheek. "Um, no, I'm not. I just thought Spanish would be useful, and I've always wanted to visit Japan."

He walked further into the room and stood in front of the larger painting hanging on the wall next to her. "*Interessant.* What is your name?"

"If I tell you my name, will you tell me yours?" Abbi asked, feeling a little braver.

He nodded.

"It's Abbigayl. Abbigayl Byrne." She gave him a small smile.

He faced her and furrowed his brows. "Abbigayl Byrne?"

She almost laughed at how her name sounded in that thick accent. "Yes, that's right."

"My name, it's Kristian. Kristian Wolf." This time he returned her smile.

She tried not to get too caught up in how cute he looked when he smiled at her. No, he wouldn't be interested in someone like her anyway. Her mother and sisters had made that point abundantly clear about any man who interested her. She would always be the single sister who would take care of their mother when the other two were married. It was the fate she had resigned herself to. No point wishing for something that'd never happen.

"What brings you here during this time of year? Shouldn't you be with your family?" he inquired.

Abbi fiddled with the hem of her apron piece and picked over her words carefully. How do you tell a stranger that the whole point of your trip was to escape your family? That would require way too much explanation, but she didn't want to be too vague where she made him feel bad. She wasn't good in these types of situations!

"Um, it just wasn't the right time for that this year."

He scratched his jaw and looked away from Abbi. "*Entschuldigung!*"

Abbi bit her lip. "Um, I don't know what that means, sorry."

Loud voices sounded from the hall and they both turned to look at the doorway. She recognized a few of the faces from the big announcement earlier. Where was everyone going? Had she actually missed something important in the announcement?

"Sorry! I've got to go! It was nice talking to you!" she called out.

As she reached the doorframe, she chanced a quick glance back, only to find an empty room before her. What?

Abbi shuddered and got pulled into the crowd, following them to the assigned rooms, and locking her own door once she was inside. Her heart was still thumping, adrenaline coursing through her veins. Never in her life had she experienced something like this. She had so many questions she wanted answered, but at the forefront of her mind loomed the most important:

What happened to Kristian?

Two

A loud crash outside Abbigayl's door jolted her from deep slumber. She rubbed her eyes as she looked around her room. Everything appeared to be as she left it the night before. The loud noise echoed from the hall again, and Abbi shot up from bed and scrambled for the door. Throwing it open, she was met with a girl her age sprawled out on the ground, cleaning supplies surrounding her.

"Oh my! Are you okay?" Abbi knelt down and assessed the girl for any potential injuries. Her first aid training might actually come in handy for once.

The girl sniffed and nodded, her blonde hair bouncing in its pony-tail holder on the back of her head. "I am. I'm so sorry for all the noise, I didn't mean to wake you up."

Abbi waved her off. "It was time I get up anyway. I have so much of this castle to explore." She smiled. "What's your name? I'm Abbigayl, but you can call me Abbi."

"I'm Ingrid. Thank you for being so kind." Ingrid wiped at her brown eyes and started collecting the supplies around her.

Abbi picked up the tools at her knees and handed them to her new friend. They worked in relative silence until all the pieces were back in the supply basket.

"Thank you again for helping me and just being so nice." Ingrid smiled and stood up.

Abbi followed suit before putting a hand on Ingrid's shoulder. "I'm happy to have made a new friend. If you ever want to talk or just need some help, you know where to find me." She gave her shoulder a pat. "That's if I haven't managed to get lost in this place!"

They both laughed and Ingrid nodded.

"I still get lost sometimes too, and I've been working here two years now!" She scratched her cheek and sighed. "I should probably get back to work. I still have a few other rooms to clean before moving on to my other chores."

"I totally get it! It was nice talking to you, and I hope we meet again while I'm here," Abbi replied.

She turned and strode back into her room. *All right girl, time for a new day with new adventures just around the corner.* She grabbed her phone off the dresser and checked her text messages. There were three from companies she had subscribed to updates from, and a few from her family. She opted to look at the bath treats sale text instead of the impending doom that awaited her in her mother's texts. Pretending to scour the websites sale, she huffed. Focusing was going to be a problem that day. No matter how hard she tried, she couldn't get Kristian off her mind. There was something so old-fashioned about him, and it drew her in like a princess to a castle. Why was he lingering there, and why did he seem surprised when she walked in?

Ding!

Her phone buzzed in her hand, and she groaned when her mother's face flashed on the screen. Pressing the green button, she closed her eyes and sighed. "Hey, Mom!"

Abbi prayed her mom couldn't hear the fakeness of her joy.

"Hey sweetheart! I wanted to check in and see how you were doing!" Her mom's voice was shrill through the small speakers.

Abbi didn't give it long before it would disappear. "It's going great, Mom. The castle is just as beautiful as I thought it'd be." She smiled as she thought about the way her chest felt at seeing the castle in person the day before.

"Abbi!"

She jolted and scrambled to grab her phone as it slipped from her grip. "Yes, Mom?"

A deep sigh settled against her ear. "It's no wonder you're still single. You never know how to listen. Brain always off somewhere else."

Despite her multiple attempts to erect a shield around her heart for her mother's words, it never seemed to work. Abbi blinked away the tears pooling in her eyes. "Sorry, Mom. What were you saying?"

There was that sigh again. How many times has she heard that in her lifetime? "I asked if you wised up and are coming for Christmas." The coolness in her tone could have turned water to ice.

Abbi closed her eyes. *Please help me, Lord.* "No, Mom. I really like it here, and I still have so many places to explore."

"You're not a child anymore. You need to think about your future and spend time with your family. Not go off galivanting around Bavaria!"

She sucked in a breath at the dagger piercing her heart. *Why can't I ever be good enough for her? Why must everything be her way?*

"I'm sorry, Mom. They're serving breakfast, and I don't want to miss it."

A soft "Watch how much you eat" echoed from the phone before Abbi pressed the red button and tossed the device down onto the bed, watching it bounce against the comforter. *Way to go, Mom, first full day, and you've already ruined it.*

She sighed as she stood up and started to gather her clothes for the day. Maybe a warm shower would help her feel better. She nabbed a towel from the rack and started her morning routine.

In less time than it took to annoy her mom, Abbi stood under the spray and let it beat away the cobwebs and frustrations. With a clearer head, she dressed and reminded herself that she was far away from her family, and she could easily turn her phone off if it got bad enough. She had more important things to think about anyway. There was still so much of the castle to see before she went home. She adjusted her bodice before stepping out her door and locking it. She made her way to the main gathering room from the night before. As she passed by the gallery, her mind wandered to her time with Kristian. Would she get to see him at all today? All her thoughts were on him as she joined the crowd for breakfast.

Three

Breakfast was a loud affair for Abbigayl. There was so much excited chatter throughout the room that it was hard to hear herself think. *How long is this supposed to go?* Her leg bounced as she moved the food around her plate. Maybe no one would notice if she sneaked out before everyone finished.

After the morning she'd had so far, socializing wasn't really in her realm of interest at the moment, anyway. Wandering the halls and taking in the sights sounded like a more enjoyable time to her. She slid her chair back as slow as she could, but it still made a loud screech. Everyone's head turned to look at her, and the room went quiet. Abbi sank lower in her seat.

"Are you headed off somewhere?" The man who made the announcement last night peered around the person next to him to look at her.

Abbi sighed as she scratched at her arm. This was the last thing she had wanted, and now all the attention was on her. "Um, I'm just eager to start exploring the castle. There are so many rooms to see, and I wanna make sure I can find as many of them as I can before this is over."

The man clapped his hands with a broad smile on his face. "Ah! I'm glad someone appreciates the art and history within these walls!" He turned to the others at the table. "If you are all done with your breakfast, you're free to explore the castle! Lunch will be served at two."

Chatter filled the room once again as the guests dispersed, heading off to explore the castle. As she stood from her seat, Abbi looked around to see if she could spot Kristian, but she didn't see his brown head in the crowd.

Maybe he chose to skip breakfast?

Sighing, she placed her napkin on her plate and followed everyone into the hall. Their voices echoed off the walls, and Abbi resisted the urge to cover her ears. She split off from the group and made her way down the less traveled hallway in search of peace and quiet.

The dark tones of the interior fascinated her. Most castles she read about were bright and almost cheery. What was going through King Ludwig's mind when he was designing this place for himself? She desperately wanted to run her fingers along the walls and feel the history beneath her fingertips.

The sound of humming stopped her, and a chill shot down her spine.

"Hello?" she called out.

The humming continued, not even a slight hitch in the tone. She moved to the closest doorway and peered inside.

The room was dark, without much outside light filtering through the window. *It got cloudy quick out there.* The fireplace was lit, flames dancing within the hearth, providing a comfortable warmth to the room.

"It's you."

Abbi spun around and saw a familiar face standing in the corner.

"Hello Kristian!" She smiled at him.

He returned her smile. "Hello again, Abbigayl."

She blushed at his use of her full name. "You can call me Abbi, no one really calls me by my full name."

"It's a pretty name. It suits you."

The heat on her face increased, and she had no doubt that even her ears were red.

"Thank you."

He nodded, still smiling. Abbi watched him as he went back to examining the room. He stood so straight, like it had been ingrained in him that he must do so. His attire was different than what she had seen the other men in the group wear. *Maybe he brought his own since he's a local?*

She was startled out of her daze by the sound of someone clearing their throat. She noticed Kristian was staring at her. Was he waiting for something from her?

"I'm sorry, I was lost in my thoughts there. What did you say?" She tugged the hem of her bodice piece and picked at the seam.

His warm laugh filled her with a sense of giddiness she didn't expect. "I asked how you are this *morgen.*"

"Oh! I'm all right, I guess. Had a rather unpleasant phone call with my mom this morning, but that's usual." She scratched at her jaw and looked around the study.

"I take it you aren't on *froh* terms with her?"

Abbi bit her lip. "I don't know what *f-froh* means. I'm sorry."

He furrowed his brows. "Do you know any German at all?"

She shook her head. "I don't. I'm sorry." *Why does apologizing come so easy for me? What am I sorry for?*

He moved closer to her, scowl set on his face. "What is an American who speaks no German doing here?"

What am I doing here? Abbi stared at him. "Um, I'm here for the Christmas party. I paid to be able to come and see the famous castle just like everyone else."

Instead of relaxing, his expression grew firmer. "Others? There are no others here. What are you talking about?"

Abbi took a step back. Her heartbeat quickened against her chest, and she struggled to take deep enough breaths. *What's going on? I-I don't understand why he's acting this way.*

Her eyes darted behind Kristian. The door was close enough for her to escape. She just had to be quick. *I can do this.*

She looked over at the wall next to her, and he followed her gaze. She took the opportunity to give him a quick shove before sprinting to the door. Throwing it open, she dashed down the hallway. Her lungs burned as she ducked into a nearby room. She panted and slid down the door, clutching her side. *Athleticism was never my strongest skill.*

"Woah, are you okay?"

Abbi glanced up and saw an older man holding his hand out to her. "Oh, um, yes. I'm fine. J-just had a slight scare." She grasped his hand and rose to her feet with his assistance.

He chuckled. There was a comforting tone to it, and her heartrate slowed some. Her shoulders relaxed. The pain in her lungs subsided with minor coughing.

"I can breathe again!"

He patted her shoulder with a smile on his face. "Breathing is a good thing. Can't have you dying on us now."

She returned his smile and glanced around the room. Pictures of the castle in various states of repair lined the walls, and blueprints covered the desk in the far end of the room.

"Do you work here?"

The man nodded. "I do, indeed. Part of the restoration team working to keep this place in pristine condition." He winked at her. "Someone has to make sure the magic in this place stays intact. What good's a castle without the magic it holds within its walls?"

His words filled her with a sense of peace. This was clearly someone who loved his job and took his role in caring for the castle seriously. *If only more people cared about keeping these monuments of history alive.* How many beautiful pieces of architecture have been lost over time, never to grace the public with their beauty again?

"I don't think I caught your name."

Abbi's attention snapped back to the man in front of her. "Sorry, my name is Abbigayl, but I insist you call me Abbi." She smiled, "All my friends do."

"Well, it's a pleasure to make your acquaintance, Abbi. I'm Jacob." He held out his hand once more, and Abbi shook it.

She was grateful when he led her back to the main room where everyone else was. When lunchtime came, she sat picking at her food, lost in her thoughts. The encounter with Kristian rattled her. What had caused him to flip and made him turn on her like that? That curious part of her just had to know.

Four

I ngrid sighed as she stepped into the castle restoration planning room. She pulled her hair band out and let her blonde hair spill onto her shoulders. She massaged the sore spots left behind from the tight ponytail. Jacob chuckled as he glanced up at her from his chair by the desk.

"Today didn't go as planned, did it?" Jacob asked before taking a sip of his coffee.

She shook her head. "It most definitely did not." She groaned and tugged on her hair. "Why'd he have to go and scare her for? Poor thing looked so traumatized running out of that room."

She walked over to the desk while pulling her hair into a looser ponytail. She sighed and sorted through the paperwork on the desk. Abbi's picture was paper clipped to the top of the folder. The castle's newest addition to the wall of the specially chosen. There was a reason the castle wanted to bring her and Kristian together. The staff members never questioned it. They only worked to help make the match happen.

"I think this will be one of our more challenging cases. I don't think today was a good indicator of how this will go." Ingrid toyed with the corner of Abbi's photo.

Jacob sighed and placed his hand on hers. "Don't worry, child. The castle knows best. Its plan has never failed, and I don't think it will this time either." He patted her hand. "We'll just have to watch, see what happens, and play our part."

Ingrid nodded. "I know. It was just hard to see her so spooked. I heard her on the phone with her mother earlier." Ingrid scrunched her nose. "That woman is awful. You wouldn't believe the things she says to her own daughter! Despicable."

Jacob nodded. "It's a sad reality that not all parents can appreciate their child's uniqueness and gifts. I just met the girl and can already see that she has a heart that is unfailingly kind."

Ingrid nodded. "She was super sweet to me this morning when I dropped all my cleaning supplies outside her door on accident."

Jacob pinched the bridge of his nose and sighed. "Child, you are really going to hurt yourself one of these days."

She giggled. "Sorry, Papa."

The two lingered in silence, reflecting on their conversation.

Ingrid looked up at the wall and gasped. "Is that really the time? I have to go help serve lunch!" She darted out the door but stuck her head back in the doorway moments later. "Catch you around, Jacob!"

The old man laughed and shook his head. "That kiddo is always so full of life. I don't know where she gets all that energy from." He took a sip of his coffee. "Makes me tired just watching her."

He returned his focus to his work for the day. The castle wasn't going to repair itself, after all.

Abbi poked and prodded at her lunch, her earlier interaction with Kristian overtaking her thoughts. *Why did he react so strangely to what I said?* There were plenty of Americans who had no clue how to speak German. Most of the people in her life had no interest in learning the language, and Abbi had no reason to take it up either. But he seemed almost offended that she was so clueless.

"Not hungry?"

Abbi jumped at the voice. She looked back to see the dark-haired man who made the announcements last night and this morning. She should know his name since he seemed to be in charge, but she hadn't been paying much attention when he introduced himself to the crowd.

"Um, not really. Had a scare earlier and lost my appetite."

He pulled out the chair next to her and took a seat. "I can understand that. This place has a lot of ghosts." He leaned in closer. "My first day working here, I swore I saw a ghost. It kept appearing in the different rooms I went in."

Abbi giggled. "I can imagine that was quite the experience on your first day here!"

"The staff who had been here for a while thought it was hilarious. They even take bets on the new guy, and I made some people lose pretty quickly."

"That's pretty mean, but it's also kinda funny." She looked down and picked at her fingernails. "I have to apologize. I don't remember your name."

He laughed. "It's all right, most people don't even call us by our names. They just order us about. My name is Paul."

She stuck her hand out. "Nice to meet you, Paul. I'm Abbi! Well, Abbigayl, but I prefer Abbi."

He took her hand and gave it a firm squeeze. "Welcome to Neuschwanstein." He let go of her hand and motioned her closer.

Abbi leaned in.

"This castle has many secrets—some good, some bad. There's so much magic here for you to discover." He smiled and set a hand on her shoulder. "Please don't let what happened today discourage you from seeking that out."

"I'll do my best. That man was scary though. You'd think he would know why I'm here when he had to pay to get in like I did." Abbi huffed, crossing her arms against her chest.

Paul smiled, a glimmer of mischief in his green eyes. "That man is not a guest of this Christmas party."

Her gaze bore into Paul. "If he's not a part of this party, then who is he, and why is he here?"

"That's one of the secrets this castle holds, and a mystery you'll have to solve for yourself, Miss Abbi." He stood up and gave a slight nod. "Until next time."

A quiet "bye" left her lips as she tried to process what he had just told her.

What is going on in this castle? What game are they playing here? So many questions swirled around in her brain, and none of them had answers that made any sense. What had she gotten herself into by coming here for Christmas? Would this be a decision she'd come to regret by the end of the week?

Abbi could only hope she didn't.

Five

⁓

Abbi woke up the next morning with a pounding headache. Sleep had been elusive for most of the night making nausea curl in her gut.

No breakfast for me today.

Abbi rolled out of bed and stretched her fingers towards the ceiling. Her lower back produced a quick succession of pops. *I'm only twenty-six, and I already sound like I'm eighty.* She chuckled to herself. After grabbing a new set of the clothes from the dresser, she made her way to the bathroom to get ready for the day. A shower should help calm her rolling stomach.

She stepped back into her room with a newfound calmness she hadn't experienced in some time. Something told her that today would be a good day, or better than the last few at least. She headed out the door and off toward the main room. Along the way she spotted Paul and Ingrid whispering to each other. As she grew closer Ingrid gave a startled yelp when Abbi made eye contact.

"Good morning, Abbi!" Her voice sounded way too chipper for how early it was.

Abbi gave a small smile. "Good morning, Ingrid. Did you sleep well?"

"I did! Thank you for asking! You're very kind."

Paul pretended to tip a hat in Abbi's direction. "Good morning, Miss Abbi."

"Good morning, Paul. I hope you slept well too."

He gave a firm nod. "As cozy as can be with all the blankets to keep me warm."

The group laughed and walked toward the main room where breakfast would be served in an hour.

Ingrid turned to Abbi. "You're more than welcome to join us in here if you want. We don't mind."

Abbi shook her head. "I'm very grateful for the offer, but I think I'm going to do a little bit of exploring before breakfast. See if I can shake off the tendrils of sleepiness still in my system."

Ingrid and Paul nodded, bidding Abbi goodbye until later.

Abbi wandered down the hallway hoping to find the study from the day before, but she couldn't remember how she had made it to that room. After walking for a good five minutes, she gave up and chose to wander around until lunch time.

She floated from room to room, enjoying the unique design that each one had to offer. One of her favorite rooms had walls covered in artwork and a chandelier that still held real candles. The gold piece paired wonderfully with the neutral tones of the walls and brought out the colors of the paintings. This was a place she truly felt happy.

She stepped into the next room, and her jaw dropped. The top half of the walls were covered in a powder blue design, and it paired beautifully with the beige pattens along the bottom half of the walls. The bed frame matched the pattern on the walls. The whole room felt so delicate, like it was made for a woman who was well-loved.

Abbi sighed. That wasn't something she was overly familiar with. Her family was always so critical of everything she did. Something was either all wrong or could be done better. She grew up watching movies and reading books about the handsome men who swept women like her off her feet. She dreamed of having someone like that in her life, but it never worked out. She was just not the right woman for any of the men that came into her life, and at this point, she doubted there would ever be one. Romance like that was for fairy tales and romance novels. Right now, Abbi thought her life for more akin to a horror story. *A girl can only dream.*

She spent her time between lunch and dinner examining the murals along the wall. She had never read the story of the "Swan Knight," but she found herself drawn to the tale as she watched it unfold along the walls of the castle. Every detail was so beautifully captured, and the display looked as flawless as it must have been when it was first painted.

During dinner, she found herself more comfortable talking with the other guests and getting to know them. She worried that they would find her love of art and history odd, but it seemed she was in good company here. Everyone she talked to was nothing but kind, and Abbi was able to share her thoughts and opinions with ease. Though, the compliments and praise she received for some of her statements brought a blush to her cheeks. This was all she had ever wanted from her family and friends. She was included and appreciated here. It would be hard to return home once all this was over.

When dinner was over, Abbi tried to find her way to the restoration planning room to say good night to Jacob and thank him for his help the day before. She looked for familiar landmarks, but nothing stood out. Frustrated, she decided to just scope out the room on her right. She opened the door and smiled.

It was a sight to behold. The bedroom was covered in dark wood, and elegant pictures hung on the walls. For being filled with such dark furniture, the room was well lit by the moonlight coming in through the window. It made the room comfy and homey.

"What are you doing in here?"

Abbi jumped at the sound of Kristian's voice from behind her.

"Don't sneak up on me like that!" She swung around and placed a hand on her heart. It did nothing to stop its quick beating.

Kristian's shoulders shook as he bit his lip.

"Don't laugh at me!" Abbi scowled at him. "It's not funny!"

Her indignation only made him laugh harder, no longer trying to hide it by biting his lip.

"*Entschuldige*. It's just, I'm pretty sure you jumped *drei*...um...three feet in the air," he said, still chuckling at her.

Abbi huffed. "Well, that's what usually happens when you sneak up on people!"

Kristian shook his head, a smile on his face. "To be fair, you are in my room."

Abbi looked around and noticed the luggage sitting in the corner. Her face heated, and she looked everywhere but at Kristian.

"I'm sorry. I didn't realize this was your room." She wrung her hands together against the fabric of her apron. "I didn't—I mean—I wouldn't have come in if I had known. I swear!" She continued to ramble, but Kristian reached out a hand and set it on her shoulder.

"You ran off yesterday before I had the chance to ask you. What are you doing here?" He took a step closer to her. "I asked my commanding officer yesterday about the Americans staying at the castle, and he had no idea what I was talking about. Said there were no Americans here."

Abbi took a step back, trying to push enough air in her lungs. *Oh no, this is just like yesterday! What am I going to do?*

"Are you a spy? Come to see what Germany is up to and planning?"

Abbi shook her head, the force of it making her slightly dizzy. "N-no! I'm not a spy! I'm just here for the Christmas party."

Kristian stared at her, his brows furrowed. "Party? There is no party here. My CO would know if there was. Who. Are. You?" He punctuated the last three words with a step toward her.

Abbi's whole body shook the closer he came to her. "I-I swear! I'm just here for the party! I can go back to my room and grab the ticket for you to prove it."

"How do I know you won't use that opportunity to try and run away? How can I trust you to do as you say?"

She sighed. "You're going to have to trust me. I have no other way of proving it to you, but I will come back with the ticket. Maybe then you'll stop acting so mean." She mumbled the last part to herself.

An awkward silence settled over the room as they just stood there.

"You think I'm mean?" Kristian's voice was quiet.

Abbi refused to make eye contact with him. "What else am I supposed to think when you're a perfect gentleman one day and are being all threatening the next? I thought we got along quite nicely that first day, but then yesterday you got all rude when I said I didn't know German." Abbi took a deep breath. "And today you're spouting some weird nonsense about your commanding officer and no party or Americans being on the premises." She threw her hands up. "What else am I supposed to think?"

Kristian ran a hand down his face. "*Entschuldige*...sorry. I didn't mean to frighten you. I've been charged with keeping the castle secure and safe. Imagine being in my shoes; what would you have done?" He sighed. "What would you have done?"

Abbi opened her mouth, then closed it again. She found herself at a loss for words. He made a good point, but still...would she have done the same thing? If her life were on the line, would she have become so cold at a possible threat?

"I-I don't know what to say. I guess I can see your point," she mumbled.

Silence sat over the room once more. It was like a thick cloud had settled over them. Abbi shifted her weight and picked at her fingernails.

"Um, I'll grab my ticket and meet you here in an hour, if that's okay with you," Abbi whispered.

Kristian nodded. "I will see you here in an hour. I'm going to trust you, even if my gut tells me this is a mistake."

The corner of Abbi's mouth twitched up. "You sure know how to make a girl feel good about herself."

Kristian frowned. "What do you mean?"

"Nothing." Abbi shook her head and turned toward the door. "I'll see you soon."

She strode over to the door and pulled it open.

"Wait!"

Abbi didn't bother to stop as she walked out the door.

Six

Abbi made her way back to her room, her mind going over the conversation she'd just had with Kristian. Maybe she had been too quick to judge him. But he had also scared her yesterday. Both parts of her clashed as she tried to understand just who Kristian was. He could be downright intimidating, but when he asked her if she thought he was mean...there was just something so vulnerable and gentle about his tone.

Abbi reached out and grabbed her door handle, turning it and pushing the door open. She flicked on the light switch and allowed the bedside lamp to illuminate the room. It had taken her ten minutes to reach her room with her scattered thoughts. Maybe a little bit of relaxation would prove beneficial. She strode over to the bathroom and turned the water on in the tub. She pulled her favorite rose petal bath bomb from her toiletry bag, unwrapped it, and dropped it in the water.

The sight of pink spreading through the water combined with the floral scent filling the air caused her shoulders to drop and the tension in her muscles to ease slightly. She pulled her hair back and twisted it up before clamping it in place with her clip. This is just what she needed right now.

Thirty minutes later, she was drying off and redressing in her clothes from earlier. On her way to the door, she made sure to grab her receipt and ticket, stuffing them in her pocket. The moon cast a beautiful glow across the walls of the castle. She smiled at the way the colors reflected off the gold tones in the decorations that lined the walls. She thought back to what Paul had told her yesterday at lunch. "This castle had some secrets, good and bad," she repeated to herself. *What does he want me to do with that information? What secrets do the walls of this castle hold for me?*

She traced her steps from her post-dinner stroll. She had five minutes to spare. She turned the handle and slipped into the room.

"Kristian? Are you here?" Abbi called out as she turned the light on in the room. The fireplace was no longer lit. In fact, it didn't even look like it had housed a fire in the past several hours. *What is going on here? What happened to the fire?* The room was cold, no longer holding the warmth it had before. She sat down on the chair in the corner of the room and waited.

And waited.

And waited.

Somewhere in the hallway, a clock chime rang out. Nine chimes reverberated in the quietness of the room. *He's not coming.* Abbi blinked back tears. He stood her up, so to speak. He didn't believe what she said, so he didn't even bother to show. *Is this really even his room, or was that a lie?* She pulled the papers from her pocket and smoothed out the fold lines. Why hadn't he shown?

She waited a few minutes more, but there was still no sign of him. Sighing, she folded the papers up and stuffed them back into her pocket. She used the bottom of her apron to brush the tears away.

No. This man was not worth her tears. She spent too much of her time being the topic of other people's jokes and snide comments. This man stood her up, so he was not worth her tears. She marched out of the room and went right back to her own.

She changed into her pajamas before climbing into bed, desperate to sleep the horrible day off.

A knock on the door roused Abbi from her sleep. She hissed as her bare feet made contact with the cold wood floor. *I must have kicked my socks off last night.* Abbi sighed, knowing she would have to scavenge around her sheets to find them.

The person at the door knocked a little louder.

"I'm coming!" She called out and grabbed the dressing gown from the hook by the door. She wrapped it around herself before answering whoever was at the door.

A familiar head of blonde hair and brown eyes greeted her. "Good morning!" Ingrid chirped.

Abbi ran a hand down her face. "Good morning, Ingrid. Not to be rude, but why are you here so early?"

Ingrid tilted her head and laughed. "Early? You slept through breakfast, so I came to see if you were okay."

Warmth blossomed in Abbi's chest and spread throughout the rest of her body. A sob pushed its way up her throat and the waterworks triggered in her eyes.

The blonde girl was quick to pull her into an embrace, hugging her tightly and rubbing her back. "Shh, you're all right. Everything's okay."

Abbi's cries quieted down until she was sniffling against Ingrid's neck. "I'm sorry for crying all over you." Her words were muffled by Ingrid's shirt, but she understood anyway.

"It's just a shirt. It can be washed no problem. You're more important anyway." She pulled Abbi back slightly and used her sleeves to wipe the tears from Abbi's eyes. "There you go, good as new." Ingrid beamed at her and gave her face a soft pat.

Abbi sniffled. "Thank you, you've been so kind. I really don't deserve it." Abbi ran her sleeve across her nose and cringed at the snot that transferred with the motion.

"It's okay, we can wash it."

Abbi gave her a small smile. "Thank you, Ingrid. I've never really had someone care so much about me. Most people don't even notice I'm missing."

Ingrid frowned and took Abbi's hands in hers. "That's because people are missing out and don't know how amazing you are. Don't worry, that will change. I just know it."

Laughter forced itself from deep within Abbi. "I think you have way too much confidence in me. I don't know where you found it."

Ingrid winked. "Call it intuition. Now come on, let's go get you some food."

"Let me change first," Abbi gestured to her clothes and giggled, "I don't think I want to wander the castle like this."

"I mean, you look adorable, but you're probably right."

Abbi ducked inside and changed into the first outfit she could find. "All right, I'm ready!"

Ingrid linked her arm with Abbi's, and they took off down the hallway. "Off we go!"

Seven

A bbi decided to explore the other side of the castle and see what secrets it held. *Maybe I can avoid any more encounters with him too.*

She walked along the hallways, taking in each painting that graced the walls. How she wished she could put a brush to the canvas and create a masterpiece like any one of these. No, her talent didn't lie in creating art, so she settled for admiring and studying it. She loved that each part of the castle was different, how King Ludwig II's style steeped into every part of its design. While it might clash in some places, there was just something so enchanting about everything. It made her want to get lost in the castle, never to return to the real world. *What a dream that would be.*

She opened the door at the end of the hall and stepped through into the room. Instead of housing paintings, the walls were lined with photographs. There were glass cases lining walls along the room.

"What is this place?"

She walked over to the first case on the left side of the room and peered down into the cases. Set along the velvet lining were medals and other smaller pieces. The plaque screwed into the table had information etched into it. She leaned closer and read, "Artifacts from World War I and World War II."

"Wow." Abbi gazed down at all the little trinkets that were nestled within the soft fabric. She continued around the room, looking at all the glass cases and the pieces of history they held. She started around the room again, this time taking in the images that decorated the walls. Young men stood in lines, pictures of both sides hanging in memoriam.

Tears streamed down her face at the sight of the men, frowns on their faces. Some were embracing their families. Others were of families who never got to see their sons, brothers, or fathers again. There were pictures of prisoners of war and bodies strewn across the battlefield. As she reached the center of the room, a photo from 1914 made her stop. The picture showed a group of German soldiers lined up in front of the castle. At the very end, the second to last person on the left, was a familiar face. A scarily familiar face. The defined jaw and scowl was undoubtably Kristian.

Abbi's head spun as she stared at the picture. There was just no way it was real. It had to be his ancestor or something. She took a step back, then another, and another before bolting out the door to find someone who could help her make sense of what was going on. Someone had to have the answers she so desperately needed.

Abby skidded around the corner and entered the main room where dinner was being served. At the center of the group was Paul, and she spotted Ingrid standing at the far corner of the room.

Abbi weaved her way through the tables and stopped in front of Ingrid.

"Ingrid!"

She jumped at the sound of her name being called. "Abbi! You scared me!"

Despite the gravity of the situation, Abbi couldn't help but laugh at how spooked Ingrid was. "Sorry! Sorry! I didn't mean to scare you!" She placed a hand over her mouth to stifle her giggles.

Ingrid pouted at her and crossed her arms over her chest. "That wasn't very nice."

Abbi pulled her into a big hug. "I'm sorry. I didn't think it would scare you. I wasn't exactly quiet."

"You're forgiven."

The two girls stood there for a minute just staring at each other before bursting out in laughter. The wait staff gave them funny looks as they walked by, but neither of the girls could really bring themselves to care. They were having too much fun.

The smile slipped from Abbi's face as she remembered why she had come to Ingrid.

"What's wrong?" Ingrid placed a hand on Abbi's back and guided her to a set of empty seats nearby. They both sat down, Ingrid setting her hand on Abbi's knee. "You okay?"

Abbi shook her head, her hands starting to shake. "Do you know if there is anyone here that is a descendant of the soldiers that once occupied this area?"

Ingrid's brows furrowed. "Not that I know of. As far as I know, most of the guests here are Americans, and the few people from here are the regulars that attend each year. Why? What happened, Abbi?"

The shaking in Abbi's hand increased, and her guts twisted. Nausea curled its way up her throat. If there were no descendants here, the man in the photo couldn't be Kristian's ancestor. *Is it just coincidence that he looks almost identical to the man in the picture?* Her breathing quickened, and she struggled to take a deep enough breath to fill her lungs. Black spots danced across the edges of her vision. The room spun around her. She could faintly hear someone saying something to her, but she couldn't make out what they were saying or even who it was talking to her. The darkness crept closer, threatening to overtake her completely.

"Ingrid?" She choked out before her eyes closed and she lost consciousness.

Her eyes blinked open, but she squeezed them shut as the bright light overwhelmed her vision.

"Hey, dim the lights a little bit. It's hurting her eyes."

Abbi thought it sounded like Ingrid, but she couldn't quite tell if that's who she was hearing.

"I-Ingrid, is that you?" Abbi forced the words out. Her mouth was dry, like someone had shoved cotton balls in her mouth. It was hard to talk around that feeling, but she tried to anyway.

"Hey, hey, let me get you some water."

Something was pressed to her lips, and she could only assume that it was a glass of water. She drank it down as quick as she could manage, but it was pulled away from her lips before she had finished it.

"Woah, slow down! You don't want to make yourself sick!"

Abbi opened her eyes, blinking them a few times to adjust to the faint lighting in the room. Ingrid sat beside her, cup in hand, while Paul, Jacob, and the lady from her first day here hovered behind her.

"What happened?" Abbi reached up and rubbed the blurriness from her eyes.

Ingrid smoothed down the rogue strands of hair on Abbi's head. "You asked me a question about descendants of soldiers being here, and when I told you no, you kinda freaked and then passed out."

"Gave us a right good scare there, love." Paul chimed in.

Jacob smiled, "Glad to see you're looking fine now."

Abbi gazed at all their faces. Each one of them was smiling, but concern lingered in their gazes. *I'm about to make it worse.*

"Um, if what you say is true, Ingrid, then something is terribly wrong." Abbi stated.

Ingrid scooted closer, the rest of the group following suit. "What is it, Abbi? What's wrong?"

"Um..." Abbi fiddled with her hands, picking at the skin around her fingernails. "I don't know how to say this, so I'm just gonna come right out and say it.

The group nodded.

"I think Kristian, the man I keep bumping into, is a ghost."

Eight

The group all stared at her in silence. They exchanged looks with each other, but no one said anything. Abbi wondered if they were trying to silently get their stories together. They had information she needed, but would they willingly give it to her? *Let's find out.*

Abbi looked up at Ingrid, and she was the first to break the silence.

"What do you mean he's a ghost?" Ingrid asked.

What kind of question is that? Abbi sighed, "It's just what I said. I think he's a ghost."

Jacob piped up next, "What makes you think he's a ghost?"

"Yeah, just because no descendants of soldiers are visiting doesn't make him a ghost," Paul added.

Abbi ran a hand down her face. "I found a room full of World War I and World War II memorabilia. I was looking at the pictures along the wall and saw one taken in 1914. The castle was in the background of the picture with the men all lined up. He was in the picture."

"Honey, are you sure it just isn't someone who looks like him? There are many cases like that throughout history." The old woman turned to the others. "What's that celebrity that everyone thinks is a vampire because he looks like so many people in pictures they've found?"

Ingrid giggled. "You're thinking of Nicolas Cage, Grandma."

"Yes, that's him!" Grandma snapped her fingers.

"I've seen those pictures. While they look like him, none of them are an exact match to his face, just eerily similar. The man in this picture is a perfect match for the man I've been seeing in the castle. The way he was talking even fits what would be going on at that time." Abbi threw her hands up in the air. "How else would you explain all of that? The only logical conclusion is that he's a ghost!"

No one said anything, and Abbi wanted to pull her hair out. Either they thought she was crazy, or they were hiding something from her. She'd seen the glances they'd exchanged earlier. They had to know something. If that was the case, she would get to the bottom of this. She wouldn't let them keep all this hidden from her when she was already so involved. She had just as much of a right to know what was going on right now. She had a right know why the soldier in the picture was scaring her one moment and then being friendly to her the next minute. None of it made any sense. All she wanted was for someone to explain what was happening to her. *Is that too much to ask? I just feel so lost.*

She sighed and took in each one of the people surrounding her. They had at least some knowledge on what was happening to her, who the man was, and why he was out to make her miserable during her much-needed Christmas vacation. No matter, she would find out in the end. All she had to do was bide her time and wait until she had the chance to pry the information out of one of them.

She already knew who her first target would be. Ingrid was shifting in her seat. Yes, the weak link was obvious. Abbi could do it, but she would have to come up with the perfect plan to make it happen.

"Stop it. You'll overwhelm the poor dear. She's been through a lot today already. You're just making it worse." The old woman from Monday night pushed her way past the others and settled on the chair beside Abbi's bed. She took Abbi's hand in hers and gave it a gentle pat. "We haven't been properly introduced. I'm Gerda. I know you're confused, and you want answers, but there are some things that are better left alone." She smiled at Abbi. "Trust me on that. When God decides you're ready to see what secrets this place holds, He will reveal it all to you in the way He has deemed best."

Abbi just stared at the woman for a few moments. The motherly tone in her voice soothed Abbi a little, but the battle within her still raged on, though not quite at full strength anymore. *God has never given me cause to doubt Him and His plan for me, but at the same time, I'm so desperate to know what's going on here.*

Acceptance and curiosity clashed in her brain. The answer was obvious, but it wasn't one she wanted to choose. She wanted to do what was right, but it was so hard to resist trying to find the answers on her own. She'd have to wait and see what was in store for her. She could do that, right? *Please give me patience, Lord. I don't think I can get through this without You. Help me to trust in You and Your plan. You've never let me down.*

"Fine. I guess I can wait a little longer to get my answers. Who knows, maybe the next time I run into him I can see if he'd be willing to answer all my questions. "

Ingrid smiled and helped pull Abbi to her feet. "Let's get you some dinner and then you can join me and the gang for a round of cards. How does that sound?"

Abbi gave each one of them a tight hug. "I'd love that. Thank you guys for coming to my rescue, and for being amazing, caring people. There aren't enough people like you in this world." She smiled at them. "The world would be a better place if there were."

It was nice to feel cared for and wanted. When she'd booked her time for this Christmas experience, she had no idea she'd meet such incredible people that she hoped would be her friends for years to come. They were already one of her biggest Christmas blessings this year.

"Let's go play some cards!"

Nine

Abbi woke up that Friday morning to the sound of a commotion outside. The voices carried through the door, making Abbi giggle.

"Those aren't the right tablecloths! I told you the deep red ones!" That had to be Paul.

Ingrid's voice followed. "These are deep red! I grabbed the ones you told me to!"

"These are burgundy, not deep red!"

Abbi stood up and walked over to the door. She grabbed the dressing gown off the wall before wrapping it around herself. She opened the door, startling the two arguing outside her door.

"Good morning you two," she said, biting her lip to keep from laughing.

They both sighed, and Ingrid clutched her chest.

"You seriously need to stop scaring me. One of these times you're actually going to give me a heart attack." Ingrid stuck her tongue out at Abbi.

Paul huffed. "It would certainly be much quieter around here then."

They started bickering again, and this time Abbi couldn't hold back her laughter.

"What's so funny?" They both said at the same time.

That just made Abbi laugh even harder. "You two argue just like siblings. You sound like children."

Paul and Ingrid stared at each other before they joined in and laughed too. The three stood there in the hallway just laughing while the other guests passed by them and gave them weird looks. As they settled down Ingrid smiled at Abbi.

"How are you feeling today?"

Abbi shrugged with a smirk. "Better since I stomped all you guys at cards last night."

She was met with two scowls.

"It was beginner's luck," Paul shot back with his arms crossed.

"Yeah, you're just proving my point about you being children. That's called being a sore loser." Abbi giggled.

"Or just a loser in general," Ingrid muttered.

"I heard that!"

Ingrid took off down the hall and Paul chased after her. Abbi just shook her head, feeling lighter than she had the night before. She looked at the cart with tablecloths sitting in the middle of the hallway. She pushed the cart against the wall so no one would get hurt. Heading back to her room, she muttered to herself, "Those tablecloths are definitely burgundy." Her thoughts wrapped up in the strange occurrences she'd experienced as she got dressed for the day. She grabbed her coat and left her room, making her way to the castle entrance.

Abbi headed out the large front doors. She hadn't had the chance to walk around the area in front of the castle and admire the building that inspired the castle for her favorite Disney princess. A walk along the front of the castle would be the perfect remedy for a noisy mind. The air was cool and crisp against her skin, but the coat protected her from the cold and kept her warm. She felt so small compared to the exterior walls of the castle. And really, in the scheme of things, she was small. Her problems always felt so monumental to her, like the world was against her. It made it easy to forget that she wasn't the one in control of her life. Someone much bigger and wiser knew every path she would take and was there every step of the way. If only she could cling to that as tightly as she wanted to.

The sight of the castle never ceased to amaze her when she'd seen pictures, but seeing it in person took her breath away. If this were her castle, she would have left enough room for her to be able to walk around the perimeter of the castle. *Why did he build it with no surrounding outdoor space? Did he have something against fresh air?* Abbi snorted. She couldn't say she'd blame him if he did. It wasn't really her favorite thing either.

The cold finally became too much, and Abbi had already spent more than the normal amount of time staring up at the old building. She pushed her way through the front door and looked for the closest room with a fireplace. She gave a contented sigh when she stepped into the room and warmth embraced her like the most comfortable blanket in the world. She shrugged her coat off and hung it on the hook by the entryway. She yawned as she settled herself down into one of the chairs by the fire. The heat from the fire staved off the lingering chill that followed her inside.

Between a comfortable temperature of the room and the way the fire danced in the fireplace, sleep crept its way along her consciousness. Her eyelids felt heavy. *I just need to close my eyes for a minute.*

Not able to fight its hold on her, Abby succumbed to the pull of sleep and closed her eyes.

Kristian stepped into the room for a moment of quiet. With all the preparations for invasion, his brain threatened to burst from his skull with each throb. He noticed the familiar redhead asleep in one of the chairs. He couldn't deny how beautiful she looked, especially so at peace. He really should wake her up. It wasn't safe for her to sleep there.

Her eyes flew open when he shook her shoulders, and her scream that followed reverberated within the small room.

Kristian held his hands up and took a few steps away from her at the sudden loud noise.

"Entschuldige!"

Abbi set a hand on her heart and used the other to wipe her eyes.

She blinked then peered up at him standing in front of her. Kristian watched her, waiting for another sudden outburst.

"It's you! I've been hoping to bump into you, even though you didn't show up the other night."

His scowl deepened. "What do you mean I didn't show up. I waited there for you. I never left the room, but you never came back."

Abbi shook her head. "That's not true! I did show up, and I made sure to keep my receipt in my pocket in case I got to see you again another time."

She reached into her pocket and pulled out the little slip of paper. Hands shaking, she unfolded the paper and handed it to him.

He pulled it from her grasp and brought it closer to inspect it. "This is fake. Do you think I'm a fool?"

Abbi raised an eyebrow. "It's not fake. I got that from their website and printed it out. It's legit."

"I don't know what most of what you just said means. But this says 2019. That's how I know it's fake. It's 1914."

She gasped. "Oh my gosh, oh my gosh, oh my gosh," she repeated, each time growing louder.

Kristian moved toward her, his arms reaching out for her. "What? What's wrong?"

"It's not 1914, it's 2019." She grabbed his hand and pulled him out of the room and down the hallway.

"Where are we going?" he asked, making sure to keep his stride even with hers to avoid bowling her over.

"You'll see!" she called over her shoulder.

Their footsteps echoed down the hall as she tugged him along. She made a few wrong turns and had to backtrack. Despite his confusion and concern, he couldn't help but laugh a little whenever that would happen. She'd sigh, apologize then redirect them.

The more time he spent running around with her, the more comfortable he became. These weren't the actions of someone who was trying to use him for their ulterior motives. Everything she did exuded genuineness. The way her eyes lit up when she would find the correct path, or the embarrassed laugh that escaped her when she would make a wrong turn. All of it was so endearing to him.

But his mind couldn't get over the paper she handed him. It just didn't make sense. It was 1914, and war was breaking out. But here she was with a paper that said 2019 and talking about websites and printers. He just couldn't keep up.

"Aha!"

Abbi's shout jolted him from his thoughts and caused him to plough right into her. They both hit the floor in a jumble of limbs.

"*Entschuldige!*" Kristian said as he pulled her up from the floor.

Abbi ran her hands over her tailbone trying to soothe the sore area. "I think I've finally figured that one out."

Kristian tilted his head at her. "Figured out what?"

"What that word you said means. It's 'I'm sorry,' right?"

Kristian laughed. "Yes, you have that correct."

Abbi cheered and did a little dance. "See, I pick things up pretty quickly!"

Kristian just shook his head. "What made you so excited to stop without giving me any warning?"

Abbi pointed to the door next to them.

He raised an eyebrow. "What's this?"

"Well technically it's a door…" She giggled.

Kristian was less than impressed with her attempt at humor.

"Fine, party pooper. It's something I stumbled across the other day. I, um, found something interesting that I wanted to show you."

"What is it?" She piqued his interest.

She sighed, hand on the doorknob. "Well, you're gonna think I'm crazy."

He just stared at her.

"Fine, fine," she waved her hand at him when she answered. "Um, well, I think you're a ghost." She rushed through the sentence, squeezing her eyes shut.

"A what?"

Ten

"You think I'm a ghost?"

Abbi nodded.

"All right, *die Prinzessin*, you're going to have to explain this to me because I don't understand what's going on."

"I'll show you, come on." Abbi turned and gripped the door handle. Her hands were shaky, making the metal beneath her fingers rattle. She took a deep breath. *You can do this.* Then she pushed the door open.

Kristian followed her inside the room, eyes wide at all the photographs lining the walls. "*Ich bin verwirrt,*" he whispered.

Abbi bit her lip as she watched Kristian take in his surroundings. "I found this when I was wandering the castle the other day. I was so surprised to see so many artifacts here. It's a good reminder of where we've come from so we can work to keep it from becoming where we're going."

Kristian stopped and looked at her over his shoulder. "Learning from the past, *ja?*"

Abbi nodded, a small smile on her lips.

He returned her smile and continued looking at the walls and glass cases.

She enjoyed this, this quiet softness between them. She was mad when she thought he had stood her up, but with her new suspicions, Abbie realized it wasn't his fault. Something had shifted between them, and no one could accuse her of being unhappy about it. *But how will this change when he sees it?*

It was then she noticed how quiet the room was. Kristian's footsteps no longer reverberated within the small room. She looked up and saw him staring at the pictures in the center of the back wall. Her stomach dropped, and nausea swirled in her gut again. It was a chore to swallow even her own spit. *What is he thinking right now? Should I approach him and check on him?* Sniffles broke her inner battle, and she watched his shoulders shake.

Before her brain could register what she was doing, she crossed the room and pulled him into her arms. He tucked his face against her neck, and she felt the wet patch forming against her skin. All she could do was hold him. This is a cry he needed to get out, not repress. There wasn't much she could do, but she could hold him while he cried.

She rubbed his back until his sobs turned to sniffles against her. She reached up and ran her hand through his hair, doing whatever she could to help soothe him. To let him know he wasn't alone. She was there, and she would be there for as long as he needed her to be. She felt responsible for his current state. *Was showing him this a mistake? Would it end up being better for him in the end?*

She felt him move in her arms, and he leaned back, straightening himself up but remaining close to her.

"*Entschuldige.*" His voice was raspy, barely above a whisper.

Abbi peered up at him. His eyes were bloodshot and puffy, and the skin underneath them was red and patchy. She grabbed the bottom part of her apron piece and lifted it to his face, wiping the remnants of his tears. "Why are you apologizing?"

Kristian sighed. "I got your clothes wet, and I cried like *der Säugling.*" He pinched the bridge of his nose, sniffling again. "It's not becoming of a soldier."

Abbi rolled her eyes. "I don't care about my clothes right now. I care about how you're doing. And I'd like to see any soldier who is confronted with something like this not panic or cry."

The corner of his lips twitched up. She rubbed her hand along his arm and smiled.

"*Danke.*"

Abbi nodded and pulled him in for another hug. His arms encircled her waist, and he pulled her against him. She wrapped her arms around his middle and laid her head on his chest. His heartbeat was rapid against the side of her head, and she found comfort in the fact that she made him just as nervous as he made her.

She didn't know how long they stood there like that, but she didn't care. She didn't want to move away from him just yet. For the first time in her life, she truly felt safe. There was just something about the way Kristian held her that made her seem untouchable to the world. No nasty comments from family, no flaky friends, no feelings of inadequacy compared to others. It was just her and him.

He eventually pulled back and stared down at her. She reached up and cupped his face, wiping away the last few stray tears. He leaned into her touch and closed his eyes.

"Will you explain it all to me?"

Abbi cocked her head to the side. "Explain what?"

"The wars. It said there were two of them, called them the World Wars. The way they described Germany doesn't seem good at all. And the castle. I don't understand what is happening, and how I can be a ghost if I don't remember dying."

Removing her hand from his face, she worried her bottom lip between her teeth. "I can explain about the World Wars, but I'm as lost as you are about what's going on in this castle." She pulled away from Kristian, wrapping her arms around herself. "I've never truly believed in magic. As a little girl I thought fairy tales were true, but the older I got, the more I realized that they were just pretty lies told to little girls to give them false hope in life."

She turned to the door. "We passed by a room with some chairs by the fireplace. We can go sit in there, and I'll tell you what I know about the wars and Germany's part in them."

This time he took her hand in his. She looked up at him, and he gave her a soft smile.

"Lead the way."

Eleven

Abbi woke the next morning with a pounding headache. She and Kristian had both shed tears over the atrocities of the World Wars. When she left him to go back to her room, he looked so lost and conflicted. Abbi wished she could have stayed with him longer, but she was falling asleep in her chair. He needed time to truly process things anyway. He needed time alone for that.

She closed her eyes, massaging her temples to try and soothe the pain. It didn't work.

Abbi huffed as she threw the sheets off of her and slid out of bed. The cold air greeted her with an icy hug, making her shiver and rush to change into warmer clothes. She left her room and trudged through the hallway to the first aid room.

Abbi opened the door and saw Gerda laying things out for the day.

"Good morning, dear!" Gerda said, a welcoming smile on her face.

Abbi gave her a strained smile. "Good morning, Gerda."

Gerda gestured to the chair in the corner of the small room. "Have a seat, then you can tell me what's troubling you."

Abbi nodded and sat down in the chair. She closed her eyes and leaned her head back against it.

"Hmm, if I had to venture a guess, I'd say you're here with a headache. Am I right?"

Abbi gave a small nod.

"You poor thing. Don't worry, I've got just what you need." Gerda rummaged through her cart until she found a red bottle. "Ah! Here it is!" She opened the bottle and tipped out two white pills. She handed them to Abbi before filling up a small cup of water at the sink.

"Here you are." Gerda smiled and handed Abbi the cup.

Abbi tossed back the pills and downed the cup of water. She sat there, silent, for what felt like a long time. The pounding slowed and lightened until Abbi could no longer feel it at all. She opened her eyes and saw Gerda filling out paperwork at the desk.

"Feel better now?"

Abbi smiled. "So much better! Thank you, Gerda, you're a life-saver." Abbi gave her a quick hug. "I'm off to breakfast. Can't take pain meds on an empty stomach."

Gerda smiled and called after her, "Say hello to your soldier boy for me!"

Abbi's face flushed, but she nodded all the same and scurried to the main room before Gerda could embarrass her any more.

With pain meds in her system, Abbi was ready to take on the noisy dining hall. She opened the door and made her way to the food table. She picked out several pieces of soft bacon and grabbed a few slices of sourdough toast. Her eyes lit up when she spotted hashbrowns available as well. With a full plate, she sat down next to some of the others. The three guests were exchanging stories on what they had seen here.

"I swear I felt something push me," the young man next to her said.

The woman sitting next to her rolled her eyes. "You tripped over your own feet, and you're trying to use a ghost as an excuse. Have some dignity."

Abbi snorted. They all turned to look at her.

"See Mark, she knows I'm right." The woman reached across Mark and held out her hand. "I'm Zoe. It's nice to meet you."

Abbi swallowed the bit of hash brown she was still chewing. "I'm Abbigayl, but you can call me Abbi."

They shook hands before Zoe gestured to the others. "This is my husband, Mark, and his dad, Ryan."

They each shook Abbi's hand and smiled at her.

"So, Miss Abbi, see anything interesting here?" Ryan asked her.

Abbi nodded, setting her fork down with a smile. "They have a room full of World War I and World War II memorabilia. It was both amazing and horrifying at the same time."

"I can understand that. It's amazing to see pieces of history but horrifying to remember what they're connected to."

"Exactly! Thank you, Ryan, I couldn't quite put my thoughts into words." Abbi gave a nod.

"Have you seen any ghosts? I swear I felt something push me yesterday." Mark looked at her with wide eyes.

Abbi bit her lip. *Should I tell them about Kristian? I don't really want to share that little secret, but he looks so hopeful.*

She sighed. "I have actually seen a ghost. I don't know if he's going around pushing people though."

Mark's eyes sparkled. "You have? Oh, please tell us about it. I love ghosts."

"You love ghosts because you're clumsy and it's something you can blame," Zoe answered with a giggle.

Abbi couldn't help but laugh too. Mark looked at his dad for support, but Ryan just shook his head.

"I'm with the ladies on this one. Sorry kiddo."

Mark pouted at his dad. "Some help you are," he mumbled.

Zoe, Ryan, and Abbi burst into laughter, and Mark joined in after a little bit.

"Sorry, honey. You know I enjoy teasing you. Anyway, tell us about this ghost!" Zoe turned to Abbi with smile.

"I think he's a soldier from the First World War. I spotted him the first evening here in his uniform. I thought maybe it was security, but he's the only one I've seen. And I found something else that confirmed it for me."

They leaned closer, hanging on every word she said.

"While I was looking at the pictures on the wall in the memorabilia room, I spotted it."

"Spotted what?" Zoe asked.

"Yeah, what did you see?" Mark's eyes were wide.

Abbi looked around, pretending to be nervous to hype up her story. Ghost stories were her favorite to tell after all.

"It was a photograph of soldiers outside the castle in 1914. And guess who was in that picture?"

"Was it the soldier from the first night?" Zoe asked as she scooted her chair closer.

"Yes, and he looked exactly the same. Not looking a year older than when the picture was taken."

The group gasped.

"Wow," Mark whispered. His eyes were full of awe as he sat there.

"Are you guys done with your plates?" Ingrid's sudden question made the whole group jump.

Ingrid took a sudden step back. "Sorry! I didn't mean to scare you. It's just, breakfast is over, so I'm cleaning up the plates."

The four of them looked at each other before laughing.

"Sorry, Ingrid, I was telling a ghost story, and I think we all got a little too into it." Abbi smiled up at Ingrid.

Ingrid smiled back and laughed. "So that's what all the whispering was about over here. I thought maybe you four were conspiring against us waitstaff."

Mark's eyes widened. "No, not at all! You guys have been awesome. We appreciate your hard work."

Zoe facepalmed. "She was teasing."

Mark blushed and ducked his head. "Oh."

"It's okay. It's hard to know when someone's teasing sometimes." Ingrid smiled.

Zoe gave Mark's leg a pat. "It's okay, honey."

Abbi handed her plate to Ingrid before standing up. "I hope you enjoy your time in the castle!"

The others smiled back at her. "If you see the ghost again, you have to let us know," Mark pleaded.

Abbi laughed. "I will! Bye, guys!" She waved and walked away.

She was on a mission today. She wanted to see Kristian again. *Will he still want to see me?*

She could only hope.

Twelve

A bbi went from room to room, revisiting her favorite ones. She entered the study with the ornate fireplace, settled in front of the flames, and relaxed. She wished she had a fireplace like this in her home. She would never leave it during wintertime. A good book and a cup of hot chocolate would be her constant companions.

The door creaked open, and Abbi turned to see who was entering her place of solitude. Kristian's face peered around the door, bringing a smile to Abbi's face.

"Hey Kristian! How're you?"

He stepped into the room and closed the door behind him. "Hello, *die Prinzessin*. I'm about as good as can be expected today. How about you?"

Abbi scrunched up her nose. "You called me that yesterday. What does it mean?"

"It's just a nickname." Red dusted along Kristian's cheeks. Abbi thought even his ears were red.

"Are you blushing?" She peeked up at his face, but he kept turning away from her.

"*Nein*! You avoided answering my question. How are you today?" He lowered himself and sat next to her on the floor.

"I'm doing good today, actually. Woke up with a headache but took some meds to keep that pain away." Her eyes lit up as she turned to him. "Oh! I made new friends at breakfast too. Mark and Zoe are married, and his dad Ryan is with them."

Kristian smiled. "Oh? What did you talk about?"

She giggled, covering her mouth as she did so. "Mark swears there's ghosts in this castle. Said one pushed him over yesterday. Zoe says he's just clumsy and uses ghosts as an excuse."

Kristian laughed too.

As their laughter died down, Kristian scooted closer to her. "You told me when we first met that it wasn't the right time to be with your family. What did you mean by that?"

Abbi blinked up at him. He remembered that? Why did it have to be that part of the conversation he remembered? She sighed and pulled her knees up to her chest. Wrapping her arms around them, she answered him. "I, um, don't have the best relationship with my family. I've always been the outcast. I've never really fit in with my mom and sisters. They constantly remind me that my differences make me unlovable to any romantic interest."

Kristian frowned. "That's horrible. I don't blame you for not wanting to spend Christmas with them. I'd hate them."

Abbi sighed, resting her head on her knees. "I don't hate them. They're my family. But first and foremost, if God can love them, then so can I. God loves me despite how horribly I've treated Him, so how can I hate them?"

"That's strange. You don't hate them because God doesn't hate you?" Kristian furrowed his brows.

"In the simplest terms, yes. God sent His only Son to die for those He called. He made Himself like us, like those He made. He suffered during His time here, suffered greatly, yet He never complained. If He can do it, I can strive to do it the best I can. I'm not perfect. Far from it really. But I want to try and honor that sacrifice."

She looked up at Kristian. "I don't want to spend my life so caught up on hating people when I can love them and hopefully make a difference in their lives."

Kristian stared down at her. "How are you able to look at it that way? People have been horrible to you. I just, I don't understand."

Abbi smiled. "Because it isn't me. I can only do it because of Christ, because of what God sent His Son to do for me."

She took his hand in hers. "It's confusing and a lot to try and understand. I can try and explain it to you if you want. Tell you the account from start to finish."

Kristian nodded.

She was calm as she went through each part of it with him, stopping to answer the questions she knew the answers to. It was something she never thought she'd experience and something she'd be forever grateful for. Not only did she get to share the love of Christ, but she got to spend time with someone who wanted to be around her and listen to her talk without getting annoyed or bored. *Maybe Paul was right about this castle's magic.*

Abbi leaned back against the chair staring at Kristian. "What about you? What's life at home like for you?"

Kristian sat back in his chair too, turning to look at her. "There's tension there, but that's my fault. I wanted to enlist alongside my friends. My parents spent hours trying to talk me out of it, but I never wanted to listen. Now, I'm wishing I had."

Abbi set her hand on his arm. "I'm sure they still loved you, Kristian. You're their son."

He nodded, his other hand coming to rest on hers.

"If you could turn back time, would you choose a different path?"

Kristian pursed his lips. "I don't know. Part of me wishes I could go back and stop myself from enlisting, but the other part of me says that it led me to you. I'm glad I got to meet you, and I don't know that I want to give that up."

A blush spread across Abbi's face. She lowered her gaze but couldn't keep the smile from her lips. "I'm glad I met you too, Kristian. It's been an interesting experience, getting to know you, but one I can now say I'm enjoying."

"You can now say? What, you haven't enjoyed it before now?" Kristian teased.

Abbi laughed. "I mean, you did scare me out of a room the other day. I think I'm entitled to my opinion on this one."

They talked for hours, just basking in each other's presence, moments spent talking about anything and everything. As the night wore on, Abbi's eyes began to droop. She yawned and stretched in her chair.

"Maybe you should retire for the night," Kristian suggested.

Abbi shook her head. "I don't want to go just yet. I want to spend more time with you," she mumbled.

"You're falling asleep. Your back will hurt if you sleep there."

When he received no response, he looked over at her. Her eyes were closed and her breathing soft and even. He admired how adorable she looked while sleeping. "Let's get you back to your room."

He slid his arms beneath her head and knees, pulling her close and tucking her into his chest. She hummed and snuggled closer in her sleep, and he smiled down at her. She just looked so peaceful.

He opened the door and stepped out into the hallway. It wasn't until he started walking down the hallway that he realized he had no idea where her room was. With a sigh, he headed for the room where he first met her. It was a safe assumption that she was wandering near her room that first night. From time to time, she'd mumble in her sleep, and each time he couldn't resist a chuckle.

Kristian stopped outside the door to the room he'd met her in. Looking around, the halls were empty. How would he find her room without waking her?

"Abbi?"

He turned to look at the owner of the voice. A young woman stood there, brows furrowed.

"Do you know which room is hers? She fell asleep while we were talking, and I didn't want to just leave her there."

She watched him for a moment before nodding. "It's just through here."

She led him to Abbi's room and pushed the door open for him. Kristian laid her down on the bed and pulled the sheets up to her chin.

"Good night, *die Prinzessin*. May your dreams be sweet ones." He leaned over and pressed a kiss to her forehead before turning around and marching out the door.

Thirteen

A bbi rolled over, a startled yelp escaping her as she hit the floor in a tangle of sheets. She took in her surroundings, confusion muddling her mind at the sight of the familiar room. How had she got back here? The last thing she remembered was talking to Kristian in one of the studies, curled up against one of the chairs in front of the fireplace. *Did he carry me all the way back here?*

She turned on her phone and looked at the time. Breakfast would be served for another hour.

Ding!

Abbi's phone went crazy with all the notifications rolling in from her mother and sisters. She sighed as she opened them and read them. She expected most of these, reminders of her shortcomings and her lack of presence at the family gathering this year. What she didn't expect was the long voicemail from her mother detailing all the ways in which Abbi was being selfish and ruining Christmas for everybody else. The harsh words brought tears to Abbi's eyes.

Why am I never good enough for any of them?

Last night she had felt seen and appreciated as she talked to Kristian. Any lingering happiness she had this morning evaporated like snow on a warm spring day. She spent so much of her life trying to please those

341

around her, only for them never to appreciate her efforts or even acknowledge them.

She closed her eyes and set her head in her hands. *Lord, help me remember to be a light to them. That I should love them because You first loved me. A love I will never deserve or earn.* She sat there in silence for a few minutes. If the Lord could love her despite her shortcomings and failings in the face of the wonderful gift He gave her, then she could love her family despite their treatment of her. *With your strength, Lord, I can do all things.*

She pulled herself up off the floor and gathered her stuff to start a new day. While getting cleaned up, she opened her Bible app and had it read the entirety of Philippians chapter four to her. It's just what she needed to adjust her mindset and go about her day with a better attitude. She wouldn't let their mean-spiritedness bring her down.

It was a warmer day, and her walk to breakfast refreshed her a little. There was nothing more beautiful than seeing the sunrise over the surrounding hills and shining through the windows. The beauty of the scene before her once again made her want to be a painter. She wished she could capture this sight in her mind and re-create it to enjoy for a long time to come and for her future family to enjoy long after she was gone. It was the perfect thing to cheer her up after her depressing morning.

There were so many things about this castle that Abbi was grateful for. She never expected Ingrid to be such a big one. Abbi hadn't expected to make so many new friends or meet a man who made her feel special for the first time in her life. The blonde bounded over to her the moment she stepped foot in the room. Her eyes were bright and her expression giddy. The joy and excitement on her face filled Abbi with warmth.

"So, I saw something rather interesting last night..." Ingrid smirked.

Abbi rolled her eyes, a playful smile on her face. "Yeah? What'd you see?"

Ingrid bit her lip and giggled. "Oh, you know, just this handsome dark-haired man carrying a familiar ginger I've become rather fond of."

Abbi's eyes widened. Her hunch had been correct. He had carried her all the way back to her room. That must have been how he knew which room was hers.

"I'm assuming you're the one who let him know which room was mine?"

"Well, he looked a little lost, and he was rather adamant about not leaving you propped against the chair. He just looked so sweet and sincere, I had to help him." Ingrid bit her lip, shifting her weight.

Abbi placed a hand on Ingrid's arm. "Thank you. I appreciate you helping him and looking out for me. Truly. It's not often I'm shown this kindness by anyone."

Ingrid threw her arm around Abbi and pulled her into a tight hug. "You are the kindest person I know, Abbi, well, maybe except for Grandma Gerda. Anyway, you deserve to be treated better than you have been by those around you. Don't let them bring you down. You. Are. Loved."

Abbi sniffled against Ingrid's neck. "I really needed that today. My, um, my mom left me a harsh voicemail this morning. It hurt my heart, not gonna lie."

Ingrid pulled Abbi closer and squeezed a little tighter. "I'm so sorry, Abbi. I'm glad I could make your day a little brighter."

"I've been so blessed to get to know you while I'm here. I've never known kindness like this before. Thank you."

Both of them stood there sniffling for a few moments before Ingrid pulled back and wiped her eyes.

"Are you going to see Kristian today?" Ingrid asked.

Abbi shrugged. "I hope to, but I never know when our paths will cross. I want to see him." She let out a sigh. "I wish I could help him somehow, but I don't even know how to help a ghost."

Ingrid bit her lip. "You'd be willing to help him?"

Abbi nodded. "Of course, I would. Why? Do you know something?"

Ingrid shook her head but wouldn't look Abbi in the eye.

"Ingrid…what do you know?"

Ingrid's eyes widened. "I don't know anything! I just wanted to gauge your thoughts on him. I think it's cute." She took a step back.

"I've got to get to cleaning! I'll catch you later!" She sprinted out the door.

Abbi took off after her. Ingrid knew something about this whole situation, and she was going to find out.

She kept some distance between the two of them to keep from being spotted. Ingrid stopped and looked back, and Abbi darted down behind one of the larger decorations. It was silent for a few minutes. Abbi held her breath, her heart thrumming against her rib cage.

Footsteps echoed in the hallway again, but they weren't getting louder, closer. She peered around the edge of the decoration and saw Ingrid running off.

I wish I was more athletic. Abbi huffed and stood up before heading after Ingrid at a slower pace. She made it in just enough time to see Ingrid slip into one of the rooms. Abbi thought she recognized this area of the castle, but she couldn't place which room she had visited over here. She tiptoed up to the door and cracked it open a little bit, pressing her ear closer so she could hear better.

What is she hiding from me?

Ingrid stepped into the restoration planning room with a sigh.

"You'll sigh your life away if you're not careful," Jacob said, looking up at her from the desk.

She rolled her eyes at him. Slipping off her shoes, she made her way to the chair on the other side of the desk.

"Abbi told me she wishes she could help Kristian somehow. I had to use all my willpower to not just spill everything right there."

Jacob gave her a stern look. "The castle will reveal everything in its proper time. We best not take matters into our own hands. They'll find everything out soon, don't worry."

"The solstice is in two days. It's hard not to worry. Is that really enough time for this to all come together?" Ingrid folded her arms on the armrest and laid her head down on them.

Jacob nodded. "Everything will happen as it's supposed to."

They sat in silence, each lost in thought about the current case the castle had assigned them.

"This is a rather strange one. Don't you think?" Ingrid asked, breaking the quiet of the room.

Jacob raised an eyebrow. "What do you mean?"

Trailing her fingers along the chair pattern, she answered, "Usually the match is between current guests of the castle, not a current and former guest. I didn't even know that was possible."

"The castle is mysterious, but it's never been wrong before. For whatever reason, these two are meant to be brought together." Jacob winked at Ingrid. "And I think they looked good together if I do say so myself."

Ingrid laughed. "He was adorable wandering the halls trying to figure out how to get her back to her room. Had to help the poor guy out or there could have been an awkward situation."

Jacob laughed.

"How do you think the castle will reveal the secret to them?" Ingrid questioned.

Jacob hummed. "I don't know. Maybe the library? I've noticed some things have been moved around in there, but I can't say for sure."

"I really want this to work out for them. Abbi needs some love and happiness in her life, and I'm sure Kristian does too."

"I do too, kiddo. I want to see them both happy. We'll just have to wait and see what is decided at the end. That's all we can really do." Jacob ran a hand through his hair.

Ingrid sighed and stared at the wall. She sat in silence while Jacob sorted through bills and design plans.

"It's almost time for lunch. Shouldn't you be getting back to work now?" Jacob raised an eyebrow at her.

"Fine. I'm going." She huffed and put her shoes back on.

She marched to the door and swung it open before heading to the main room. She thought she saw a familiar head of ginger ducking around the corner, but there was no one there when she walked by.

Abbi retreated and ducked around the corner, narrowly missing being spotted by Ingrid.

A dull pounding formed at the base of her skull as she processed what they had said. Kristian wasn't a ghost? She was lost. If he wasn't a ghost, then what exactly was he?

She roamed the halls, trying to clear her thoughts and figure out what it all meant. What option was there other than ghost in this type of situation? Maybe a trip to the library would help answer her questions. Jacob mentioned things have been rather odd in there as of late.

She was so wrapped up in her thoughts, that she failed to notice the person approaching from the other end of the hallway. It wasn't until she had bumped into him and felt herself falling backwards that she realized what had happened. A strong arm curled itself around her waist and kept her from hitting the floor.

"Are you all right?"

Abbi blinked up at her savior and smiled. "Kristian! Thank you for catching me. I thought I was going to hit the floor for sure."

Kristian shook his head and laughed. "I should have been paying attention. *Entschuldige.*"

Abbi waved him off. "I wasn't watching where I was going either, so I'm just as much to blame as you are."

He smiled down at her. It was a minute before they realized what position they were in and separated. Heat spread across Abbi's face and up to her ears.

I miss his arm around me already. I've never felt so safe and comforted in my life. She bit her lip and looked back up at him.

Kristian coughed, breaking the spell she was under.

"What had your thoughts so captivated?" Kristian asked.

Abbi perked up at that. "I just overheard the most interesting conversation." She looked around to see if anyone was around. "Let's go in here."

She dragged him into one of the rooms nearby and sat down.

He listened without interrupting as she explained what she had just overheard Ingrid and Jacob discussing.

"Hm, it seems like the library is a visit we must make." Kristian pressed his fingers together and held them against his lips.

"That's what I was thinking. We could meet there tomorrow. We might have to go in and out a few times until our paths cross since it seems we can be in the same room and not see each other." Abbi set her jaw in her hand. "That should hopefully work."

Kristian nodded. "We can meet at nine. That should give you time to dress and eat *Frühstück*."

Abbi scrunched up her nose. "I'm going to assume that means breakfast."

Kristian rolled his eyes but nodded all the same. "I will see you then."

He moved to get up, but Abbi stopped him. "You can stay, if you want. I wouldn't mind talking to you until it's time for dinner. That's about an hour from now."

He smiled and sat back in his seat.

They were so engrossed in their conversation that Abbi also missed the time. "Dinner starts in five minutes. I should probably leave." She sighed and hoisted herself out of the chair. "I'll see you tomorrow." She gave a small wave and made for the door. She looked over her shoulder at him.

"*Wiedersehen*." He returned her wave with a smile.

With that, she closed the door behind her. Off to dinner and then her room for the rest of the evening.

Fourteen

Abbi woke up to the sound of her alarm the next morning. She jumped out of bed and dashed to the bathroom for a quick shower. She dried her hair and got dressed as fast as she could without tripping over herself. *I wonder if I should bring some food with me to the library. I don't know how long we'll be in there.*

She grabbed her small crossbody bag and swung it over her head before heading out the door to the main room for breakfast.

The castle was noisier than ever. There were people everywhere hanging little things up and carrying items into other parts of the castle.

When she spotted Ingrid in the main room, she beelined for her. "What's going on? The castle is a zoo."

Ingrid sighed, dark bags prominent under her eyes. "Tomorrow's the solstice—when we hold the Christmas ball. All the preparations are underway and there's still a lot to do." She gave Abbi a tired smile. "I won't be able to keep you company today. Sorry."

Abbi shook her head, a sympathetic smile on her face. "Do you need anything? Water? Food?"

Ingrid shook her head. "No, but you're the best for asking. You enjoy your breakfast."

Ingrid turned and stormed off when one of the younger men dropped some glass ornaments on the floor.

"Yikes..." Abbi muttered, "glad that's not my job."

She grabbed a few small breakfast items and wrapped them in a napkin, then tucked them into her bag before anyone could notice. She nabbed a slice of toast and a couple pieces of bacon before heading out the door.

She almost bowled Zoe and Mark over in her haste.

"Sorry! I need to be more careful," Abbi admitted with a sheepish smile.

They waved her off.

"It's fine! Where're you going in such a hurry?" Zoe inquired.

Abbi leaned in closer. "I'm off to study in the library with a ghost!" She gave a wink and a wave before turning around and heading for the library.

"Have fun! You'll have to tell us all about it!" Mark called after her.

Abbi chuckled and shook her head. She was glad to have new friends who understood her for a change.

The halls were full of staff members running to and from so many different places that Abbi gave up trying to figure out where they were coming from and going to.

She creaked open the library door and gazed up in awe at the sight before her. It was like walking into the Beast's library, the one Disney princess moment she always wanted to experience. This was the closest she'd ever come. All she needed now was a prince to tell her he was giving it to her. Like that'd ever happen.

"It seems the castle is on our side today."

Abbi jumped at the familiar voice in her ear. She whipped around and smacked Kristian on the arm. "Don't sneak up on me like that!" She clutched her heart, willing it to calm down.

"*Entschuldige,* you make it too easy." He held his hands up in surrender, chuckling all the while.

She narrowed her eyes at him, but it only made him laugh more.

"You're lucky I like you," she mumbled before moving off to start searching the shelves. At this rate, they'd spend the whole day just trying to find the books they needed.

"Should we start with the ones on the table? If he's noticed books not where they're supposed to be, he might have pulled them out," Kristian suggested.

Abbi shrugged and grabbed a stack of books before sitting down in one of the chairs. She picked up the first book from the pile. She ran her fingers over the cloth cover, admiring the texture before she flipped it open.

"This is on the history of the castle. Think it might have some information?"

Kristian shrugged. "It's worth trying."

Abbi delved right in. Most of it was information she already knew. King Ludwig had spared no expense building the castle, despite the reservations of his advisors. It was no wonder he wasn't popular with a lot of people. His story meets a tragic end when he was found dead, under rather suspicious circumstances, in Abbi's opinion. This information wasn't helpful to her in the slightest, but she kept reading just in case. She found sections on the wars and the part it played in housing some of Hitler's stolen art.

But nothing on the magic of the castle.

She looked over at Kristian, whose brows were furrowed.

"Find anything?" Abbi asked.

Kristian shook his head. "It's only general information."

They both sighed.

They spent hour after hour poring over all the books they found on the table, only stopping to take a lunch break.

Abbi reached down for the last book in her pile. It had a deep red leather cover and beautiful gold lettering across the front that read, THE MAGIC OF NEUSCHWANSTEIN.

Abbi's heart leapt in her chest. This had to be it. Of course, it was the bottom book in the pile, though she didn't remember seeing a red cover when she originally grabbed all the books.

The first chapter was all on the Winter Solstice. *This is it!*

She called Kristian over, and they both began to read.

"Every year leading up to the Winter Solstice, there's a chance for the timelines of the castle to overlap, allowing residents from different time periods to meet at random. On the night of the Winter Solstice, the timelines converge and allow permanent travel between the periods when a strong enough connection has been established. One may choose to go back in time or jump forward in time and remain there."

Abbi looked up at Kristian. His brows were furrowed, and the look in his eyes was distant. Abbi kept reading.

"A word of caution: the decision must not be made lightly. For once the choice has been made, there is no going back."

Abbi turned the page, but it started a new chapter on a different topic. She closed the book and stared at the far wall.

"I didn't know what to expect, but that definitely wasn't it," Abbi whispered into the tense atmosphere. She turned to look at Kristian. She thought long and hard about the words she was about to say. She was putting her heart on the line. "Would you consider, maybe, coming to the future?"

Kristian blinked and looked down at her. "What?"

Abbi bit her lip, unsure of how to continue. "I-It's just. You'd escape the w-war. You'd be safe, and I wouldn't spend the rest of my life worrying about what happened to you."

He sighed, gazing at her with an intensity that somewhat startled her. "I want so desperately to say yes, but I'd be leaving my family behind, my country behind, everything I know behind."

"You'd be leaving behind a country that became infamous for their part in the Second World War for decades after it ended. You'd have a better chance of living a long and healthy life. Even if you didn't want to do it with me by your side. I just want you to be safe." Tears streamed down Abbi's face, and she used every ounce of willpower to hold back her sobs. He needed to make this decision on his own, not be pressured into it because of her reaction.

Kristian ran a hand over his face. The room was silent as a graveyard, an oppressiveness about it in the air.

After several minutes, he spoke slow and soft. "I need time to think about it. There's so much to consider and contemplate. I want to try praying about it."

Abbi nodded. If this is what he needed to do, she could respect that. "The solstice is tomorrow."

"I'll have the answer to you before midnight." With that, he turned and stalked through the library doors.

Abbi navigated her way back to her room on autopilot. She ignored everyone who tried to stop and talk to her. She needed to get back to her room so she could cry in peace.

The second the door shut behind her, she slid to the floor and burst out in tears.

Fifteen

Abbi woke up the next morning with dread sinking like a rock in her stomach. Today was the solstice. Today, Kristian would make his choice. She got up and got ready for the day, movements lethargic.

She was quiet all through breakfast and sat alone in the corner of the room as she ate.

Ingrid intercepted her when Abbi tried to slip out of the room.

"Hey, you haven't been yourself since yesterday morning. Are you okay?"

Abbi sighed. "I heard you and Jacob talking the other day."

Ingrid's eyes widened, but Abbi kept going.

"Kristian and I spent yesterday in the library trying to find information on what's going on."

Ingrid interrupted. "And did you find anything?"

"Yes." Abbi rubbed her eyes, hoping to keep the tears from falling. "Kristian has the opportunity to come forward in time and escape that awful war."

"That's great news!" Ingrid clapped.

"He doesn't know if he wants to do it yet. He needed time to figure out if he was willing to leave everything behind. He'll give me his answer before midnight."

Ingrid slumped. "Oh."

Abbi nodded.

"Well, why spend the day letting the "what ifs" consume you. Focus on the ball for now to get your mind off it." Ingrid took Abbi's hand. "I saw the dress you brought for the ball. You'll look absolutely stunning. Take some time and pamper yourself for the day."

Abbi gave a small smile. "Maybe that's what I need to get my mind off it."

"There you go! Smiling already. You go pamper yourself, and I'll see you tonight."

Abbi gave Ingrid a hug before heading back to her room to start prepping for the festivities.

With the final hair pin in place, Abbi sighed as she looked at herself in the mirror. For once, her hair cooperated, and the curls stayed with the help of bobby pins and enough hairspray for an eighties' revival. She picked up a tube of burgundy lipstick and swiped it across her lips with practiced precision.

There. All ready to go.

Grabbing her clutch from the top of the dresser, she found herself getting increasingly nervous as the day went on. Being holed up in her room meant that she hadn't seen Kristian yet, and she was desperate to know his answer.

For now, though, she had a ball to attend.

She walked down the hallway to the throne room, the sound of music guiding her.

Stepping into the room took Abbi's breath away. A giant Christmas tree covered with lights and shining ornaments stood in the corner. Holly and garland ran along the wall and curved along decorations. The band in the back of the room played carols that sounded almost ethereal.

It was an experience of a lifetime, and Abbi couldn't be more grateful that she was getting to experience it.

"You made it! Wow! You look stunning!" Zoe rushed over and gave her a hug.

Abbi smiled and returned the hug. "You look incredible! This room looks incredible!"

The girls chatted for a few minutes before Paul stopped the band.

"Ladies and gentlemen, it's time for one of our favorite events of the night. Please find a partner and join us on the dance floor!"

Mark collected Zoe, and they joined the crowd.

"May I have this dance?"

Abbi turned and smiled at Ryan. "Yes, you may!"

The band started up the music once more and the dancing began.

Abbi's heart was full of joy as she danced with Ryan and her friends.

Mark cut in at the next song, and Paul and Jacob each danced with her as well.

She had spent so much of her life being talked down to by her mom and sisters, and she'd struggled making friends, but here in this castle, none of it mattered.

She had friends now who cared about her. Friends who wanted to keep in touch and visit during the year. She never expected the magic of the castle to touch her so deeply, but it had.

The only thing she missed was Kristian's presence. What she wouldn't give for a dance with him here tonight.

Ingrid joined her as she leaned against the wall.

"You know, you've made enough of an appearance here," Ingrid tipped her head towards the door, "go find your man."

Abbi shot forward and wrapped her arms around Ingrid. "Thank you, for everything," she whispered.

Ingrid squeezed her back. "Now, go on!"

Abbi stepped from the room, closing the door on all the festivities inside. She dashed down the hallway hoping, praying, that she would be able to find Kristian tonight, that he would want to stay with her for the rest of their lives. She wanted him to escape the horrors he would face with the coming world wars. Their own little Christmas miracle.

She saw the light shining against the wall from an open doorway up ahead. The way the light traveled across the wall reminded her of flames. She tiptoed closer and peeked into the sliver of the open door.

A large fireplace stood lit at the far side of the room. Flames danced away in its hearth, bathing the room in a soft orange glow. Brown hair poked out from the top of a chair in front of the fireplace. Abbi's heart beat faster. She knew that head of hair anywhere. This was the moment of truth. Either he'd stay with her, or he'd head off to war.

She pushed the door open enough for her to slip through and stepped into the room. The warmth from the fire wrapped around her. Its embrace comforted her as she drew closer to the man in the chair.

Kristian turned his head to look at her. A smile spread across his face, and he rose to his feet. He reached out to take her hand in his.

"You're here."

She smiled and nodded. "I was hoping the castle would allow me to see you tonight. They said it would, but I couldn't bring myself to completely believe them."

Kristian laughed. "It is still hard to believe we are in a castle overflowing with magic. Still, I'm glad it brought us together over your week here."

Abbi blushed. "Me too. I've been so happy spending time with you here. Happier than I have been in a long time."

Kristian pulled her closer to him, wrapping his arms around her waist. He leaned down and pressed his forehead to hers. "I've never been as happy as I am now, *der Schatz*."

She giggled and placed her hands on his chest. They stood there for a moment, just basking in each other's company and closeness.

Desperation clawed its way up her belly, and she couldn't wait any longer to know what his decision was. She pulled back enough to look up at him but didn't stray out of his hold on her.

"Kristian? I can't wait any longer. I need to know what you've decided."

He chuckled, and she felt the knot in her gut loosen a little.

"I can't give you up now that I have you. This week with you has been the best week of my life." He tucked a piece of hair behind her ear. "I'd be a fool to refuse the chance to be with you for the rest of my life."

Tears welled up in Abbi's eyes before trailing their way down her cheeks. Kristian held her face in his hands and wiped them away.

"You are the best Christmas gift a man could ever ask for. You have shown me nothing but kindness, love, and Christ."

Abbi closed her eyes and leaned her head into his touch. Her body shook a little as tears continued to flow down her face.

"I've spent so long thinking no one would ever want me. That my mother and sisters were right." She let out a bitter laugh.

He pulled her closer and squeezed lightly.

Abbi looked down. "They were wrong. I took my love life into my own hands too many times instead of trusting God to bring the right one along." She looked at him and smiled. "I'm glad I figured it out in time."

Kristian leaned forward and pressed his lips against hers. Her heart soared, and she wouldn't be surprised if there were fireworks going off in her brain.

Abbi had never believed she'd find someone who would love her the way she ached to be loved. Her family always made it seem like she was someone a man would end up settling with because his first choice wasn't an option.

But no, for once, she was someone's choice. He wanted her and loved her for who she was, and that was more than she could ever ask for.

Ingrid and Jacob peered around the doorway, watching as the couple talked and laughed.

They smiled at each other and closed the door with a soft click. They walked down the hallway and joined the rest of the staff members in the restoration planning room.

Everyone turned to look at them as soon as they came through the door. When Ingrid and Jacob smiled and nodded, the whole room burst into cheers and applause.

They hugged and toasted before heading back out to check on the main party still taking place, the rest of the guests completely unaware of the miracle that had just happened within these walls.

Ingrid removed a painting on the wall to reveal a hidden board behind it. She grabbed a pin and the photograph she printed earlier and stuck it to the board.

"Another successful match," she said, looking back at Jacob.

He nodded and smiled. "This was my favorite one so far."

"You say that about all of them." She laughed, her hair swaying as she shook her head.

Jacob shrugged. "Each one is better than the last, but I think this one will remain my favorite for a while."

Ingrid smiled as she looked at the pictures on the board. She thought so too.

"C'mon, let's join the party." Jacob held his arm out for her, and she accepted.

The two walked down the hall to the main room, both looking forward to what the next Christmas would bring.

About Denise L. Barela

Denise L. Barela is a twenty-something-year-old writer with a passion for fiction, her faith, and just being creative in general. When she's not working away at her desk, you might find her reading a good book or following Alice down the rabbit hole...

Learn more about Denise's books at: http://www. celebratelitpublishing.com/denise-barela/

facebook.com/AuthorDeniseLBarela

instagram.com/artisticnobody1996

pinterest.com/artisticnobody

amazon.com/author/denise-barela

bookbub.com/profile/239822666

Crystal Clear

MARGUERITE MARTIN GRAY

For those who love to travel and discover small treasures along the way.
To all my traveling buddies through the years.
And to those I've yet to join on the journey.

One

Late September, 1879, London

With the slightest of knocks, a lady's maid entered the parlor, interrupting Rosalind and Princess Beatrice.

With her nose a bit in the air, Beatrice used her princess voice. "What is it, May? You know we do not like being disturbed."

The maid curtsied and bowed her head before reaching out her hand with an envelope. "I am sorry, your highness, but this is an urgent missive from Miss Rosalind's groomsman."

The elegant yellow papered sitting room in Buckingham Palace suddenly shrank. What could be wrong? Rosalind bunched her skirt in her fist and rose. Her cheeks warmed with anticipation. "For me?"

Her name in her mother's handwriting glared at her.

By her side in an instant, Beatrice looked at the sealed note. "Open it, please. If you do not, I will."

Biting her lower lip, Rosalind hesitated as her imagination grabbed images of injury or death. Why the urgency? Her parents had only just left her in London to return to their estate. Never before had they sent such an early letter and not with a warning of immediacy.

Her nail flicked the seal loose. With a shaking hand, she began twice as her vision clouded and then cleared. Her voice sounded far away.

"Dear Rosalind,

Your father and I have startling and devastating news. But first, everyone is fine. Do not worry about our health."

Beatrice guided Rosalind to the sofa. Their eyes locked as Beatrice patted Rosalind's arm. "At least they are well."

Rosalind pulled in a deep breath. "Yes." With trepidation, she continued her task.

"Your sister has eloped and left the country..."

What? Margaret? Why?

Beatrice giggled. "That is so romantic. She was engaged to that handsome viscount. No wonder. They loved each other so much..."

Rosalind jumped to her feet and paced. "No, Beatrice. That is not what happened."

She didn't mean for her words to come out harsh. The next few words blurred.

"Margaret ran off with a Portuguese sailor. All we know about him is he is the youngest son of a shipyard owner. In Portugal of all places. The Viscount Reynolds is furious. He is threatening to ruin us because of the breach of contract."

"Oh, Beatrice, why would she do that?"

Rosalind's steps led her to the tall window overlooking the Buckingham Palace gardens. A few of the palace residents meandered the paths as gardeners attended the plots of fall vegetation.

"Love?" Beatrice's calm response carried a possible reason. Would love cause such devastation? A family's ruin?

The letter hung by Rosalind's side, a burden she wished to release. Bringing it close again, she wondered about their fate, her fate.

"My darling girl, we'll send word soon. Your brother will remain at school. We will decide what the best course is for you. Most likely your season will be terminated before it begins."

The words smudged. Her mother's tears? *Oh, Margaret, what have you done?*

Rosalind held her melancholy stance, focusing on nothing except the extreme folly of love. She bade good riddance to the season that would have most likely landed her in a loveless contract.

Beatrice joined her, linking arms and resting their heads together. Rosalind's twenty-year-old lack of wisdom equaled Beatrice's twenty-two years of no solution. A great pool of nothing. No answers or reasoning.

Beatrice sniffled. "If Alice were alive, she'd have an answer." But sweet Alice, Beatrice's sister, had passed away last year. "I'll ask Maman what to do."

Through tears of her own, Rosalind laughed. "Your mother has a country to run. A silly domestic entanglement is not worthy of her concern."

"Perhaps not, but you are. Let me share this with her. It might take her mind off state matters."

"The queen has her hands full with you. Remember, she has not allowed you to marry. *Baby* needs to remain with her."

Beatrice's half smile never reached her eyes. "She approved of one man, but he was killed this summer."

"I know. I'm sorry. Would you have been happy?"

Her friend shrugged. "I'll never know. It doesn't matter. We need to find a way for you to come out unscathed. Margaret knew better. Her actions are attached to your family."

Rosalind lifted her face and gazed at the billowing clouds in a deep blue sky.

Father God, Your answer is best. I'm listening.

Throwing off the bed covers, Rosalind could not stay in her quarters when her life was falling apart. She had no say in its direction. So many others controlled her next move—her parents, the queen, God. But never her control.

What would I do if I could choose? Go hide in the country? Run away like Margaret? Face the gossip of London by participating in the season?

Her feet dangled over the edge of the bed. Her body shivered though she doubted her robe would warm her heart or prepare her for the day.

Putting her feet into her slippers, Rosalind wouldn't seclude herself in these four walls. It didn't matter that she resided in a palace for a few months. Society's hold quelched the fairy tale. Her best friend was a princess. That offered no protection from the criticism from the upper echelon. She shuffled at a snail's pace across the plush Turkish carpet to a window and pulled back the curtain. Gray, foggy, dreary, of course. But that wouldn't hinder her morning walk through the gardens.

Standing before the wardrobe, Rosalind cared not about her attire for the day. No one would be awake at this early hour. The sun barely turned the black of night to gray. Her heart mimicked the drab colors of the dawn. A fog draped her person. Perhaps she should dress in black like the queen and mourn her future. Her assortment of dresses contained not one black or gray one. Blues and greens, always her favorites, won out over pinks and yellows.

Remember, no one cares or will care.

The marriage mart, that ominous season of suitors, will be closed to me. For how long? Perhaps, Margaret's husband—that is hard to say—will find me a husband. No. I don't want to bring that grief to Mama and Papa.

So blue it was. For her foray alone in the gardens, Rosalind chose a light corset with a loose-fitting bodice, less full skirt, and low-heeled boots. She'd change later before any audience with the household. Grabbing her cloak, she sighed, patted her quickly swept up hair, and followed the hallway and stairs down to the gardens.

In her haste she'd forgotten her book and journal. Her thoughts descended with each step. She kept to the paths not visible from the palace. Choosing an iron bench facing a pool with a fountain, she plopped down, letting her woes crash with her.

Lord, what am I to do? You say You have plans for me. Is that true?

Two gray squirrels chattered and chased each other around and around the huge oak. Her companions didn't pay any attention to her. Yet, she included them in her conversation. Perhaps their antics would calm her.

"As Beatrice's friend and confidant, perhaps I can stay on in the background. I can avoid all the parties and balls. After all, Beatrice's reputation is of utmost importance." She sat on her hands and leaned forward. "What do you think? I sound like a spoiled child who hasn't gotten her way. And one who is awaiting punishment." She sat back and crossed her arms. "But I've done nothing wrong."

After an hour of pointless deliberation, Rosalind trudged back to the palace and entered the kitchen, one of her favorite places, although Beatrice scolded her for spending so much time there. Could she become kitchen help? A giggle escaped her gloom. Gossip would really ignite. She could see the headlines: Daughter of the Honorable Mr. and Mrs. Frederick Marrow Falls to Below Stairs Status.

"Well, good morn, Miss Rosalind." The jolly Mrs. Downs glanced from Rosalind to the tray of scones in her hand. "You are up and about mighty early. How about a cuppa and a scone?"

Rosalind's mouth watered. "As long as I can have some of your raspberry jam."

"Goes without saying." The cook placed a hot scone on a plate and set it on the table.

Rosalind retrieved a teacup and saucer before Mrs. Down's had a chance to do it. "I'll use the teapot here."

A dish of jam appeared as well as sugar and cream. Perfect. If Rosalind had come here first, her walk and talk might have been more productive. Nourishment always spurred her thinking capacity.

Even with all the servants bustling around the kitchen, Mrs. Downs had time for Rosalind. "Miss, if you don't mind me observing, I'd say you are a bit angst."

Rosalind's hands went to her cheeks, then her hair. "How can you tell?"

"Your eyes, my dear. The sparkling specks of gold have disappeared, leaving a darkness against the hazel. You've got no twinkle."

Do I usually have twinkle? "It's not the best of days." How much could the cook hear from above stairs? Did it even matter? "I'm in a bit of a quandary. Not of my making, but there anyway."

Mrs. Downs placed another tray of scones in the oven. "I hope you and your family are well."

"Oh, it's nothing physical. No one's died." Not physically at least.

"Let's say someone has done something that puts a bad light on my family. It could affect my...reputation and standing."

The woman wiped her floury hands on her apron then placed her right hand over her heart and drummed her fingers. "The only thing that matters is what the good Lord thinks. And with Him, even if you mess up, there is forgiveness. Don't you fret. God has a plan for you."

Rosalind's mouth formed an O as she tilted her head. "I mentioned that in a prayer earlier. I believe that, but I don't know what it is."

"'For I know the thoughts that I think toward you, thus saith the Lord, thoughts of peace, and not of evil, to give you an expected end.'" Mrs. Downs' words soothed her.

Rosalind nodded and continued. "'Then shall ye call upon me, and ye shall go and pray unto me, and I will hearken unto you.'"

Mrs. Downs joined her, their voices blending in like mindedness. "'And ye shall seek Me, and find Me, when ye shall search for Me with all your heart.'"

With all my heart!

Two

Checking her dress one more time in the mirror, Rosalind admired the green and white stripes, accentuating her hazel eyes and auburn hair. Stepping closer, she searched for the golden specks in her eyes. A few hours of fitful rest had alleviated a minute headache, but not her furrowed brow and listless eyes. At least her hair retained the healthy golden streaks, her main asset. She swirled from side to side, letting her skirt express vibrancy she didn't feel.

Beatrice entered with a bounce in her steps. "It's time. Mama cleared this hour for us. I know she will have an answer for you."

Linking arms, they followed the center carpeted path to the queen's sitting room. Would she have an answer? Would it be something Rosalind could accept? There was no question of rejecting the queen's suggestion. Not really.

The diminutive queen never ceased to amaze Rosalind. If God could use a short but dynamic woman to rule an Empire, then He could orchestrate a solution to an awkward, embarrassing dilemma.

Queen Victoria, in a black mourning dress, sat in a cream-colored chair. The contrast of light versus dark and small versus large confirmed Rosalind's profound respect for the woman.

Rosalind curtsied and took the queen's hand. The formality

remained after all these years. Just because she was the mother of Rosalind's best friend didn't mean she wasn't still the queen of England.

"Rosalind, come have a seat close to me. You, too, Baby." The queen motioned to the sofa to her right. "There's a lovely tea for us. Help yourselves."

"Mother, do you want me to pour?"

"Oh, please, my dear."

With tea cup and saucer in her hand, Rosalind anticipated a spill as her nerves and heart reacted to the queen's glance from her teacup to Rosalind.

Please share with me soon before I dribble my tea down my blouse.

She couldn't chance the disaster lurking in her hands. Placing the teacup and saucer on a side table, Rosalind straightened her perfectly straight skirt and stared at an enormous portrait of the late Prince Albert, the reason for the queen's mourning attire, even though eighteen years had passed.

The queen leaned forward and patted Rosalind's hand. "I can see you are weary from your ordeal. I have a suggestion."

Not a demand?

"How about you spend the season on the continent. I have a friend, Madame Pelouze, who owns a castle in France. We've shared many social occasions. Her father was a chemist and engineer. Anyway, her little château is called 'Chenonceau.' It's known as *Château des Dames.*"

Rosalind smiled. "The Ladies' Château."

"Exactly. All of the owners have been women. She is the sixth one. I would like to send a message to her. She has no children, and I'm sure she would love to entertain you for a few months."

Rosalind's mouth opened and closed. Dare she contradict the queen? "Your Majesty, I do not want to be a burden to anyone. I'm sure my parents will expect me to come home."

Contemplating the round biscuit with lemon curd in her hand, the queen took a tiny bite. The minute was long and grueling. Had Rosalind offended her?

The wisdom flowing from Queen Victoria's few words could save her months of humiliation and seclusion, although going to a small château in a foreign country spun images of hiding and escaping. But no one except the mistress of the castle had to know. Right?

While morose outcomes bounced around in Rosalind's head, the small woman stood as if a giant. Rosalind disliked being taller than the queen.

"I feel this is the best option for you, your parents, and even Beatrice." Queen Victoria nodded to her daughter. "Unfortunately, the gossip of the peerage will rattle and veer to the side of the viscount." Rosalind moaned and covered her mouth. "It's not fair, my dear, but it is fact. Go to France and enjoy Christmas and the change of scenery. Marguerite—that is Madame Pelouze—will treat you as a daughter. It's for the best."

Rosalind lowered her head, holding back tears and words of protest. The best for whom? There was no best for her.

"Yes, Your Majesty. Thank you. I'll not disappoint you."

The queen stepped in front of Rosalind and took her hands in hers. "You are not a disappointment or to blame. Look at this as an adventure. Not many young women can travel. Most are facing marriage or having babies." Her eyes flitted to Beatrice. "I'm glad you and Baby have had a few years of being unencumbered."

Taking in a deep breath and releasing it slowly, Rosalind was relieved. No more wondering about her fate—a small château in France. It could have been worse. Seclusion on her family estate with no visitors would have been almost unbearable.

As she boarded the boat that would take her to Calais and her new home, a paper boy yelled, "Read all about it. Viscount sues for breach of contract."

It only took two days for the gossip to spread. Soon the boy could add, "The youngest Marrow daughter disappears."

An older couple traveling to France agreed to act as chaperones for Rosalind's journey. Did they even know who rested in their care? For obvious reasons, the queen suggested Rosalind change her name for the journey. Not too far from the truth. Miss Rosalind Farley Marrow morphed into Miss Rose Farley. She could still be the daughter of the Honorable Mr. and Mrs. Farley. Who would know in the French countryside?

Her trunks, filled with her entire wardrobe plus items from Beatrice, rested somewhere on the boat. As the coast of England faded, she set her sight on France. Her future. Her security. Was it folly to believe the rumors and gossip would cease in her absence?

A carriage arrived for her after her brief two-night sojourn at her chaperones' residence in Amboise. Her early departure necessitated her daybreak attempt at perfection. What if Madame Pelouze cared not a wit for an abandoned, disgraced daughter of the peerage? Could she be more negative? Yes, if she had actually been the one bringing on the disgrace. What happened to innocent until proven guilty? She'd been tried and found guilty without a trial.

Her recently pressed hunter green skirt with a cream-colored blouse gave her confidence. For her travels, she opted for a small hoop and only one petticoat. Fitting into the carriage prevented the addition of the extra layers. She preferred leaning against the seat for the few hours journey than the straight back position determined by the larger hoops.

I might be going to a castle, but it is in the countryside not Paris. No one will care. I hope my fashion doesn't harm my first impression.

She piled and positioned her thick hair on top of her head as she did every day by herself, unless getting ready for a ball or a state appearance. The gas lamp and the sunlight filtering into the room gave enough light for her to see the freckles across her nose and upper cheeks. She hated wearing powder to cover the flaws. Shrugging, she added a fake smile to her image in the mirror. Although not a classical beauty, she'd pass for a pleasant-looking lady with or without freckles.

Pinning her straw hat with a green ribbon over her arranged bun, Rosalind pivoted and faced the closed door, ready for her future beyond it.

Hours later the carriage stopped at a wide boulevard lined with young plane trees. Rosalind drew in a deep breath. How beautiful. As her gaze extended to the distance, a white stone castle sparkled in the afternoon sun. Her home.

Hitting her fist on the ceiling, Rosalind garnered the driver's attention. "Monsieur, I want to exit here. I'll walk the rest of the way."

He cleared his throat. "Are you sure, Mademoiselle? It's a long walk."

The longer the better.

As the carriage turned onto the pathway, Rosalind—no, Rose—stood still in the middle of the long drive. A new name might be fitting in this beautiful place.

The road passed over a stream acting as a border. She expected silence but the swans and ducks greeted her, their honking and quacking mingled with laughter from workers in areas on each side of the boulevard. Different noises from London, but sounds of a waking community.

The smells—or lack of odorous smells—accosted her as she walked. Clean. Fresh. Green. What was that aroma? Flowery. Minty. She closed her eyes and breathed in and pushed out the foulness of London.

The white façade of Chenonceau lacked the grime of the city, even though it had to be as old as some of the buildings in London.

Ah, the recent renovations of this chateau explained its crystal clean appearance. Money and time could improve almost anything. Except possibly a reputation. She'd have to see about that.

Her steps faltered. One last glance at the château's entrance, with its turrets, chimneys, and charm oozing out of every window. Bringing her hand to her heart, she changed her tactic, praying instead.

Please, Lord, purpose my heart for what's inside. I know You can make them accept me. Amen.

Three

Captain Luc Bélanger leaned against the guard's tower. His afternoon walk around the grounds failed to regulate his frustration. Why had he supposed a stay at the château would ease his turmoil? It followed him no matter where he reposed—Morocco, Tunisia, Paris, or home. Well, he hadn't tried going home yet. He couldn't face his family and their pity. His aunt was the only one who'd not pressure him. He expected no answers from Tante Marguerite, and he'd give no details.

Clicking his cane on the cobblestones, Luc pulled himself from the wall and surveyed the courtyard. The rumbling of carriage wheels jarred his pensive state. Another of his aunt's guests? She'd mentioned something about a friend of Princess Beatrice coming for a visit.

That's all I need. A spoiled British girl flitting around the place. My stay might come to an abrupt end.

He stepped to the carriage door and reached to open it. "Monsieur, there is no one inside. Mademoiselle wanted to walk to the château."

Luc raised his hand to his forehead and stared down the long boulevard. A figure advanced slowly. He remembered his awe the first time he had seen the château before the renovations. Even then, the edifice radiated beauty and inspiration.

After two footmen unloaded the carriage, the coachman turned the vehicle around and headed to the carriage house. Luc remained close to the tower that housed his suite of rooms. His trained military eye for detail studied the girl *or* woman as she stopped, even with the massive sphinx on platforms on either side of the road.

Turning toward one, she stepped close and reached her hand to its paw. It dwarfed her. Pulling back quickly, she retreated. What scared her? The coldness? The lifelessness?

He shivered as his own cold heart pumped sustaining blood into his lifeless existence.

The pricks on the back of her neck jostled her nerves as much as the lingering coldness on her fingertips. Why wasn't the sun doing its job? Testing her nagging theory of being watched, she turned to confront whatever it was.

Nothing. Nothing in view, at least.

I'm just tired and anxious. Nothing a good cup of tea wouldn't cure or France's equivalent.

The face of the château smiled at her. The second-floor windows beamed their welcome as the huge front door opened with "bonjour." A woman in a blue dress with medium hoops waved at Rose. A warmth spread, extinguishing her cool encounter with the stone beasts.

Rose's steps quickened as the gap between them diminished. Before her stood a woman fit for the queen's parlor. Her beautiful attire and flawless skin disguised her age. Her open arms defied her British upbringing. Rose melted into the embrace.

The woman giggled, taking a step back. "I do hope you are Miss Farley. Otherwise, I've made a fool of myself."

"Yes, I'm Rose Farley." *And I hope you are Madame Pelouze.*

"Ah, you truly are an English Rose. I am Marguerite Pelouze. I welcome you to my little château." She giggled. "It has secrets yet to uncover." Madame looped her arm with Rose's, as they faced the entrance together.

"Madame..."

"Please call me Marguerite. Under the circumstances, I think formalities should be dropped. Consider me an aunt or an older sister. Now what were you going to say?"

"Oh, it's silly. But I imagined the castle smiled at me."

"That, my dear, is a good omen. Perhaps you'll be privy to her magic."

Will I have the twinkle and joie de vivre *like Marguerite? Let the transformation begin.*

As the doors of Château des Dames closed behind Rose, her fear of abandonment let go, allowing her to enter the castle free to ignore the rumors in London. Of course, the gossip could not penetrate the fairy tale that was now enveloping her. She sighed, relieved that no one here knew except her hostess. How many details? Rose had no idea.

Once the ladies entered the château, Luc exited his tower. Although appreciative of the lodgings, the circular abode brought on claustrophobic tendencies if he stayed inside too long. Sleeping posed no problem. No matter where he slept, the nightmares found him. Not every night but often enough.

The gardens of Chenonceau always soothed him. As a youth the paths and ancient labyrinth challenged his imagination, spurring him toward the role of knight or crusader. He never expected the battlefield would be his home.

He had a few hours before dinner. After checking on his destrier and giving him a rub down, Luc meandered to the vegetable and flower gardens. The scents, though having nothing to do with sounds, might distract him from the constant pounding in his left ear. Though the hammering had lessened over the months, his hearing had not returned. Well, that wasn't true because he heard the constant drumming and hammering.

Someone, or several people, cared for the vast plots with techniques and planning Luc hadn't noticed before. His family's estate could use some guidance. The produce here could feed a small village. Perhaps it did. Rows upon rows hosted flowering vegetables even as the weather cooled.

He wondered if the garden was quiet. What sounds penetrated the hectares? Birds? Cats? Singing? Workers talking to themselves? He longed for normalcy or silence that he could fill with his thoughts. The background rang the same, as far from a bird's song as possible.

A dark-green, spindly plant with tiny yellow blossoms reminded him of home. He squatted in front of it.

"Ah, asparagus." He searched for other plants he recognized. "Potatoes, uh, onions." Would the cats think him crazy for speaking out loud? His words, anyone's words, dimmed the ringing.

The distinct sound of giggling vibrated from the wide path beside him. Had she spoken to him? Smiling and still, she stood as if waiting for something. He looked around him for another object of her attention.

No, it was him.

"*Excusez-moi, monsieur.*" Her words rang clear this time.

He stood. A different dress but the same hat. He'd expected the guest to remain inside recuperating from her journey. Didn't all women prefer the afternoons inside?

"*Oui, mademoiselle.*"

"Eh. *J'ai besoin de mon...mon* basket." Her hand covered her mouth as she shook her head.

An English woman. At least, she tried to speak French. So many refused to try. "Ah, *oui, votre panier.* Your basket." He smiled, observing her crinkled, freckled cheek.

She pointed to a wicker basket at the end of the row. He walked a few steps and retrieved the vegetable and herb-laden basket.

"You must be on a mission."

Her cheeks reddened. "You speak English."

He gave a slight bow as he handed her the produce. "I do. And your French is impressive. Your vocabulary will increase. You've added a new word already—*panier.*"

"*Merci, monsieur.*"

He let her leave without an introduction. He scratched his beard before running his fingers through his hair. What must he resemble to a lady? An unkept worker. Tough clean, he had no reason to perform the extra duties on his appearance. Why even consider it now?

Her piercing, curious hazel eyes—that was why. Trouble. And were those gold specks?

She looked back once before she exited the garden. The barn would block her view in a moment. The stranger had not moved. Didn't he have work to do? If not a gardener, a field hand or a groomsman?

A very handsome one under the unruly wild hair and unkept beard. A little trim to his thick brown hair would improve his looks, though a bit untamed suited her. His brown eyes warmed her cheeks as he had studied her from his tall, possibly six-foot frame.

No, no, no! No entanglements with a French hired help. He might as well be a Portuguese shipbuilder.

Her stride lengthened, passing cottages lining a courtyard with a pond. Who lived there piqued her curiosity? But no time today. For all she knew, Monsieur Asparagus could be a resident with a wife and children.

Once she entered the formal gardens, Rose came to a halt.

"Oh, my goodness."

Château Chenonceau gleamed in the afternoon sun, white and clean. Spread across the River Cher, the castle rested on stone arches, floating on sparkling water, clear as crystal. A fairy tale portrait. From this view, the turrets, chimneys, and myriad windows begged for people to embrace and experience the nuances of secrecy and treasures.

Rose's burdens lightened as her feet danced through the paths by a fountain bordered with fall color, past the guard's tower into her fairy land.

Four

Luc pulled down on his jacket and adjusted his vest. Would his aunt approve? She wouldn't criticize in front of the guest. But he'd hear later if he messed up.

The breeze from the window, open to the river's currents, chilled his newly shaven face. It took a beautiful guest's presence for him to return to a more civilized self. He still desired to hide from society whether under a beard, common clothes, a hat, or a country château. Already, the castle offered less of a hideaway than he had expected.

"Ah, Luc, *entrez*." Marguerite ushered him forward. Her throne for the pre-dinner was a red-velvet heavily brocaded chair with thick cushions. Dressed in a golden gown, she posed as the queen of her domain.

He peeked at her as he took her hand in his and kissed it. A formal act befitting the drawing room, draped in rich velvets. Her eyes and nod directed him to the nymph from the walkway and gardens.

"May I introduce Mademoiselle Rose Farley. She will be my guest for the Christmas season. Miss Farley, this is my nephew Monsieur Luc Bélanger, my guest for an undetermined time."

Stepping to his right, he noted no proffered hand. He clamped his hands behind his back and bowed his head. "*Enchanté*, mademoiselle. I believe you are the same lady from our afternoon encounter in the vegetable plots."

Mademoiselle Farley blushed, making her powdered freckles darken. Enchanting. "Monsieur Bélanger. Finally, a name for the stranger. I must confess. I hardly recognize you."

Now his cheeks heated. Had he looked that unkept? He did and on purpose. He never expected to meet a guest in the gardens. Servants, *bien sûr*. Who sent a young lady of the house to pick the oddities for the evening meal? Only Marguerite, who probably would have gone herself if unoccupied.

Marguerite flicked open her fan and studied him through her lashes. "He does look a little better with a smooth face and combed hair."

"Tante, you know better than to discuss appearances in company. I'll consider your criticism in a private setting."

His aunt giggled and swatted his sleeve with her ornate accessories. "No need to be so uptight, Luc. I need you and Rose to get along. What better way than to discard a few formalities."

Marguerite's blue gaze turned and included the young lady, Rose. How appropriate for his garden image of her. But not a fussy, perfect, untouchable rose. Perhaps more of an English Rose, a blushing rose—cream with a pink tinge.

"*Moi*, uptight? I'm not the one dressed for a ball sitting in a Louis XIV chair like a queen."

Rose stared at them and smiled. "Do you always banter back and forth? It reminds me of siblings, not aunt and nephew."

Marguerite rose and fixed her bustle, adjusting the skirt as she stepped forward. Patting Luc's cheek, reminding him of days as a child, she laced her arm through his. "Without my estranged husband here, I tend to forget my manners. You will have to keep me in line, Luc. Your Uncle Théophile always thought he could. We see how that turned out."

Before Luc could offer his other arm to Rose, his aunt locked her to her side. He took the first step with the ladies joining his pace into the dining room. "I will never try to keep you in any kind of mold, Tante. You are the lady of this castle. No one has any sway over you."

"Well said, but you forget, God has a plan."

Luc doubted that. Was God in Vietnam or Morocco? Did He plan for Luc's deafness? What plan now that his stint with the military had ended?

"I agree," interrupted his inner tirade. Rose's strong, sure voice grated on his confidence. "His plan is sure and a promise for good. Right now, I have no idea what it is. I thought I did."

This conversation was one way to shut him out. Concentrating on seating his aunt at the head of the table dissuaded a response. Next, he helped Rose to her seat to Marguerite's left. He took his place opposite her. At least the view would be pleasant if not the conversation. He'd heard the talk of the goodness of God all his life. Had the priests ever been to war?

The servants served an aromatic, creamy asparagus soup, followed by a crusty loaf of bread sprinkled with caraway seeds. His aunt's commentary of her cook's skills steered the conversation on the right path for Luc. "I found Madame Lambert in the village. She had served in a local manor house for ten years. She's taken my family recipes and created sublime renditions. Her husband oversees the kitchen and vegetable gardens. What a couple of hard workers. So talented."

Talented? He couldn't even claim a single talent, although he couldn't honestly call cooking a simple task.

Rose observed the main course and closed her eyes, taking a deep breath as if wanting to savor everything about it. "What is this, Madame?"

"*Poulet aux oignons,* chicken with onions in a roasted garlic sauce. *Chou rouge aux pommes,* which is red cabbage and apples. And *gratin de pommes de terre à la crème*, potatoes in cream."

Rose continued her appraisal. "I knew it was something marvelous."

Luc's mouth watered at the description. He'd gain his healthy weight again if he stayed here.

If. I'm here for now. For this meal.

He relaxed and let instinct guide his knife and fork. His taste buds did the rest.

When the fruit and cheese arrived, Marguerite leaned back against her chair with her goblet in hand. Her eyes darted from Rose to Luc, and finally settled in a place where she could see them both. "I've been thinking about the possibility available to you for the next few months."

No, not a few months for him. But he clamped his lips together. Not a word.

"Rose, I think you might enjoy visits with me in the village. And I have a niggling desire to have a Christmas ball." Marguerite's eyebrows arched in question toward Rose. Luc caught the guest's look of surprise, big eyes with no words. "I think we all need a project of this magnitude to welcome the season. The château is a perfect stage for lights, music, and dancing."

Luc covered his grunt with his napkin. Delayed eye contact. Perhaps that would deter his involvement. He should have expressed his predicament with a sterner emphasis. *No social activity. I'm in seclusion, hidden away from the social whelms of the frivolous echelon. A battered warrior has no place at a Christmas ball...or a parlor, or dinner party. No.*

"And for you, Luc, I think a visit with a local farmer would do you some good. He is very productive with his vineyards and orchards as well as wheat and barley. His estate borders mine. His family began it in the 1750s."

She'd caught him anyway. So, he could escape the clutches of the ball planning. Luc crossed his arms and leaned back, not trusting Marguerite's motives or purpose. Would he really escape so easily?

"Tante, I agree with meeting your neighbor. He might be able to ignite my interest in my own estate. But a Christmas ball is beyond my present ability. I wish you success." He nodded to his aunt and then Rose, who was either a willing accomplice or a guilt-ridden guest.

Rose relaxed into her chair. Her constant grin during Marguerite's speech had reached her eyes. If she wasn't careful, her apparent joy at their playful yet serious confrontation would bubble into a fit of laughter. If he surmised correctly, the lady had fallen under the spell of his aunt.

Rose wiggled in her seat. "A Christmas ball sounds lovely, Madame. I know you have ideas that will outshine Buckingham Palace. A tree in every room. Candles and greenery. Decorations from the centuries... crystal and glass. And..." Her hands clapped and gestured as she spoke.

Luc focused his chuckle into a hiccup. He rolled his eyes at her enthusiasm. Definitely a willing accomplice. He'd have to sequester himself in his tower or move in with the farmer.

Marguerite pushed to her feet. "*Allons-y, mes amis*. We'll take dessert in the drawing room. Pen and paper await. Luc, I'm sure you can add a few suggestions."

He was sure he could not. "I'm afraid Christmas balls and crowds hold no fascination for me. Too much noise and gaiety."

As they entered the next room, Rose turned her head and dropped her jaw. But no words proceeded. Good, he had shocked her.

Only a second or two lapsed before Rose found her words. Crossing her arms, she posed as his opponent. "Monsieur, I don't know anyone who doesn't like Christmas. Think of the food and the music."

He strode to safety across the room, claiming a seat a preferable distance from the ladies. Resting his hand on the high back, he waited for them to sit before he eased into his chair, making sure his good ear could access the conversation.

Luc sighed, hoping he wouldn't growl. "I didn't say I don't like Christmas. The beauty and the songs and the meaning are all well and good. The extravagant trappings are bothersome."

Marguerite tapped her finger against her chin. "Hmmm. Why is that?"

He'd not let her figure anything out. If he unleashed the darkness plaguing his being, the petit château might groan with its weight.

"Leave it, Tante. Let's talk of your wishes, not mine."

"Ah, *cher* Luc, you are my wish. I'll just have to devise another way to coerce the boy of the past to show his face."

He laughed and slapped his knee. "That awkward boy does not exist anymore."

A servant passed out tea and dainty sweet concoctions. After the ladies chose no more than two each, he filled his tiny saucer with one of each—chocolate éclair, lemon tart, shortbread, and fruit quiche.

Rose sipped her tea as probably the queen encouraged. All manners and poise. Had she ever spilled it in front of royalty? He's likely to see that. Between bites of her chocolate treat, she studied him openly. "I like a challenge." She winked at Marguerite. "I'm adding you, Monsieur

Bélanger, as part of my project. You are going to like—no, adore—something about the Christmas ball."

He raised his brow. Did he hear correctly? Perhaps the pounding in his ear scrambled the words. "Adore? I don't think I've ever adored anything, much less anything that glitters or sparkles."

Marguerite jangled her bracelets and rings toward him. "Not even me, Luc?"

He snickered. Love? Yes. Admire? For sure. But adore? That held a higher degree of worthiness. "As tempting as it is to say yes, Marguerite, my answer is not even you."

How pathetic he sounded. The last thing he hoped to gain was their pity. They could just think of him as a tired, old warrior. No need for them to share in his nightmares.

Five

"Luc brought another box from the tower." Marguerite, dressed in a simple blue day dress, ran a cloth over the dusty crate.

Rose's heart skipped a beat every time a new treasure chest arrived. Well, she saw them as valuable treasures. Ancient decorations, some centuries old. "Where does he find all of these?" She spun around, swinging out her arms to encompass the different boxes in a spare room claimed for the sole purpose of sorting and storing the decorations.

"The first ones were from the attic of the château. But these..." Marguerite pointed to the ones lining one wall. "These are from the top floor of Luc's tower. During the renovation, I never had the opportunity to explore *La Tour des Marques*. But I've heard that is where many of the items that belonged to Catherine de Medici and Diane de Poitiers were stored. In the 1700s a guest found books and clothing dating back to the 1500s."

Rose dropped to her knees and leaned over the box Marguerite pried open. "I like the older ones." Rose imagined the stories the first owners would tell. "I'm so excited. It's like Christmas morning each time you open a crate."

How could Luc walk away and not care what he deposited? But each morning he left before Rose entered the room. If not for the occasional dinner, she'd not spent more than a few minutes with him in passing.

Under a layer of green velvet, Marguerite uncovered a colorful, though faded, porcelain shepherd, complete with a wooden staff and a sheep draped over his shoulders.

Rose sighed, clasping her hands over her heart. "How magnificent. The details make him seem alive. And look at the clothing." She grinned. "It reminds me of the costumes in Queen Elizabeth's court with the balloon knee breeches and stockings."

Marguerite ran her fingers down the statue. "I'm so glad men do not wear such silly costumes now."

Instantly, an image of Luc in stockings and puffy pants emerged. Rose nodded. "I agree. The current fashion is preferable. Though wouldn't it be comfortable on a day like this if we could put on breeches and sit on the floor?"

"What an idea! Théophile kept some of his clothes here. We could do that."

"What if someone saw us?" Rose couldn't afford to have another layer of gossip on her head.

"Phew. I'm not worried about that. I've already crossed the line of propriety by living in this place by myself. Being estranged from my husband is as damaging as divorce." Marguerite shrugged and stood. She placed the shepherd on a table. "I don't want anything I do to bring you more harm, *ma chère*."

Marguerite's gentle touch on Rose's hair soothed the separation of being alone and forever labeled in society. No one would ever know what went on in an obscure French village. From what Rose assembled, Château Chenonceau was no longer a playground for the higher-ups in France and definitely not in England. If her intuition proved wrong, she'd cross that bridge of social ruin when confronted.

Leaning in from her position on the floor, Rose secured another porcelain figure. A woman with a water jug balanced on her head, held in place by her hand. Beautiful. Oh, the content smile on the pure, unblemished face expressed a life well lived. Joy in her fate as a servant. Her simple dress of pale green boasted the puffy sleeves of the time, and a simple high-waisted costume flowed in the timeless breeze. Perhaps, she accompanied the lowly shepherd.

Marguerite sighed and arranged the servant girl next to the shepherd. "Perfect for the nativity. The first visitors."

"Here are some animals. A cow and donkey. Two sheep." Rose's breath caught in her throat as she retrieved a child leading a younger child by the hand. "How precious. I've never thought of children being at the manger."

"Well, they will be at our display. The Jesus I know would want children worshipping Him."

"*Oui, bien sûr. Les enfants sont innocents,*" Rose added.

Something happens to that innocence. Somehow, I've fallen into a world lacking that purity.

The empty box joined others to return to storage. Standing in the middle of the organized items, Marguerite crossed her arms and bit her lower lip. "Now, we need to decide on themes for each room. In about a week, we'll bring in some freshly cut trees." Her blue eyes captured Rose's intent concentration. "I think you and Luc can be in charge of that task."

Not a question. A command in the friendly way that Madame used for getting what she wanted. Tramping through the woods with Luc was scheduled without consent from either party.

I could protest. But would it do any good? I doubt it.

"How many trees?" Rose might as well sound enthusiastic. She truly was about the whole project.

Marguerite extended her hand, helping Rose to her feet. "Let's go find out."

The tour around the château's main floor included twelve trees inside and two by the outside front doors. Three of those would grace the gallery where the main ball would be held. Fourteen trees! A daunting task.

Rose channeled her overwhelming anxiety into a challenge. If they could accomplish the task, she'd gain satisfaction beyond her imagination. Reaching out her hand, Rose touched Marguerite's arm. "Let's do it."

"*Merci, mon amie.* I promise the reward will be more rewarding if we accomplish the imposing feat. I figure a tree a day will be a good goal along with the other greenery."

Rose chuckled. "At least we don't have to cook the food."

"No, but we have to make the menu."

"Oh. I don't even know how many people you are inviting."

"About a hundred."

"*Quoi*? So many?"

"Mostly villagers and the local estate owners and their families. Very few dignitaries, although my brother will invite a few of his political influencers."

Rose's smile disappeared. People outside of this remote area did not bode well for her situation. What if he brought a British diplomat or a courtier from Buckingham Palace?

Another box. This one was a bit lighter than the others. Luc might as well deposit one more. Once the tower treasure trove emptied, he'd be free of the cobwebs and dust. As much as he loved his aunt, her grand renovation campaign to bring the château back to Diane de Poitiers' sixteenth century grandeur didn't impress him. So much money and time. For what? Beauty? History?

The pounding inside his head resounded with the cannons and disturbing cries of war. Where was the beauty in the battlefield? While he fought, his aunt chiseled away at stone facades to create a time of romance. Hadn't wars and misplaced love plagued that century too? Yet, people clung to the fairy tale possibility.

How can I mesh the two? I see the beauty in the castle, the gardens, and in...in Rose, but the calamity of war invades my dreams and my head every day. Prayer hadn't worked during war, and it wouldn't work now in his idle life amid God's creation. One world destroys life and the other brings life. For what purpose?

Christmas.

Christmas would come and go, unlike the constant reminder of death.

"Where do you want this box?" He hadn't expected to see Rose in the decoration room.

Her hand went to her heart. "Oh, yes...how about right here on this table. Is it heavy?"

"Not at all. But it's fragile."

"*Oui*, I see fragile painted here. Do you want to see what's inside?"

No. I don't really care.

"*Bien*." How could he refuse her innocent curiosity?

Her delicate, long fingers unlatched the lid. Watching her reaction stirred a faint flutter of excitement for what she would find. True, he didn't care about the contents, but she did. That was enough to spike his interest. Her gasp and wide eyes coerced him to peek at the contents.

Her fingers caressed a crystal sphere with delicate etchings of lines and circles. "Oh, what a treasure. I feel I should wait for Marguerite. Have you ever seen anything so precious and beautiful?"

"*Oui*, I mean *non*." If her expressions and hands do not count. "Take it out."

She held it by the hook and ribbon at the top and let it rest in her other hand. "I think it is actually an ornament. Perhaps not originally for a Christmas tree, but it hung somewhere." She included him in her search. "What do you think?"

"In front of a window to capture the sunlight?"

"Ah, *oui, parfait*."

Rose transferred it to an open box with discarded fabric. The next crystal item resembled a perfect hexagon. The afternoon sunlight filtered through the crystal, casting a rainbow of color across the floor and wall. Tiny dots spotted Rose's face. An ethereal veil descended, draping her in its magical web.

Luc backed away, avoiding any spidery threads waiting to entangle him. He blinked. The sunlight splayed across the room, splashing reality on his gloomy wonderings. The crystals were just that. Objects with the ability to distort light. Surely, his nightmares couldn't distort beauty in the middle of the day.

Rose beamed with girlish delight. "There must be two dozen items here, all crystal."

"Do you have an idea for them?"

She surveyed her collection, each twinkling from its resting place. "*Oui*, I think I do with Marguerite's approval. The crystal ornaments would be perfect in the long gallery. The white and black checkered floor and the many windows. Light from gas lamps, chandeliers, and candles. Yes. Center stage as the *pièce de résistance*. A crystal and silver theme against the black and white marble." Her finger rested against her lips, then she reached for his arm.

Following the motion, he stared at her gesture, almost missing her question. "Are there any more boxes?"

With her simple touch he desired to give her anything but knew his limitations. He shook at her words. What she asked for was not personal at all. Boxes from an attic. His escape from her contagious presence. It was clear that he needed to run out of the room. He'd send someone else with the boxes.

"I believe there are two more similar to this one."

"Oh, let's go find them now. I want to see if perhaps there are more crystal ornaments to complete my gallery project."

No. "You stay here, and I'll…"

She placed her hands on her hips. "Luc, I insist. Anyway, I've wanted to see this ancient tower of yours. This is as good an excuse as any."

She headed into the hallway within a few seconds. His lead feet stayed his movement. Her smile turned his "no" into "what would it matter?"

"Are you coming with me?" Her voice echoed in the hall.

"Hmph. I have no choice now. Do I?"

Her eyes twinkled before she flitted toward the front doors. "Monsieur, you always have a choice."

Do I?

Six

T he tower was all Rose thought it would be, right down to the winding circular stone staircase. Up and up, a dizzy ascension. They passed two floors, which Luc said led to his quarters. The final level had a solid wooden door with an old iron latch.

Luc jiggled the handle. "Marguerite had it unlocked for our search. Watch your step and your head."

The opening dipped lower than her height. The two steps down could trip someone. Inside the circular room, Rose stood in awe of the crates, paintings, a work table, and two chairs, positioned for someone to easily examine the boxes or create the next masterpiece.

Running her hand over the old table top, Rose's imagination pulsed with questions. "Whose workroom would this have been?"

Luc ducked his upper body under the archway. "I don't know. I've cleared away some of the cobwebs and dust. It hasn't been used in ages." He straightened, leaving his head two inches below the ceiling. "The boxes are in this corner."

Rose found the identical crates and bent to lift one.

"Let me do that for you." Luc stepped beside her, brushing his arm against hers.

She whispered, "*Merci.*" Her skin tingled through her sleeve at his accidental touch.

Concentrate. Boxes, crystal, decorations. Not Luc, men, or problems.

Luc used a rag from the table to wipe the grime off the top of the boxes. He must have done that for every box he'd delivered. Did Marguerite know of the trouble and care he took?

She looked over his shoulder. "*Fragile.*" Oh, please be more crystal. A humming echoed around the room. The wind. But it was sweet and calming. She leaned toward the notes. Perhaps the objects in the box rubbed against each other. She opened the lid. A resounding sigh breathed into the room.

"Did you hear that, Luc?"

He shook his head. "No. Unless it is pounding like a cannon. What did you hear?"

He stared at her, seeming to pay attention, possibly wanting to believe her but couldn't. "Oh, well. Maybe nothing. A hum or whisper."

He raised his eyebrows. So, he *did* question her, choosing not to believe her strange observation. No matter. She knew crystal didn't sigh or hum. She assumed crystal lay beneath the velvet. Without breathing, she removed the covering. "Yes, more crystal." She clapped her hands, swaying as joy filled her places of doubt.

Seeking Luc's opinion, she saw his smirk. Why did she seek something he wasn't willing or able to give? He'd been against the ball from the beginning.

Peace. A whisper.

Yes, the task at hand. She held up a crystal dove. With little sunlight from the arrow slits, posing as windows, the overall shimmery effect dimmed. Yet, the potential remained. Placed on a tree with sources of light all around it, the dove would sparkle and shoot its rainbow on others.

"Look, Luc, this box is different. Instead of shapes, there are images. A bird. I think this one is a fox." She thought a smile surfaced but wasn't sure. "And a rabbit."

Luc leaned closer and picked up a perfectly formed rose. "A rose for you, dear Rose."

Her hands received the crystal rose, as she whispered yet again, "*Merci.*" He might not hear the peace or accept the beauty of Christmas, but somewhere in his warrior's armor there was a human soul.

Could Christmas and light melt his hardness? Was there a miracle left for him?

She prayed Jesus' words silently. "My peace I leave with you; My peace I give to you."

Rose tied another red ribbon on the red-and-gold themed tree in the front room—the first one that guests would see off the main hall. Louis XIV's room was named for his portrait and ornate, red-cushioned chair. It contained one of the trees brought in by a ground's worker. Three more were scattered around the house.

"I knew he'd accept." Marguerite rushed into the parlor, waving a letter. Her blue eyes found Rose but skittered back to the paper.

"Who accepted what?" Rose took the opportunity to plop into a chair, a reprieve for a minute during Madame's dramatic entrance. Tree number four and a thousand to finish in two weeks.

"Monsieur Debussy, of course."

Rose quickly retrieved a memory. "The young pianist."

"*Bien sûr.* And composer. The next Bach."

Rose giggled. "You put high expectations on someone so young and obscure."

"You'll see. He managed to elevate the little orchestra this summer to a level everyone wanted to hear. You should have heard the applause. I had to have an encore performance a few weeks later for all the dignitaries who missed the first concert."

"And now?" Rose's curiosity attached to Marguerite's enthusiasm.

"Well, he is spending Christmas at the château and will be here for the ball. He and a local violinist will serve as the musicians for the ball. You will waltz to the talented music of Claude Debussy. Aren't you impressed?"

Rose didn't know Monsieur Debussy from Jack the butcher. "I look forward to it. If you say he's talented, I believe you."

Marguerite pouted and huffed. "Well, if that is all the enthusiasm you can muster, no telling what Luc will say. Speaking of Luc, when are you going to pick out the rest of the trees? We'll need one for tomorrow in the chapel."

"He promised to go this afternoon."

"Good. I'm sending you across the river. There is a nice grove of firs there."

Last time Luc had gone by himself to Marguerite's chagrin. Why did she insist on Rose's presence? He really didn't seem to want Rose tagging along. He might not get his way today.

"I have some old boots for you. I'll put them on the steps by the gallery door. All you have to do is tag the trees, and Jacques will cut them as needed."

Rose laid her head against the comfortable chair, slipping into its arms. "Do you think we'll finish?"

"Oh, my dear, we have no choice. By the way, tomorrow the seamstress is coming to measure you for a dress. I ordered the material—silver and white. You will be the belle of the ball."

I'll be an ornament instead of fading into the background. What happened to my plan?

Rose joined Marguerite by the tree. "You do realize I am trying not to draw attention to myself. I do appreciate all you are doing for me. But what if one of your guests connects me with my sister's debacle?"

Marguerite gently guided Rose's chin toward her, preventing Rose from staring into the fir needles. "You are not your sister, rumors or no rumors. I cannot promise that no one will recognize you. Do me a favor and let Christmas work a little magic."

Catching a tear at the corner of her eye, Rose nodded, repeating the lady's words. "I am not my sister. I'm strong enough for whatever happens." She never let her musings go farther than a "what if" question. She had no idea what she'd do if confronted.

After a mid-day lunch of quiche filled with ham, onions, and cheese, Rose slipped into a light-brown day dress, possibly from the back of a servant's closet and put on the borrowed boots at the end of the gallery. She'd noticed the door but had never ventured through it. The large loop handle clicked as she turned it. The door was a bit heavy and awkward, as she pulled it toward her. Stone steps led to a landing with the river on either side. A small fishing boat tied to an iron post rested in the lapping water. A lazy cruise down the river would give her time to float away from the nibbling fears. Yet, at the other end, her fears would still churn and bubble.

Steps led to another door placed between a sturdy wall or barricade on each side. Where was Luc? If he didn't show up, could she continue alone? One of her favorite pastimes included walking through the woods but not ones unfamiliar to her.

The door screeched open, depositing her on a concrete platform before a tall man—Luc in worn, navy pants tied with a rope at the waist, and a stained beige or white or brown shirt, the color drained from the cloth seasons ago.

Rose threw her head back and laughed. The old clothes matched his old worn soul. At the moment, he could be fifty instead of his thirty years. Was he even thirty?

"Have I caused such a stir, Rose?" He stomped his old boots, releasing dirt globs. "It's still me."

"No, you are fine. We must look a sight in our ill-fitting attire. I didn't pack for a jaunt through the forest."

"Neither did I. It would take me years to fill out these clothes." He stretched out his arms, emphasizing the sagging sleeves of the jacket.

Although he had gained a little weight, giving his face a healthy fullness and color, she couldn't imagine Luc ever gaining enough to equal the pants or jacket.

A rumbling on the path revealed a wagon for their trees and Jacques. Rose was sure he was sent as a chaperone, helper, and messenger. It made sense—he needed to know which trees to cut down. His attire resembled Luc's but fit his true fifty-year-old form perfectly.

Luc took the first steps up a slight incline. "*Allons-y, mon amie.*"

Thankful for the sturdy leather boots, Rose gained her footing, accepting Luc's gloved hand, though more than capable of ascending the slope. His firm grip buoyed her resolve and afternoon outing.

Purpose and companionship. Would he want her company if he knew? Was her predicament a secret she should keep?

Snow had not burdened the evergreens yet this season. Strong branches spread toward the sun, reaching for the warmth. They knew the snow and cold of winter promised an entrance. Their sturdy trunks and limbs were prepared by God's plan. Some of them had the special task of adorning the château and providing warmth later.

If a tree has a purpose, so do I. What is it?

Very simple for now, she supposed. "Our goal is to tag ten trees. I have a mental idea of size and where they'll go." She compared Luc's height to the trees. "One needs to be fifteen feet or more—double your height plus some feet."

Luc nodded, understanding since he'd heard the instructions. She caught Jacques rolling his eyes. Of course, the mission meant hard work for him and his fellow hands.

Suppressing a chuckle, Rose encouraged Jacques. "At least, the giant one is going right through that door into the gallery and no further."

The man grunted. "*Oui, mademoiselle*, at least."

"We need to find two more for that room—one twelve feet and the other eight. The rest need to be around six to eight feet. These are our marching orders."

Her little speech reminded her of childish games where the participants made a pack and swore allegiance to the outcome.

Luc was a soldier so he could march—probably used to being in charge. Could he follow Marguerite's lead? Or hers?

He grinned and patted his wide-brimmed straw hat on his head. "Mission accepted, captain. I think you found your calling. Leader of a tree-cutting brigade."

She pointed her finger at him. "You laugh now but remember the general is the one with the orders and the power."

"True. Yet, you seem to be very supportive of every aspect of the project."

Her chin rose, honing in on his playful stare. "I am. The house smells of Christmas. It sparkles like the season. I've even heard whispers lingering of peace."

Her brow creased, concerned that her friend's blockade barred any connection. "Do you really feel nothing?"

"Only around you and Marguerite. Who knows? It could be the magic of the château."

"Or a miracle," she added, marching forward.

Veering off the path, they encountered so many trees—some had to be spruce, Nordmann firs, and noble firs, the ones Marguerite desired. Cutting ten trees would leave barely noticeable gaps.

"Luc, do you know the differences in the trees? I can see the nuances but Madame particularly wants the majority to have a strong fragrance."

He stood next to a tree a few feet taller than his height. "Yes, this one is a noble fir. Come feel the soft needles. They will keep longer, and this variety has a great pine odor."

"*Ah, fantastique!*" She retrieved a red cord from her pocket and tied it loosely on a branch. "Nine to go."

Luc became their guide through the forest. "This one is a Nordmann fir, which has soft needles and excellent retention, but it's not particularly odorant."

"Yet, beautiful. Do you see another one about the same size?" She spun around, spotting its twin. Two more cords gone.

Luc disappeared between some trees. His voice led her to his side. How did he know so much about trees? It proved she knew very little about him. "The spruce reminds me of Christmas. But you have to be careful and cut them closer to the date, for they will drop their needles quickly. But smell the Christmas scent."

He broke a small limb, rubbed the needles together, and lifted his palm toward her nose. She inhaled, closing her eyes. The piney scent tickled her senses, erupting images of joyous Christmases. Her family around the tree—lights and presents—and innocence.

She opened her eyes, which probably glistened with tears over the sweet memories, shattered with one decision. *Oh, Margaret. Why?*

Love.

"It sounds like you have some good Christmas memories, Luc. What happened?"

"War." He stomped off to another group of trees.

She guessed war could change anyone's outlook, as could rumors and lies.

Rose tagged a few spruces, letting Jacques know to cut them much later. *We still need the* pièce de résistance *for the long gallery.* She walked, concentrating on high tree tops, wandering through the firs until she halted. Spreading its majestic green branches stood a perfect noble fir. How could she have it cut for a ball?

For such a time as this. Decorated with crystal ornaments and draped with silver garland. It would be perfect.

She advanced, her hand out to touch a branch. "*Merci.* You will bring Christmas joy to so many." Leaning in closer, she added, "Perhaps you are the one to return beauty to Luc's life. Jesus could use you for the Christmas miracle."

Please, Lord, embrace Luc with Your peace, hope, and joy. Make Your presence crystal clear to his hurting soul. Amen.

The outing wasn't what Luc expected. Find some trees and be done. Instead, he entertained notions of celebration. Why did her presence conjure up images of a world of beauty and peace? Didn't everyone know that this world was full of death and violence? Why should Christmas change that reality? They were living in a fairy tale world in a fairy tale castle.

Do I have the right to destroy that for them?

No. Stomping off into the woods had separated him from Rose's innocent outlook. Once he and Jacques had cut down two of the trees, they wound their way back to the castle. The task completed, he could escape to his tower.

They exited the forest at a spot a few hundred yards from the castle. His breath always caught at the sight. This hundredth time was no exception. Awe at the splendor.

Rose stumbled a few feet behind him. Catching her, he rested his hand on her arm. He realized the moment she glanced at the splendor of stone, water, and light. Her shoulders rose as air filled her lungs and hesitated before release.

"Oh, my gracious. She is beautiful. But more than that." Rose bit her lower lip and tilted her head. "*Fantastique. Magnifique. Je ne sais quoi.*"

The Château des Dames sprawled across the Cher in her glamourous white reach. Four wide arches braced the long gallery. The design of a master for sure. What could he add to his emotion?

"I know. My favorite view." He released Rose's arm and pointed to a bench. "Marguerite placed benches on either side of the river from every vantage point."

Rose nodded without taking her eyes off the castle. "It's my favorite too."

Once seated, he couldn't take his eyes off of her, Rose—not the castle. While the view occupied her, he studied her expressions, the rise and fall of her lips, eyelashes, cheeks, and forehead. Her freckles emphasized innocence. Although he guessed she was part of the English upper echelon, she shed those mantles just as his aunt did at times. He imagined the real Rose sat here. Now. A straw hat. A little dirt on her gloves and cheek. He forced his hand behind his back before he made a fool of himself by cleaning her face. Not a child. But someone who understood joy in simple acts. Well, maybe decorating a château qualified for more than a single project. Her capabilities spread a wide girth.

Right now, she sighed and swayed forward. "Look, the sun is turning it a golden yellow. Her reflection is reaching out to us. What an inspiration."

"*Oui.*" Yes, Rose was an inspiration, though an unexpected one. In her presence, the pounding in his head was replaced with the gurgling of the river against the bank. Beauty sprang to life. Right now, he could believe battlefields did not exist anymore.

She eased up with her hand on the back of the bench. "There goes Jacques. I almost forgot about our mission. He might need some help."

Walking in silence allowed a few more minutes under Chenonceau's spell.

Once at the steps, Rose's hand stayed his advance at the door. "*Merci*, Luc. You were so helpful."

Her smile forced his own. "*Mon plaisir, mademoiselle.*" He added a slight bow.

"I apologize for anything I might have said that hurt you."

"Eh, *mon amie*. You're not to blame. Let's just say the battles of war plague me and show up at the most inopportune times."

Lowering her eyes to examine her gloved hand, she whispered, "I'll pray for you then."

"Well, that would be an awfully long prayer with no results."

"Challenge accepted. My God is bigger than we are. I'm not deterred. But He doesn't promise the answer I want, only an answer and a plan."

"His answer for an angry old soldier would be interesting."

"You're not old."

"I feel it, and I'm sure I look it."

Her hand reached for his cheek and caressed it. Heat from the gloved touch trickled to his heart, bypassing his mind. Touch. Her touch could melt his cold soul.

"Open your heart to possibilities—Christmas promises."

She turned, pushed the château door open, and disappeared into her fairy tale land, leaving him basking in a spring-like warmth.

Seven

Rose endured the pinning and draping of fabric to humor her host. The satin against her body cooled her comments. She ran her hand over the soft, slick, white material.

Marguerite circled Rose, waving the pattern of a Parisian design as the seamstress took notes. "Silver accents. I don't want the dress to appear white. Enough silver lace and buttons to highlight the skirt. The fringe needs to be made of pearls and crystals dyed silver."

Could Rose comment? Did she have a say? Probably not her place, but... "Madame, what if you left the crystals untouched? Use clear crystals whenever possible."

"Hmmm." Madame rested the folded pattern against her chin. "You have a point. The crystals would reflect the light whenever you move. Perfect. *Merci*, Rose."

A small bustle, with a silver satin overlay, tight bodice, and modest V-shaped neckline. Rose could live with all of that. Compared to Princess Beatrice's sessions with a seamstress, Rose had it easy.

"And add two day dresses of blue and burgundy."

The seamstress adjusted the last of the pins. "*Oui*, Madame. I'll have the dresses ready within the week. The ball gown will be ready to alter in two weeks."

403

"*Parfait*. You always produce grand creations, Madame Roux."

Rose slipped on her green-striped skirt with no bustle and her flowing white blouse. She saved the tight, well-fitted attire for dinner and formal occasions. The rest of the day would find her on a stepladder or on the floor sorting and placing ornaments.

She put the boxes of crystal, silver, and white decorations on a long work table in the gallery. The long rectangular windows allowed ample light. The only problem was she spent too much time peering at the water below, the forest of evergreens, and the bench where she shared pleasant moments with Luc.

Concentrate. I have trees to decorate. Luc is an individual I cannot help. But God can.

She'd sorted the first box for the smallest tree of the three noble firs for the ball room. As she unwrapped a crystal sphere, a slight hum wrapped around her. The same pleasant hum from before. Only with the crystal ones. She held the item toward the ceiling and the light. Rays sparked through the crystal-clear sphere. Rose's hum joined the chorus as she placed the balls among the silver fabric garland draping the trees. Strings of tiny crystals looped the branches. Silver and white ornaments calmed the blaze from the crystals.

Stepping back from the first tree, Rose steepled her fingers under her chin. The crystals sparked and rang out peace.

"I will call you 'Peace' and pray that all who see you will hear you and feel peace."

Luc slowed his gait as he walked along the bank toward the château. Processing all the information he'd gained from the bordering estate manager. Luc shuffled the ideas around in his head. Categories emerged —orchard and vineyard schemes as well as fields for staples like wheat and barley. He could have warmer climate fruit trees. If he could make his family estate more productive, he'd consider staying and settling down.

Settle down? That meant his mother finding a local girl from Roussillon or at least the Provence region. Was he ready? Although the prospect wasn't the nightmare he gained from battles, the reality of a wife and domestic life was daunting. After Christmas, it would be time to travel home no matter his state of mind.

He stuffed his hands deep into his pockets and forced his gaze outward. The rattling had lessened, allowing other noises to invade. From an open window in the front drawing room, Luc recognized elaborate compositions on the piano, though he couldn't name the composer.

Stalling for a minute, he remembered today was the day of Claude Debussy's arrival. Marguerite must have situated him at the piano right away. Luc didn't know enough about music to critique it, but in his unprofessional opinion, the notes floated above the river as if they were part of the flow—part of nature itself.

Changing his farmer's attire for an afternoon suit, Luc followed the music. Marguerite and Rose stood on either side of the grand piano, swaying with the rhythm. Neither looked up at his entrance. A bit mesmerized? He had to admit the youth played with expertise and flawless effort.

His aunt raised her head at the end of the piece and motioned Luc forward. "Monsieur Debussy, this is my nephew, Monsieur Luc Bélanger."

Luc accepted Debussy's hand. "*Mon plaisir*, monsieur."

"Please, call me Claude. I feel at home here. Any friend or relative of Madame's is an automatic friend of mine."

Luc glanced at Rose whose stare included Luc, not Debussy. Her raised eyebrows asked a question. "Rose." He bowed and promised himself he'd ask later her thoughts about the young artist.

Marguerite clapped her hands, drawing all eyes to her. "I propose an after-dinner concert with Christmas carols and dancing."

Tilting her head, Rose shrugged. "How can there be dancing with so few guests?"

"Well, Luc can dance with you and then with me." Marguerite laughed. "Does that not suit you, Luc?"

"I will admit that I need the practice. Soldiering rendered little time for social events."

What have I done by coming here? Christmas, singing, dancing, Rose...

Dinner proved entertaining. A small party of four. To Rose's right sat Luc, dashing in his black jacket. On her left was Claude, charming in his gray jacket. Seventeen seemed so very young to her twenty years. Marguerite carried the conversation, causing each of them to comment. What did Rose know of the quality of music or farming or battle techniques. Who would want to talk about decorations and nature, crystal, and flowers?

If only she could concentrate solely on her *poisson au beurre blanc*, fish smothered in a white butter sauce, and *champignons au four et pois vert*, mushrooms and peas.

Marguerite twirled her silver goblet and leveled her chin. "Claude, have you seen the beautiful trees around the castle? They are Rose's creation."

He set his fork on his plate and smiled at Rose. "You have created music with your skills."

"*Merci*, Claude. It's funny you should say that because I hear the crystal ornaments humming. And I hum along. Sometimes a Christmas carol."

"*Vraiment*? I, too, hear music in beauty. Whereas I transcribe it into compositions, you create for aesthetic beauty."

Luc dropped his knife. It's clunking pushed the compliment down a few notches. "I'm sorry. I guess all the flowery words startled me. I wish I could hear music and see beauty as all of you can. I feel I have a long way to go before my imagination takes over."

On impulse Rose placed her hand over his and squeezed. Not at all appropriate unless the present company allowed her *faux pas* in the familial atmosphere. "At least you are progressing. Anyway, hearing humming from inanimate objects might be considered crazy. Do you think I'm *une folle*? A fool to grasp at beauty whenever I can?"

His fingers twitched under her hand. "*Non, mademoiselle. Tu n'es pas folle mais une femme intelligente et belle.*"

Rose broke the bond and replaced her hand in her lap. Intelligent and beautiful? Perhaps he was hard of seeing too.

Madame rose, pushing her chair at an angle. "I've had a fire prepared in the gallery. If you don't mind the petit grand piano, Claude, perhaps you can play a few familiar carols with a waltz in the midst." She winked at Rose.

What did her host expect to happen? Surely, she had no match-making plans. Not for Rose. One foreign romance in the family was enough.

As they walked out of the room arm in arm, Marguerite whispered for Rose's benefit, "Humor me, *mon amie*. Luc needs to feel free to enjoy himself. You are friends now. Make him smile for a few minutes. A few days."

So not matchmaking but the rescue of a weary soul. Hadn't Rose tried to do that since her arrival? By concentrating on Luc and the château, her dilemma had faded. It helped that no mention of the fiasco appeared in letters or conversation. Even Beatrice ignored mention of the fateful episode.

Claude played a few runs. Rose's ear for correct pitch lacked a professional's, but he played with satisfaction as his fingers produced harmony in their perfect elocution. He began with "Adele Fideles."

Rose forgot her resolution to remain quiet as her less than adequate singing joined Marguerite's in Latin, then English, ending with a French verse. "O Come, All Ye Faithful" tied as her favorite with "Joy to the World."

Luc sat close to the fireplace, staring into the flames. Was he oblivious to the music? Rose assumed he could hear it. Most likely, he cared little for the Christmas merriment. "What carol do you like, Luc?" Probably not the question for someone brooding in his own world.

Slowly, he raised his head. A grin? How could she have been so wrong? "'Hark! The Herald Angels Sing.'"

Before he finished his words, Claude filled the room with a lively prelude. What appeal did Luc find in the song? Glory, peace, joyful, new born King?

Luc hummed along as Rose and Marguerite's words cadenced with the notes. Would she ever sing this carol again without these memories? "Join the triumph of the skies; with angelic hosts proclaim, 'Christ is born in Bethlehem!'"

A Christmas miracle unfolded.

As Claude flowed into a composition unknown to Rose, Luc presented his hand to her. Before she could evaluate or protest, he swept her into a waltz. The black and white checkered floor swam under their feet like the river through the arches. The music faded in and out as they traversed the long gallery toward the two decorated trees. The crystals shimmered in the gas light from various sconces.

Peace hummed in her ears as she twirled close to her peace tree. The pressure on her back shoulder blade warmed her quicker than the fire. Was this what peace felt like? A waltz? The composition? Or Luc's arms?

Swinging by the other tree decorated with the crystal birds and animals, Rose heard a different word of promise—hope. The name of this tree echoed through her. Hope.

"Do you hear that?"

Luc glanced down at her and continued his excellent foot work. "Don't tell me you hear more crystals speaking to you?"

She wouldn't say speaking. "It's more of a feeling when I see their beauty and light. But yes, this time it translated hope."

"And the other is peace, *n'est-ce pas*?"

She nodded. His crinkled brow could either be he thought her foolish, or he struggled to understand her. Well, since she didn't understand herself, she shrugged. "It's clear that these ornaments meant something to someone long ago."

"And now they reach out to you. There is nothing wrong with that. Sometimes, a painting does that for me. Or did in the past."

"Can you not see or hear beauty anymore?" Immediately, she clamped her lips together. Too many words. Perhaps, she should just concentrate on the moves. Surprisingly, they could spin and talk with ease during the dance.

He chuckled. "Don't grimace. I like your honesty. What if I admitted it's getting better?"

"Why is that?" How many times had they passed the windows on each side and glided by Claude and Marguerite?

"I'm afraid to admit my summation."

"Please."

"All right. Christmas. These trees. The outdoors. Distance from war. And...you."

Her lower jaw dropped. *I wasn't expecting any credit. What does he mean? I'll not ask, but he could tell me.*

The music stopped. The spinning left her out of breath. Or his words had. Clapping drew them apart.

"Brilliant. You will lead our first dance at the ball." Marguerite took Rose's hands in hers and pulled her close enough to kiss her cheeks. "You are working wonders with Luc."

Rose whispered back. "I don't mean to. I haven't figured him out yet." Rose cut her eyes toward him as he spoke to Claude. "He's full of emotional surprises. It's not me. It's this castle."

Pointing toward the trees dancing in the gaslight, Rose diverted Marguerite's attention to the whimsical tableau. "There is the Christmas magic seeping into unexpecting hearts. I see Christ's promises in the beauty of the crystal rays—some hope, others peace. If a person comes with an open heart, even the tiniest crack, God can spread the Christmas spell and warm the coldest soul."

Marguerite leaned the side of her head against Rose's and squeezed her elbow. "*Oui*, and perhaps He uses people too. What a combination. It would be hard to escape that pull."

Rose tried to divert any of the credit. If Marguerite chose to believe Rose was a source of thawing Luc's shield, then Rose could not change her mind. *I don't have to believe her.*

They turned around together, witnessing Luc's stare and incredible smile directed at them, or at her. Suddenly, Claude introduced a grand prelude to "Joy to the World." Luc leaned against the grand piano on one side while Marguerite joined Claude on the piano bench, and Rose stood opposite Luc.

All four voices echoed up and down the gallery from the ceiling to the floor. French, English, and French again. Rose hummed or made up words or sang English when the French escaped her memory.

Pure joy.

That's what I'll name the huge bare tree in the middle of the two crystal ones, Peace and Hope. Joy!

"Joy to the World! The Lord is come."

Eight

Nothing could topple or surpass the continuous elation from the evening with Luc—and the others, of course. Dancing, singing, dreaming. A week later and Rose still basked in the glow of acceptance and friendship. The mystery of Christmas.

This morning, a mere week before the big event, she wore a simple wool day dress of dusty-blue. Before her stood the noble fir rising high. She had no idea of the footage—twenty, twenty-five feet? Luc with a sturdy ladder had wrapped the white garland around the tree and placed the silver star on the top along with a few white and silver ornaments on the high boughs. Had he enjoyed the exchange of glances, words, and shared purpose? He hadn't stayed the course for the rest of the decorating.

She stood alone with the remaining crystal ornaments. Joy deserved a bell right in the center. Rose rang it before, looping the silver bow over a branch. She placed spheres with delicate etchings, hearts, diamonds, and angels. She didn't want to position the last object, eliminating her time decorating his tree. Joy, the tree, would have to now be shared with others. As it should be. Covering her heart with her hand, she stepped back.

Beautiful. Magical. *Fantastique*.

In direct contrast to her simple attire with more of her hair down her back than remained pinned high. Being alone had its advantages. Soon enough she would be on display amidst the noblest of firs.

Clapping from the entrance of the gallery startled Rose. Her moment of awe faded. Marguerite should be in the chapel putting final touches on the golden tree. And Luc? Probably visiting a local farmer.

She turned, smiling at the approval from the visitors—a man and a woman, standing beside Marguerite. Their travel attire of top quality labeled them equal to Marguerite. Rose was not ready for guests. Tempted to pat her hair and straighten her skirts, Rose did neither. Too late for a better first impression.

Moving forward, she met them halfway. Marguerite beamed her approval of the gallery's decoration. "Gorgeous, Rose. Perfectly wonderful."

"*Merci, madame.*" Rose wondered at Marguerite's use of her English praise.

"Let me introduce my guests, Mr. and Mrs. Wilbur Leister." Rose nodded. "From London."

London? Oh, no! What if...

"This is Miss Rose Farley."

Please. Nothing else.

Rose couldn't breathe. The man took her hand and kissed it. His eyes shadowed and his brow furrowed. Mrs. Leister tilted her head and studied Rose. Too late. They knew something.

Mr. Leister stepped back and tapped his finger against his bottom lip. "Are you the missing lady from Kent? You favor a Miss Rosalind Marrow."

Rose coughed when she failed to take in air. Her hand covered her mouth. She wasn't ready for this.

Mrs. Leister raised her chin and looked down her narrow nose at Rose. "You are the sister of the girl who ran off with a foreigner. And here you are hiding in France." She scrutinized Rose's figure up and down. "You probably have a few secrets to hid yourself." The haughty woman turned toward Marguerite. "Did you know about this? You are housing a wayward woman."

In two steps Marguerite braced Rose with a firm arm around her back, pasted on a smile, and calmly, ever so assuredly, faced the enemy. "I assure you that Rose has done nothing wrong. The gossip you encourage even across the sea is a virus that we do not want here at the château. As long as Rose is my guest, you will refrain from insults and insinuations, or you will leave."

Rose froze, begging her tears to hold.

Mrs. Leister fidgeted with her gloves. "Well, I never."

Marguerite chuckled. "Well, you never what?"

Please don't encourage the woman to spell out her complaint.

"Mr. Leister, we are not welcome here."

"As you wish, my dear."

The unwanted visitors exited the gallery. Squeezing Rose's side, Marguerite whispered, "I will see them out. All will be all right. You will see."

Rose stood alone. Again. Her elation shattered as broken crystal. Too many pieces to make whole. She ran up the marble stairs to her room where she watched the carriage disappear. Wanting to escape the now cold stone walls of a once warm home, she headed down the stairs, out the front door to the gardens. Nowhere could shelter her from the cruel whispers of gossipers. Now the rumors included her. Mrs. Leister's insinuations about her condition infuriated Rose. How was her life any concern of this woman whom Rose had never met before today?

The cottages blurred as Rose trudged toward the barn. A solid place of warmth for animals. Even they were protected and cared for by humans. Rose took two wool blankets from a stack by a partition and laid one on a bale of hay before sitting on it, curling against a strong bale. Another blanket covered her lap. Tears rushed contrary to her will. She'd become soft to the dilemma, assuming with Marguerite's care that her reputation was safe in France. Of course, there had been no guarantee. British friends and acquaintances of Marguerite probably showed up all the time to catch a glimpse of the charming castle and friendly host. And now of the ruined debutante. Hiding had made the rumors grander and more risqué, not less.

An orange cat jumped on the bale and rubbed his head against her arm. Her only counselor. Rose petted him and encouraged him to curl in her lap.

Why did it always seem to take so long to recognize God? Shouldn't He have been the first one she had turned to in her room or in the presence of the intruders? Instead, she let the embarrassment and fear chase her to a place farther from her friend. But not far enough away from God.

After drying her tears with her sleeves, Rose focused on the sunlight, painting the barn floor a patchwork of orange, gold, and yellow. "Here I am again, God. Apparently, not much has changed since this all started. I thought it had. I hoped I had changed. Why am I still fearful of what people will say?"

Hadn't Marguerite, Beatrice, and even Queen Victoria accepted her innocence and used their power and reason to help her? Yes. That should be enough. Why wasn't it?

Luc. He doesn't know. What if he finds out? Should I tell him and let him shun me too?

"Help me, God, please."

She closed her eyes and ran her fingers through the cat's long fur. Rose's heartbeat steadied with the purring and warmth.

The barn door slid open a bit, letting in more light. Rose opened her eyes to a shadow in the opening. She'd run so no one would see her fall apart. The being elongated as he advanced.

"Rose?" Luc's voice echoed in the cavernous barn.

He hadn't expected to find Rose in the barn of all places. Without asking and without a care for his clothing, Luc climbed up next to her on the hay. "You've been crying." More like weeping. He rubbed a finger across her cheek, nothing but dried streaks. The silence and the sighs of her pain battled for shared space with cannons and battles. He willed for her words and feelings to drown out his own concerns and nightmares.

"We've been looking for you. I'll have to send word soon that you are all right. That is true, *n'est-ce pas*? You are not hurt physically?"

"No, Luc. I am well in that sense."

He sighed. Her hand stroked the cat, who was faking sleep as the animal stared at Luc with one eye open. "Fine. Rose..." He started but paused, gaining confidence. If he asked the wrong questions or caused her more pain, he'd negate his purpose. "I am a good listener. During the battles, I heard many a man's story and many confessions."

He failed to anticipate his true desire to enter Rose's realm, whether in joy or pain. But here he was, wanting to be a part of the solution. He might be the one weeping later, wishing he had backed away. Yet, he doubted it.

She sniffled. He could handle that with a quick retrieval of a fresh handkerchief. "Here, Rose." His dear Rose. Not hardly. He'd given her little cause to embrace his wounded character.

She adjusted her skirt around her legs as she dangled them over the edge of the bale. "I guess you might as well know. It's not a long story, and it's really not mine. I'm just a victim of someone else's folly."

He stretched out his legs as he leaned against the opposite side. Now he could study her face. "I'm listening."

Pulling in a deep breath, she pushed out her words. "My name is Rosalind Farley Marrow, the youngest daughter of The Honorable Mr. and Mrs. Frederick Marrow of Kent."

His eyebrows rose as his eyes widened. That explained her manners and dress. "*Enchanté*, Miss Rosalind." He brushed his booted foot against her ankle. "I rather like 'Rose' myself. It reminds me of the beauty in the gardens here."

"Yes, well, it had always been a nickname and appropriate in the circumstances. Since I answer to it anyway, it works."

"I assume there is more to this story." He felt, as well as heard, her sigh ripple to her shoe as she crossed one ankle over the other.

"I really do wish I were deserving of this censor." She pouted. "It's been a lot of heartache for something I didn't do."

That didn't make much sense. Why would anyone want to get what he deserved? "You're stalling. Out with it. I'm not the queen or your best friend, but I promise to be open to your plight. I might be able to help."

Her guffaw croaked between a cry and a chuckle. "All right. Since you insist. I had agreed to reside at Buckingham Palace with Princess Beatrice for the London season. We are, or perhaps were, the closest of friends. Dresses and parties and dance lessons—all scheduled, leading up to the big events. Then it all came to an abrupt halt. At least for me it did." Her eyes clamped shut.

What images did she see that forced the darkness? He had enough experience to know shutting out the light did not dispel the images. When he shut his eyes, all sorts of demons from the war emerged, preventing needed sleep. Hopefully, she didn't suffer the same way. Lately, visions of crystal trees and shimmering rivers occupied the space behind his eyelids more than battles.

"You see, my sister Margaret decided to upend my life while pursuing her own dreams. She eloped with a Portuguese shipbuilder while engaged to a viscount." She looked at him through squinted eyes, then snapped them shut.

He refused to grimace at her story, afraid she'd mistake it for a personal assault. All he wanted to do was hold her until the pain left her forever.

Her shoulders shuddered as she released a moan. "Everyone's solution was to hide me away until the gossip subsided and restitution to the viscount was made. The man has threatened legal procedures for the breach of contract. My parents returned to their estate, and my brother remained at school. And here I am."

"I'm glad that you are here." His whisper crept across the void. He was glad, but he didn't know if Rose wanted to hear that.

She leaned forward, out of her trance and her painful story. "Oh, Luc. I thought I was safe. Marguerite did too. How was she to know two of her acquaintances from England would visit and bring the worst kind of gossip. They...they insinuated that I...well, that I was hiding away because of my own...indiscretions. The couple looked me over like I was a brood mare. How humiliating. Now I know what the rumors are around London. Instead of protecting me, my disappearance has sparked the gossip mill. No different than Margaret except at least she is married."

Her tears flowed as her hands covered her face. Luc retrieved another handkerchief from his jacket and pushed it between her fingers. Although he'd never taken part in a season in London or Paris, he could imagine the brutality lurking behind the matrons' critiques. No one was immune, not even a beautiful, innocent young lady.

He joined her on her side of the hay stack and draped his arm over her shoulder, pulling her close. She leaned into him, dropping her hands to her lap. His head rested on the hay behind him. Slowly, her sobs morphed into short breaths.

"What...do..." Her words hiccupped as her shoulders rose and fell. "...you...think of me...now?"

Guide me, Lord.

"No differently than before in regard to your reputation or character. I would change all of those ugly circumstances for you if I could. For some reason, society latches onto the misfortune of others and spreads the rumors with lightning speed. It is more alive with the bad news than the good."

"But that is so unfair." Her speech slowed and landed in a whisper.

"Unfortunately, when the gossip about you has faded, some other soul will be the next victim."

"Did I do wrong by fleeing the court?"

"It seems you had no choice with the queen and your parents making all the decisions. I meant it when I said, I'm glad you are here."

Her lashes glistened with the remnant of her tears. "Even with the Leisters' harsh words, I am too. But what do I do now? Marguerite has invited many of her British friends living in France for the winter to the château. Also, I have a feeling Mrs. Leister will let her friends know about my whereabouts."

The idea sprang with such certainly that Luc assured it was an answer to prayer or a brilliant scheme. Would Rose?

He nudged her forward, then put his hands on her shoulders. "Look at me." Her hazel eyes sparked with gold from the sunlight, stealing through the door. "I have an idea. Let's form an attachment of sorts to last through the Christmas ball. That way if anyone accuses you and says one word about your family's situation, he, or most likely she, will have to report to me. I'll protect you from slander. This way you can enjoy the season. What do you think?"

Rose laughed. A deep, cleansing, continuous song of laughter. Not what he expected. Laughter? Perhaps "thank you" or "I don't know." But a string of giggles and chuckles and true laughter? And more tears. Of joy?

"What Rose? I don't understand."

"Luc, you are a dear. Marguerite will be amused and take credit for your actions."

He ran his hand through his hair. "Now, I really don't understand."

Rose took his hand and held it, rubbing her fingers over his. He'd rather look at her face than the top of her head. She pulled in a huge breath. With a few more words maybe he'd comprehend the spectrum of reactions—tears, laughter, smiles, sighs. Shouldn't she give one of those at a time instead of all together? Someone else would be better for Rose right now.

As she slowly raised her head, her portrait covered a gamut of details: her sparkling eyelashes, rosy cheeks, a piece of straw on her shoulder, and a quivering smile. "I cannot believe you haven't picked up on Marguerite's intentions. Silly man, she wants you to form an attach-ment. Perhaps not a permanent one with me, but one that would bring you out of your doldrums."

Her smile and slight chuckle were contagious. "She told you all of that?" His ignorance surprised him. Reading men's motives in battle wasn't nearly as complicated.

"Not in so many words. Hints, pushing me to speak, to dance, to include you. She smiles and winks when you are not looking. If she can infiltrate your nightmares with the magic of Christmas, she will have done her part."

How much of Rose's attention was actually play acting or doing his aunt's bidding? He might not like the answer, but he had to know. He'd exposed too much of himself, his heart, to Rose to have it all be false. "And your part, Rose? How much have you invested in this charade?"

Her grip tightened on his hand as her head shook. "Oh, Luc, it's not like that at all. She never asked me to do anything special. Not really. Don't you see. She suggested we find the trees, the decorations, and dance." She poked her bottom lip out in a pout. "I see that this disturbs you. I won't hold you to your plan. I just wanted you to be warned about Marguerite and her possible elation."

She tried to pull her hand away but he grabbed both of them and leaned his forehead against hers. "Sweet Rose, my offer still stands. I will enjoy seeing her smile for a week. Will you enjoy the play attachment? I promise we'll tell her everything after Christmas. We'll not prolong our fake association."

Her smile twitched as if deciding between that and a frown. Did a false attachment unnerve her? "You would do that for me?" Her voice quivered.

"Most assuredly. Who knows, you might enjoy my attention."

I will certainly treasure yours—vrai ou faux. *I'd rather it be true.*

Nine

⁓

Luc helped Rosalind down from the hay bales. His hands on her waist sent prickles over her skin as spikey as straw. Fortunately, her day dress lacked the awkward bustle and made climbing less cumbersome. Her long cloak hid some of the wrinkles and remaining straw. If someone saw them walking about, would they guess she'd been in a barn with a man?

His hands brushed off her back. "I think you are free of evidence. What about me?"

He turned his back to her. Her hands performed the same service, relaxing with the intimate activity. It shouldn't be seen as anything special since servants did it all the time. But in the barn after revealing her secrets, the wall had crumbled. Who would have guessed Luc would make such a sacrifice?

He looped her arm with his. "*Allons-y*. We'll face the menaces of society together. Are you ready?"

The twinkle startled her. Was he truly enjoying this scheme? "*Je suis prête.*" *I think I am. To have his attention for a few days.* Why not let the lightened burden buoy her spirits?

Their stroll arm in arm past the cottages would start rumors of different kinds. She didn't mind, but did Luc mean to carry on even outside of the château? "You do realize, Luc, that workers have their own rumor mills."

"I do." He patted her hand. "Smile if you see anyone. Better yet, smile anyway since you're on the arm of a handsome soldier."

"Who is full of himself. Who told you about your good looks?"

"Well, my mother, Marguerite, and perhaps you just did."

Her laughter escaped. This could be amusing. *Flirting when no one is listening. It gives me practice.* "I don't disagree, especially when you smile."

"Even with my long hair?"

"It's shorter and tamer than before." He ran his free hand through the misbehaving waves.

As they approached the stone wall with the entrance to Catherine de Medici's Garden, Rose pulled his arm, halting their steps. "You can back out. I'm sure I can handle myself better after the shock."

He stooped to her level, his brown eyes probing. "Are you scared of an association with a worn, grim, military gentleman?" He winked, convincing her jaw to relax and her eyes to bulge.

"*Pas du tout.* I'm proud to be on your arm. It's just...we...what if some lady, a French lady, attracts you...and you are stuck with me?"

"Stuck with you is hardly how I see it. If no *dame française* has attracted me yet, what are the chances now?"

She blew out a pent-up breath. "All right. If you are sure, I'll not mention it again. On the count of three, let's enter the gardens and our make-believe fairy tale." She glanced at him and melted in his gaze. "*Un, deux, trois.*" They stepped into the ancient garden with roses waiting for spring to share their beauty and color. Possibly, she was like that flower with potential to bloom where she was placed. God had a plan. If Luc played a part, Rose would welcome God's humor and purpose. For some comforting reason, she believed He orchestrated more of her placement than her sister's fiasco, Queen Victoria, her parents, and Marguerite combined.

The next morning, Rose joined Marguerite in the grand entrance hall. Marguerite stood with hands on her hips, staring at the empty table set under a huge tapestry of a medieval version of a picnic with lords and ladies talking and laughing.

"What if we made the *crèche* the major emphasis in the hall?"

Rose observed the scene. "*Oui*, the large pieces in the front room?"

"I think so. Perhaps, the guests will associate the ball with honoring Jesus. A time of celebration."

Rose skipped into the front room and returned with a solid eighteen inch or so model of Joseph. Marguerite draped a green velvet piece of cloth over the table. "Maybe we can use a few of the tree branches to form a shelter."

Placed in the center all by himself, Joseph begged for his family, his purpose. Rose backed away and bumped into a solid body who held her firmly by the shoulders.

She gasped at her near fall. She knew that touch and whispering breath. Her imagination embraced the familiarity of Luc's presence. "I don't want you falling before our premiere dance."

Rose swatted at his jacket front. "I'm not going to miss that moment for anything."

Marguerite stood with crossed arms and a tapping foot. "If you have finished whispering and flirting, we have decorations to finish." Her tone was anything but impatient.

The reprimand with a huge grin spurred Rose to action. "I'll bring the other nativity pieces."

"Except Jesus," Marguerite stressed. "Hide him in the chapel. He can't arrive until Christmas Day. You and Luc can figure out how to make a stable out of branches or something else."

"*Oui*, Madame." Luc pivoted with his marching orders.

Giggling about Marguerite's orders, Rose retrieved Mary and a lamb. Four trips later the table resembled a barnyard with animals and shepherds. The angel and the empty manger signified that it wasn't an ordinary barn.

Luc returned with branches woven around sturdy limbs, forming a frame around the couple and the crib. Rose wanted to bring the baby

Jesus to His family. She had wrapped Him in a gold cloth under the tree in the chapel. Safe, warm, anticipating His reunion with the world.

If Jesus could face a hostile world, Rose could do her best to confront a few rumors and individuals bent on malice. He suffered much more than she could ever endure.

Marguerite placed the wise men and their camels at one end of the table, awaiting their turn to see the baby king. "Now, what else do we need?"

"People." Why did Rose let that slip? For her, the fewer the better, preferably no Englishmen.

"I have guests from the village coming for dinner tonight. The minister with his wife and daughter and the couple from the adjoining estate, Claude, and a local violinist, Paul Hebert. That evens out our numbers."

Rose shook her head, amazed how her host only shared details when she wanted, dropping tidbits along the way. At least tonight, there wasn't a single person to ruin her evening. "I'll finish Joy this afternoon."

Luc laughed, brushing her arm with his nearness. "You mean that huge tree needs more attention?"

"Just a bit. I found a string of white beads that will finish off the front."

Marguerite scrunched the velvet one more time, giving the manger scene a textured base. "Afterwards, Claude has promised a mini-concert. Monsieur Hebert might accompany him on the violin. I do hope so."

Rose noticed a blush as Marguerite mentioned the violinist. What age was the man? Surely, not a youth like Claude.

Why do I question Marguerite's motives? Why lean on the side of speculation or gossip? No more. Lesson learned.

Rose pointed to a box by the front door. "I have one more tree to decorate. Do you want to help me, Luc?" She peered out the hallway window. *Yes, it is in place.*

He bowed and grinned. "*Mon plaisir, mademoiselle.*"

"*Bien.* You can bring that box, *s'il te plaît.*"

He followed her through the front doors toward the tower, joining her stride. He watched her instead of the scene unfolding in front of them. "Stop gazing at me. Look ahead."

It took him a second to follow her command. She captured the moment as he grinned one of his rare, brilliant smiles. "Ah, a tree for me."

"*Oui, pour toi*. We have so many in the castle. Why shouldn't you have one to grace your entrance, and I think you can see it from your living area." Had she made a mistake? Did he want to see a reminder of Christmas all the time?

A twinkle. A genuine reflection of joy. Perhaps she hadn't been mistaken.

She clapped a childish response. "Let's make it special. I saved some of the sturdier, less sparkly ornaments. You liked those carved and painted ones." She pulled out a wooden chalet and a deer. Filling his hands with her selection, she rummaged until she found the gold garland, more like a yellow braided rope.

Rose hummed "Joy to the World." Perhaps the pounding in his head prevented his participation. She expected too much, even though Luc had warmed up a bit to Christmas.

Taking one end of the garland, Luc helped her drape the tree, back and forth. A deep humming startled her, but she regained her grip on the rope and sang the words. Before long one carol led to another. Luc changed into someone she'd hoped existed. He could hear and carry a tune. Smile, laugh, and experience Christmas. With her.

An empty box behind them, Rose reached for Luc's hand, pulling him backwards. "Our perfect creation. A little of the forest amid the bows."

He squeezed her fingers laced with his. "As pretty as the elegant ones inside. Perhaps more so." He focused on Rose, not the tree. "Because we did it together."

His words and actions fit so naturally. Was it part of the charade? She thought not. Then what was this...this display of affection...of togetherness?

Oops...I'm the one who grabbed his hand. Should I apologize? A fake attraction has so many wavy lives.

She could end the most recent connection. Freeing her hand, she picked up the empty box. "I need to dress for this evening. I don't want to embarrass Marguerite."

Luc chuckled. "I doubt that is possible. Even in your day dress, you look beautiful."

Too much. In a week, he'll forget all about her.

She tilted her head before turning away. "Well, I will see you this evening."

"*À bientôt. Merci pour l'arbre de Noël*. Your gift is just what this old soldier needs."

She pivoted to face him. "Luc, you look younger every day."

"And I feel it, too. A Christmas miracle?"

"*Peut-être*." Perhaps her prayers for him were being answered.

Ten

As he studied his figure in the long mirror in his room, Luc waited for an image of a twenty-eight-year-old to face him. His face had lost the worn gray tinge and deep lines of fatigue and pain. Maybe he could pass for thirty-five instead of fifty now.

But why would a fresh, freckled faced beauty with specks of gold in her eyes and streaks of gold in her hair choose him over someone like Claude or any young man. She was light to his shadow. He listened for the constant hammering and heard nothing except the ticking of the clock on his bureau and the carriage wheels on the cobblestones.

Time for daydreaming about miracles and golden hues had to be set aside. His gray pants, black vest, and jacket over a crisp white shirt with a black tie should suffice for the dinner. He didn't have many choices anyway.

As he exited his tower—the Marques' Tower—he joined the Reverend Armand and his wife in the courtyard entrance. "*Bonsoir, Monsieur et Madame Armand*. I'm Luc Bélanger."

"*Oui, bien sûr*. We've seen you in church but haven't met. This is our daughter, Louise."

"*Enchanté.*" Perfect for Claude. Luc felt relieved to have "an attach-ment" to Rose.

Marguerite welcomed them at the door. "*Bienvenus, mes amis. Entrez.*"

Luc expected she yearned for their comments and approval of the elaborate, striking beauty of Christmas gracing every room.

After discarding coats, hats, and gloves, the tour began. Madame Armand clapped her hands at, well, almost everything. The crèche. The chapel tree. The greenery and trees in each room.

Marguerite paused at the end of the grand hallway. "We'll save the gallery for later. The others are in the front parlor with drinks and *hors d'oeuvres.*"

Trailing the guests, Luc quickly licked his lips. The food at the château far exceeded what he encountered in the military and even at his estate. He needed to find someone with culinary skills for their kitchen.

Before he made it to the appetizers, Luc blinked twice as Rose came into view. Such a beauty in a deep, watery blue dress. It flowed as the river, catching streaks of light. He preferred her fashion with less bustle and train. Her laughter turned him away from the refreshments. Once by her side, he grasped her elbow with his fingers. Was he allowed the privilege of her side as her beau?

"*Bonsoir*, Luc." Rose's cheeks pinked. "We were discussing the scavenger hunt in the village."

He smiled at Claude and Monsieur Hebert. What else were they planning? He'd make sure he tagged along, though two Frenchmen didn't pose a threat of gossip. Yet, he'd rather Rose spend her time with him.

Ouch. I'm not really courting her, but she must remember for appearance's sake to prefer me.

"Gentlemen, have you met the Reverend Armand's daughter?" Luc indicated with a jerk of his head to where she stood.

Claude looked around Luc. "Where has she been hiding? I was here all summer and never met her?"

Luc shrugged. The whereabouts of the young girl failed to interest him.

Monsieur Hebert added, "She's been away at school. I'll introduce you."

The men strode in the innocent girl's direction. Rose giggled, then faced Luc. "That was clever."

He smirked, raising innocent eyes at the accusation. "What? Louise is perfect for Claude." How could she argue?

"Perhaps. What other motive could you have?" Her head tilted, allowing her a clear study of him.

Her scrutiny agitated him as she searched out the truth. His hand guided her toward the table. He hoped he could eat and swallow. *It's only Rose. Not a princess. And, I'm not jealous. Am I?*

Pointing to some delicacies, Rose leaned toward the table. "The pâté and cucumber are tasty as well as the cheese puffs and biscuits with caviar. I'll take a cup of punch while you choose."

Choose? He took one of each. Perhaps with his mouth full, he'd refrain from speaking overly much about her beauty or bizarre phrases that exit unbidden. If he yelled out loud, "This is a fake attachment," would he revert back to normal?

Normal wasn't so bad. A world to himself with his nightmares, battles, fatigue, and pain. What he felt now was a fairy tale of light, music, beauty, and Christmas. Would it disappear when Rose left?

He searched for Rose but found Reverend Armand by his side instead. "We hope you are enjoying our little village. How long will you be staying?"

Luc swallowed a bite of biscuit quickly, hoping not to choke. "I must return to my home after Christmas. My parents are anxious about my acclimating to estate affairs."

"I see." Reverend Armand motioned his cheese ball in Rose's direction. "And the young lady, will she go with you?"

Luc choked and coughed. "With me? I imagine she'll return to England."

"But I thought I detected an attraction and possible attachment."

"Well, yes, but we've no plans beyond this time." Luc placed his plate on a small side table. "Excuse me. I need some punch."

What had he expected? If he was to protect Rose from rumors at the ball, questions would arise.

The call for dinner couldn't come soon enough. Marguerite partnered with Monsieur Hebert, followed by the Armands, then Louise and Claude, and last, Luc and Rose.

He whispered, "Our plan is working. Maybe too well. The Reverend asked about my future plans, including you. We have to be careful. I told him I didn't know."

Rose nodded. "I see. It's not as if we're engaged, only interested. Right?"

"Of course." *Only interested, very interested.*

Dinner proved a delight, from conversation to each bite of the château's *haut cuisine*. Rose gleamed as the savory spices mingled, playing in harmony with her senses. The French mastered presentation and taste at a higher level than the English ever could. What did the cook say? It was all in the sauces—butter and cream.

Hard to determine her favorite. Scallops *au gratin* on half shells followed by *soupe d'asperges vertes* with asparagus straight from the garden. Then *poissons de rivière en beurre blanc*. She probably saw the fishermen this morning. Everything came from a local source—no faraway market. After the fish, Rose's eyes widened at the *poule au pot* with a *tarte de pomme de terre*. Chicken with a slice of potato tart.

Luc raised his glass to Marguerite. "Excellent, Madame. Fit for a king."

Marguerite's face radiated sincere pride from flushed cheeks to a wide grin. She nodded and joined the toast. "Eh, you are not far off. The recipes are from the cuisine of kings in the châteaux de la Loire. Some go back to the sixteenth century."

Chuckles around the table mimicked Rose's own. Of course, only the best for the guests at the petit château. Chenonceau boasted many such jewels as to rival the grands châteaux.

Rose appreciated the culinary art, hoping to steal some secrets from the cook. "Cook says the secret is in the sauce, but I add it's in the spices."

Marguerite winked at her. "*Bien sûr*. And it magnifies the effect since they are all grown here."

Servants replaced their dinner plates with a medley of three desserts —*madeleine chaude avec fraises*, *soufflé au citron*, and *pain d'épice au miel*. Which to try first? Rose chose the madeleine with strawberries since it was hot. Would the cook share her secrets?

Luc leaned toward her. "They are all fine choices. My favorite is the lemon soufflé, but the honey spice bread is a house specialty."

"Let me guess. Bees from the château."

He gave a slight nod while staring at her mouth. Did she have crumbs or cream there? She licked her lips, which resulted in an abrupt jerk of his head away from her. Would she ever understand him? Attentive one second and distant and awkward the next.

Instead of figuring him out, she finished her scrumptious desserts, leaving tiny crumbs on her plate.

A few minutes later, Marguerite stood. "We will now adjourn to the gallery where Claude and Paul...Monsieur Hebert will entertain us with carols and pieces of their choice. Chairs have been added for our comfort. Enjoy the time to wander, chat, or just listen."

Following the group into the gallery, Luc partnered with Claude. Not knowing much about music—the main topic of the young man's conversation—Luc listened, not trusting his inadequate responses.

Hands behind his back, the lanky youth continued, "Music is the space between the notes." His dark eyes forced Luc to focus on the words. "What do you think, monsieur?"

What? About music? "I believe you need to use that expression as a motto for your pieces." He'd have to dissect the phrase later.

"Hmmm. You might be correct. Did you know while I spent the summer here, I composed two piano pieces based on the poems by Alfred de Mosset? They are to be accompanied by voice. *Ballade à la lune* and *Madrid, princesse des Espagnes*."

Did Claude Debussy realize the details were wasted on Luc's lack of expertise in the art? "I'm sure you will perform them at the ball."

"*Bien sûr*, especially for you and Mademoiselle Rose."

"*Merci*. I look forward to dancing to your compositions." Luc patted the youth's shoulder before Claude settled on the piano bench.

Luc gladly traded conversation partners, seeking Rose's side. Her blue dress accentuated everything in her path. All other treasures faded, even the twinkling trees dominating the far end. Rose motioned for him to join her at one of the windows overlooking the river.

The mirror image of the moon rippled below. He imagined a moonlit walk with her in the gardens. But Reverend Armand stood on the other side of Rose, sharing the moment.

The man clicked his heels and steepled his fingers. "Then the angel sowed me a river with the water of life, clear as crystal, flowing from the throne of God and of the Lamb."

Rose whispered, "Revelation, I assume."

Reverend Armand turned his head toward her. "*Oui*." His voice posed as calm as hers. "I believe sometimes we try to make life too complicated. When really it is as clear as the flow of the River Cher. God's plans can be heard without a loud voice."

Luc didn't fit into this conversation either. *What are You trying to tell me, God? It's not clear to me. Not yet.* Rose's steady gaze on the speaker glowed with understanding.

The reverend's steady voice carried more truth. "Perhaps, it is as easy as trusting He will hold us above the water like this gallery rests firmly over the river."

Returning her gaze to the river, Rose smiled and blew out a gentle breath. "How did you know I needed your perspective tonight?"

The man chuckled and faced the center of the room. "Don't give me any credit. Perhaps I was speaking to myself."

Luc wondered at the insight. Ignited by the discourse, he dug deep for a verse of old. *Everything you have heard and seen is trustworthy and true.* And clear.

Hands stuffed in his pockets, Reverend Armand said, "I believe I'm not needed here anymore." With a nod and a crooked smile, he humbly strode away.

How could Luc add another word?

Rose linked her arm through his. As the music started, Luc bowed to his partner. "Would you care to dance?" Tchaikovsky, Chopin, Debussy. It mattered not to him. He had what he desired in front of him.

"With you? At any time."

His reflection in her eyes shone clearer than the moon on the water.

Eleven

"Are you sure you don't need me, Marguerite?" Rose looked around the room. No more boxes to unpack. A bit confused without a project, she had found a new one.

"No. You go. I'd join you, but I don't like to bake." Marguerite shuddered. "I avoid the kitchen unless totally necessary. Cook is waiting for you."

Rose skipped out of the room. To think she would spend the morning under the tutelage of the cook. For some reason, Madame Lambert had accepted the challenge and allowed Rose to join in the task of baking Christmas sweets and bread. She, an English guest, had the privilege of entering the woman's domain.

As she rounded the corner from the stone staircase, she gasped at the spacious kitchen with copper pots and pans hooked on the wall, a large brick fireplace, and a huge modern stove. The aromatic whiff of French spices greeted her along with the tall, silver-haired Madame Lambert. Weren't cooks supposed to be round and short? Rose shook her head at her generalization. Rumors and gossip were not always true.

"There you are. I was hoping you'd join me. Not many upstairs guests want to venture down here."

Rose's cheeks flushed from the warmth. "Oh, I feel honored." She rubbed her hands together and barely caught herself from clapping and smacking her lips together. "I love baking. Adding a few recipes will be a great Christmas gift. I hope you truly don't mind."

"*Pas du tout, mademoiselle. C'est mon plaisir.* We are making butter *bredele* which is a butter biscuit flavored with either orange and cinnamon or lemon. Here are the cutters."

Rose peered into the tin—star, tree, diamond, circle, even a person. "Do you think I'll be able to do this?"

"*Pas de problème.* Four ingredients." Madame Lambert pointed to the table. "Butter, flour, sugar, and eggs. The icing is powdered sugar and egg."

"They sound delicious."

"You know what the French say, *n'est-ce pas*?" The cook winked at Rose.

Rose giggled. "All in the butter and sauce."

"*Exactement.*"

Tying an apron over her blue-striped skirt and white blouse, Rose washed her hands and followed the expertise of the cook. After cutting out the shapes, they brushed each biscuit with the egg yolk.

Rose could hardly wait the ten minutes before the first batch finished baking.

Finally, her creations were ready.

"Now, sprinkle the biscuits with the sugar and *voila—bredele!*"

The buttery concoction melted in her mouth. Rose would be a round, plump cook if temptation confronted her all the time.

Madame Lambert smiled, but she never stopped to taste the biscuits. "Now on to my favorite sweet to make—*pain d'épices.*"

Rose licked the sugar off of her lips. "Ah, in English that is gingerbread."

Snickering, Cook shook her head. "I don't like to cook the bland English food. Look at all these spices. I'm going to show you a true masterpiece with a special blend."

Soon, eight medium loaves rested securely in their pans. Stepping close to Madame Lambert, Rose inched up on her tiptoes and kissed the woman's cheek. "*Merci.* You've given me a gift I can take home, recipes for life."

After wiping her hands, Cook opened her arms for an embrace. Her mother, Marguerite, and the queen would disapprove, but Rose sank into the hug. Here she was safe.

Would she feel so safe this afternoon in town?

Bien sûr. How many Englishmen would be wandering in the village?

The town scavenger hunt began at two in the afternoon. Luc found Rose racing down the marble staircase, skidding into the hallway with a hand on her untied hat.

Reaching to brush flour from Rose's chin, Luc steadied her by the shoulder. "Slow down. We still have time to join the townspeople."

She placed her hands on her hips and pouted. "But don't you want to win."

He laughed as he tied the straps under her chin. "I'd prefer to enjoy the event as a casual participant."

Grabbing his hand, she pulled him toward the door. "Not me. I want to come in first as I enjoy myself."

Who was he to dislodge her enthusiasm? So much for a leisurely stroll through town with like-minded citizens. Or perhaps the towns-people were more like Rose, eager to complete the task in first place.

"All right, mademoiselle. I accept the challenge of a brisk walk. Lead the way, and I'll match your pace."

One step for her two. She settled into an easy gait as her breathing calmed. By the time they arrived at the church, they had ten minutes to spare. A crowd of locals gathered, some he had met or seen at church or in the shops. Rose secured a scavenger hunt list from Reverend Armand and joined Luc by his acquaintances.

"I'd like to introduce you to Monsieur and Madame Martin. They have been very helpful and given me lots of ideas for my own estate." How at ease he felt with them. Mutual admiration and trust surfaced and stuck after a few visits. "This is Mademoiselle Rose Marrow."

Jean Martin turned his hat in his hands. The humble man must not be used to praise.

"*Enchantée*. Luc speaks highly of you." Rose dipped her head, adding her welcoming smile.

Madame Martin, a decade older than Rose, grinned back. "Please call me Ella."

"If you will call me Rose."

Could they be friends that easily? Why not? Luc had warmed to the couple immediately. He needed a dose of Rose's spontaneous acceptance and charm in all of his dealings with the townspeople.

Although younger than the Martins, Luc bore the footsteps of a grandfather next to them. His emotional load stooped his being. But did he have to bend under the weight? Why had Rose wanted to go with him to the scavenger hunt? Then he remembered—Marguerite.

Couples separated from the crowd, each determined to win the hunt. Rose led him to an elm tree and quickly read the list to him. Her gaze penetrated his wandering mind. All he had was the present not the future. A trivial scavenger hunt, instead of a well-run estate with a qualified spouse by his side. The Martins had a unique relationship that Luc envied. He *had* himself.

For now, he had a fidgeting partner, poking him in the ribs. "*Écoute-moi*. I need your attention, Luc. Couples are already fanning out."

Shrugging out of his daydream, Luc concentrated on Rose's contagious drive. "All right. The list."

"Old wagon wheel, white flower, blue door, a swing, a willow tree, cow, cat, dog, red ribbon, and a book. We write where we see them on this paper."

"Do you have a pencil?"

Rose clicked her heels. "I do. The list and pencil are provided as our only tools. Now, think."

Before the first thought entered his mind, Luc had to take double steps to catch up with Rose. How much time had she spent in the village anyway? More than he had, for when they turned into an alley, Rose halted in front of an old wagon wheel propped against a house with the remnants of a summer rose bush wrapped around the spokes.

"Number one. Done." She pivoted and left him in the dust.

Her giddiness rubbed off on him as he passed her and guided her toward a small barn. The "moo" gave them a clue.

Rose jotted down the information. "Where there is a barn, there's a cat, *n'est-ce pas?*"

Luc pictured the kitten in Rose's lap in the castle's large barn. He spied a small black kitten in a corner. "*Voila.*"

"*Fantastique.*" She spun around, out into the road again.

Reaching for her hand, Luc slowed her pace. "Let's enjoy the search. I want to walk and talk as we go."

The list dropped to her side. "Oh." A momentary frown on her otherwise animated face countered his rash decision to curtail her speed.

Walking backwards in front of him, Rose waved her paper to the sky, lifting his concern as her smile erased any negativity. He'd almost ruined the outing. "Captain Bélanger, I think you've forgotten how to play."

"Play? Well, I hope so."

Why the giggles? Playing took too much suspending the heaviness of the world.

"Look around. What do you see?"

Was this another game? "People. Houses."

She huffed, her eyes darting about seeing things he guessed he should see. "People doing what?"

Now, he huffed and puffed out his frustration. He'd lose this game, not knowing the rules. "They are holding hands, running, laughing, talking."

"And playing, competing, participating in an activity together."

Bowing his head, small inklings of understanding slipped through his closed memory. "You're telling me it's all right for me to set aside my serious nature and scutter about town like a child chasing a ball."

She bounced in place and clapped her hands. "*Exactement.*"

He shrugged in acceptance. "You win, *mon amie*. What's next?"

Her vision blurred as Luc acquiesced with little more than her suggestion. This man shed more of his armor every day. Surely, some of his bending was for insignificant things like a village scavenger hunt. But other layers promised adjustments that could make his life whole and purposeful again.

"Now, you find the next one. A blue door."

Luc grabbed her hand and gave a brisk jolt toward the other side of the street. He pointed as he urged her triple steps. "There. The bookseller's shop."

"*Parfait.* And that settles where to find a book." She peered at the display in the window and wrote *Gulliver's Travels* on the sheet.

Looping her hand through his arm, Luc guided them onward. "Did you mention a white flower?"

"I did."

She smelled the winter rose before she saw the bush.

His hand reached out but stopped just short of the flower. "I'd pick one for you, if I didn't think forty others would do the same, leaving the bush bare and the owner distraught."

She blushed. "The gesture is noted."

His bold stare—so familiar yet new—proceeded a kiss on her cheek. She'd take a kiss instead of a rose any day. "Uh, Luc," she stammered. "We best continue the hunt."

"Ah, *oui,* mademoiselle. We must not be caught smelling the roses."

She swiveled out of his reach. "Over there. A swing in an oak tree. I wish we had time to try it." Would he think that childish too? Too much play? A little boy and his dog stole her chance anyway.

"A dog." She added notes to her list. "That leaves a red ribbon and a willow."

Luc secured her hand around his arm, escorting her back the way they'd begun. "You look in all the windows for a Christmas bow, and I'll lead us to a weeping willow in the church courtyard."

"Ah, I'd forgotten about that beauty."

Rose halted abruptly, pulling Luc to a standstill. "There. A big red ribbon in the baker's window." After jotting down the whereabouts, she stored her pencil in her pocket, and turned her steps into a jog. "*Allons-y.*"

Their brisk pace through the wooden gate deposited them in front of an old willow tree, weeping with age though crowned with beauty.

The bench begged for a moment's repose. Even if it cost her the win, she accepted the offer—one of peace with someone dear to her heart.

Rose patted the space beside her. Once Luc's long form followed her example, she relaxed.

"You do realize..." Luc raised his eyebrows and gestured toward the church.

"Yes, I do," she whispered, closing her eyes. *I claim this moment as a gift with no regrets. For one minute, I'm imagining breathing this magical air, whistling through the hanging tresses of the willow, whispering hope, peace, and joy with Luc and no one else.*

Peeking through her lashes, Rose formed a memory, one to travel home with her. "Ah. That's better." She stood and yanked Luc to his feet. "*Allons-y*. We might still come in second or third."

Running up the steps of the church, Rose checked her list, signed their names, and handed the sheet to Mrs. Armand. The woman wrote and circled "2" at the top and handed her an envelope. Rose smiled and shrugged. It was worth the pause in the garden.

Luc leaned against a white fence post, watching her advance. His quirky grin and lazy stance made her wonder. How did he feel about being "attached" to a silly girl, playing games? Well, at least she wasn't the only participant. Squeals of glee or frustration clamored around them.

"I assume, mademoiselle, by your unchecked smile, that you are happy with your place."

She'd be content with third, tenth, twentieth, if she could spend it with Luc. So, second was grand. "*Formidable*. We are second."

His brow scrunched. "And the prize is?"

"I don't know." Nor did it matter. Opening the envelope, she read, "A dinner for two at the local inn."

"Hmmm." Luc stood straight and adjusted his jacket. "Am I in the running for your guest?"

She faced him and patted his chest lightly. "You are the only one on my list."

So very true. And so very confusing.

Twelve

The day of the ball dawned crisp and clear. Rose prayed a silent "Thank you." With perfect weather, not a rain or snow cloud above, the guests would be able to attend and celebrate Christmas at the château. Well, not quite Christmas since it was still three days away. Celebrate the season. Recently, she'd felt as if Christmas came every day. With Christ in her daily life, it did.

Throwing on a loose day dress of dusty rose and a warm shawl, Rose descended the marble staircase to the main floor. No one was about, which suited her desire to be alone. Rays of yellow light spilled from the gallery entrance. So much better than gas or candle light. Her feet followed the enlightened path.

She paused and clasped her hands in front of her heart. A round of giggles released. The light from the nine eastern windows danced across the floor, vying for positions on the checkered tiles. The streaks of sunrise color had no need for music. God orchestrated their dance.

Rose twirled her way, colliding with the flickering rays, her arms flaying with an inner rhythm. Pulled toward Joy, Rose yearned to embrace the elegant tree decked in silver, white, and crystal. Instead, she held out her arms and curtsied. A silly, childish motion that tickled her from head to toe.

Upon rising, she caught her reflection in a large crystal sphere at eye level. A crystal-clear image stared back. For the first time in a long time —or maybe in forever—she saw radiance, confidence, and security. She was free. Her future belonged to God's divine purpose—no one else could steal it.

Her whisper wrapped around the evergreen. "What joy for those whose record the Lord has cleared of guilt, whose lives are lived in complete honesty." Could the verse from Psalms envelope her this day?

Peace and Hope echoed the Joy chorus.

Now, let my new journey begin.

Luc picked a bouquet of hot house flowers—white roses, lavender, and baby's breath. Turning them into a nosegay for Rose posed a bit of a problem with no skill or supplies. After leaving the garden, he found the head gardener's wife and explained his predicament. With little diffi- culty, she used twine and white satin ribbon, creating a brilliant piece of art.

"Absolutely beautiful, madame. *Merci*!"

"Ah, monsieur, it's God who made it beautiful."

"Why, yes, I agree."

All his senses sparked with the melding of lavender and sweet rose. Would Rose like his gesture?

He placed the flowers in a vase at his tower. The cool mid-morning air spurred his walk through the gardens and the wooded paths. Rose had worked incredibly hard beside Marguerite, adding her unique touches. They'd created a winter fairy land of gold and silver, red and green, black and white. A masterpiece. Did she feel like a princess among the beauty? Rose fit so well into the château life, as if born to it. She was fully capable of running a household like Marguerite. It must be an innate mechanism, wanting to bring beauty into the every day. Though the decorations dripped with precious items, most of them emerged from the past. Few of Marguerite's funds produced the wonderland. Talent, time, and vision.

Would my manor house in Provence interest someone used to palaces and castles?

What was he thinking? Rose? Could he invite her to his home? What would that mean? Her reputation would spiral again.

But can I leave her here?

Rose flitted and swayed as she dressed for the ball, giddy and light. Remaining still for the maid's help with her dressing and hair proved a challenge of her will. Was she somehow sixteen again at her first ball? She had at least twenty-five of them behind her.

But not any with Luc.

If the butterflies in her stomach failed to cease their flight, she'd float right down the stairs and hide in the kitchen. No one would miss her.

Except Marguerite. And Luc?

A knock preceded Marguerite's entrance, and a kitchen maid with a tray of light foods—sandwiches, cheese, and tiny buttery biscuits. *Feed my jitters or not?*

"Oh, *mon amie*, your hair is perfect. Emily does such a splendid job with tight curls. I love the way she has let it hang longer in the back. Aren't you glad we don't have to wear a hat tonight?"

Rose touched her flushed cheeks. The compliments and the attention as well as the gown elevated her emotions. It was almost too much. "There are so many things I'm thankful for this evening." Their eyes met in the long mirror. "You, Marguerite, are a blessing. You've made me a princess as elegant as Princess Alexandra or Beatrice."

Marguerite shimmered in her purple gown with gold trim and lacy sleeves. "All I did was supply a gown. You are the beauty. I'm glad you are not a real princess. I think that status is highly cumbersome. There's enough pressure in life without adding royalty."

"I do agree." Rose swayed her hips back and forth, watching the silver threads glimmer. Her white lace sleeves with silver edgings extended to her elbows. Her tight-fitting bodice had a straight front neck line with a V in the back.

"Thank you for letting me be fitted with a light corset and small bustle."

"My pleasure. It's important to feel comfortable. Let's spin around the room in a waltz. The train can be tricky."

Giggling at the silly suggestion, Rose let Marguerite take the lead. The extra material glided with her, causing no missteps or concern. She'd been right in testing out the dress.

"*Voila*. As long as Luc doesn't have a long train attached to him, you should be fine." Rose shook with laughter at the image.

The pearls from her grandmother and a silver fan were Rose's only adornments, except for the sprigs of baby's breath in her hair.

"Let's eat and fortify ourselves to meet the guests." Marguerite placed her hands on her stomach and breathed deeply. "We've worked hard on this gala." She pulled Rose into a light hug, avoiding messing with any of their gowns and hair. "Our work, your work, will shine tonight. *Merci* from my grateful heart."

God had used a special medley of people to orchestrate His plan from the queen's suggestion to Marguerite's acceptance. All the rest contained unexpected threads woven just so. Ones Rose would not have been able to weave into the fabric of her life without help.

Joy. Hope. Peace. A peace that passes understanding. I think one of the epistles says, "Let the peace of Christ rule in your hearts."

From her experience these past months, she realized that anger, jealousy, stress, and gossip were not partners with peace. She chose peace.

This evening, I choose peace.

Thirteen

T he first sound of carriages drew Rose to the front window in the red parlor. Her heart raced with the anticipation of a child wanting to open a present. The only present she needed had already been opened. Her time in the château with her new family. Acceptance with no strings attached.

Oh, the gowns and jewels boasted of celebration. The laughter and chatter pronounced friendships and happiness. And...

And the language she had dreaded hearing—English. Did it matter now? Her heart sputtered but righted itself. She no longer cared what her sister did or didn't do. The gossip could not disable her purpose and hope anymore.

Her Christmas miracle was hers to keep.

Luc discreetly joined the other guests crossing the courtyard. He blended in perfectly with his black pants and jacket with a white shirt and tie. Not much distinction among the gentlemen. But the ladies? He spotted every hue of the rainbow. Some gowns leaned toward the ridiculous with large bustles and long, cumbersome trains. If Rose chose that style, he'd not snicker or complain. But really, he hoped the fashion changed soon.

The bouquet gripped in his hand guided his mission. *Rose.*

To his right inside the entrance, a splash of light caught his eyes. Her smile was extremely contagious. He cut away from the receiving line toward the front parlor.

Nothing in the entire house compared with *his* Rose. Her silver and white gown pulsed with rivulets of motion.

"*Joyeux Noël*, Rose. *Tu es magnifique. Non, parfaite.*" Even perfect appeared too tame. "Are you sure you're not a princess?"

"I'm sure, sweet Luc. It's still just me." She lifted her arms out from her sides, tilted her head, and shrugged.

Still a princess. He presented the nosegay, which a royal would probably not accept. But he believed the real Rose stood before him. Surely a gown, no matter how elegant, could not change the lady he knew and...loved.

Love? I can't ruin the evening with my fantasy.

"*Merci*, Luc." Rose brought the flowers close. Her fingers released the fragrance so their shared air smelled of rose and lavender—a detail he'd never forget.

He took his place beside her, noting her train was ever so much shorter than others. He'd not have to fight with the fabric. Instead, he could enjoy the feel of her in his arms while dancing.

As they strolled down the long hall arm in arm toward the gallery, he noticed the stares and whispers of a few couples and especially among the women. *English guests.* He wanted to confront them and end the rumors before they reached Rose's ears.

A small, sweet voice whispered, "Luc, don't concern yourself with them. I'm not." Her eyes sparkled with something pure—peace? "Their comments and faces are a blur to me. The music and the beauty of the château will work their magic. If I'm not concerned, neither should you be. I want this evening with you to remember forever. I think you can give me that. Consider it your Christmas present to me."

"Well, if you can block their voices, I can too. And by the way, who said I was going to give you a present?" He crinkled his brow and winked.

She squeezed his arm and giggled.

In front of them, the gallery opened, dispelling light and color. Beauty radiated from the trees, the music, the river, and Rose. All of these replaced the darkness and noises of tragedy. Gone. Was the healing a miracle or Rose? Or both? God was definitely the author of this peace, allowing His people and this petit château a role in the peace he now experienced. That truth was crystal clear.

Claude Debussy began his angelic performance solo as the guests mingled in the gallery. Rose guided Luc with an ever-so-slight pull toward the glittering trio. The other visitors had not proceeded that far yet, so the view remained unobscured.

Before they escaped the crowd, a woman stopped Rose with her fan, then stepped to face them. "Aren't you Margaret Marrow's sister? We've heard you ran away too. Isn't that right, Mr. Ward?" The woman hit her partner, most likely her poor husband, on the arm with the offensive object.

What gave Rose away out of all the people in the room?

Mr. Ward squinted at Rose. "Well, I don't know, my dear. You know more about these things than I do."

Luc completed the circle. His scowl proceeded his growl. "I assure you, this lady is exactly where she should be." His arm rested on her back. She could feel the heat from his fingers. His protective gesture gave her courage to face all the others, most likely wondering the same things. "I promise you Miss Marrow's future is none of your concern. It's ours."

The fan flitted in front of the woman. "I see. Well, congratulations. We didn't believe it any way."

As the couple left, Rose stifled a giggle but not for long. Her laughter broke free of her gloved hand. "You were marvelous, Luc. I was ready to use the same tactic. It is definitely no one's business."

He secured her hand through his arm again and patted her hand. Or was it more of a caress? "You weathered that rather well."

"God and I had a little talk. I'm reclaiming my purpose and life from the negative rumors. I'm ready for the next phase as I face the future." She nibbled on her bottom lip. "What did you mean about my future being our concern?"

This time Luc led her forward toward Joy, standing tall between Peace and Hope. Their images reflected from the crystal objects, making designs on their clothing and the floor. Luc's face glowed with the play of light. His usually dark eyes shone with golden sparks.

He faced her and took her hands in his. She stared at her reflection in his eyes—eyes she never wanted to leave. "I meant every word. Rose, I want to spend every Christmas with you. Every day of every year. You are my Christmas gift. For a stubborn, hard-nosed soldier to see things as clear as these crystals is..."

"A miracle. My Christmas miracle is you."

"*Je t'aime, mon amour*. I've loved you from the first box of Christmas decorations."

"*Je t'aime aussi*. And I've loved you since our traipse through the woods."

"Oh, Rose, my Rosalind, dare I kiss you here?"

"You might as well. My reputation is already tarnished. What better way to seal it?"

Joy looked on as Rose accepted her first kiss from her Frenchman. All the warmth of a summer day pierced her thawing winter being. His probing kiss only lasted a second but promised many more days and nights to explore their love.

Claude and Monsieur Hebert played the introduction of the first dance. Deftly, Luc took her in his arms and danced her across the gallery. No one else existed. No rumor pierced her soul. This love of a soldier answered all her dreams.

Tonight, she was a princess in a silver gown with a future as sure and steady as the river beneath them.

Epilogue

JANUARY 1880

S tanding in the drive with the plane trees weaving their arms towards each other and forming a future canopy, Rose already knew she would return one day. The sphinx on their grand columns would guard the Château des Dames through the centuries. The magic—and in Rose's case, the miracle—of the château could lend its aid to someone else. She'd found her purpose, ready to move safely into the world.

Luc—her love, her future—stood in the courtyard, a vague image with the white stone entrance and turrets surrounding him. Even at this distance, she imagined the details of his handsome face, the feel of his hand in hers, and the wonder of his unconditional love.

Even the gardens in their winter state waved a soothing farewell. She'd be back in the summer for their full bloom, alive with color and perfume.

Her wedding.

She twirled in a circle and stretched her arms upward, laughing at the circumstances enabling her to rejoice amidst the drama.

I'm marrying a foreigner, a Frenchman. Someone who found me at my lowest and loved me anyway.

Each step toward the shadow confirmed the details of God's plan.

Luc was her future. His image remained crystal clear against the château's façade. He wanted her, faults and all, with rumors attached. And she, Rosalind Marrow, cherished his commitment. She'd forever be his Rose.

Although they would leave the magical place of their budding romance among the twinkling lights of the trees and crystals, they'd forge a new life in Southern France, returning here for their wedding.

Luc's arms opened wide, allowing her to fall into his embrace. "The carriage awaits, *ma chère*."

Her eyes glistened with a watery haze. "*Oui*. To whisk me off to my future home."

"Are you nervous? I promise my parents will love you."

"Nervous, *non*. A flutter of excitement, *oui*."

Rose held Luc's hand as they departed. Turning her gaze back toward the Château Chenonceau, she winked and nodded at the exquisite castle, whispering, "I'll return soon."

La Fin

Author's Notes

Le Château de Chenonceau impressed me as an eleven-year-old on a tour of the beautiful, perfect castle in the Loire Valley in France. Back then, I had no knowledge of the role the château had played over the centuries or what it would mean to me. I fell in love with a fairy tale castle, one I would return to many times. As with true love, I want to know more, see more, experience all aspects of the history, the gardens, the rooms, present and past.

Welcome to this Christmas novella set in 1879. The historical background includes the sixth woman to own the castle, Marguerite Wilson Pelouze. She followed a long line of dames who owned and occupied the petit château including Queen Catherine de Medici and Diane de Poitiers. It is a bit strange having one of the minor characters named

Marguerite, but the facts speak clearly—she has to have her place and proper name, one I proudly share.

Claude Debussy, at age seventeen, really did spend the summer of 1879 at the chateau where he composed two of his ballads. I take advantage of the fact and have him return to entertain at Christmas of the same year.

Every year at Christmas, the present-day château comes alive with trees, lights, decorations, and activities that would make any of her ancestors proud. Enjoy your journey in time to my favorite place in France. *Joyeux Noël*!

About Marguerite Martin Gray

Marguerite enjoys the study of history, especially when combined with fiction. An avid traveler and reader, she teaches French and Spanish and has degrees in French, Spanish, and Journalism from Trinity University in San Antonio, Texas and a MA in English from Hardin-Simmons University in Abilene. She has two grown children and currently lives with her husband in north Louisiana. She writes historical fiction.

Learn more about Marguerite's books at: http://www.celebratelitpublishing.com/marguerite-martin-gray/

facebook.com/Marguerite-Martin-Gray-261131773910522

instagram.com/margueritemgray

bookbub.com/authors/marguerite-martin-gray

goodreads.com/margueritemartingray

amazon.com/author/margueritemartingray

The Weary World Rejoices

NAOMI CRAIG

Introduction

When I was first married, my pastor always held to the view that the wise-men didn't arrive on scene at the same time as the shepherds to the nativity scene. He would set the wisemen and their finery over on the piano instead of at the communion table with the rest of the nativity set. I personally had this belief growing up as well. In fact, there is an indication in scripture that they would have shown up much later—one to two years later.

In Luke's account, Jesus is circumcised at eight days old, and dedicated in the temple after the days of Mary's purification (thirty-three days) where we meet Simeon and Anna. Joseph and Mary also give a poor man's offering of two turtledoves or pigeons.

In Matthew's account, when the wisemen do arrive, they show up at a house where they see the young child. Of course, their gifts are familiar: gold, frankincense and myrrh. These items were so costly it would have instantly bumped Joseph and Mary to a new tax bracket if you will. They would have been required to offer a lamb.

Joseph and Mary flee to Egypt shortly after the wisemen return home another way, but they couldn't have made it back to the temple at the appointed time for Mary's purification and Jesus' dedication if they had left directly after the birth.

All this is not to convince you to change your mind, but to show you my reasoning behind the timeline in The Weary World Rejoices.

I hope you enjoy Amal's journey as he seeks out Truth.

Naomi

One

In the days of Herod the king, behold, wise men from the East came to Jerusalem, saying "Where is He who has been born King of the Jews? For we have seen His star in the East and have come to worship Him."
Matthew 2:1b-2

Jerusalem
6 B.C.

Crash! The ornate, imported cedar door cracked with force as it slammed against the wall.

Amal crouched and flung his arm over his head, heart leaping to his throat and his pulse ramping to an unprecedented speed.

"Where is it?" The veins in King Herod's neck bulged as he crossed the *bibliotheca* in three strides. With a feral growl that rivaled the lions in Caesarea's hippodrome, he yanked a scroll from the torah section. The other documents clattered together to fill the void.

Amal clutched the edge of his copy table and drew in a shallow breath. His knees audibly creaked as he pushed himself up and bowed at the waist. "How can I serve you, my king?"

King Herod ripped at the scroll, to no avail, and hurled it across the room.

Amal's body seized, the cramp in his hand forgotten under the force of his trembling.

"My king!" He stepped over the crumpled scroll. "What are you searching for? I can find it for you."

Ignoring him, the king rifled through the piles of scrolls with no regard to their sacred teachings.

Amal prostrated himself on the cold tiles. There was nothing he could do to protect his life's work, as the ethnarch pulled more scrolls, only to throw them violently at him.

"Where? Where does it say? Stop cowering, you imbecile and show me!"

King Herod's venomous tone evoked a sweat on Amal's back. He scrambled to his feet and wedged himself as a feeble barrier between the king's raging hands and the costly work represented in ink.

Studying the ornate embroidery dancing along the hem of King Herod's purple silk robe, Amal's breath puffed out in relief as the king paced frantically.

"What do you know about the Messiah?"

Amal blinked at the frenzied accusation. "The Messiah? We hope for the Messiah to come and redeem His people—"

"I know that. Is he said to be the *King* of the Jews?"

A faint-remembered scripture niggled at his memory as understanding and dread registered. "If you would allow me to search out the scriptures, I'm sure I could find a satisfactory answer, my king. What is your entire query?"

It was a stall tactic for sure, but Amal knew no other way to mollify the king's wrath.

"From where does the Messiah hail?" King Herod whirled, his robe swooshing as he pivoted.

"Why does this trouble you, my king? The Messiah won't arrive anytime soon. Not in your lifetime, surely."

The vein on King Herod's forehead bulged, and his face turned an unnatural shade of purplish-red in the lamplight. "There is an entourage of Magi come from the east—on palace grounds—searching for the 'King of the Jews.'"

"You must be mistaken. Clearly they seek to honor you."

THE WEARY WORLD REJOICES

"You would think so, wouldn't you?" King Herod stalked closer and his voice dropped ominously low. "These men were insistent they had seen the star announcing the birth of the King of the Jews. Now you tell me that isn't a threat."

Amal gulped as the king's hot breath assailed his face with the scent of rotting fish, and the hand spotted with age pressed against Amal's airway.

"I will look into the matter." Amal's voice squeaked out.

"I await your findings with bated breath."

The veiled threat hindered Amal's breathing as the frigid clasp released. "Yes, my king."

"I want to know when. Where. Where the birthplace of the Messiah is predicted. What his intentions are." King Herod slammed his fist against the door. "I want to know who he is."

"I will consult with the chief priests and the temple scribes." Amal hesitated. "May I confer with the visitors to see their basis for this claim?"

King Herod spun around so fast his curled hair bounced. "Do what you must. I want answers. No one sleeps until I know. You have until the sixth hour. I am *obligated* to give an answer to our distinguished guests' query as to where."

"Yes, my king." Amal whispered to the king's departing back.

The king's footsteps clattered through the corridor and—if his standard mannerisms were displayed—the bellowing that would distress the whole of Jerusalem would soon give way to cunning manipulation. The halls of the palace would be silent. Eerie was the tomb while the servants moved around like a whisper, completing their assignments and not drawing attention to themselves.

Amal's shoulders sagged. He smoothed out a crumpled scroll and rerolled it gingerly. Faltering before its rightful place, he surveyed the stacks upon stacks of scrolls tucked into the niches.

There was no merit to the claims of the Messiah coming *now*, was there?

"What happened in here?" Amal's aide, Sofar's tone was as incredulous as his expression. As he stepped into the dimly lit room.

"The king has tasked me with…research." Amal slid the document into the slot and tucked his hands inside his dark sleeves.

"Appears as if he's done some 'research' of his own." Sofar muttered and nudged a parchment with his toe.

Amal shot a glare at Sofar and scurried to the doorway. He peered both ways down the hallway before swinging the heavy door into place.

The walls themselves were rumored to have ears. Sofar's accusatory tone could deliver them both into Herod's Roman torture chamber.

At Sofar's side, Amal hissed, "Guard your tongue. Speak not of what you don't know."

With a defiant glance at the door, Sofar's chin dipped in acknowledgement, though his eyes still sparked with hidden thoughts. "What are you meant to research?"

Would it be a valuable resource to include Sofar in his task? Though deniability was an intriguing cloak, rarely did it result in higher favor. Amal pressed his lips together and rocked back on his heels. "The Messiah."

Sofar scoffed. "Yahweh has been silent toward our people these four hundred years, with not a sign of Elijah's return, and you think the Messiah will arrive now to deliver us like Moses did in Egypt?"

"The king sees reason for concern." Amal bobbled his head.

"Yahweh has forgotten His people. We are languishing under oppressive rule and the king is babbling on about myths—"

Amal clamped his hand over Sofar's mouth. "You will bridle your words or you will send both of us to the dungeons."

Sofar's eyes glittered as he tore himself away from Amal's grasp.

"Besides," Amal breathed. "Wouldn't this be a good time for the Messiah to come? Please, help me clean this up."

With a grunt, Sofar squatted and began rolling the scrolls.

After the *bibliotheca* had been restored to orderly fashion, Amal straightened his lower back. "Find Micah's scroll and the section you referenced. I will consult the king's honored guests and then go to the temple. If Elijah has returned, the priests will likely know."

At least, that was Amal's prayer. If he couldn't find direct answers by the sixth hour, his life was already over.

Two

Know therefore and understand, that from the going forth of the command to restore and build Jerusalem until Messiah the Prince, there shall be seven weeks, and sixty-two weeks; the street shall be built again, and the wall even in troublesome times.
    ~Daniel 9:25

"Do you even believe in the God of my people?"

"We are here, are we not?" The Magi called Gaspar gently rotated the wine goblet under his nose.

"Well, of course. But you could be on assignment from your king." Amal rolled his shoulders back and stretched his neck. The reasoning sounded weak even to his ears.

Melchior leaned back against the silk cushion and stroked the hair sprouting from his chin until it jutted out like an arrowhead. "We have come seeking the way of truth. Did not your prophets declare how this king will restore peace on earth? We were guided by a star to this land. It lines up with the prophecies. This is the time of salvation."

"You observe a star in the night sky and come up with 'the Messiah.'" Amal scrubbed his ink-stained fingers against his black outer robe before wiping what was surely an incredulous look off his face.

Melchior leaned forward and stared at the scroll he had brought from the land of Persia—Isaiah's words. "Your holy texts say that the stars are placed in the sky as signs of the times. Yet *you* do not believe."

Amal stood so quickly he disrupted the scroll on his lap. He strode out on the balcony where Balthasar stood with his neck craned back studying the heavens. "Which star?"

"Are you aware of how long our journey was?" Balthasar's low voice rolled from his deep chest like a shallow stream tumbling over rocks.

"What does that have to do with a star?" Why did exceptionally wise men speak only in riddles?

"We study the stars. The path of the stars changes nightly. If you look now, you can determine where they will line up based on the established pattern." Balthasar's gesture toward the heavens did nothing to clarify the pin-pricks of light strewn across the sky.

Amal lowered his gaze to the courtyard below—unusually busy for this time of night. "We do not put credibility in the stars. They hold no power over the future."

"Then put credibility in your scriptures." Gaspar glided out to join them, his heavy robes sweeping against the floor.

Words of defense rose inside Amal as he shifted to allow room at the railing. Who was this man to assume Amal did not put trust in the sacred words of Yahweh's prophets? "Your accusation is unfounded. I have dedicated my life to the words of the prophets and the law. You could learn much from me."

"Perhaps you are not *looking* for the Messiah." Melchior stood behind Amal, silent and imposing even with his short stature. "You see the words. You copy the words faithfully, yet you do not see the pattern or the fulfillment."

Gaspar clasped his hands behind his back and turned to Amal. "Let me ask you, scribe, how old would a faithful priest be?"

Amal blinked twice. What did priests have to do with the coming of the Messiah? "Thirty years of age, but I don't see what—"

"You are correct!" Melchior clapped his hands and shuffled his feet in a little jig. "Then I will raise up for Myself a faithful priest!"

"The words of Samuel." Amal pondered the meaning. "He shall walk before My anointed forever."

"From the time of the angel Gabriel's arrival to the prophet Daniel, till now has been nearly sixty-nine periods of sevens. The prophecy declares the Messiah will be struck down at the end of sixty-nine sevens." Gaspar clasped the railing and tilted his head toward the heavens again.

"Naturally the man has to be born before he can die." Melchior's tone sobered. "We subtracted thirty years from the four hundred and eighty-three years."

The Messiah had barely made His appearance and now they spoke of His death? If the man would be a priest, and the Magi had calculated thirty years, that would mean—"You seek an infant?"

"When the stars aligned nearly two years ago, we knew. The time is now. He will be a child now."

"You do not use the past to show the way to the future." Amal stepped back and felt the press of the balustrade from behind and the weight of the magus's knowledge in the front.

"Do not ignore the signs. They still occurred in the past, despite your refusal to see their significance." Balthasar seemed to grow taller with each step.

"Couple that with the prophecy from the fourth book of your Torah." Gaspar tapped the rail, staring beyond the courtyard. "A star shall come out of Jacob, a scepter shall rise out of Israel—"

"Shh!" Amal held up his hand and peered down into the courtyard. The shiver of someone's gaze made the back of his neck prickle. His breath quickened, and he peered inside the guest quarters. "You cannot speak of other kings in the palace of Herod the Great. That—I am certain—even you can understand."

Gaspar sighed as if his past had been exposed. "Seeking out the Messiah comes at a cost. What are you willing to risk? Your comfortable position? Your reputation? Your life?"

"The Faithful Priest has come. What are you going to do about it?" Balthasar tipped his head away from the night sky.

Amal resisted the urge to shield himself from Balthasar's probing stare. His well-practiced words failed him.

"Search your scriptures against the facts we share." Melchior opened his arms as if to embrace Amal. "You are a learned man. You hold a valuable position expounding knowledge. Seek with the goal of understanding."

This conversation was getting no further on finding where the Messiah was to hail from. He scanned the horizon. Was the skyline lighter, or just Amal's imagination?

A shiver ran down Amal's back. He whipped his head around and furtively searched the dim interior. People had...disappeared for seemingly less than fulfilling the king's assignment. He rubbed his neck where he could still feel the imprint of King Herod's bony fingers digging into his flesh.

Swallowing hard, he scanned the now empty courtyard. His discomfort grew. Had anyone below heard? A servant? Did someone lurk on the next balcony? He cleared his throat twice and shuffled backward. "Perhaps I could document your findings, then I can investigate amongst my scrolls and my colleagues."

Balthasar pivoted and blocked Amal's retreat. He shifted his torso to the side so light poured onto Amal's face, his own face hidden in shadow.

Amal stepped back, feeling as if he were a boy again, and his Rabi was about to make a public display of Amal's mistakes. His gaze darted over the somber—yet expectant—expressions of the other two. He stole another glance around the courtyard. The shadows bulged with suspicious shapes.

Bringing his attention back to Balthasar, Amal found the tall man towering above him.

"Search your scrolls, yes. Seek the prophesies." Balthasar leaned closer to Amal. The lines around the scholar's mouth softened and his eyes shone with an intensity that caused Amal to flinch back from its glow.

Balthasar reached out a single finger and placed it against Amal's chest. "But here. Here is where you must search in order to know." He touched Amal's temple. "Not here."

Amal's breath lodged in his throat.

"Messiah has come to bring salvation to all people. Find the truth of what we speak in your heart."

Three

When Herod the king heard this, he was troubled, and all Jerusalem with him. And when he gathered all the chief priests and scribes of the people together, he inquired of them where the Christ was to be born.
  ~Matthew 2:3-4

"The Messiah?"
   "Here?"
   "Now?"
Amal bowed slightly to the chief priests who had been summoned from their beds. Was it wrong to feel relief that they also were not expecting this news?

How was it that they all had been caught unaware? What significance was it that Gentiles had informed the Chosen People about this momentous event?

"They were extremely confident, my lords." Amal discreetly covered a yawn with his sleeve.

"You must be wary of prophets who prophecy in their own name." The Captain of the Temple rubbed the back of his hand across his eyes.

Prophets by their own right. Of course. Why hadn't Amal thought of that? A weight lifted off his shoulders and a nervous laugh burbled up. People had been predicting the Messiah's arrival with a frenzied passion—the Good Lord knew they could use relief from Roman occupation.

Yes, this *would* be a good time for the Messiah to arrive—even as he had told Sofar.

Amal glanced behind him and laughed aloud at his own foolishness. His thoughts were not announced to the room.

His relief was short lived.

The priests may guarantee the errancy of the claim, but King Herod would be less than satisfied when his direct query wasn't explicitly answered. The feeling of being hunted returned.

Amal shifted his gaze in both directions. "Where would the birthplace be documented in the scriptures?"

A crease deepened between the captain's eyes, creating a chasm. "We have been quashing these rebellious tales for years. It only makes things worse to elaborate."

"Yes, my lord. You can understand my need to return to the king with some sort of information." Amal narrowed in on the sleepy expressions of the priests.

The Captain of the Temple huffed and paced with his hands behind his back. "The scriptures identify hundreds of prophecies for the Messiah's arrival and tasks. According to the data, the chances of all the prophecies coming true are impossible—"

Amal flitted his gaze around the room while the man lectured. The other priests blinked heavy eyelids, and one stifled a yawn.

The youngest man stared back at Amal, and the muscle in his jaw bulged.

Rubbing his grainy eyes, Amal narrowed in on what could have sparked a reaction, but the priest's face was devoid of any expression.

The morning light inched across the floor from the high window, and the gong indicating the third hour sounded.

Amal lifted his face to the slits of the windows high on the walls. "A place. Please!" Sweat beaded on his forehead as the sun's rays spilled in through the high windows.

The captain heaved a sigh. "You understand we highly discourage this line of thinking."

"Of course. I must report back to the king."

Frowning, the captain crossed over to the wall and sorted through the collection of scrolls that rivaled the palace's assortment. He selected one, untied the leather strip and unrolled the papyrus, his eyes skimming the words. With painfully slow precision, he rerolled it and replaced it.

Amal shifted his weight to his left side as the man pulled out the scroll below and repeated the process. Two other priests appeared to have mentally returned to their beds. One scratched his gray beard and yawned. The youngest priest stared steadily at Amal.

Pressing his lips tight, Amal glared back. "I'm sorry, who are you? What do you wish to say?"

The priests—including the young man—turned quizzical looks to Amal.

The captain glanced back over his shoulder and tracked Amal's line of sight. "This is Lior. He is the director of the daily courses. What is your concern?"

Was Amal so jumpy that every glance aroused suspicion?

He shook his head briefly. "I lost the direction of my thoughts."

People began to filter outside the library. Amal restrained himself from glancing at the rising sun creeping steadily toward the fourth hour.

The captain returned to his perusing as Amal took a swig from the nearby water jar.

The prickle of a gaze traveled down his spine and he involuntarily shuddered.

"Bethlehem."

Amal swung around to see Lior staring at him again.

"According to the prophet Micah," His voice grew in strength. "Oh you, Bethlehem, though the least of all..."

Amal blinked.

The director of daily courses continued to recite the words with an expression of nonchalance. Did these men not understand Amal's well-being was at stake? Perhaps even his life.

He nodded at the words. "Yes, I am familiar with the passage. But how do you know that is the location?"

"Think about it." The director tapped his head. "Tribe of Judah. Line of David. City of David."

Amal surveyed the bored faces of the priests. The captain of the temple nodded his agreement of the assessment.

Bethlehem was good. There was no indication of any royal upstart in Bethlehem. All Jerusalem could rest at ease.

"Very good." Amal released his tension through a long breath. "I shall report back to the king and be sure to set his mind at ease."

Bowing swiftly, he took his leave.

The anxiousness he expected to leave behind with the proclamation of the wrong time only heightened as he maneuvered through Jerusalem's narrow alleys.

There were definitely footsteps in the shadows behind him.

Amal lengthened his stride as he rounded the corner. He pressed himself into the arched doorway, his dark robes blending in with the deep crevices not yet illuminated by the morning's light.

The sound of footsteps hastened closer, matching the tempo of Amal's pounding heart.

Someone rounded the corner and stopped, breathing heavily, their shadow extending sharply outward.

Amal's lungs burned. After more than a minute, he heard nothing. An overwhelming desire to peek around the archway coursed through his veins. Had the stalker passed by?

"You didn't ask why I knew that so well."

Amal lurched back into the uneven stone with a gasp.

"I've researched all the prophecies in the last two years."

After catching his breath, Amal peered out to find Lior. "Why didn't you say that in the counsel of priests instead of nearly killing me?"

"For the same reason, you think your actions are being monitored."

Amal shrugged and peered down the alley.

The director leaned conspiratorially close. "He has come."

"Who?" Amal braced his hands on his knees and tried to regulate his breathing.

"The Messiah is here!"

Four

But the angel said to him, "Do not be afraid, Zacharias, for your prayer is heard; and your wife Elizabeth will bear you a son, and you shall call his name John."
~Luke 1:13

Why did the man whisper? What proof did he have? Before Amal could organize his thoughts, Lior was speaking again.

"The priest Zacharias was chosen to present the incense offering. He came out, unable to speak, and wrote he had seen a vision—no —a messenger who stands in the presence of God. The Lord said he would have a son."

"Zacharias' son is the Messiah?" Amal combed his fingers through his beard.

"No. The messenger. The one who prepares the way for the Messiah."

"Zacharias is the messenger?"

Lior snapped the edges of his outer cloak. "No."

Amal rolled back heavy shoulders. He had to report back. His time was nearly expired. "I'm sorry. I don't understand. What are you trying to tell me?"

"Zacharias is old, his wife is past the time of childbearing. This child is a miracle announced by the angel who stood in the presence of God." Lior leaned on the balls of his feet, searching Amal's face.

"So, neither Zacharias nor his child are the Messiah? What does that have to do with anything?"

Frustration crept into Lior's eyes. "Zacharias could not speak until the child was born. When he came back for his service a year later, he could talk—he wouldn't stop talking. When his wife still carried the child in her womb, their cousin came from Nazareth and she was with child! Zacharias' child leapt in his wife's womb. At her arrival, the child knew."

Amal shook his head and scrubbed his face, trying to reassemble Lior's words in some sense of order.

"All the prophecies line up. The messenger of the Lord, Elijah the prophet, the virgin giving birth, Bethlehem." Lior's voice rasped out in an excited whisper. "Do you remember Caesar's census?"

How could he forget that season two years ago? It had been every scribe's nightmare attempting to organize all the documentation. Amal slowly nodded.

"There was an old man, Simeon, who announced all over the place, that the spirit of God had come upon him. He saw the Messiah dedicated right here in the temple—"

Amal held up his hands and talked over Lior's verbal flood. "Where is this Simeon now?"

A shadow passed over Lior's face, and he cast furtive glances both ways. He pressed his lips together. "He died shortly after."

A chill crept up Amal's spine.

The sun flared over the rooftop and into Amal's eyes. If he delayed much longer, he'd find himself with the same fate as the old man Simeon.

Time was running out, yet a niggling curiosity stirred deep in his soul. "Where can I find Zacharias?" Amal heard the words as if they came from someone else's mouth.

"He is not here."

Amal's stomach dropped like the times scrolls were supposed to be copied and his deadline had passed.

"No, no. Not like that. He only serves twice a year, and for special events. And feasts."

A chuckle forced its way out of Amal's throat. "When does he return?"

Something clattered around the corner and both men tensed.

Two men began to argue in the alley, their voices echoing against the walls of stone.

Amal swallowed and wiped his hands on his robe. "I must return to the palace. Please send a messenger when Zacharias next serves."

Amal dodged around Lior and hurried down the cobblestone street.

"Do you believe what I am telling you?" Lior's voice arrested Amal's forward motion.

Did he? It was all so new—so anticipated. Yet unexpected. Amal pressed dry lips together and glanced back at Lior's discerning gaze. "It's a lot to take in."

That muscle bulged in Lior's jaw again and imprinted in Amal's memory as he sped the rest of the way to the palace.

I won't expose Lior in my report. Amal scanned the road behind him, but it didn't ease the pressure behind his eyes. He waved aside the musty scent of indecision. There was work to be done.

Mentally, he rehearsed the words he would say to the king. *Bethlehem. Not relevant. Many predictions, none true. This was another desperate attempt to break free from Rome's tyranny.*

Probably best to not say that last part—the king enjoyed his plush assignment from Rome. Was it any wonder that news, regardless of validity, of a king of the Jews would undermine his authority?

The priests were right. This was merely a false alarm.

Weren't they?

The magi and their impossible claim were no threat to Herod's precarious perch on the Judean throne.

And what of the old man Simeon?

Lior hadn't indicated the cause of death.

As much as Amal tried to convince himself, something didn't sit right. Every detail did not align.

As the exquisitely designed façade of the palace loomed above Amal, a deepening sense of dread shrouded his footsteps. Such beauty, yet concealed behind the pristine workmanship, a cold, ruthless tyrant lay in wait for him. As always, his gaze skimmed the thirty-cubit high walls. Only the most trained eye could determine where one marble brick ended and the next began.

Amal shuddered as he walked briskly through the grove of trees lining the canal. Even here on palace grounds, with water trickling through the brazen statues amongst the lush greenery, the peaceful atmosphere seemed contrived.

Why did he fight with everything in him for the prestigious position of chief palace scribe if everything about this place was a façade? No, he could not afford to entertain such thoughts. This was his purpose—his life's work and his only goal.

He refocused his thoughts on ensuring the security of his position. One wrong step, one thing he did not observe and document as relevant and Sofar would be the chief palace scribe, not him. After he reported to the king, he would settle in once again to his bibliotheca and his routine and brush aside the curiosity Lior kindled.

His presence was announced, and he entered the throne room from the servants' hallway.

All confidence fled as Amal prostrated himself before the elevated marble throne draped with the luxurious purple cloth, and the ethnarch draped with disdain.

A storm cloud of rage brewed on King Herod's face. The servants all retreated to the shadows—common protocol for avoiding the king's thundering after a sleepless night.

"Oh, King, live forever." Amal's voice squeaked past his dry lips.

"What did you discover?" King Herod's words stabbed into the tension filled air.

Amal hadn't thought to bring the scrolls to hide behind. Even his immaculate memory threatened to abandon him. "My king, the scribes and the priests at the temple are conclusive in their findings. And may I point out, they are united in the belief that this brazen suggestion is a false alarm—"

"Are you indicating I am wrong? Where does he hail from?" Bony fingers clutched at the armrests.

"Bethlehem, my king." A sense of uneasiness settled in Amal's gut.

"Ah, the city of David." King Herod brooded.

"Yes, my king. According to the prophet, Micah, A ruler shall be born—"

The king's growl rumbled through the throne room like the roar of chariots during a race in the arena.

Amal pressed his hands on the tiled floor to still the shaking in his arms. "But all the scribes agreed. This isn't the right timing."

"Should I ignore a threat to Israel's security?" King Herod turned his predatory visage toward Amal.

"No, my king," Amal mumbled.

"Silence. Let me think." King Herod drummed his gnarly fingers on the throne's armrest.

The back of Amal's throat stretched, and a yawn threatened to burst from his mouth. His eyes widened, and he shook his head in an attempt to restrain the unsanctioned reaction.

The king narrowed his eyes and Amal squirmed internally under the calculating scrutiny. "That is all for now. Leave me before you disrespect me with your insolent yawns."

"Thank you, my king." Amal rose and backed away, still bent at the waist.

At the appointed location, Amal straightened and left, making way for the king's son, Archelaus. The crown prince was as calculating and violent as his *abba*, yet without King Herod's shrewd managerial sense.

Amal's thoughts and footsteps were heavy as he stumbled to his sleeping quarters. He groaned as he sank to his elevated cot. There had been a time he had been able to go without rest for a day and a half straight. Indeed, he used to relish the quiet of night to work uninterrupted. But those days were long gone.

His weary body and mind sank into slumber as soon as his head rested on the cot.

Five

Then Herod, when he had secretly called the wise men, determined from them what time the star appeared. And he sent them to Bethlehem and said, "Go and search carefully for the young Child, and when you have found Him, bring back word to me, that I may come and worship Him also.
    ~Matthew 2:7-8

Dusk deepened outside the high window, as Amal paused mid-stride outside the king's private chambers.

Voices filtered out through the thick door. Who had called this meeting and which scribe documented it?

Anger and betrayal bubbled up in his chest. *He* was the chief scribe. Who had the audacity to make this executive decision? He could have been woken from his slumber and evaluated whether he wished to rise and attend, or to delegate the duty.

He leaned close to the wooden door. Could he find the servants entrance to the room and discover what was being discussed?

Muffled footsteps approached the door. Amal retreated to a dark corner and pressed against the cold stone.

The door creaked open and light spilled into the hallway. Amal narrowed his eyes at the king, holding the door open for the Magi. No servants? What did King Herod discuss with the visitors?

"Your arrival has indeed been providential." King Herod smiled benevolently and clasped his hand over his chest.

"Yes, oh king." Gaspar bowed at the waist. "This is an exciting time. The time of the Lord's favor."

"Indeed."

Amal shivered at the lethal undercurrent in the king's tone. What could they have discussed that warranted such deceptive speech?

The Magi regally floated past Amal's hiding spot. Clearly, they did not seem to recognize the king's potential for maliciousness.

The heavy cedar groaned mostly to a close and a sliver of light shone through. Amal stretched his neck side to side and fisted his hands. Whichever scribe emerged would feel the heat of Amal's scorn.

The inner door of the king's private quarters shut with a resounding clang. Amal waited another moment, but no one else emerged. In addition to the planned lecture of the hierarchy of the scribes, Amal would have to educate the interloper about haste in exiting the king's presence. The ethnarch did not abide dallying.

Still no one exited the receiving chambers.

Creeping close, Amal tipped his ear to the wooden frame to listen. Beyond Herod's stirrings in the inner chambers, there was no movement.

Amal sucked in a breath—and his stomach—and squeezed inside the receiving chambers. He pivoted and cast a fierce glare to the scribe's usual place, but found it vacant. In fact the entire outer room was empty.

With trepidation, Amal glanced at the king's closed sleeping quarters, and tread lightly to the scribe's cushion where the clay tablets and styli sat waiting and untouched. Just as he had left them.

What had transpired here? King Herod would not conduct any business without documenting everything for the annuls. Would he?

Amal retreated and latched the door behind him. There had been no scribe. No documentation of what had been said.

A chill crept over his skin. It was as if the meeting had never happened. How would one know the king's intentions if there was no record of what transpired?

Walk away. It is not intended to be known.

But Amal could not shake the quickening of his spirit. How could he walk away from this uncovered mystery?

"It is merely another conspiracy." He folded his hands into the sleeves of his robe, unconvinced even of his own thoughts spoken aloud.

The intrigue drew him to the lavish guest quarters where Balthasar carefully wound lengths of cloth around his grand instruments and the magi's servants bustled around packing up their robes and possessions.

A sense of loss shrouded Amal. "You're leaving?"

"First, we seek the new king to worship." Balthasar didn't seem surprised at Amal's unannounced arrival.

"Surely not." The words escaped Amal's mouth before he could censor them. "That is, surely King Herod advised you of the improbability—"

"On the contrary." Melchior glanced up from his maps. "King Herod has directed us with his blessing."

"With his blessing." Amal guarded his tone and restrained himself from searching the room. In the palace, there was no telling where loyalties lay at any given time. Distrust was bred amongst the servants as surely as the royal animal handler whelped hunting dogs. Everyone regarded one another with skepticism and suspicion.

"He has asked us to report back, so he too can worship the child king." Melchior rolled up the parchments in a protective cloth.

Amal narrowed his eyes. Why the secret meeting then? Why not publicly declare it? Something was amiss. "So you depart in the morning?"

Balthasar paused on his way to the balcony with an expression of disbelief. "We will wait and pray for your God's will to be revealed. We delay until the star appears to guide us."

What was Yahweh's will? Was it His plan to have the treacherous king eliminating every threat to his reign? Was it His will for a man to abandon all comfort and lifestyle to trek across the vast desert at an unprovable hope of a Messiah?

"Won't you come with us?" Gaspar clasped Amal's shoulder.

Amal scanned the room behind him. "Where? Bethlehem still covers a significant amount of land. How will you find this child?"

"The God who brought us this far will surely equip us for what we need." Gaspar continued to pack the exotic food he must have brought along.

Melchior tipped his head and crossed his arms. "Join us in prayer. See what your God does."

Amal calculated the duties he had neglected, but the curiosity refused to be tamped down.

"Aha!" Balthasar shouted from outside. "I knew it would appear."

Excitement burbled up in Amal's chest, and he rushed with the others to the balcony. Even without the help of Balthasar's equipment, Amal could see the star increasing in light set against the backdrop of the velvety black sky. "Incredible."

"That is the direction of Bethlehem?"

"Yes. Off to the southeast." Amal pointed beyond the steep valley to the east.

"Come with us."

Panic surged inside Amal's belly, like mice scurrying for shelter. "Now? It is dark, we won't be able to find the way—"

"The Almighty God will show us the way." Melchior clasped his hands around his portly middle with assurance.

Outside the wind, whipped up to a frenzied pace. Amal shivered as the air chilled.

"Will you come with us?"

In the span of moments since the star appeared, the room had been packed and servants began taking the trunks to the camels waiting in the courtyard below.

What if the king found out he considered abandoning his post? Amal rubbed his neck and gulped. "I can't. Not now. Perhaps in a day or two."

Balthasar stared at Amal with an unreadable expression then followed suit as the other two dipped their heads and strode away.

Six

Get wisdom! Get understanding! Do not forget, nor turn away from the words of my mouth. Do not forsake [wisdom], and she will preserve you; love her and she will keep you.
Proverbs 4:6-7

"Your presence is requested." The temple servant bowed low.

"Of course." Amal set down his carved feather quill and blotted the ink. He pushed off the ground and rose, rolling his shoulders back. He gave Sofar instructions for his absence and followed the servant through the streets of Jerusalem.

The sun beat directly down on them when they emerged from the shaded alleyways. Midday and still they heard nothing from the Magi. Had they found the one they sought? They should have arrived in Bethlehem at the zenith of night—if they had not fallen off the steep cliffs.

Amal's insides curdled with the sinking feeling that he had missed something important. He contemplated the curious loss that accompanied all the unknown factors, but couldn't identify the source. Was his body more attuned because of the lack of restful sleep the last couple of days? The imbalance felt deep. A rift the size of the Hinnom Valley.

The servant led him to the room where a priest worked quietly, portioning out grain.

Amal waited by the door for several minutes without the priest acknowledging him. He cleared his throat. "You summoned me, my lord?"

The older man turned slowly and evaluated Amal from head to toe. "Walk with me."

Amal dusted his hands on his robe and stepped carefully around the sacks of grain.

"I hear you were inquiring about my son." The man gave Amal the woven basket.

"Are you Zacharias?"

The man dipped his chin and counted out seven more scoops. "Are you ready to emerge from the darkness in which you sit?"

Did he sit in darkness? His life seemed pretty illuminated. Copying the scrolls was enlightening and documenting daily happenings around the palace was satisfying. His *abba* had been proud of Amal's accomplishments. He had little to complain about. "I don't believe I am in darkness."

"Then I have nothing further to say." Zacharias held his hands out for the basket, tucked it against his side and returned to portioning out the grain.

Amal had disrupted his work and his day for this? He did not restrain his indignation. "*You* were the one who summoned me." He turned with a swirl of his robes and marched the way he came.

The slap of his sandals echoed through the Solomon's Portico and he fisted his hands. "Waste of my time. Who is he to say I am in darkness? What right does he have to criticize me?"

Every step toward the temple entrance felt like one step further away —from what?

Why did his spirit grow heavier?

Amal shook his head briskly. This was foolishness. Nonsense. He'd become too invested in this paradox.

The Magi would bring word back, and King Herod would seek out this child and life would proceed, as normal.

The ugly feeling in Amal's gut surged. Whatever King Herod

planned with the new king—if it was truth—would *not* end with everything returning to normal.

Amal's body slammed into an unseen wall. He stepped back, and he braced his hands on his knees. No matter how much he tried to ignore the King's intentions, for some reason he remained connected with this unfurling narrative.

Think. Amal grimaced and tapped his fist on his forehead.

Scribes were trained to search out the nature of a thing. The words unsaid, and the intonation all played a part in the full message.

Right now, he could sense something missing. Something the priest, Zacharias, possessed—a lamp that would shed light on the whole affair.

If Zacharias could shed light, then perhaps there was indeed some darkness inside.

Amal closed his eyes, seeking out the unfamiliar emotion lurking around the edges of his thoughts. Dissatisfaction? Unfulfillment?

Perhaps that could be described as darkness.

He stepped back. *This is foolishness.*

Though it cost you everything, seek out understanding. Amal turned and strode back to where he had left Zacharias.

Before his hesitation took hold, the words burst from his lips. "There is darkness around the edges of my life. An unspoken emptiness. A lack of purpose and fulfillment. If that is darkness, then yes, I am ready to be free of it."

Zacarias stroked his graying beard and contemplated Amal. "Very well."

Amal stepped into the dim room and scanned the corridor behind him as priests walked by piously. "Should I be documenting this?"

A pained expression crossed Zacharias' face. He heaved out a breath and thumped Amal's chest. "I'd prefer you document it here."

Amal frowned. "Why all the secrecy?"

"In asking about the son of my old age, you are putting his life in danger. What man would risk his only son's life for someone who probably won't believe his message and purpose." Zacharias drummed his fingers on the shelf before him. "I'm only human."

"I can appreciate that." Amal stepped closer and extended his hands for the woven basket.

"His name is John. Yahweh is gracious. Indeed, Yahweh has visited and redeemed His people."

The basket nearly slipped from Amal's grasp. "You mean *will* redeem His people."

Zacharias' eyes sparked in the dim light. "No. Not in the future. Yahweh's promises have been fulfilled. My son is the forerunner of the Messiah. Already—even in my wife's womb—he was filled with the Holy Spirit in the spirit and power of Elijah."

"How?" The basket's weight seemed to increase with every revelation from Zacharias' lips. "How do you know this?"

"The angel, Gabriel, appeared to me these two and a half years ago—"

"Wait. The angel's name was Gabriel?" Amal's thoughts tumbled over themselves. "According to the Magi...According to the prophesies of Daniel, that was the name of the angel who delivered the timing of the Messiah in Babylon!"

Zacharias paused and broke into a grin, crinkling the edges of eyes full of aged wisdom. "It had not occurred to me. You are correct, learned scribe. Gabriel has always had charge of delivering this good news. He also appeared to my wife's young cousin. Mary resided with us in the last months of my wife's confinement."

The angel Gabriel, the cousin Mary, the spirit of Elijah. Amal rubbed his forehead. His legs trembled, and he set the basket carefully on the shelf and gripped the sides of his head.

Zacharias leaned close. "And Mary was with child!"

Amal closed one eye and tried to maintain a level of skepticism. "As young women tend to be."

"She was not yet married to her husband." Zacharias crossed his arms with a satisfied smile.

"That doesn't explain anything but her lack of fidelity." Amal sighed. Seeking out understanding resulted in more questions.

"And the virgin shall be with child and give birth to a son."

Amal shifted with growing uneasiness. "I know the words. I know the prophecies. Who can understand their meanings?"

Zacharias slumped his sack on the shelf, and grain spilled out. "That is where you will have to step out in faith. Is it logical that an old man and his wife, past childbearing years, should have a child to take away our reproach? No. But time and again the Lord has given the same blessing to couples for furthering His purpose. Is it logical for a man to be struck mute for disbelief and be restored in God's timing?"

Amal inched back. The queries denied logic. He shook his head.

"Yahweh has spoken through the holy prophets since the world began." Zacharias leaned forward and gripped Amal's shoulders. "The messages are there that we should be saved from our enemies. The words of the Lord proclaim the mercy He promised to our fathers so that we would forever remember His holy covenant. Why not now?"

Amal closed his gaping mouth.

"There is salvation in the Lord. Step out of the shadow of death and be guided into the way of peace, my brother! Believe. Accept the tender mercies of our gracious God."

"It is too much to take in." Amal scrubbed his palms over his eyes, trying to comprehend.

"Promise me you will consider all I have said." Zacharias took the full basket into his arms. "Walk with me. There is someone I'd like you to meet."

Seven

And [Anna] was a widow of about eighty-four years, who did not depart from the temple, but served God with fastings and prayers night and day. And coming in that instant she gave thanks to the Lord, and spoke of Him to all those who looked for redemption in Israel.
  ~Luke 2:36-38

Amal followed Zacharias into the inner sanctuary where he deposited the grain offering and discussed the duties of the day with the priests.

What could Zacharias possibly share that would decrease the skepticism Amal felt? The spring sun warmed the scent of temple worship—grain roasting, incense, and people—The familiar aroma of routine.

Finally, Zacharias peeled away from the conversation and nodded to Amal. Without a word he led the way to the South entrance of the temple.

All this and he had changed his mind? In what way was Amal a threat? What could a scribe do to inflict harm?

Life was a lot simpler when he only copied words from the Scriptures and recorded the annuls.

Zacharias halted abruptly and looked back at Amal with raised eyebrows and a sweep of his hand.

Amal sidestepped to avoid careening with the priest. When he had righted himself, he surveyed the courtyard. People mingled near the open gate, chatting and going about their daily routine, oblivious of Caesar's ever-present golden eagle above them.

"What are you expecting me to notice, Zacharias?" Amal's shoulders sagged. "The Roman Eagle boldly displayed?"

Zacharias frowned and stepped aside, revealing an aged woman.

Amal inadvertently glanced between the two. Was this Zacharias' wife? She appeared more aged than the priest.

"This is Anna. She has faithfully served the Lord in the temple since her husband's death." Zacharias reached into the pouch at his waist and pressed a round of bread into her hands.

Nodding respectfully, Amal cleared his throat. "And you are the mother of John?"

A smile lit up Anna's rheumy eyes. "I have no children—my husband is the Lord God, husband to the widow and father to the fatherless, the consolation of Israel."

Amal regretted the chuckle that emitted from his mouth. "Forgive my rudeness. I didn't know what to expect."

What does this have to do with the situation of Zacharias's son? Amal slanted a glance at the priest's expectant look and crossed his arms.

"While it is an honor to meet you, woman, I do not understand. It appears you expect me to say something, yet I'm unclear as to what." Amal glanced at the shadow of the sun. Had the Magi returned yet?

"Anna has held in her arms the Messiah."

Zacharias' words slogged through Amal's thoughts like thick ink not properly mixed. *Anna held the—*

"You *held* the Messiah? A child?" Amal gaped at Anna.

"Well, Zacharias isn't telling you he has too." She leaned forward in a joyful laugh.

Amal swung to face Zacharias so fast, he lurched off balance.

Zacharias reached out to steady him. "You still haven't grasped my son's purpose and role. You wouldn't have heard the other part. Yes. I have held the Messiah. My wife's cousin, remember?"

"How did you know?" Amal shook his head. As fantastic as the story was, he couldn't very well discredit two witnesses.

All his stoic doubts became hazy and the lines between absolutes and fanciful longing blurred. *Now is the time of salvation.* His chest swelled at the quickening in his spirit. The fledgling seed of faith took root, not by his own power.

He gingerly took Anna's outstretched hand. The soft skin dipped low, accentuating the frail bones. "Tell me your story, woman."

Anna patted his hand. "Not my story, dear. *His* story. Yahweh's anger is past. He has consoled His people and will subdue our iniquities once and for all."

Amal's vision blurred and hope leapt to his weary soul. He smeared the tears from his eyes and cleared his throat. "Truly?"

"For the Jew and the Gentile." Zacharias murmured as a Roman soldier, marched past hobnailed shoes clacking on the quarried stones.

"For all that seek the redemption of Israel." Anna's voice rang loud and clear, attracting the glances of passersby.

His whole life, Amal had awaited these words, for they meant Messiah had come. But now that he heard them, he could not believe it. He would not. If it were true, it would be like Joash of old. Blood would stain the stones of the Temple. He turned his thoughts once again to Zacharias' words.

"—delivered from our enemies that we might serve him without fear in holiness and righteousness all the days of our lives. For the remission of sins."

"What does it mean? Redemption from our enemies? From Rome's oppression?" Amal glanced at the soldiers across the courtyard.

Anna shook her head. "Our oppression does not come from outside sources. It is our own sin that enslaves us. He has come to release us from our sin, to lift the dark shadow clouding our vision and usher us into the light. All our lives we have waited and hoped for his coming. But we have not understood His true purpose. John has come to prepare the way as the Scripture foretold. Now the Messiah has come to bring His kingdom."

Eight

When Herod the king heard this, he was troubled, and all of Jerusalem with him.
  ~Matthew 2:3

Amal's pulse raced at the implication and magnitude of what Anna and Zacharias had said. How could this be? And in Amal's lifetime?

He turned down the corridor that led to the kitchen. Repast first, then the scriptures for more insight.

Zacharias said the Messiah had come. He had been given the name Jesus—for He will save His people from their sins. Salvation had come in the form of a small child with impoverished parents.

Amal peered into the ornate throne room as he passed by. Nothing like the opulence of this king, who was not Jewish by blood. A hushed conversation drew his attention as he approached the servants' entrance to the kitchen.

"The king has ordered a silent sweep."

"—he was dragged out of the chambers and straight to the executioner."

Normally Amal pretended not to hear the words whispered in

secret. Today they took up permanence like a dried line of print. Against his better judgment, he approached the huddle of kitchen servants.

The woman facing him stopped talking and her eyes widened. She jerked her head.

The second woman stiffened and turned her head slowly. "Is there something we can help you with?"

Amal recognized his own reaction in the underlying suspicion and narrowing of their eyes. None of the servants ever lost their vigilance here.

Surely there had to be a better way. A hope to counteract the fear and make the caution worthwhile.

"Forgive me for intruding." Amal scanned the kitchen. "May I please have some bread and some watered wine?"

The women moved silently around the kitchen, to Amal's disappointment. They had no reason to trust him and carry on the conversation in front of him. He sat in the presence of the king.

The women approached him, and his reason to linger expired.

"I couldn't help but overhear. What was the man's charge?"

The women exchanged a glance, their fear palpable.

"In truth..." The truth was, anything he said further could be used against him. "...I wish to know what action to avoid. I've been out this morning."

Another tight-lipped glance.

Amal puffed air in his cheeks and turned on his heel. Took three steps. *Light to those who sit in the shadow of death.* He returned to the women to their apparent regret.

"You have no reason to trust me, I understand. Was it regarding the elite ambassadors? The magi?" Amal kept his voice a mere breath.

One woman remained stoic but the other's eyes widened slightly.

Amal swallowed and took his leave.

Everything he had been doing and learning this morning would send the signal of treason. His life held no value if his clandestine appointments were made known.

The rest of the day, Amal shoved aside every thought of the magi's anticipated return and jammed away every reason to think about Zacharias and Anna.

But the questions refused to remain locked in the treasury of his mind and kept oozing out—a pot of ink with a crack in its side.

He has come to save His people from their sins.

The mantra of pure lives seemed to hold more weight than delivering people from their enemies.

How could this be?

Once Israel had deliverance from their captors, then they could focus on the state of their hearts. Right?

He reread what he had written. His troubling thoughts spilled out onto the scroll. *Deliverance from our captors.*

"Ack!" Amal purposely made a blotch of ink so he could scrape off the words when the ink dried, and re-read over the whole section. There was seven—no eight—misprints or letters touching.

He drew in a sharp breath and stared at his shaking hands.

Footsteps approached the doorway, making him jump. He shielded his sloppy work with his body.

They wouldn't be able to see it from the door, fool.

A nervous laugh escaped as a servant passed by without so much as glancing into the room.

Wiping off the quill, he wedged the cork on the ink jar. He was no good in this state.

"Where is my mental clarity?" Amal could practically hear his *abba's* voice. *If you can't do it right the first time, then you don't deserve the position. No one will employ an incompetent scribe like you.*

The rows upon rows of meticulously copied scrolls and his prestigious position as Chief Palace scribe, did blessed little to negate the haunting voice on a good day—let alone the day when everything Amal knew to be routine had been disrupted.

Amal unfolded his legs and rolled his shoulders back while rotating his stiff neck. The persistent inner nag of not doing enough—and not doing it properly—weighed him down like a yoke.

This was why it was best to keep his head low. To do his work without looking around. Then nothing could distract him—or put his position or life in jeopardy.

Had the magi returned yet?

Even while glancing around to see who had discerned his rogue thoughts, Amal found himself marching up the hall to the guests' quarters. The female servant didn't even glance up as she swept the room devoid of even the exotic aroma from the easterners. It was as if they hadn't even been there.

Who else would know their whereabouts? The stable hand, perhaps?

Amal blended in the shadows all the way down to the stables where, as he figured, the camels had not arrived.

Would they return? And why did their absence arouse his curiosity? The future lurked before him like a dark cliff. Now that he had met Anna and Zacharias—now that he accepted their testimony of the Messiah—what could he do with the knowledge? Did it change anything?

Unsure of his next plan, he stood in the stable yard and another matter vied for equal attention—what of the widow, Anna? Her dedication was commendable to come to the temple every day for so many years. Did she need accommodations or support?

If Amal had the good fortune of living that long, would he possess the peace that Anna had? In his mind's eye, his dedication would rival Anna's, but instead of the peace she displayed, he perceived a gruff old man, bent on perfection and derogatory to those who would fail.

He would become his *abba*.

The disturbing thought scraped the weary places in his soul.

What was Anna's source of peace? Was it solely the knowledge of the Messiah's arrival that guided her and gave her the deep-seated purpose?

He had to see her again and draw out the heart of the matter. If he could make a choice in the matter, he'd rather be in the court of the Lord, than in the dark *bibliotheca* hunched over his writings.

A palace guard passed the stables, his marching feet matching the cadence of Amal's heart. The king's stallion nickered, giving Amal a legitimate reason to inspect the magnificent animal. As soon as the guard was out of sight, Amal drew his cloak over his head and snuck out the gate into the streets of Jerusalem heading east, back to the temple.

Nine

For among My people are found wicked men; They lie in wait as one who sets snares; they set a trap and catch men.
~Jeremiah 6:26

Amal clutched his cloak low over his face as he crept near the entrance to the temple. Surely he drew attention to himself and stood out as one from the palace grounds. How did a man of lesser status walk?

His back tensed as the familiar apprehension returned. He swiped the sweat from his temples and refused to look back. Keeping to the wall, Amal glanced in and saw Anna's folded legs. A crowd of Levites debating the merits of the levirate marriage passed by. When they had gone, Amal stepped inside and lowered himself beside Anna.

The old woman did not stir.

Tilting his head back slightly, Amal surveyed the courtyard from under his cloak. The cluster of Levites continued on to the Court of the Women clearing a wide path amongst the common people milling around and a bored Roman soldier passed at the far end of Solomon's Portico.

"I am Amal." He tilted his shoulder closer to Anna. "I came to you earlier with...the priest."

Anna did not reply.

"Forgive the secrecy. I wish to know more about what you saw." Amal slanted a glance at the woman.

Perhaps she had dozed off. He peered from under the cloak and glanced at her profile.

Her mouth gaped open and her head was propped back against the wall at an odd angle.

"Anna?" Amal's whisper did not wake her. He winced at the unnatural angle of her neck. She would have a terrible ache when she awoke.

He patted her frail hand. "Anna"

Still no response. Poor woman probably didn't rest well at night. When he was as old as her, he'd probably be dozing off during the day too. Even now, the longer he sat in the afternoon sun, the more drowsy he felt.

He sat up and scrubbed his fists across his eyes.

Anna hadn't shifted positions.

Frowning, Amal shook her shoulder gently.

The aged woman slid down the wall to the side and crumpled forward.

"No!" Amal lurched forward and caught Anna before she made contact with the stone floor. "Help! I need help."

A stout Levite turned and his eyes grew wide as coins as he trotted over. "What have you done?"

"I didn't!" Amal gasped out.

"Here, let's lay her down gently. Gently."

Together they rotated the woman down as a crowd gathered, buzzing with questions.

The Levite lowered his ear to Anna's mouth and watched her still chest. He shook his head. "She has gone to Sarah's bosom."

Amal sat back on his heels, loss digging through him as though he had known the woman all his life rather than a few hours.

"What happened?" The Levite stood above Amal and crossed his arms with a scowl.

"Nothing." Panic clawed inside Amal's chest as more surly faces pressed in around him. He swallowed. If the palace guards were nearby, they'd recognize him. "I sat beside her."

"Why?" The Levite jabbed a stubby finger at Amal's chest, knocking him back.

Amal's gaze darted around the crowd.

A temple guard rushed forward his hand on his sword.

"I sought her wisdom about a matter. I thought she slept. Then she fell over." Amal searched the Levite's face for compassion.

Ac priest plowed through the gathering and after the story was repeated, he folded pious hands and tilted his head back to the heavens. "The Lord gives, and the Lord takes away."

"Blessed be His name," the cluster responded in unison.

"Anna has been faithful in her service of the Lord. She has devoutly hoped in the promises to come."

Someone draped a cloth over Anna's legs, and Amal pulled it gently over her chest.

The sight of discolorations on her neck gave him pause. A chill snaked up his spine. He turned his head slightly to see the crowd still watching him, and pressed himself low over his knees in a show of mourning. From this angle, the dark spots were clearly bruises—in the shape of three fingers—hidden to the casual observer by leathery wrinkles.

The implicating marks blurred as moisture filled his eyes.

Anna did not slip into death peacefully. She was assisted.

Amal sucked in a breath through his teeth and lifted his face to the priest. "Forgive me—" He broke off at the sight of a beggar in the street outside. The man with a lame leg gave a slight shake of his dusty head.

Amal narrowed his eyes and opened his mouth to speak again.

The beggar raised a grimy finger to his lips and mouthed "*Later.*"

Narrowing his eyes, Amal nodded slightly and lowered the sheet over Anna's face. "Rest now. You have borne witness faithfully." He straightened his arms and pushed himself off the ground as temple servants trotted up with a stretcher.

Deep loss clutched his chest as they took her away. He swallowed but couldn't dislodge the lumps in his throat. Did she have anyone to attend to the burial? He pressed himself against the wall and dug his fists into opposite sleeves.

When the crowd had dispersed Amal stepped gingerly over to the beggar. His nose wrinkled, and he tried not to show the reflex that made him gag at the man's stench. "What do you know?"

The man rolled his head along the wall and stared at his leg. "I wish I could tell you but this pain..."

Amal rolled his eyes and produced a coin from his money pouch.

The beggar grunted and fiddled with the wrapping of his bandage. He raised incredulous eyes.

"Fine." Amal retrieved another coin. "But not a denarius more. What did you see?"

"I *saw* nothing." The man's tone rose.

I didn't hand over two denarii for 'nothing.' Amal expanded his chest, hoping to appear intimidating. "What do you know?"

The beggar glanced pointedly at Amal's moneybag, but finally conceded. "Anna had begun talking again after this morning when you visited. Every person who came through that gate, she drew them with her tale of seeing the Messiah."

Amal surveyed his informant's ragged clothing. "Were you here that day?"

The man's head jerked back and forth.

Another roadblock in his quest. Amal's shoulders sagged. "Go on."

"She was spreading the story to all, even to people who wouldn't listen."

"Then what happened?" Amal leaned against the wall and scanned each person in the courtyard.

"Then there came a man in a cloak—of course, I knew who he was. I know things nobody thinks I'm worth anything, but they don't realize—"

Amal broke in. "They don't realize what a wealth of knowledge you are."

The beggar glanced up and blinked a couple of times. "That's right."

"The man in the cloak." Amal gripped his hands to prevent from shaking the man.

"He came and squatted directly before her. He appeared to be listening to her story, then quick as a serpent, he lashed out his hand to her neck and squeezed the life out of her." The beggar shook his head. "Pity. People ought to be able to speak without getting killed."

Amal shifted, sniffed back the moisture and cleared his throat. "Who was it?"

"What does that matter?"

He had a point. Anyone under Herod's thumb would have done the same. He shuddered.

Another thought slammed into him threatening to send him to his knees.

What about Zacharias?

Ten

Then, being divinely warned in a dream that they should not return to Herod, they departed for their own country another way.
  ~Matthew 2:13

For the first time in his life Amal lacked purpose. He wandered away from the temple, without a clear direction of where to go. The beggar knew nothing of Zacharias' status.

Should Amal investigate the priest's health? Would that draw unnecessary attention to him—or them both?

He squeezed his head with his hands. What was the next course of action?

A man with a slack jaw slouched unmoving on the side of the narrow street sending Amal's heart to his throat. *Not again!*

He crept closer, afraid of what he'd discover. His hand shook as he stretched it out.

The man's eyes flew open. "What are you doing? Trying to steal my pittance?" He clutched his jar, jostling the long, matted beard across his chest.

"My apologies, I thought—"

"You thought you could take advantage of me sleeping and steal from me!" The man squawked and shook a rough, grimy hand. "Get away!"

Amal backed away quickly, taking care to study the next beggars he passed for signs of life before approaching.

Search from here. Amal rubbed his chest where Balthasar had jabbed.

"It's hard to search with your heart when you are shaken to the core." He muttered. "This is all madness. I'm beginning to think as foolishly as a child."

Or perhaps Anna's death had thrust him so far beyond his comfortable position that now he was beginning to see reason.

On the other side of the city, Amal studied the sprawling palace influenced both by Greek and Roman design.

Discontentment surged up, and he couldn't contain the urge to pace.

"Where am I to go if not to the palace?"

The sundial in the courtyard indicated the ninth hour.

He could go to Bethlehem directly and discover what had become of the Magi.

Amal scoffed and turned towards the servants' entrance, but the thought would not be uprooted. He studied the sky. If he took a donkey, he could make it there and back by nightfall. He pivoted and strode to the palace stables before he fully comprehended what he intended to do.

Uncertainty assaulted him as strong as the scents of hay, dirt and sweat wafting from the stalls causing him to pause at the entrance to the dimly lit stable.

Confidence. You've taken donkeys out before.

Amal drew in a breath and signaled a stable boy. "Ready a donkey for me."

"Yes, my lord." The boy made haste of the task and Amal was on his way within a quarter of an hour.

When he exited Jerusalem, he lifted the cloak from his head, and flapped it back and forth away from his neck.

What am I thinking? He wasn't the one to venture out on a whim.

Amal fortified his resolve. Right or wrong. He had made this choice.

He held his head high as he passed travelers on the road.

Traveling away from Jerusalem, the psalms resonated with his soul. What better way to seek with your heart than to familiarize oneself with the holy words?

"—if You Lord, should mark iniquities, who would stand. But there is forgiveness with You." Amal hummed the next line and the donkey pricked her ears back.

Amal leaned forward, scratching the soft fur at the base of those long ears. "Did that mean something to you girl?"

The next verse of the song practically jumped off his tongue.

"I wait for the Lord, my soul waits and in His word, I do hope."

Lord, I do wait for You as eagerly as the watchman for morning. I feel I am on the verge of—what I don't know. Discovery?

No, it was more than that.

His very being had awoken from a deep slumber. What if he was to behold with his own eyes, the Messiah as Anna and Zacharias had?

"For with the Lord there is mercy, and with Him abundant redemption."

All those who look for the redemption of Israel. Anna's vacant expression replayed in Amal's mind. He brushed away moisture from his eyes.

"Oh, God! When will You console Your people? When will You vindicate those who have been wronged?"

And He shall redeem Israel from all iniquities.

The donkey planted her hooves and brayed, the sound echoing across the hills.

"What is it?" Amal looked across the rocky ground, but didn't see a wild animal or snake. Kick as he might, she still didn't move.

Amal heaved a sigh, swung his leg over and slid off. "What was the point of bringing you if I am walking anyway?" Snagging the reins, he led the donkey onward.

Lord God, Master of the universe. You have long established that we, Your people, are a stiff-necked people. Is this really the time You will redeem us from our iniquities? Our nation could once again use Your merciful intervention.

Amal climbed back on the donkey as the road grew steep and crested the hilltop overlooking Bethlehem. Many hills sprawled out before him, some dotted with sheep and whitewashed homes. They weren't far from the heart of the town now.

The donkey brayed, and began trotting, jostling Amal with every downward step. By the time they had reached the well in the center of town, his teeth ached from clacking together.

His spirit sank, and he dismounted. He eyed the empty courtyard. The sounds of pots being stirred and the aroma of suppers cooking wafted out from the surrounding houses.

The rumbling of his belly did not overshadow the foolishness that consumed him.

How would he even find the magi or the Messiah? This whole trip was a waste.

He tipped his gaze past the yellowing horizon to the pale blue sky. "I wait for You. Oh Lord, my soul waits. If You would show me the way I sure would appreciate it."

Amal folded his hands and waited for another star to guide him.

A small boy no older than three years approached from in front of the house where he played, clanging together two metal bells. "I like your donkey."

"Thank you." Amal turned in a circle, surveying the sky. Still too far away from sunset.

"Sheeps are my favorites. The babies are so cute."

"Mmhmm." Amal expelled a breath. *It doesn't have to be a star, Lord. I'll take any sign.*

"All animals are my favorite. Even camels."

Amal snapped to attention. "Camels? You've seen camels?"

The boy nodded and zoomed around in a circle.

"How many camels? Where are they?"

"Six." The boy held up all ten fingers and his eyes grew large. "Last night when I was sleeping there was...there was a loud noise. I think the camel was burping."

Amal covered his chuckle with a cough as the child demonstrated with a fake belch of his own.

"Three *fancy* men—I think they were kings—and then they walked by. *Galumph. Galumph.* And the camels were sleepy and hungry."

"How did you see all that when you were sleeping?" The sign he had prayed for from the mouth of a small child.

"Well...I was looking out the window. But everyone else was sleeping." The boy glanced over his shoulder as if his *ima* would hear.

"Can you show me where they are?" Amal surveyed each house he could see with intense interest.

"When I get big, I'm gonna ride a camel. So high up like a mountain."

"Yes, yes. Where did they stop?" *Search with your heart and not your head.* Amal drew in a breath and crouched down to the child's level. "Do you think they'd be smoother to ride than a donkey?"

The boy's brow furrowed. "I haven't ridden a donkey. But you jostled a lot."

That was certainly true. "Would you like to ride on this donkey?"

"Could I?" The boy hopped up and down and clapped his hands.

"Of course." Amal hoisted the boy up "Where to, young sire?"

The boy clutched the donkey's mane and laughed a great big belly laugh as Amal led him in a circle.

A woman leaned out of the door of the house the boy came from. "Eli, come in! Time for supper."

"Yes, *ima.*" Eli began to slide off, while the donkey was mid-stride.

"Allow me to help you." Amal pulled the donkey to a halt and lowered the boy until his sandals plopped in the dusty road.

"*Ima!*" Eli barreled home, leaning forward so his shoulders led the charge. "Did you see me? I rode the donkey!"

Amal blew out a breath. Taking time to befriend Eli had not produced any benefit for him.

At the pathway to his house, Eli turned and ran backward. "The camels went that way." He flung his hand to the east.

"Thank you, Eli!" *And thank You, Yahweh.*

Amal walked quickly down the street Eli indicated and he laughed. He could nearly skip like Eli.

The donkey followed amicably, as if she too were eager to see the result of the quest.

"In Your word, I do hope—" Amal puffed out as he jogged along, searching for the camels.

To soon, he came to the end of the street.

No camels. Nothing remotely large enough to house camels.

Amal dug his heels into the packed dirt, halting in the middle of the road. The donkey nudged his back with her broad head. He absently patted the side of her face and slowly pivoted, taking in every detail of each whitewashed house in the lane.

There, off to the right!

Amal bent over and examined the scattering of large round dung.

He laughed and looked over his shoulder at the donkey. "These aren't yours, are they?"

The donkey grunted and lifted her tail, adding some plops for Amal to compare.

From camel burps to scrutinizing donkey dung. His *abba* would certainly disapprove of the deviations from scribal duties. Amal rested his arm over the donkey's withers and did what he knew best —observed.

The plops and the indentations in the dirt clearly showed Magi had been here, but weren't any longer. If they had returned to Jerusalem, he would have passed them on the road. Logic indicated they had gone home a different way.

Had they intended to return to Jerusalem, or had they understood King Herod's inner rage from the start?

A young woman stepped out of the doorway and tore off some stems from the herbs growing by the door. "Joseph, supper." Her call was reminiscent of Eli's *ima*.

Amal stepped back and turned his face, so the woman would not think that he stared at her.

The timing was wrong.

What even would he say?

I have come to see the Messiah.

His cheeks heated. What right had he to interrupt their family meal?

A broad-shouldered man exited the structure to the side, his workspace it would seem, and walked to the main house, closing the door firmly behind him.

Spirits sinking, Amal turned away.

Tomorrow. Tomorrow I will return and introduce myself.

Eleven

Then Herod, when he saw that he was deceived by the wise men, was exceedingly angry; and sent forth and put to death all the male children who were in Bethlehem and in all its districts, from two years old and under, according to the time which he had determined from the wise men.
  ~Matthew 2:16

"Your presence is requested by the King."

Amal jumped as the shadows in the stable materialized into the form of a man.

"Absolutely." Heart pounding in his chest, Amal handed the reins to the stable boy and followed the servant. The man's stiff back gave no indication of the matter at hand.

It's probably some unforeseen meeting or decree requiring documentation.

But if Amal wasn't on palace grounds, his aide, Sofar, would suffice. There was no reason to delay setting something for tomorrow's agenda.

Rather than turning toward the king's private quarters, the servant led Amal to the throne room.

Trepidation weighed his steps. His mouth grew parched, and he dared a glance at the king's brooding expression.

Amal prostrated himself before the throne "Oh, King, live forever."

"What did you find?" King Herod's voice sent chills down Amal's spine.

"My lord?" Amal pushed himself to his knees and lifted his gaze to the king's fingers tapping on the armrest of the throne.

"You went to Bethlehem." The king's tone dared Amal to deny it.

Amal dug his fingers into his palms. "Yes, my king. I sought the Magi to see why they had not yet sent word."

King Herod leaned forward, and Amal felt the weight of his penetrating gaze. "And? What excuse did they have for not upholding my request?"

"None, my lord." Amal studied his white knuckles. The truth most certainly would be ill received.

"Explain yourself."

"They weren't there, my king." Amal's nose began to drip. He lifted his chin and kept his eyes at the level of the tapping fingers.

"Hmm. It's unlikely they changed their minds to seek out this child. Did they even make it to Bethlehem or did they get lost along the way?" The musing ended with an upward inflection indicating Amal was meant to respond.

"I saw the place where the camels knelt in Bethlehem, oh King." Amal pressed his lips together. "They were there and now they are gone."

The hand shot off the armrest and clutched Amal's hair and his head was yanked up.

"Did they get the idea to not return from you, Scribe?"

"No, my king." Amal gasped out. "I was just as surprised as you are."

"Surprised doesn't begin to describe what I'm experiencing." Herod's hand was replaced by a soldier's strong grip and a blade at Amal's throat.

Amal drew in sharp breaths as the king prowled around the dais. He threw back his wine goblet, gulping the contents.

With a snarl, King Herod flung the goblet square into Amal's face.

Wine splashed in his eye and the heavy gold cup cracked against Amal's nose.

Pain consumed Amal's head and warm metallic liquid trickled down the back of Amal's throat. *Oh Yahweh, have mercy on me.*

King Herod's face turned purple and the vein in his neck bulged like a worm. He advanced and his extended fist shook. He leaned over Amal and screamed at the soldier, "I want them all killed! All the baby boys in Bethlehem and in all the nearby districts."

No! Amal struggled to speak, but the fear clogging his throat was a stronger deterrent than the blade at his throat.

Amal was dragged to his room and shoved inside. He pressed a damp cloth under his nose to staunch the bleeding.

A rap on the door accelerated Amal's pulse. He mumbled around the cloth, "Who is it?"

"The physician. I hear you've come into a bit of trouble."

Fear clutched at Amal's chest tighter than he gripped his water jar. Was it a ploy to get his defenses down? Did someone wait outside with the physician to coerce him to share the location of the child?

The pain inside his nose felt like a thousand bees warring. How much more of his body would they break before he caved in like a coward?

The latch lifted, the physician pushed the door open and stepped inside.

Amal scanned the empty corridor as he shut the door. *Keep your guard up.*

The physician gestured for Amal to sit and began probing his nose.

"Ow!" Amal jerked back.

"Be still." The physician clutched Amal's chin and surveyed his face. "It will have to be set. Breathe in through your mouth."

Before Amal had gathered a breath, the physician had tented his fingers together and firmly raked them down the length of Amal's nose.

All the blood in Amal's head seemed to pool into his stomach and nausea surged. "I have to lie down." The floor tipped up as his arms grew weak. He squeezed his eyes shut and felt the physician's hands guiding him down.

A moment later, a foul-smelling ointment was pressed into the open wound beside Amal's nose.

The sting on the tender flesh was dull compared to the searing pain in his soul.

"What have I done?" Amal pounded his fist against his forehead. Jostling the physician's hand into his nose.

He sucked in air through his teeth and his eyes smarted.

"You will be sore for quite some time." The physician's gravelly voice announced as he collected his supplies. "Likely you will have black eyes—like you got into fistfights and lost. But all things considered, I'd think you are fortunate."

What fortune was there in preserving his own life at the cost of all those boys in Bethlehem?

Amal fought the dizziness, hauled himself up and accompanied the physician to the door. The night guard in the hallway brought on a fresh wave of nausea.

He slammed the door shut, hating himself for his indecision. "Coward."

What could he do? If he tried to distract the guard, there would be no way he could make it to Bethlehem before the soldiers' swift horses. And in the slim chance they didn't find the house, Amal would lead them directly there.

Even if he was able to warn the family, what good could come of it? He'd be killed too.

It would have been better if he'd never gotten involved.

Amal crouched in the corner and wrapped his arms around his stiff knees. His whole face blazed with fire and his failure and cowardice paraded in his thoughts.

How could he be so ignorant? Why hadn't he taken more caution in his journey? All those children.

"Oh Yahweh! Have mercy on those children as You have mercy on me. They don't deserve to die for my transgressions. Have mercy on Your chosen one—Your Messiah. Surely it isn't in Your plan for him to be killed for my shortcomings."

What kind of man was he? How could he continue to turn his head away from the king's evil deeds?

He would be dead, but at least he would have died without the load of guilt and shame of chosen ignorance.

Amal pried the door open a crack.

The soldier met his perusal with a menacing gaze and a step toward him.

Shoving the door shut, Amal leaned his forehead against the door. His heart raced and his nose throbbed.

"Oh God! What would You have me do?" Amal scurried to the window and stood on the tip of his toes to peer out to the abrupt drop ending in thorny bushes.

He paced the room until he could no longer push down the nausea and the hideous shame. Like the surge of vomit, guilt reared its ugly head with a force that pushed Amal to his hands and knees before his waste pot.

Coughing up bile and blood, Amal began to sob between gasping breaths.

When the retching subsided, he pressed his face to the ground, instantly regretting it. He flopped over on his back, whimpering, as his fingers explored his nose.

How long he lay there he couldn't tell. An inkling jiggled on the edge of his awareness, growing until it resembled a full prayer.

"Oh God, I've spent my whole life keeping my head down, pretending injustice didn't happen right before me. I am a mouse and I am tired of hiding. I want to follow Your ways from here on out. Have mercy on Your chosen ones."

Twelve

Then it was fulfilled what was spoken by Jeremiah the prophet, saying "A voice was heard in Ramah, lamentation, weeping and great mourning, Rachel weeping for her children, refusing to be comforted, because they are no more."
    ~Matthew 2:17-18

On Amal's ascent to Bethlehem in the morning light, he couldn't shake the increasingly familiar sensation of being watched. He cast a wary glance over his shoulder to the Herodium.

The dome-shaped mountain dominated the flat plains southeast of Bethlehem. One of King Herod's magnificent architectural master-pieces, it was made on the backs of thousands of slaves. The Herodium was a palace and a den of exotic pleasures.

Amal shuddered at the unpleasant memories of the things he had seen inside the walls of the fortress.

The thunder of horses' hooves approaching brought Amal's attention back to the road. An *ile* of King Herod's cavalry plowed toward him, led by Archelaus, the Crown Prince and King's heir.

Amal yanked the reins and kicked the donkey's sides, and they made it off the road just as the horses came abreast of them. A cloud of dust accompanied the riders, swirling around Amal with the force of a summer storm.

He lifted his sleeve to cover his nose and mouth from the dust—and from any recognizing glances.

Archelaus's head swiveled as he thundered past, and his narrowed eyes honed in on Amal.

He knows. Amal took a swig of water as the cavalry pounded past, losing count after one hundred men.

Was that blood on the soldier's sword or merely the early morning sunlight playing tricks on his mind?

The water skin jostled into his nose and he sucked air through his teeth.

Why so many soldiers? Was there a soul left alive in the town?

Finally, the *ile* disappeared leaving a haze of disturbed dust.

Amal stared at the crest of the hill. He dreaded going forward, yet he couldn't bring himself to return to Jerusalem.

Unprompted, the donkey stepped onto the road and broke into a jarring trot.

Knuckles white on the reins, Amal tried to decipher the sounds rising amongst the donkey's grunts. She plowed to an abrupt halt at the first set of houses, lurching Amal forward over her neck.

Dismounting with growing horror, Amal clutched the donkey's halter but the stalwart beast looked at him with the whites of her eyes showing and nostrils flaring. He would not receive support from her.

The sound he could now identify as wailing rose and fell on the morning breeze. The closed, slatted doors could not contain the anger and sorrow and despair.

The dirt was wet with puddles of darkness.

Gasping and heavy breathing filled Amal's ears—his own. He tore his gaze away from the dark liquid before him. Horse hooves tracked the blood in every direction.

Oh God, have mercy.

Tying off the donkey, Amal stumbled down the narrow street. He came to the square and his feet skidded to a stop at the sight of a woman hunched over, wailing.

Eli's *ima*.

Amal couldn't breathe.

A small, limp hand flopped into view from the woman's arms.

Unbidden, Amal's feet carried him over. He peered over the woman's quaking shoulders.

Eli's blood covered his *ima's* tunic and hands.

Amal gazed upon the frozen expression of horror on the boy's face and he retched, narrowly missing the woman's tunic

"Why? Why my only son?" She swiped at her tears leaving a smear of blood across her cheek. Her eyes widened as she noticed Amal. "You were there with the donkey. Eli couldn't stop talking about riding—" She keened, clutching her son to her chest.

Amal crouched before the pair. His extended hand blurred as his own tears fell and he touched Eli's lifeless cheek.

"I'm sorry. I'm so sorry." Amal couldn't prevent his gaze from returning to the gash ripping open Eli's small belly.

This is my fault. If she knew, she'd despise me. Amal pushed himself off the ground and stared at the blood on his hands.

"I have to go." He felt obliged to say though Eli's *ima* didn't seem to hear.

Amal could hardly breathe as he stumbled down the street Eli had pointed out mere hours before.

The house where the camel dung marked the path was strangely quiet. Dark.

Had the girl he'd seen last night protested? Had her husband fought back?

The door hung as if it had been kicked open. Amal fell to his knees before the door, afraid to see the carnage within.

A footstep ground on the packed dirt behind him.

Amal scrambled up. How could he be so foolish? He led them directly to the house to confirm they'd killed the right child.

He stumbled down the pathway the husband had come from, dodging around a shaded carpenter's work space. His lungs already burned, but he kept running.

"You there!"

Amal dug deep within to find a small reserve of energy. He couldn't keep up this pace much longer.

The footsteps behind pounded ever closer, gaining on him, but he didn't look back.

His side ached, and his lungs burned. His legs wobbled like fresh goat cheese and refused to carry him any further. He deserved whatever fate lay before him.

Wheezing, Amal braced his hands on unstable knees and looked under his arm to see his pursuer.

A shepherd, barely a man with wispy hair on his chin, bent over, mirroring Amal's position. He pressed on his side. "Who are you?"

You are asking me? "Why are you chasing me?"

The young man circled around him. "You *are* from the palace, aren't you? Why are you here? Come to inflict more pain on the people?"

He knew. Something akin to relief relaxed Amal's shoulders. "I didn't mean to. I didn't mean to turn the King's attention to Bethlehem. I merely wanted to understand what the Magi knew. I wanted to see Him."

An unreadable expression filtered across the shepherd's face.

"I should have come sooner. I could have warned them."

"Warned the whole town?" The shepherd clasped his hands behind his head and drew in a breath.

"I was too afraid. There was a soldier standing guard." Amal heard his words spilling out as the incoherent inkblot that they were, but he could not restrain them.

"What happened to your face?" The shepherd jabbed his finger near Amal's nose.

"Ow." Amal winced as if the shepherd had made contact and proceeded to touch it himself. His eyes watered but he still caught the boy's smirk. "I didn't move fast enough."

"Why were you at that house?" The shepherd circled around him.

Amal heaved a sigh. "I knew the camels—the Magi stopped there. I wanted to make sure —" Amal's voice choked and moisture clouded his vision.

The boy leaned close and lowered his voice. "Come away from here."

Amal scanned the ground they had covered. By the time he turned back, the shepherd had darted away like a gangly lamb.

"Hold up." Amal wheezed out. "I'm coming."

When they had gone what felt like halfway to the Great Sea, the shepherd stopped amongst a flock of sheep with one final scan.

He leaned forward. "They weren't there."

Thirteen

When they had seen [Jesus], they made widely known the saying which was told them concerning this Child. And all those who heard it marveled at those things which were told them by the shepherds.
  ~Luke 2:17-18

"What do you mean they weren't there?" Amal gingerly rubbed his beard. "I saw them last night."

The shepherd travelled in a tight circle. "Then you know!"

Amal paced, bouncing off the full wool of a sheep's side. "I know nothing. I thought I was on the verge of knowing, but now all I know is..."

The vision of Eli's bloody body cradled lifeless in his *ima's* arms, threatened to make him loose the contents of his stomach again. He sank to the ground and rested his elbows on his knees. This time he welcomed the pain spreading across his face. What pain did Eli's *ima* have? Amal deserved worse than this superficial pain.

All the way up from Jerusalem, Amal had trusted Yahweh's providence. He would deliver His children from King Herod's destruction.

Yet Amal had been wrong, fatally wrong.

Why hadn't he found a way to leave his room? That guard was always there. It didn't necessarily even mean Amal was under surveillance.

Through the tumult in his mind, the gentle strumming of a stringed instrument gently breached his self-loathing. Amal dabbed at his wet cheeks with his sleeve and sagged into the strange, undeserved comfort.

He rubbed his weary chest and his eyes weighed heavy. If only he could sink into a deep sleep right here and forget about the last couple of days. He felt his body lowering.

Baa.

Amal's eyes jerked open to find a sheep tongue connecting with his face.

"*Argh.*" He jerked back, bounced off another woolly side and struggled to his feet, only to have sheep claiming all extra space now vacated by his backside.

He twisted at the waist. There was the shepherd watching, strumming on a harp. "Who are you?"

"I am Neri."

"Why did you bring me out here?"

Neri glanced up, still strumming. "You look like you could use a reason to rejoice."

Amal's shoulders sagged. His craving for long lasting peace had only been accentuated by the massacre in the town. "What do you know?"

"May I first tell you a tale? When my sheep are agitated, nothing soothes them quite like a story."

A story? Amal waded through sheep to get to the perimeter. "I don't know—"

"What else have you to do?" Neri didn't wait for an answer. "One spring night, not too different from a week ago, there was no moon, and we had settled the sheep. We had just put out the campfire."

Amal shoved a sheep aside and sat before Neri. The sheep bent its front legs and plopped its back end beside Amal.

"The night had reached its darkest, then a blinding light appeared in the sky. Like staring at lightning, only it stayed lit." A sheep nudged

Neri's hand away from the strings of the *kinnor*. The shepherd rubbed the animal between the eyes.

"What do you mean?" Amal took an experimental poke at the sheep's wool to test its softness. His finger compacted the springy wool slightly.

Neri returned to fingering the strings. "Well, lightning flashes once then disappears, though you still think you can see it, you know."

"Mmhm." By the time this boy came to the point, the sheep would be shorn for summer.

"You aren't paying attention. You've missed so much already." Neri jabbed his fingers into Amal's shoulder. "Are you willing to risk it once more?"

Amal blinked. The boy had probably not attended Torah school, yet spoke with authority and confidence. "Forgive me. Please proceed."

"A messenger, glowing from having been in the presence of God." Neri's face took on a glow, as he recounted the events.

Could this be what Amal's soul-deep emptiness stemmed from? Lior, Zacharias, Anna, and now Neri had this air of confident expectation about them.

"This angel said the Savior had been born. For us—shepherds, the lowest class. The Messiah would be wrapped in swaddling clothes, lying in a manger." Neri's eyebrows rose, and he paused expectantly.

Amal blinked. "I don't understand." Oddly, the part of the angel no longer gave him pause, but Neri seemed to think the manger would mean something to him.

Neri rose to his feet and offered an arm to pull Amal up. They waded through the sea of sheep—Neri pausing to scratch the ears of this one, patting the other one.

"They like you." Heat crept up Amal's ears. Perhaps that was obvious.

Neri shrugged. "They know my voice. They trust me."

They stopped in front of a stone tower near the edge of the town. Neri traced a brown calloused hand over the stone. "This is the watchtower for the priestly sheep. We raise the sacrificial lambs for the temple."

Amal nodded, trying to appear interested. The youth ducked inside and Amal followed. A staircase carved into the wall led to the second story but Neri stood before the stone manger.

He swiped a tear from his cheek and spoke through deep emotion. "This is where the lambs are birthed. We wrap them and lay them in the manger until they are calm. A temple sacrifice must be pure. No broken bones."

"Fascinating." Amal brushed off the hay dust from the manger's rim.

"We found the baby wrapped in swaddling clothes in *our* manger. The sacrificial lamb to make atonement for our sins."

Mercy promised to our fathers, the redemption of Israel.

The magnitude of the concept swept through Amal's body and his legs weakened. He sank before the manger gripping the stone edge. "Oh Yahweh! The beauty of Your plan for men here in our humble position."

The fresh tears streaming down his face reminded Amal of the travesty back in Bethlehem. He groaned. "But the soldiers."

Neri's strong hand clamped onto Amal's shoulder. "The family made it out."

Amal gripped Neri's wrist, desperate to understand. "How?"

"Joseph had been warned in a dream. My guess? The same angel." Neri crossed his arms with a satisfied look. "They came through the field last night. We got to say goodbye."

Amal expelled the air in his lungs and slumped forward. "Praise be! Did you know them?" He shivered at the possibility.

Neri's expression proclaimed Amal daft. "Course. After that first night, we visited with them often. Told everyone in Bethlehem."

"Did they believe?" It is all too wonderful. Amal could hardly breathe.

"Some did. Others think it is too impossible. But the angel told Mary nothing is impossible with God." Neri caressed the crude manger.

Amal studied the shepherd. His own life had languished, hiding in the shadows, too afraid to stand for right, and this youth told everyone in town. "I admire your bravery."

Neri shrugged. "When you have an angel and a whole multitude of heavenly host praising God, you get a new perspective. What is my life if Yahweh sends His son for redemption?"

"Where did they go?" Amal held up his hand. "Never mind. I don't want to hear in case I am questioned."

Together they returned to the flock. Neri—wise beyond his years— let Amal contemplate everything.

The thought nearly struck the breath out of him again. "But the baby boys. Bethlehem will be forever scarred because of what I have done. If I hadn't come searching last night, this wouldn't have happened."

Neri frowned before his face dipped low. "Seeking the Messiah comes at great cost. Some more than others."

If that was meant to make Amal feel better, it failed miserably. "Why must the *imas* and *abbas* pay for my seeking?"

Neri's knuckles grew white against his *kinnor*. "Do you suppose the king would have not sent out his army, if you hadn't come?"

Amal studied the dirt. "Not as quickly."

"But he still would protect his throne, right?"

"Yes. He was deeply...troubled." Amal's heart pounded, and he peered over both shoulders.

"I don't know why the innocent ones had to suffer." Neri drew in a shaky breath. "But I choose to believe Yahweh has a plan. The bitterness will make the redemption all the more sweet."

"What do I do now?" Amal was an educated man asking the shepherd theological questions. But something about Neri's simple faith and absolute assurance drew Amal in.

"That's the question. Do you take what you have seen and heard and ignore it like you did before, or do you use the evidence to give you faith? To hope in that promise." Neri's gaze pierced Amal to the marrow.

He pondered Neri's words as he retraced his steps to the simple house on the edge of town.

This time he stepped through the door and looked around. He held his breath afraid to disturb the air. The house was empty and there was no sign of a struggle.

"I don't know why I'm looking for one. I trust what Neri said."

The soldiers must not have thought it was worth their time either, there was no sign of entry beyond the splintered door.

This was the place?

The Messiah in an impoverished town in a tyrannical province. The Redeemer of Israel, whose birth was announced first to shepherds?

A savior for the lowest of men to the wealthy magi.

Even for him, somewhere in between.

Was there hope for these grieving parents in the promises fulfilled from a God who pursued His chosen people—no, the Magi were not Jewish—a God who pursued *all* people with a reckless love?

Amal pressed his fingers to his lips and then to the mezuzah. "May God keep my going out and my coming in from now on and ever more."

He made his way back to the square where Eli's *ima* still rocked back and forth holding her son. More of the towns people had gathered, their wailing and tearing of garments a haunting cry that rose and fell over the swells of the land.

Devastation had spread the length of the town and the outlying areas like raging waters overcoming all in its path. Amal paced helplessly in the square, aching to bring comfort yet overtaken by a strange guilt that he had not suffered loss.

Where would these precious children be laid to rest? Perhaps he could be of use with the burials. He approached an old man who stood apart, wringing his hands and moaning. "I will begin to dig graves. Tell me where."

Dirt streamed off the man's head as he stared at Amal. He blinked and nodded. "Yes. From dust we come and to dust we return. So many children. So many...murdered. If the king had decreed something we would have complied. Why?"

What of the carpenter's land? The house was currently vacant. Was there a better place to bury the boys of the town than the place where the Messiah had played?

"Come with me." Amal took the old man's arm and led him to the end of the street. He scoured the carpenter's workspace and collected the tools that had been neatly set aside.

When he emerged into the sunlight, the elderly man had been

joined by a handful of men with red-rimmed eyes and tunics torn at the neck.

Wordlessly, Amal dispersed the tools and led the grieving fathers to the shady spot behind the house.

The rest of the day was spent digging a mass grave. Time and again, a man would collapse, overcome by the tides of grief. Others would work fiercely fueled by rage.

Amal refused to rest until the dirt had been packed down on the bodies of the boys. A whole generation lost.

When there was nothing more he could do, and the muscles in his arms and back clenched tight in agony, Amal staggered to the edge of town where his donkey was still tied. He clambered on and turned her towards Jerusalem.

He tucked his wrists inside the leather reins and stared at the blistered, shaking hands. All his strength drained from his limbs, weak from the lack of water and sustenance. A thick fog seemed to encompass Amal's thoughts, and he slumped forward, embracing the donkey's neck, his whole body and spirit weary.

The pain set in from his shredded hands. These hands that were trained in the fine art of writing, were no better than raw meat.

Fourteen

But when [Joseph] heard that Archelaus was reigning over Judea instead of his father Herod, he was afraid to go there.
~ Matthew 2:2a

Thwack!

Something blunt struck Amal's back.

"Where were you all day, Scribe?" Another blow knocked Amal off the donkey's back.

Amal flopped to the floor, and the breath was knocked from him. He wheezed for air, staring up at the ornate archway decorating the entrance to the palace stables. Sparks flashed into his vision.

The shadowed form lurked over him with a long pole. Archelaus shifted into the light.

Amal rolled over and struggled to his hands and knees. "My Prince."

"I know you were out to Bethlehem. Don't deny it." Archelaus struck Amal on the side.

Pain snaked around Amal's body and stole his breath. The straw and dirt dug into his raw hands as he struggled to keep himself upright. "I don't...deny...it."

"What were you doing there? Inciting rebellion amongst the locals?"

"No!" Amal sucked air through his teeth and the expansion of his lungs felt like fire in his chest. "The people are in no condition to revolt."

Do you take what you have seen and ignore it as before?

Neri told everyone who crossed his path about the Messiah. If Amal believed—truly believed—could he speak any less boldly?

"What were you doing all day?" Archelaus raised the pole.

"I was digging graves with men and women who had just lost their sons." Amal couldn't bridle the disdain in his voice as he displayed a hand.

"You disagree with the assignment from the king?" Archelaus cracked the rod against Amal's thigh sending him sprawling.

Amal struggled to his knees again, breathing heavy. "Yes. These are not a threat to the king's throne." He braced himself for another blow.

Instead, Archelaus barked out a laugh. "You think you can make the decision on what is a threat to *my* throne?"

"They are a peaceful people." Sweat stung Amal's eyes.

Another blow slammed on his spine. Amal tried to rise again, but the strength sapped out of his arms and legs. He collapsed on his swollen face and his body began to succumb to the pain.

"Did you get permission before stealing my *abba's* donkey and stepping away from your position all day?" Archelaus' accusation filtered as through a thick wall.

"Duties...delegated." Amal pushed out.

"The next time you delegate, consider the ill effects of meddling in things that aren't your concern." This time the blows rained within increasing force.

Amal cried out and tried to shield his face and head, but his arms couldn't respond to his command. The pain faded, and he stopped fighting for control and yielded to the blackness.

Every part of Amal's body objected with each jostle. The constant sway produced relentless agony.

Wooden slats beneath him creaked and groaned, and the aroma of straw became evident.

Why did the stable sway and rock like a cart?

Light began to register through his eyelids. He opened his eyes to the searing brightness.

Amal whimpered and tried to shield his face, but his arms lay heavy on his chest.

His fingers inched up the cloth covering his face all the way to the sides of an oxcart. The cart bumped over a rock and landed with a thud jolting Amal and sending tears to his eyes.

Why did his muscles ache so and his hands burn? Amal shifted the covering slightly until he could feel fresh air on his throbbing face.

After a long while, he pried one eye open to see blue sky over the sides of an oxcart. Amal tipped his head back to see the driver, but couldn't discern the man's identity. Why did the set of his shoulders and the grey hair peeking from under the cap look familiar?

Amal's eyes closed, and he took inventory of his aches. His head throbbed—even to the roots of his hair—his face, his ribs. He muffled a groan and clutched at his bruised side. The fibers of his robe scraped across the raw flesh on his hand.

The rod.

Archelaus.

The killing of the innocents.

Amal's head pounded harder with each memory.

Oh Yahweh, preserve me. Will You leave my soul here in Sheol? It hurts so bad, make it stop.

Where was his determination for boldness as his body withered in pain? Was courage only for the times when there was no threat to his person?

Why would Archelaus cover him? If this cart were on the prince's assignment, he would be displayed for all to see. A warning to other dissenters.

Who had taken the time to rest him on a bed of straw in an attempt to cushion his discomfort?

The rapid thoughts took their toll, and fatigue slowed Amal's mind.

He jolted awake as the cart jerked to a stop.

The aches intensified and Amal could not restrain his whimper.

"I'm sorry my friend. I know you are in bad shape." The wagon creaked to the side as his benefactor climbed down. "I must prepare your place inside. I won't be long."

Amal couldn't muddle through whose voice was attached to the narrow form.

A shadow fell across him. His eyes opened again and a woman's face, lined with time and worry, hovered over him.

"Zacharias, this poor man. Quickly, we must get him inside."

Though their hands were gentle, Amal's body knew no relief as they scooted him to the edge of the cart.

"Do you think you can stand?"

Amal closed his eyes and concentrated on his legs. "I think so."

Zacharias pulled him to a sitting position, ducked under Amal's arm, and braced him at the waist.

A gasp escaped Amal's clenched teeth.

"It's just going to have to be brutal until we get you inside." Zacharias hefted Amal off the cart with a grunt of his own. "I could carry you—"

"Don't you do it, old man. Then I'll have to care for the both of you."

Zacharias tipped his chin to the woman who draped Amal's other arm across her shoulders. "My wife, Elizabeth."

Amal's legs caved under his weight, and the three of them staggered Elizabeth's direction.

"I am so sorry" Amal gripped Zacharias' thin shoulder and shifted as much weight as he could away from the woman.

With much effort, they made it into the house.

Sweat soaked the front of Amal's tunic and the air grew thin.

One final agonizing push and Zacharias lowered him to a cushioned mat while Elizabeth fluffed cushions and fretted like a mother hen.

Blackness crept around the edge of Amal's vision again and he sank once more into oblivion.

When he awoke, the late afternoon shadows were long from the high window.

"*Ima,* he wakes."

Amal shifted his head to meet the glittering black gaze of a toddler, barely older than Eli.

Tears stung the back of his eyes. He blinked rapidly as Elizabeth bustled over.

"Thank you John. Run and tell *Abba.*"

"This is John?" Amal cleared his throat. "What a miracle."

Elizabeth's smile sent warmth into his weary heart. "Indeed. As you are, Amal."

The image of the *imas* and the *abbas* tearing the necks of their tunics and the sound of their grief, gouged a fresh wound in his broken body. "I'm not anything special, but I thank you for your kind care."

Elizabeth rubbed Amal's arm with her calloused hands. "What is it? What has happened?"

Zacharias emerged from outside, hand in hand with John.

"I went to Bethlehem to..." Amal paused. The real reason. He would no longer hide. "Seek the Messiah. The king knew and sent soldiers."

Elizabeth covered a gasp and Zacharias gripped her hand.

Amal stared at young John and censored his words. "All boys John's age and younger."

After a stunned moment, Elizabeth squeaked out. "And my cousin?"

"The angel appeared in the night and warned them."

"Those poor *imas.*" Elizabeth pulled John into her arms and rocked him back and forth, tears forming in her eyes.

Zacharias embraced his small family. "Oh Yahweh, have mercy on our king for his choices. Show him the need to divert from his evil ways and turn his heart to You."

"So be it." John's little voice eased the burden.

Amal chuckled and Elizabeth laughed, spilling her tears down her cheeks.

"How did you find me?" Amal clasped Zacharias' wrist.

The priest helped Amal to recline. "I was emptying the temple's ashes on the trash heap outside the city. You were being left for dead."

Emotion clogged Amal's throat. He swallowed hard. "Thank you for risking...everything...for me."

Zacharias shrugged. "When our great God loved us enough to come for restoration, how could I not act in love as well? Just as He *gives* all to us so we could have peace with Him. To be made right. There is nothing we can do to earn His favor. He gives generously, much like I give good things to my son."

Amal pondered this as Elizabeth served a simple fare of unleavened bread and lentils. He continued to think on Zacharias' words

From his angle below the window, Amal could see the stars flung across the sky.

"Yahweh. My life is characterized by order and fear of not upholding it. I wish I could easily put that aside. I want to pursue You. It's hard for me to not be in control of my surroundings. Help me to trust in Your plan when I cannot see the way."

A yawn split his face, and he slipped into a restless sleep.

Fifteen

When Israel was a child, I loved him, and out of Egypt I called My son.
~Hosea 11:1

The next two days passed in a haze of resting and pain as Amal began to heal under the constant watch care from Zacharias' wife.

On the third day, Amal found he was able to stay awake longer and even grew restless.

He fought the agonizing pain and pushed himself up to a seated position.

"What do you think you are doing?" Elizabeth emerged from the outside with her jug of water and John in tow.

"Please, just a moment," Amal panted, secretly glad for the scolding. Already exhaustion crept up his limbs.

"You lie back down immediately!" Elizabeth set her jug down and marched toward him with her fists jammed on her hips.

Amal moaned as he lowered himself. His heart slammed against his bruised chest and his shallow breathing filled his ears. He mashed his eyes closed and drew in deep breaths until he settled into the cushions and felt less faint.

He opened his eyes as Elizabeth fussed over his pillows.

"If you try that sort of thing again when my husband is not here, I'll..." Her stern expression faded and her eyes crinkled. "I'll let John sit on you."

Amal flinched. He had observed John "sitting" on his *abba's* chest. "I'll behave."

John charged three steps, jumped—his little feet barely leaving the ground—and plopped on the floor with a triumphant cackle.

"I will wait for Zacharias." Amal watched the boy without a care in the world. He brushed away the moisture pooling at the corner of his eye.

"You're thinking of the children?" Elizabeth dipped a cup into the water jar and brought it to Amal.

He leaned on his elbow and drank, trying to be rid of the lump in his throat. He pressed his lips together and couldn't meet her gaze.

Elizabeth sighed heavily and sat beside the cushion. "I know Yahweh has a plan. And I know He is working, even now. But I think of all those broken *imas*—" She wiped her eyes with the corner of her outer tunic.

John wandered over and straddled Elizabeth's lap, chortling as she buried her face in his neck and playfully buzzed her lips. The child flung himself backward, trusting his *ima's* arms would be always be there.

"He is so precious."

"John is a miracle." Elizabeth pressed another loud kiss on John's chubby cheek before he clambered off and darted away on some adventure only he could see. "The Lord has looked on me to take away my reproach among people."

"Does he already know? Is he aware of the great tasks and honors he will do?" Amal studied Elizabeth's thoughtful expression.

"He was filled with the Spirit even in my womb. There are times as he sits beside Zacharias I can see the scripture sinking into his heart." Elizabeth laughed as John buzzed around like a bee searching for honey. "But he is also very much a child."

Together they watched the child-prophet being more child today.

"It reminds me of our people enslaved by Pharaoh of old. The senseless killing of our baby boys because of a jealous ruler." Elizabeth rose with heaviness around her eyes.

A chill ran down Amal's arms, raising the hair. "Elizabeth! Does Zacharias have access to the scriptures?"

Elizabeth pivoted and cocked her head. "Of course. Let me know which scroll I can have him bring home. I can send a messenger."

Amal's eyebrows met in the middle. Absently, he rubbed the wrinkle between and winced. *How long will it take for me to remember my injuries?*

Which scroll? Which prophet? Amal glanced toward John, who studied him with a deep expression older than his years.

"Do you know where the Messiah has gone? Or which prophet said it?" Amal whispered with a sideways glance at Elizabeth, sweeping across the room. Was it wrong to test a child?

John shrugged and toddled off.

Amal closed his eyes, picturing the rows of scrolls in his library.

Moses sent to deliver the chosen people from slavery. The Messiah sent to give knowledge of salvation by remissions of sin—a form of internal slavery.

He summoned Elizabeth. "Would you please send for the scrolls of the prophets Isaiah and Micah?" If Micah's prophesies told where the Messiah would be born and of little John's ministry, would it also say the words Amal could nearly picture?

Anticipation fluttered in his chest as Elizabeth fetched a runner.

What great mystery was this? So many times, Israel and Judah had strayed from Yahweh like an unfaithful wife. So often, the Lord had drawn His people back to His embrace. And now, through the ultimate act of love, He sent His son to visit and redeem His people.

An unfaithful wife.

"Hosea!"

Amal's shout accosted Elizabeth's attention, and she ran out the door after the messenger.

"Wait! We'll also need the scroll from the prophet Hosea." A moment later she returned and leaned against the door frame with a triumphant grin. "I caught him!"

"Thank you." Hope swelled in Amal's chest at the anticipation of searching out the scriptures once more.

This time, so much more rode on his discovery than sharing knowledge with fellow scribes. All the knowledge that Amal had stored up cried out for a soul-deep level of application. The printed words paraded through his thoughts with a new meaning.

As if walking from the dark wine cellar directly into the garden decorated with Roman statues, the truths kept blinding him with unfailing precision. *Sing for joy and be glad, O daughter of Zion; for behold I am coming and I will dwell in your midst.*

Emotion surged inside Amal's chest. He gently pinched the moisture from beneath his nose. God on high had come to live amongst the people. "Oh God, my God! You have looked upon the afflictions of Your people. I don't deserve Your mercy or favor, but I'm so thankful You saw fit to send Your Messiah. And in my lifetime!"

Finally, the runner returned with three scrolls tucked inside a basket.

Elizabeth paid the boy a coin and brought the treasure to Amal's side.

Amal skipped over the largest scroll that would be Isaiah—and picked up one of the others.

"The word of the Lord came to Micah of Moresheth—" Not this one. He rerolled it and picked up the last one. What if he didn't find it?

Confirming that these were indeed the writings of Hosea, Amal began scanning the words.

It was here all along, God's promise of redemption for His wayward people. Deliverance of His people, despite the many times they had sinned against Him.

Amal stopped skimming and began consuming the life-giving words with tears streaming down his face.

Oh Yahweh, I am a sinful man. How long have You presented my sin directly before my eyes in Your holy scripture? And I have disregarded it. I have read, written, and memorized Your words of life and not seen them as applicable to me.

Tears came afresh, this time with an unbelievably clean feeling of restoration.

His eyes roved over the next section. *Out of Egypt. I will call My son.*

"Ah ha!" His shout brought Elizabeth and John running, and Zacharias walked in at that moment. "Zacharias, help me up!"

"Your side. You must rest." Zacharias squatted before Amal's cushions.

"Elizabeth made me promise, when you came, you'd help me."

"What?" Zacharias glanced at his wife.

"How can I lie here when I know? I know." Amal had to dance.

"Help him up, Zacharias, before the man injures himself." Elizabeth clapped her hands like a small girl and John jumped up and down.

"Alright." Zacharias hoisted Amal up. "Now, just what has riled you up, my friend?"

Amal pointed to the scroll still laying on the cushions. "May I see that?"

Elizabeth bent to retrieve it before John could grab it with eager hands.

"Out of Egypt I will call My son." Amal tapped the section. "You see, Elizabeth had it right. It's like the Israelite boys being slaughtered in Egypt. I knew it. I knew it. I've spent the afternoon reading Hosea's scroll. They traveled to Egypt."

Amal gripped Zacharias' arms and shuffled his feet from side to side, laughing. Elizabeth and John joined the celebration, laughing and holding hands.

"How do I get to Egypt?" Amal pressed on his side and motioned for Zacharias to lower him.

"I admire your commitment, my friend." Zacharias grunted as he eased Amal to the cushion. "And if Yahweh is clearly placing this on your heart, then I will not dissuade you. Consider this. Believing in your being the Messiah has come is enough. You do not need to be present with him to believe."

"Yes of course—"

"I don't have the ability to send you to Egypt."

Amal frowned. He had no access to his money either.

Elizabeth's hand pressed on his arm. "We also have been given a different task to raise up our son and instruct him in the ways of the Lord, so when the time comes, he will be able to prepare the way for the

Messiah's ministry. We don't have to be *with* him to do what Yahweh has assigned us."

Zacharias straightened and his knees creaked. "Seek the Lord. I do not intend to discourage you. If it is in His will for you to join up with our relatives, He will make a way."

Elizabeth tapped her cheek. "If the scriptures say He will be coming back, perhaps *then* you will meet the Messiah."

Could that be the plan? "Will He—they—return to Bethlehem? Do you suppose?"

Elizabeth worried her brow. "It seems awfully close to Jerusalem."

"Even when Archelaus reigns, I can't imagine they will find Bethlehem safe." Zacharias tugged on his beard.

"Their families are in Nazareth." Elizabeth offered.

Amal pondered this. He had to see the Messiah with his own eyes. But how would he get to Egypt? And how would he find them if he did?

Elizabeth was right about Bethlehem. It felt too close to the Herodium's overpowering presence. Amal would only draw attention to the already broken community.

But Nazareth? It was still a gamble. It still might not unfold in his favor.

But perhaps in some small way, he could help prepare the way for when the Messiah came and began his ministry.

"Could they use scribes in Nazareth?"

Epilogue

And he came and dwelt in a city called Nazareth, that it might be fulfilled which was spoken by the prophets, "He shall be called a Nazarene."

~Matthew 2:23

4 **BCE**

Nazareth, Galilee

The marketplace bustled with merchants crying out their wares, clinking coins, the scraping of stone upon stone grinding grain. Amal leaned his back against the uneven wall of the synagogue, and absently ran his fingers across the bump on his nose as he did each time, he contemplated the slower pace of the village. "Thank you, Yahweh for the provision of Zacharias and Elizabeth. May they have wisdom and Your protection as they raise John."

The passel of boys, laughing and running toward him, made him amend his prayer. *And may I have wisdom and Your protection as I teach these boys Your words.*

"Good morning students." Amal motioned with both hands for the boys to find their places. He dipped his spoon into the honey jar and went row by row—the little ones first, to those nearly ready for their Bar-mitzvah ceremony—putting a dollop of honey on each slate.

He washed his hand in the water dish and twisted off the lid of the jar protecting the words of Isaiah in the Holy Scripture.

The boys watched with wide eyes, their reverence producing pride and joy in Amal's chest.

He unfurled the scroll on the slanted desk and smiled at his pupils. "You may eat the honey." He nodded to his newest student. "Zev, why do I give you honey?"

The boy stood, his finger still shoved in his mouth. "Because the word of the Lord is sweeter than honey and the honeycomb."

Amal smiled. "That is correct."

He nodded to the eldest boy who stood to recite.

"Today's passage from the Prophet Isaiah. The spirit of the Lord God is upon me, because the Lord has anointed me to preach good tidings to the poor—"

Thank you, Yahweh, for the good tidings. Keep Your Messiah safe. My heart longs to see Your consolation and redemption, if it is in Your will. Amal searched the eager faces of the handful of boys before him. Since he had arrived in Nazareth a year and a half prior, he had established himself as part of the community.

Truly, teaching the little ones to recognize the works of God most high was like honey on his lips.

Perhaps we each have some part in the Messiah's ministry. Elizabeth admonition was his constant reminder—the standard he strove for each day as he sat before the boys in the community.

"—to proclaim the acceptable year of the Lord."

"Excellent recitation!"

The youth beamed under Amal's praise.

"Is anyone else prepared to recite—" Amal caught sight of a woman and her young son thumping on the melons at the stand on the edge of the market.

The woman bent down out of sight, her stature triggering a memory. The hairs on Amal's arms rose.

The boys turned as one to see what arrested Amal's attention.

The small boy glanced their way and then tugged on his *ima's* skirts.

The woman lifted her gaze and assessed the school and nodded.

Amal's heart pounded in his ears as the small boy made his way over. "Do any of you know this boy?"

The students exchanged glances.

Zev shrugged and shook his head. "No, Rabbi."

"They must be newly arrived in town."

The newcomer halted at the pillar supporting the reed roof.

"Shalom young man" Amal stared hard. The boy was younger than the five-year-olds sitting in the first row but not by much.

"Hello." The boy glanced back at the woman. "My *ima* told me I could stand here."

"Of course, you are most welcome." Amal's words came as through the thick wall behind him. "Students, greet our new friend."

"Shalom, brother." The voices blended and staggered over each other.

"He can sit by me." Zev piped up.

"That is very kind." Amal could hardly breathe as the boy sat at his feet.

"We are studying the prophet, Isaiah. I am Amal, the Rabbi." *Boldness. Do not look away and ignore.* "Tell us about yourself. Have you just arrived in Nazareth?" Amal managed to squeak out.

"Yes. We came from Egypt."

The students' admiration masked Amal's intake of air. A sheen of moisture blurred his vision. He swiped it away and found himself kneeling before the small boy, his hands framing the small cheeks, but not touching.

The boy returned his open gaze and Amal sensed a similar depth as the lad, John.

"Rabbi, are you well?" Zev patted his arm.

"I have never been better." Amal smiled at Zev, never breaking the connection with the boy before him. "I have been waiting for you."

The boy's serious expression gave way to a boyish grin. "I am here."

"Do you know him, Rabbi?"

Amal rose, begging his thoughts to align coherently.

"I...wait for every boy to come to our *Bet-Seffer*. I desire to teach young men the joy of the Lord's holy words in our house of learning."

Amal glanced back to the small boy. "It is how I can prepare for the Messiah's ministry by preparing your hearts to recognize Him."

"What a beautiful way of putting it." The boy's *ima* stood just under the awning with a gentle smile, cradling a melon.

Amal crossed to her with two strides and dug his fists into his robes to prevent from clasping her hands. "We welcome you to Nazareth. Your boy is inquisitive. He will have a place among us when he is ready."

The woman blinked and her eyes narrowed slightly. "That is kind, but my son is not yet of age."

"It doesn't matter. I have been waiting—" Amal pressed his lips together to halt the words spewing out of his mouth. "Forgive me. Zacharias and Elizabeth send their highest regard."

The woman's eyes widened. "You know my cousin?"

"Yes, they cared for me when I was weary and downtrodden two years ago."

"Why were you downtrodden?" Caution laced the woman's tone.

"I had missed connecting with the One I sought by mere hours." Amal gazed upon the boy's upturned face and his throat grew tight. "I have been waiting to see with my own eyes. For He who is mighty has done great things for me."

Understanding flickered in the woman's eyes. She scanned the faces of the students then flicked her gaze back to Amal and murmured. "And holy is His name."

Amal pinched the moisture from under his nose. He must look the blubbering fool.

The woman smiled. "Thank you, Rabbi for...welcoming us back into our town. Good day, children."

"Shalom, the boys replied politely.

The woman reached down for her son's hand. "Come along, Jesus."

Tears streamed down Amal's face as he watched the small boy depart. He turned and faced the students, but could not temper the grin that split his face. He shuffled in a dance step as he walked down the aisle to the front of the class.

Holy is His name.

His heart rejoiced.

Author's Note

Thank you for joining me on Amal's Journey to seek out Truth.

The Scriptures say Herod consulted his Scribes and the Chief Priests about the location of the Messiah's Birth, but beyond that, Amal's character and journey is fictional.

There are several theories regarding the star the Magi followed. Some say it was a new star with the sole purpose of spotlighting the Messiah's birth. Some say the planets aligned in a way that appeared to touch creating a singular bright star. Along with that the path of the planets would have looped back and "touched" again a while later. Some say it was the Shekinah Glory of God. Regardless, it was a miraculous sight. 6 the miracle is the Magi knew to look for and seek out the star.

Why did the wisemen asked the location of the new king if they had the scriptures and prophesies of Daniel? The Lord told the prophet, Micah, where the Messiah would be born *after* the Jews had returned to the land of Israel. Scholars in Babylon would not have had access to later prophecies given in Israel.

I found it fascinating that the angel Gabriel who appeared to Mary and Zacharias was the same one who told Daniel about the seventy weeks till the chosen one's demise.

Nowhere is it mentioned what became of Anna. In light of the horrible things Herod did to secure his throne, it would not come as a shock to me if he got wind of Anna's proclamations and had her killed. However, that is the musing of my imagination.

This is a work of fiction, and in no way is intended to replace the scripture. My prayer is that the words I write would send you to the Bible to check for accuracy.

Jerusalem and Bethlehem are about six miles apart. It made me wonder if Jesus showed up in the next town over, would I set aside my schedule and make the journey?

About Naomi Craig

Author of Biblical fiction, avid reader, pastor's wife, Naomi loves reading the Bible and imagining how things were at the time. When she's not serving in various areas at church, trying to stay on top of mountains of dishes or convincing her rescue dog, Freeway, to be cute on command for Instagram reels, you'll most likely find her enjoying a good book and a cup of coffee. Naomi co-hosts #BehindTheStory with Naomi and Lisa, an author interview show on YouTube and your podcast platform of choice.

Learn more about Naomi's books at: http://www.celebratelitpublishing.com/naomi-craig/

facebook.com/Naomicraigauthor
instagram.com/Naomicraigauthor

Did you know there's another volume?

Don't miss Keeping Christmas: Volume Two releasing October 18!

Featuring

Chautona Havig

Tabitha Bouldin

Susan K. Beatty

Jennifer Sienes

Melissa Wardwell

Stacy T. Simmons

You can get your copy on Amazon!

Made in the USA
Middletown, DE
04 April 2023